WHERE SOULS COLLIDE

STEFANIE WORTH

LEISURE BOOKS

NEW YORK CITY

A LEISURE BOOK®

August 2007

Dorchester Publishing Co., Inc.
200 Madison Avenue
New York, NY 10016

ISBN-10: 0-8439-5970-3
ISBN-13: 978-0-8439-5970-3

Printed in the United States of America.

SURPRISE BIRTHDAY

"Do I detect the birthday girl?" The trespasser's baritone-deep voice boomed beyond the cubicle.

She gasped as the generic "And you must be..." that left her lips tumbled silently into stunned surprise.

No way.

"Maxwell McKnight." He grinned like he'd caught her pulling up her panties. "Great to finally see you again, Navena."

Navena grabbed hold of her composure and thrust forward a handshake to her former teacher and long-ago lover.

Maxwell was even more handsome than the first day she'd seen him fourteen years before. Jeri Curls had given way to a clean shave. He seemed even taller than the six-foot seven demigod she remembered—folded into her desk the way he was—but no less impressive in a Coogi sweater and khakis than he had been in rolled shirt-sleeves and crisply starched jeans.

That unforgettable smile brought flash-back recognition and stirred memories and sentiments she swore were long resolved....

DEDICATION

I breathe. I pray. I dream. I write.

Thanks to the people who love me enough to let me live my mantra:

Critique partners who've been secure enough to support me, savvy enough to guide me and smart enough to question me. . .

True friends who know who they are by the amount of conspiring, consoling, whispering and wishing we've shared. . .

Brothers who never seem as far as they are because they're always here for me. . .

Parents who taught me the value of hard work, high expectations and faith. . .

Kids and a husband who keep me grounded and push me to reach. . .

I breathe, I pray, I dream, I write
—because of you.

WHERE SOULS COLLIDE

Prologue

May 9, 1990
St. Louis, Missouri

"Daddy's dead!" Navena came running through the kitchen, back screen door slamming in her wake. "I saw it, Mama. I saw it."

Then she fainted at her mother's feet.

"Not my husband! Not today!" Audrey Ann Larimore spun toward the window above the sink.

Outside, the wind hissed. Silence pierced the air. There were no strains of "God Bless the Child" that always accompanied her husband's work. No click-chop whirring from his manual push mower. Audrey Ann hopped gingerly over Navena's sleeping body and ran toward the backyard.

Hurdling the porch, skipping down the stairs, sprinting across the freshly mowed grass, she screamed into the suffocating afternoon, stopping, exhausted, at the yard's edge where the mower and her husband both lay still. She knelt beside him and prayed.

In a little while, she'd call her pastor and the sheriff. But, first, she had to deal with her daughter's psychic sense, which had grown too powerful for an eighteen-year-old to manage. And she had to undo it now, before her husband's body left Larimore Manor and before Navena awoke.

The air chilled her, despite its heat. Muggy breezes shoved the willow tree branches at the yard's edge and tousled her shoulder-length brown hair. She ran one hand down the other sleeveless arm to smooth away sudden goose bumps and returned to the house.

Quick thinking accompanied deliberate steps as Audrey searched her ancestral legends for an answer. *I should've known this was coming. Pity I can tell futures for everyone except my own family.*

Desperation and sadness attempted to overtake her. Still, she continued her dogged trek, maneuvering around the pantry's jars of fruit preserves, vegetables in bushels, canned milk, and bags of sugar and flour. She crossed the kitchen into a narrow hallway, and opened the seldom-used door that led to the attic.

There, she removed a favorite quilt from the guest bed and dug through her sewing box to find her good shears and leftover cloth from the first dress she'd made Navena. Then she turned her search to an antique hope chest. Inside, Audrey soon found a red satin box and a container of her daughter's childhood keepsakes.

Gathering all her items, she made her way back to the kitchen, detouring into Navena's room to pluck an old-fashioned rag doll from her bed pillows. "Come on, Vee."

Dropping her finds on the kitchen table, Navena's mother held on to the quilt, returning quickly to the willow tree and Navena's father. She tenderly wrapped him in the handmade bedcover and ran back inside.

Afraid that time might undermine her efforts, she quickly carried Vee to the sink and held the heirloom up against the light of the kitchen window for one final look. Handcrafted by a slave ancestor generations before, the doll's spotless white pinafore, curly yarn hair, black button eyes, and cocoa-brown face represented the Larimore spirit—strong, smart, and sovereign. Each mother since Vee's creation had lovingly and faithfully passed the doll to her own daughter. Doing so ensured continuity of their legacy.

"I wouldn't break the chain other than to save my child."

Without hesitation or remorse, Audrey Ann Larimore laid the doll on the kitchen counter. She placed the tip of the shears at the hem of the doll's pinafore and cut quickly upward through her body, dividing it into slightly uneven halves so that the heart remained intact.

Yes, doing this would change her daughter. But Audrey had heard stories of Larimore women who'd lost their minds under the weight of their gifts. Not all futures are filled with joy, and tragedy takes it toll on some seers. No child should have to predict her own father's passing, she scolded herself. She would spare Navena the aftermath if she could.

"In time, when the moon calls, you will remember that you are one." Taking a half in each hand, she moved toward the dining table and sat down.

She emptied Navena's keepsakes onto the surface, spreading them out for better viewing. Then she opened the red satin box, removed a spool of thread, and wove one end through a large embroidery needle.

For the doll's heart-bearing half, she rustled through the collectibles and selected items symbolic of her daughter's abilities: a four-holed button resembling the doll's own eyes, a dried ear of corn, a stray three of hearts playing card, and a page torn from Navena's *Mother Goose Nursery Rhymes*. The Man in the Moon stared up at Audrey as if asking for a reprieve from his imminent sentence.

"Happy birthday, sweetheart," Mama whispered. "I can't believe you're eighteen. I swear it was just this morning God answered my prayers for a child." She sighed and lifted a wrist to wipe one sentimental tear from her cheek.

Using a kitchen knife, she pierced the corn to create a small slit. Starting with the "moon," she laid the "eye," then "ear" and "hearts" atop it, and wove the items together with the thread. Making sure the doll's heart remained unharmed, she lifted Vee's larger half and wove both ends of the thread through her hand, tied off the string, and started on the other body half.

Rustling through the keepsakes once more, she selected another playing card. This time it was the joker, dancing beneath the word "wild."

Because in the right circumstances, anything is possible, Mama reassured the doll half and herself.

Lastly, she chose a bird feather crudely glued to a ballpoint pen. She smiled at Navena's long ago attempt to make a quill-type writing instrument. "This should help in case you need to draw up a plan of your own."

As with the other half, Navena's mother used the thread to bind the pieces to each other and then to the doll's hand. She then gathered the disjointed doll and skirted each half in Navena's dress cloth.

Nearly finished, she glanced at her daughter, still in a faint on the floor, to be sure she had enough time. "I love you."

One last rummage through the keepsakes turned up a bottle of red nail polish, thick from nonuse. Mama painted an "N" on the heartless doll half and a "V" on the other. It seemed unfair that the doll with the heart, "V," also received the gifts—empathy, prophesy, sensory perception. However, true power required great heart. That left "N" with wit, wisdom, and a need to search for what she lacked inside.

Mama returned the assorted items to their respective containers, placing the "N" doll half among Navena's keepsakes to make sure her life continued on its current path—minus the Larimore gifts.

"V" went into the red box. Mama tied it with a string and headed back to the attic. Navena's gifts were safe here—locked away beyond the reach of her memory and use—until she was instructed to call on them once more.

"Eventually, Navena, you will be whole again and have all that is yours."

Chapter One

Monday, May 9, 2006
Detroit, Michigan

Navena forced open her Jeep's rusty door and slid out. Rocky pavement sucked in her heels and poked at her soles as she strolled past a gathering of pigeons, pecking for—what?—among cracks in the bloated tar. Most mornings even scavenging birds ignored this once historic neighborhood, now pocked by transient hotels and homeless men pushing carts of stolen bricks.

Empathy for the area's degeneration tangoed with a deteriorating love life she was glad to leave locked in the gated lot each morning. Her heart belonged to each day's deadlines waiting inside the *Detroit Dispatch*.

With a one-handed strum on her air guitar, she silenced the last strains of Lenny Kravitz rocking on her iPod. The screaming electric guitar matched her kick-butt mood.

Inside the weathered architectural gem revolved a world in stark contrast to the street it called home. Fresh paint heralded the arrival of a new executive editor. Her soon-to-be-boss had also prompted repairs to broken windows and installation of a security keyboard for entry.

Just gotta show 'em what you've got, girlfriend. Stooping to peek in the rearview mirror, Navena adjusted the chestnut-colored head wrap constraining her matching dreadlocks. They flopped in the breeze, bouncing against her cheeks. Brushed with bronze powder, her face and lips glistened in the reflection. *We will feel as good as we look today.*

Anger flashed at the thought of being passed over for the promotion. As managing editor and second-in-command, she deserved that job. But Cullen—an old-fashioned publisher with a mentality to match—hired from the outside.

"You're good at doing the work," he'd said. "But I need somebody else to do the thinking."

Navena input her private code and bolted up the lobby stairs to the building's second floor. The last to arrive in the newsroom she found, once there, a makeshift birthday banner strung across her cubicle, roses on her desk, and a man hunched over her computer.

Must be my new boss. Everybody else knows better than to use my desk for anything.

Now the mysterious editor would finally be revealed.

Navena dropped her bag and two years of frustration beside the desk, making enough noise to be noticed.

"Do I detect the birthday girl?" The trespasser's baritone deep voice boomed beyond the cubicle.

She gasped as the generic "And you must be . . ." that left her lips tumbled silently into stunned surprise.

No way.

"Maxwell McKnight." He grinned like he'd caught her pulling up her panties. "Great to finally see you again, Navena."

Navena grabbed hold of her composure and thrust

forward a handshake to her former teacher and long-ago lover.

Maxwell was even more handsome than the first day she'd seen him fourteen years before. Jeri Curls had given way to a clean shave. He seemed even taller than the six-foot-seven demigod she remembered—folded into her desk the way he was—but no less impressive in a Coogi sweater and khakis than he had been in rolled shirtsleeves and crisply starched jeans.

That unforgettable smile brought flashback recognition and stirred memories and sentiments she swore were long resolved. Feelings of coed adoration ambushed her career woman demeanor. Lingering resentment over the staffing imposition helped her resist the impulse to hug him.

"And what brings you to the *Dispatch*?" she asked with feigned nonchalance. *If he's really the—*

"New executive editor. Not sure why they kept it quiet, but here I am."

"I thought you were a rebel—not a writer." There was no way she could report to this man although she could not release his hand.

"Always told you I could change," Maxwell said.

"So, since you've overtaken my space, does this mean I get *your* office?" Blood raced through Navena's palm. She slipped her hand hastily from his.

"After my job already?" Maxwell asked with a smug grin.

"Should have had it to begin with," she said, feeling emboldened by their previous relationship.

Despite the cocky reply, a rising current of unrest began to boil in her belly.

He laughed. "You may be older, but you're just the way I pictured you."

"Thank you," she replied. "It's been a long time since Hillstone College. You're looking . . ." Her voice trailed. She wanted to say something silly like *absolutely scrumptious*, but refused. "well, You're looking well these days, Professor," Navena finessed.

Nervous perspiration trickled down her back. This was the man, after all, she once dubbed "my only vice." She wanted to sit, assess this coolly as serendipity, but Maxwell hadn't budged.

"Maybe we can spend some time catching up over lunch," he offered.

The ends of a salt-and-pepper mustache stroked the corners of his full mouth, the barber-groomed facial hair contrasting his now smooth scalp. She studied his baldness for a moment.

Maxwell ran a hand across his bare head, slowly from front to back as if seeking her unspoken approval.

"Wednesday, please, if I have a choice," Navena answered. "Not to rush you, but will you need my computer much longer? I have work to do." She felt a sudden urgency to let Maxwell know she'd come a long way from being his starry-eyed protégée. Mentor and all, he was on *her* territory now.

"Of course," he said. "My computer isn't quite set, so I grabbed yours to e-mail the team about a quick editorial meeting. Hope you don't mind."

"I do if it's this morning. We meet on Wednesdays. Everybody's on deadline today." She folded her arms.

"Gonna make me pull rank? I will." Maxwell rose and turned away. "Nine-thirty. Conference room. See you then."

Watching him walk away, Navena realized it took him all of ten minutes to make her angry.

Swallowing a roiling mix of kismet and resentment, Navena maintained her poise and walked the other direction toward the cell-like company lunchroom. She navigated a square metal table and four mismatched folding chairs to slam a handful of change into the vending machine. Two strawberry Pop-Tarts and a twelve-ounce cola dutifully plopped from the dispenser. She popped the can and took a long mind-clearing swig. Both the burning bubbles and the caffeine were welcome.

Remember, she thought, *you know how to rattle his buttons same as he knows how to push yours.*

With her confidence slowly being restored, Navena took another long drink, shook off the room's unusual draftiness, and returned to her cubicle as the in-charge managing editor staff knew her as.

Forget Maxwell. She allowed her memory a flash of his body atop hers and smiled in spite of her annoyance. *My turn to be on top.*

It was 9:00 AM already and Navena hadn't accomplished a thing. She settled in and reviewed her computerized task list for the day. There was nothing she couldn't conquer, except that Maxwell had her totally distracted. Trying to focus, she logged in to the system and picked up the phone to return calls she'd put off from Friday.

Before she'd had time to make a dent in her voice mail, her on-screen alarm sounded. Navena's stomach knotted. She headed for the meeting, absentmindedly twisting a pair of stray dreads as she hurried down the hallway.

Scattered "happy birthdays!" greeted Navena's entrance into the conference room. She nodded her appreciation and slid into a padded chair alongside Fern Davis, the paper's Youth section editor.

Anderson Cole strolled in and sat across from them. Right behind Anderson trailed Spence Hale, his penny loafers clippety-clapping across the scarred tile floor. The two men were sworn editorial enemies. Spence, the Economy editor, considered himself a journalistic purist and despised everything relating to Anderson's

Lifestyles pages—particularly Anderson. The rumor mill tattled that Spence's new fiancée was Anderson's ex-wife. Their predictable bickering was generally the highlight of the news team's regular meetings.

Remaining news team members quickly assembled around the table, stumbling over a rush of exclamations related, Navena deduced, to the NBA playoffs. The reporters divided and took seats flanking Maxwell, settled at the head of the oblong table, finishing a cup of coffee.

"All right, then," he said, glancing at the latecomers. "Let's call this meeting to order." Maxwell rose from the table. "You should all know by now that I am Maxwell McKnight, your new executive editor." He threw a smile Navena's way.

Her face remained impassive.

"I am really pleased to be here and I'm really looking forward to creating changes at the *Dispatch* that will get this paper the respect it deserves."

He paused, though not long enough for the attentive group to digest the implications of change. He plowed forward with his speech.

"If you want my curriculum vitae, look it up on the Web. Just know I got my undergrad at Dillard, master's at Northwestern. I went from prelaw to NBA, then MBA. Any questions about my credentials for this job?"

He is so arrogant. Navena surveyed her team's expressions. All eyes were on Maxwell. Nobody was even doodling in their notebooks. She met Anderson's eyes as recognition dawned across his face.

"Man, I knew you looked familiar!" he shouted. "Rookie of the Year. All-Star team. Knocked out of the championships by the Lakers three years in a row. Landed on your leg after a helluva slam dunk."

Anderson cupped his hands and released an imaginary basketball across the table. The room's mood lightened. Even Maxwell laughed.

"They call it a *season*-ending injury, but that bad knee cost me my career," he said, peering wistfully above the reporters' heads into a place he seemed to long for.

"I had made a point of picking up the local black paper in every city we played in. And after I . . . lost my job, I decided to pursue publishing."

"Why not broadcasting?" Anderson asked.

"Not interested in being another fly-by-night color commentator. Might as well be sitting on the bench. I was looking for an opportunity to make a difference. I put the word out. Cullen called."

Navena frowned at the mention of her publisher's name. All these years working her way up the food chain and he shut her down with him.

"As a result, I became a long-term, long-distance fan of each of yours. So you can all relax." He paused briefly to laugh. "I am fondly aware of your individual styles, unique story preferences, your successes . . . and your weaknesses. Now I'm ready to play hardball and put my money where my mouth is. I will also be majority owner of the *Dispatch*."

No mention of Hillstone College made its way out of his detailed biography. Why not? Navena felt oddly slighted, as if her memories of that special place and time were perhaps not so memorable for him. Yet she shared his vision of the changes her colleagues longed for at the paper.

No longer pacing, Maxwell stood centered at the head of the table with its rounded vertex hitting squarely between his knees. Arms folded, brow creased, he rattled off a list of new administrative must-do's effective immediately: Monday morning meetings, weekly time sheets, monthly expense reports, source lists for each story, dress code every day.

Maxwell paused and offered an enthusiastic smile. "That ends our first editorial meeting. Let's hit the streets and change the world."

Navena counted living in the new millennium as one of her many blessings. Spending her woman-years in such a time, meant she could lead the life she wanted without fear of social constraints that outdated norms and mores dictated. She could sleep with her man outside of marriage. She could pursue the career she loved. She could ignore her mother. These times allowed her choice: the freedom to follow her mind or forgo it, accept her world or better it. And putting her mark on society—without the family crutch—was what mattered most.

Journalism seemed the most logical route. Far removed from her mystical southern roots, reporting was fact-based, objective, and rooted in rationale. After college, she sought a faraway job at a small northern paper and lucked up on the *Dispatch* in Detroit and edged her way onto the staff by working without pay writing weekly editorials in exchange for bylines. She took a job at UPS and spent weekends telemarketing home improvement in order to pay the rent on her downtown studio apartment.

When she officially hired on—and took home her first paycheck from the paper—it was as city desk editor, a post she commanded for five years. A penchant for school board stories and feel-good youth articles led Navena to the Lifestyles section where she juggled junior columnists, calmed concerned teachers and parents, highlighted positive kids, and waged war on sex and drugs until three years ago when she was promoted to managing editor. She was finally in a position to make a real difference at the paper.

Located in the heart of Detroit, the *Dispatch* commanded prestige as one of the oldest and largest

African-American newspapers in the country. The publication provided a voice for grassroots activists, family reunion organizers, and Missionary Wives Societies that wanted to publicize happenings within the black community. Its weekly pages filled a void for good news, editorials, and human interest stories that seldom rated attention in the larger daily papers.

The *Dispatch* operated with a lean staff. A news team of nine occupied the second floor. On the third floor worked a sales force of five whose cumulative experience totaled more than ninety years. Three graphic designers, four secretaries, one receptionist soon to celebrate her thirtieth anniversary there—all resided on the first floor. And the publisher, Richard Cullen, who occupied one of only two offices in the building, sat in the westernmost corner of the first floor. Still, the few employees managed to put out a twenty-page paper (with color front page) every Wednesday.

A faithful following buoyed the *Dispatch* through depressions, recessions, and plentiful times. Many subscribers renewed faithfully every six months, often pulling children and grandchildren into the ranks of its readership.

Now, away from work, Navena wondered what kind of changes the new man in charge would bring to the paper and her life. She collapsed into an overstuffed sofa, safe amid the comfort of her den's book-lined walls and surround-sound TV.

She allowed herself to contemplate the "what if it had worked?" that she'd kept at bay all day. Or, more specifically, the death knell in her relationship with Maxwell. "What if Maxwell had been free?" Not legally separated with lingering obligations, but hers to have and hold whenever, wherever, however they chose. Would he be hers today?

Instead, as bad as it hurt, she released him to tend to

Lila, his almost ex-wife, and the loose ends a difficult divorce brings.

Even hoochies have scruples, Navena thought with a laugh. She dropped onto the Berber-carpeted floor, using the sleek glass coffee table to unpack her chicken lo mein and cola.

What were the chances of Maxwell McKnight showing up out of nowhere and falling smack dab in the middle of her comfort zone? *What's that saying about letting someone go? Guess they do come back.*

Today, she didn't notice a wedding ring. *So, of course, he's available since I'm trying to figure out my relationship with Luke. Fate's a trip.*

As if cued, the phone rang, forcing her to check the clock on the VCR across the room.

"Boy, talked you up, didn't I?"

"Hey, there," she said evenly. Background noise flooded the telephone receiver. Not-so-muted music and voices pierced the serenity of the scene outside her window.

"Navena . . . hon . . . you there? Can you hear me?" Luke shouted over the din and into her digression. "Happy birthday to you!" He began to sing Stevie Wonder's ode to Martin Luther King.

Stunned, she stood as he serenaded her. She wanted to smile at Luke's foolishness. Instead, his singing seemed silly with everything else she had on her mind.

The doorbell rang.

"Hang on, Luke," she murmured. "I gotta get the door."

Holding the phone, she greeted a tuxedoed deliveryman at the door. Surely, some extravagant birthday gift from Luke.

"Sign here, please, ma'am," the gift bearer instructed, shoving a clipboard and pen into her waist.

She scribbled her shorthand signature. He thanked

her, with a sweeping gesture, stepped aside, and directed her gaze toward the driveway.

"Luke, what have you done?" A giant red bow topped a brand-new car. She moaned inwardly and stepped outside in her bare feet. "You are crazy, you know that?"

"You got it?" Luke asked loudly. "It was supposed to be there this morning, but the paperwork got fouled up."

"This is really too much." Navena circled the car, glancing at the rear bumper to identify its make and model. She sighed into the phone. "A Lexus, huh? What's wrong with my Jeep?"

She shaded her eyes and looked inside, then decided to try the door. The deliveryman followed each footstep and finally succeeded in getting her attention.

"I think you'll need these." He handed over a set of keys, bound on a chain with her name scripted in gold. She smiled politely and waved him off. A cab pulled up to the curb and swept him away.

"I knew you'd like it." Luke sounded pleased with himself, as if he'd satisfied her heart's desire.

"My truck is perfectly fine. And I thought you agreed not to do this kind of stuff anymore." His penchant for buying bling in times of trouble exposed his past life with younger girls who preferred expense over emotion.

"I always gotta come up with new tricks and treats for you, girl." Luke laughed. "You keep a brother on his toes. Besides . . . I love you, Navena."

"I know you do, Luke." Though Navena didn't see that a man who constantly ignored her wishes cared about her at all. Distant thoughts of love notes from Maxwell crept into her mind.

Luke's apology interrupted her drifting thoughts. "Hey, hon, I know it's late and you want to talk, but I'm on my way to meet these folks about finalizing the groundbreaking ceremony. I won't be back till day after tomorrow." He paused. "Are you okay?"

He really doesn't get it. And tonight she wasn't up for fighting. "I'm fine. See you Wednesday."

"Happy birthday," Luke said. "Sleep tight."

"I will. Good night."

Luke hung up and left Navena staring at the top-of-the-line gold Lexus 300 he'd bought. Beautiful, but pointless.

"It's just a bribe. Next thing you know, he'll be proposing again." How do you convince your man you're not the marrying kind? She'd seen too many couples abuse their vows to make the commitment seem worthwhile.

Yet, intrigued by the gift, Navena extended a finger to touch the SUV she had no intention of driving. "No harm in checking it out before I send it back."

Unlocking the door, she hopped inside. She glanced around sniffing for cherry air freshener or some hint of new car scent. Instead, a hint of smoke tickled her nose. Ignoring a brewing uneasiness, she shoved the key into the ignition.

The car's engine roared to life amid a sudden vision of shattered window glass and gunshots. Navena released the steering wheel as if it were fire and thrust herself against the seat, leaning as far back as she could. Leaving the key in the ignition, she fumbled with the lock and tumbled out of the car. Nearly falling onto the driveway, Navena slammed the door behind her and ran back into the house.

Chapter Two

"I can't let you die."

"Do it," he choked.

"I won't."

"If I live, he'll come for you."

Navena's eyes flew open, and yet, the nightmare continued. Mouth wide and dry, pulse booming in her ears, she swam through layers of gauzy confusion, clawing at the window between dream and reality.

"Let me save you!" she begged as the wounded man floated beyond the glassy border.

Frightened shouts, grief-stricken screams, bullets flying, and people fleeing, the vivid scene darted between realms. Real somewhere but theatrical through her sleep-filled lens.

She turned the man's face toward her own, struggling to shift his bulk evenly across her lap.

Footsteps approached from behind.

A gun trigger clicked.

Dampness oozed across her skin, dripped into her lap. A blended odor of mud, blood, cologne, and lipstick filled her nose.

She felt herself scream.

She choked, finally awake. Safe in the lower apartment of the two-family flat she rented from Luke, Navena sat hunched in the recliner, waiting until the vision dissipated. Her sights settled on the tidy row of daffodils vased on the window seat. The scorched smell of gunpowder and the stench of old blood in her nostrils were replaced by the scent of vanilla bean candles and cinnamon apple potpourri from a nearby candle.

Wanting to be sure she was in her den—not in the middle of the street—and that she was not covered in someone else's blood, Navena forced herself upright, fingering her unbundled dreadlocks and surveying her surroundings.

An infomercial pushing cooking gadgets filled the room with chatter. A cool breeze caressed the wind chimes outside the picture window. Fragments of starlight sprinkled the dark room and glittered atop the glass coffee table. Navena shuddered, muddy-minded and cold, as if to toss the vision from her mind and warm her body in wakefulness.

"Shake it off," she told herself. "You fell asleep."

Thrusting her arms outward, she searched for red splatters on her goose-pimpled skin. Finding nothing but remnants of guilt, Navena wondered if her subconscious was punishing her wayward thoughts of Maxwell by killing off Luke.

"I don't want him dead. Just don't want to be his wife," she reassured herself aloud. "Luke's in St. Louis. Safe. Sleeping, I'm sure." She parted her lips and blew several rapid puffs of air until her pulse slowed and the sea inside her ebbed.

Scared to be afraid, deeply worried that something was about to happen to her boyfriend of five years, Navena felt her panic surge on a wave of nausea and nostalgia.

From the first time she'd walked up the front stoop

to check out the flat for rent, Luke commanded her attention—savvy and sexy, though a bit chauvinistic. They'd carved out a friendship that evolved into late nights up and down the stairs in and out of each other's beds.

Without fuss or formality, they blended their lives, assuming fidelity and friendship without promises of forever. Part of her resented the fact that he'd raised the stakes and bought her a ring.

Still, instinct urged her to call him, make sure she hadn't launched some self-fulfilling prophesy. She also wanted to confirm that he was all right without letting him know she feared otherwise. Navena reached toward the end table, picked up the cordless phone, and dialed Luke's cell phone. As it rang, she walked across the room to turn off the TV, pressed the dimmer on the light switch, and strolled to her bedroom.

"Hey, sleepyhead." Navena greeted Luke with relief, stripped out of her work clothes, and sat on the bed in her panties and bra. She stroked the vacant pillow beside her.

"Navena? What time is it?"

She listened as Luke yawned, picturing him wound naked in the hotel's king-sized bedsheets, with two pillows scrunched mercilessly beneath his broad chest. Not wanting to voice the alarm in her heart, still visible in her head, she lied. "I couldn't get back to sleep. I thought you might be up."

"At four in the morning?" Luke laughed. "Didn't you have an imaginary friend when you were little? Call her up."

The shutters rattled.

"You're right. She'd be good to have around about now." Faded memories of an old doll made Navena smile. She became an imaginary friend when Navena couldn't take her along to school or church, and developed into an alter ego during her teenage years. "But I haven't 'talked' to Vee since I was fifteen or sixteen."

"Can't conjure her up like your mother would?"

The dig at her mother's fortune-telling business angered Navena. "Kiss off, Lucas."

His teasing elicited painful singsong remembrances of playground games gone awry. Too many days, "Ring Around the Rosie" became "Ring Around the Witch Girl" as Navena stood within the circle of spinning children.

However imaginary, Vee saved her every time, feeding her strength to cuss out hecklers bigger and stronger than she was. Now spitting those words at Luke rekindled bittersweet memories.

"At least advice never cost you six-ninety-nine a minute." Luke continued his taunting.

"You know . . ." She stemmed her anger because she knew he knew better than to joke about her family's line of work. However, her vision repeated in her head.

Did it signal some future tragedy? Navena tried to recall the fading nightmare scene, wondering if the victim was even Luke, and why she'd have such a horrible dream at all. "You're right. I should let you go."

"Hey, I'm sorry." He paused. "How was your day at work with the new boss and all?"

She didn't dare tell. Luke knew nothing about her college affair with Maxwell and she intended to keep it that way. Few men would be comfortable with their woman reporting to a former lover.

"If first impressions hold true, we're in for quite a ride. He came in talking about big changes. Conceited. Kind of a jerk if you ask me."

"You should've been outta there anyway. Your talent's wasted at the *Dispatch*. So here's your chance to split."

"Translated to what? Stay home and work for you?"

"Something wrong with that?"

"Everything, Sugar Daddy. PR for your company wouldn't be enough. Journalism gives me a life that I like."

"I'm offering one you'd love."

She tried to lighten the tone. The middle of the night was not the time for their ongoing argument over why she should be his wife. "I have you and that's enough."

"That's your problem, Navena. Low expectations."

Here we go, she thought, and sighed aloud. "Thanks again for the car, hon. It's beautiful, but you need to take it back." Truth was, it could be burnt to a crisp in the driveway. She hadn't turned back or peeked out once since she ran into the house. But she wanted to seem appreciative.

"Just giving you what you deserve," he said.

"We have a steady relationship, Luke. A friendship with benefits. I have your back and you've got mine—ring or no ring, right? We don't need to give big gifts to prove how we feel." She changed the subject. "So anyway, how's the conference? Any leads?"

"Plenty. Business will be jumping when I get back. Probably won't be seeing me too much."

"What did you get lined up?" She fished for specifics since she'd be creating promotional materials for his upcoming grand opening event.

"Might have a couple of suburban accounts to bid on."

"For?"

"You know what I do," he said, sounding aggravated. "People want a building. I make it happen. What's up with you tonight? Calling late. Crazy-ass questions. You really *are* checking up on me, aren't you?"

"Just trying to be sure you meet my expectations." Her reply dripped with sarcasm.

"Uh-huh. Then you won't have a problem giving me what I expect when I show up downstairs in a couple of days." He laughed, a raw, throaty chuckle that made Navena shudder in repulsion rather than quiver with attraction. It was hard to think about sex with the feeling of the dream's blood on her hands and hearing the gunfire in her ears.

"Yeah, well, we'll see. I'm going back to sleep. Sorry I woke you."

"No, you're not. I owe you one." He laughed again. Lighter, more Luke-like this time. "Night, babe. Love you."

"Same here. Night."

Click.

"Well, that was a waste of perfectly good worry." She fussed at herself aloud, feeling silly for being concerned. Luke was Luke. So, of course, the conversation went from worry to horny to aggravated. Thus, she sat, still haunted by her dream. No answer in sight.

He was right about one thing. Mama would be awake. Not manning her late-night psychic hotline anymore, but always on call. It seemed to Navena that she never slept.

Still, Luke's well-intentioned teasing began to unleash a hailstorm of realities Navena preferred to deny. All of them linked to her mother the phone psychic and Gramma the fortune-teller.

In the days before 1-900 call-in lines, Mama made her living by reading tarot cards and tea leaves for people around the neighborhood. On a good day, she'd make twenty or thirty dollars. Then she'd take Navena to the market and get crowder peas and greens for Sunday dinner, buy Navena a new hair ribbon for church, and sometimes treat them both to ice cream.

Eventually Mama took over a psychic shop in Sikeston. Word spread of her uncanny accuracy and her popularity grew. Unfortunately, she had as many clients as naysayers, all who seemed to have school-age children.

She used to hate her mother for the playground tears, that cruel classmates evoked. Growing up in a normal family would have been a welcome relief.

I'm not like them, I'm not, Navena insisted, unnerved to even think that the Larimore gift she hoped had passed her by might have circled back to roost.

The phone rang.

"Hi, Mama," she answered, tentative, yet certain. A small, curious voice in the back of her head didn't want to wonder how she knew who phoned without checking the caller ID.

"Are you okay?" Mama's high-pitched tone betrayed her anxiety.

"You know about the nightmare, don't you?" Navena flung the words into the receiver, hoping to release the burdensome feeling of premonition swallowing her. Yet the tremor in Mama's voice told Navena she might not be much help.

"I'm so sorry. It wasn't supposed to happen like this."

Her mother's words tumbled into the space between them. They didn't seem to have any connection to the moment. *Why would Mama apologize for my nightmare? Unless . . .*

"Mama, What's happening? What have you done?"

"It wouldn't unlock—" Mama began to sob. "It was the only way—set aside your gifts and they'd restore them in time. I did what I was supposed to."

"Who made you take *what* from me?" Navena had never heard her mother sound this way. Audrey was always cool and in control. Now she was crying and apologizing, babbling about—"My gifts? Like yours and Gramma Livia's? Getting vibes and seeing ghosts?"

"Or having dreams."

A stiff breeze blew in through the balcony doors, rattling their shutters and stroking Navena's face.

"Oh, that?" She sighed with tickled relief. "I just talked to Luke. He's fine. Must've heard some movie in my sleep. Spooked me at first, but—"

"It's not that simple, sweetheart." Mama sniffled and breathed heavily into the receiver. "See, thirty-three years ago today, you entered the world after thirty-three hours of labor. This birthday begins your Moon Year—the point at which every Larimore woman receives the full extent of her gifts."

"And here I thought maybe it would skip a generation." Navena closed her eyes and fell back against her pillows. "Tell me I have a choice here. That if I say 'pass,' the Larimore Legacy ends without me."

"No. It's your birthright. Like the way we only bear daughters. Or how we're tall, thin, and appear ageless. Each Larimore woman receives one gift. It's always been seeing the future, sensing emotion, reading minds, mentally moving objects, or communing with spirits. But, honey—" her mother took a deep breath—"*your* birth marked a new era for us." Through the wistfulness in her voice, Navena detected a smile. "You arrived on the day of a dark moon, just like tonight's."

With Mama's words, Navena noticed the orb in the black sky, its light shining through the French doors and curtained windows to illuminate her entire bedroom. Drawn by the glow, she stepped out of bed, stood in the room's center, and absorbed the moonbeam.

"Gramma Livia noticed your caul before the rest of us. Yours was the first in ten generations, she said. Some call it a veil. Doctors nowadays say it's just a membrane. Still, it's very, very rare." Mama's pace picked up. "Once she laid you in my arms, I saw it for myself, what Grandma was so excited about."

Warmth surged through Navena's belly, firing upward and outward into her arms and face; spiraling downward between her thighs and through her legs. Her fingertips sparkled.

"Even though medicine thinks it's nothing, we Larimores know that a new moon baby who wears the veil can see in this world and the other realm, cross from dream to reality and back." Her mother continued, despite Navena's speechlessness. "With that comes access to all gifts that each Larimore before you possessed."

"The ones you said you got rid of, right?" Navena laughed, entertained by the moon's display and her mother's saga. "Well, then, what are you worried about? I'm free from the legacy, right?"

"If there had been no dream tonight, I would have said yes." Mama's voice faded as if coming to Navena from afar. "Was there a window?"

"Yes." Navena stopped playing in the moonlight. Fear rose in the stillness around her.

"That's the border. Asleep or awake, glass will let you cross from here to there and back. *Remember that,*" her mother whispered, punctuating the statement with a sense of foresight. "Now, were you in the dream?"

"Kind of," she replied. "You know dreams. Familiar people and places turn out to represent something completely different."

"Not in *that* kind of dream. And not with us Larimores." Mama seemed preoccupied. "Tell me what you can remember."

Navena closed her eyes and reached for dream fragments.

"I was cradling a man in my arms. Someone approached us and shot him."

"Was it Luke?" Mama asked.

"Couldn't tell. The face was familiar, but distorted."

"Luke's out of town?"

"Another engineering conference." Confused and terrified, Navena attempted to scoot beyond the moon's surveillance, escaping only three feet to the bed's edge. She twirled her dreadlocks with her free hand, round and round, mimicking her emotional angst. "Who else could it be? And if my gifts are gone, what does that nightmare have to do with me?"

"We're dealing with two things here—your inheritance and the dream," Mama explained. "Your gifts must have continued to grow while waiting all these years. They are beyond my power to unlock. You are the only one who can retrieve them now.

"As for this dream murder, I have to tell you that our legacy, unfortunately, brings pain with its power. It's much the way a savant is brilliantly musical, but otherwise disabled. We all have a challenge to overcome."

"You expect me to stop this from happening? Is that my 'challenge'? To stop someone from dying?"

"Your dream took you to the other realm. Each time you cross, you bring a piece of that realm into your own reality. Now the death you saw waits here."

Walking to the window to prove her mother wrong, Navena fully opened the shutters and pressed her palms against warm glass. Unexpectedly her hands sank through, shattering the glass and sending her hand into the dark space of the dreamworld. Blood oozed between her fingers.

Navena withdrew her hands. "Mama!" she screamed into the telephone and tumbled onto her bottom on the floor. "What's happening? This nightmare is real?"

"You, Navena, are the only one who can change the future. *You* have to find and undo the death."

Mama was headed down the wrong road with this Larimore thing. Navena wanted no part of it.

"So, what? Now, I'm like you? And Gramma?" Navena scoffed and tugged mercilessly at her hair, as if it were attached to a doll's scalp and not her own. "Not only that, you expect me to save someone from something I know nothing about without any of these family gifts I'm supposed to have?"

"You need to get them back."

"How *do* you get rid of family gifts?" Navena snapped at her mother and released the captive dreadlock spun around her finger. It sprang free and bounced wildly against her shoulder. "What did you do with them?"

"Look under your pillow."

The moonbeam floated from the center of the floor to her headboard, illuminating the rumpled pillows she'd sat on minutes before. Caught between curiosity and skepticism, Navena turned toward the light. Her heart pounded in her chest. Sweat trickled between her breasts. Eyes closed in fear, she inhaled and reached out, snatching the linen from her bed.

The doll magically appeared as she opened her eyes.

"Vee! How—" Her childhood rag doll and imaginary friend lay mangled on the sheet. Her half body was wrapped in a skirt Navena remembered, with a quill pen and a joker card sewn to her only hand. The sight nauseated Navena. "This is sick, Mama."

"That, Navena, is you. It represents the half-life you live now. Your gifts and the life that comes with them are on the other side, a place I couldn't unlock."

She listened as rain began to splatter the balcony beyond, splish-splashing atop the teak decking, Adirondack chairs, and potted hydrangeas. Typical Michigan weather: foul and unpredictable like today's many surprises.

Navena picked up Vee and fingered her yarn hair. "I have a good life," she said absently. "No psychic anything could make me more content."

Mama chuckled. "When you find the other half, you'll see how incomplete your world has been."

"Uh-hmm." She tossed the doll on the bed. "That's enough, Mama. Really. I'm tired. I have to get up in the morning and, thanks to you, the nightmare doesn't matter anymore."

"You can be hardheaded and let that man die if you want to. Or, you can find your gifts, follow their lead, and undo this dream death," Mama said. "Otherwise, what you see will be."

"And if I don't?"

"He will die and you will never be complete."

Mama knew how to irk her daughter. Give her a challenge and dare her to fail. Navena thrived on winning—be it a man, a job, or disproving a dream. She'd play along and show her mother that she was destined to be different all right, by ending up exactly the same. "What do I do?"

"It started with the nightmare. Other dreams will follow." Mama spoke to Navena as if teaching her to read. "Let the trail lead you to Vee. Start there."

"So. I'm on the hunt for half of a doll that can change the world," Navena scoffed.

"How this dream comes to pass—what happens along the way—is in your hands." With a semiscornful laugh, Mama took a deep breath into the space between them. "Like it or not, you have until the next dark moon to claim your inheritance as a true Larimore."

Navena flopped onto the bed next to her half doll. Her palms tingled. She tucked one beneath her bottom for safekeeping. "Never pictured myself a visionary."

"You'll be that and more once you connect with Vee." Mama yawned. "You can do this. Call when you need me."

Relieved to be free of the conversation and its apparitions, Navena submitted to Mama's fatigue—and her own. After a quick exchange of "good night" and

"I love you" she pitched the cordless phone onto the floor and reached to turn off the lamp.

Maybe this is one of those dreams where you think you're awake, but you're not, she thought, then decided to leave on the light.

Navena crawled into bed, pulled the covers up to her chin, and pondered her mother's instructions. The only thing to do now was sleep. She was semiconvinced that by morning, the sun would shine, and all this would be forgotten.

The moonbeam dissipated as stars returned outside the window, winking as if they shared her secret. *Thirty days from now, my life will be just the same. She'll see.*

A veil of sleep descended on the sky beyond, cloaking the Morse code sparkles that tried to warn her otherwise.

Chapter Three

Tuesday, May 10
St. Louis, Missouri

Vee deciphered the code, twinkle by twinkle, letter by letter, feeling helpless.

Disoriented, she lay motionless, watching the nightmare melt into the sunrise outside her window. Blue jays and chipmunks chattered in the tree beyond the screen. Mixed smells of morning dew and leftover lovemaking assured her she was home. Nervous perspiration dampened her forehead.

Dismayed by the dream, Vee rolled over to reach for her husband. His sand-tone skin sank deep into the red satin sheets, the image he cast mirrored the death dream she'd just witnessed: her Mack lying dead in a pool of blood. Tears welled in her eyes.

It didn't matter that the dream was not her own, that she just happened to witness someone else's nightmare. What she watched—whether fate or coincidence—frightened her.

She'd never dreamed herself so clearly before. Even with dreadlocks and all new details, Vee recognized her own spirit inside the woman she watched all night.

The pictures in her mind played vividly, erasing her husband, their life, and the world as she knew it, without ceremony or explanation. Everything from her home to her hairstyle belonged to someone else.

She freed her hand from Mack's and felt for the satin head wrap constricting her layered shag. Poked a finger beneath to check its texture and length. *I've never considered dreadlocks.* The thought—and sight—amused her, though little else from the dream did.

Seeing Mama made her sad. Vee missed her so. Her job at the paper seemed exciting, but the life portrayed, overall, felt empty. Especially without Mack.

She eased her arm over his broad shoulders, hugging him close and listening to his deep peaceful breathing.

Of course he's here. The same way he'd been every night for five years. Vee relaxed with a tickled sigh.

Crazy.

Scary.

Mack murdered?

Cupping her body against his, Vee pressed her nose into the nape of his neck and rubbed it against the prickly edges of his close-cut fade. This was reality. Mack had not died in her arms as they slept.

Vee held her palm up against the encroaching dawn, spread her fingers, and admired her wedding band. In the diffused light, its elaborate etchings glistened like stars. Glow, twinkle, shadow, glow, twinkle, shadow, as she rotated her hand back and forth.

Mack stirred and scooted into her hips' heat. "Feels brand-new, doesn't it?"

Marriage, yes. Especially since moments ago, you weren't even alive.

"Amazing." She continued wiggling her fingers. Glow, twinkle, shadow. "How it shines in this dimness."

"Like us." Mack ran his hand up the length of Vee's outstretched arm and grasped her fingers in his own.

He pulled her hand to his lips and kissed it. "I would know you from a million miles away."

"I hope so," she whispered, remembering their nonexistent love in the dream and the dying man in her arms.

"Promise." He answered the unspoken prayer as if he'd witnessed her vision.

Swept by a sense of urgency, she hugged him tightly, inhaling the smell of unscented soap and unwashed sex, committing the moment to permanent memory.

I can't imagine me without you.

Sleep began to tug at the fringes of her mind even as she traced her name across his bare back.

"Don't start something you can't finish," Mack teased.

"Bet I'll outlast you," she said, kissing him on the shoulder to seal the deal. "Please make love to me."

He turned to face her. Dawn spilled orange rays on his bare chest.

Vee smoothed his eyebrows with her thumbs, studying his model-square jaw and the beard that outlined it. She absorbed the affection pouring through his eyes, soaked in his sensuality.

"I love you" floated from her mouth.

Mack captured her tongue with his own, kissing and climbing atop her. His large hands found her supple breasts. They touched. Explored. Seeking out the familiar places that made their love real.

A moan escaped. He kissed her harder, forcing his tongue deep inside her mouth. She opened wide to receive him, anticipating what came next.

Mack clenched her head and tilted it back to expose her neck. Running his tongue from ear to collarbone and back, he lapped between her breasts and down to her navel. Uncontrollable shivers shook her thighs.

Sliding the satin fabric above her hips and up to her shoulders, Mack punctuated every step with a kiss. Vee shivered. He cupped her breasts. Squeezed her. Hard. Pushed the gown over her head to expose her entire body and returned his mouth to her breasts, lapping hungrily at the right nipple, then the left.

Vee writhed, moaning and reveling in her reality. Light poured through a gap in the drapes, illuminating her sweat-dampened body.

Tracing a heart on her forehead with his finger, he whispered, "You are so beautiful."

On cue, Vee spread her legs to invite him in. Explosions began the moment he entered her, releasing shameless primal screams, part fear, part love. She moaned and shivered, writhed and screamed, as he seared her again and again. The bed heaved and shuddered beneath their frantic lovemaking.

When she thought she might die from the unbearable pleasure that started between her legs and ravaged her entire body, Mack grunted, biting her softly on the lip. She squealed in pain and orgasm, arched her back, scratched his. They tumbled, liberated and satiated, until every ounce of love they held for each other had been shared between them.

I love you. She inhaled his essence, fighting fatigue as the nightmare faded, afraid that if she drifted too far, she might not find her way home.

"Hey, sunshine, how's it going?" Mack's voice crackled through the cell phone.

"Great," Vee answered, squinting against the afternoon glare. "I could learn to like this freelance journalism stuff."

"So, what did they say?"

"Drumroll, please." Carefully avoiding the sidewalk

cracks, she fished for a pair of sunglasses inside her oversized tote, slid them on her nose, and cleared her throat. "Guess who's got the cover of the fall *Made in Missouri* magazine?"

"I knew they'd catch on quick," Mack said. "What's your assignment?"

"Did you know Missouri was America's second Motown?" She paused. "Yep. Right behind Michigan in car production after the World Wars. But Missouri missed the Motor City's slump by diversifying its industry. I get to find a family to talk about what Michigan should've done differently and how it's affected them."

"Gonna make some folks angry?"

"Now, you know I like it that way." She laughed. "Can you come to Detroit with me for a few days?"

"As long as I'm back in time to prep for my Youth Basketball Camp in three weeks."

"See, that's why I love you. Always got my back."

"No doubt. Make the arrangements. Just tell me where to be and when."

"Later, love."

They each hung up. Vee stopped midstep and turned her face skyward. *Thank you, God.*

Finally, it seemed all the waiting had paid off. What she'd hoped for long ago when Mack left to teach at Millstone University, halfway across the country, now belonged to her. His love, his loyalty, his life. Even giving up his tenure proved only a minor setback.

Choosing her world over his ended his education career, but he was still awesome on the basketball court. And luckily, the blessed fathers at Ignatius Preparatory Academy appreciated his coaching ability.

Through Mack's diligence, the team earned its first state title in twenty-five years and Vee won the man of her dreams.

* * *

"What's going on down here today?" Vee asked the travel agent.

Through wall-sized windows beyond the low-walled cubicle, men in business casual blue and khaki strolled in groups, chatted on street corners, and darted through midday traffic. She loved her city's resurgence, but regretted choosing today to venture outdoors instead of online.

"Society of Black Engineers convention." The travel agent spoke between keyboard strokes, interrupting Vee's musings. "I've been taking in the eye candy all day."

"No women in SBE?" Vee asked, scoping the scenery.

"There are, but they're probably smart enough to be inside, out of the heat." The woman laughed and spun her computer monitor toward Vee. "This is what we've got for Detroit."

Vee scanned the screen's offerings of fares and departure and return schedules. Dates and appointments flipped through her mental calendar. She needed two weeks to work and Mack would appreciate a few days before his basketball camp. So much for a seven-day advance.

"We'll leave Saturday afternoon," Vee decided.

She turned her attention to the men on the sidewalk. One in particular.

He was head and shoulders above his companions, his red conference badge swinging in side-to-side unison with his confident strides. Dark-skinned. Athletic build. Fine as hell.

Luke! She instantly recognized her dream twin's boyfriend.

He stopped, rotating his head as if he heard Vee think, and looked right into her eyes. The lingering gaze told her he knew exactly who she was.

Impossible.

Already at the corner, but less than twenty feet away, Luke seemed to beckon, no, *dare* her approach.

Vee stood and called Luke's name.

A gust of wind tore through the intersection, scattering leaflets and lost lunch napkins. Heavy traffic signals groaned at the upheaval, swinging with precarious lethargy over unwitting passersby.

"Walk across," the wind whispered, pounding against the window, startling Vee.

"Are you okay, ma'am?" asked the embarrassed-looking agent who wore a look that said she'd rather not get involved. "Do you want to come back and finish another time?" The woman began shoveling printouts and brochures into a brightly colored folder and offered the package to Vee.

Sunlight glinted from the amber traffic signal. In a flash, the light turned green, Luke disappeared, and Vee returned from the glitch in time that crossed their paths.

I swear Gramma told me what to do if this ever happened.

Well aware of her intuitive sense, Vee had grown accustomed over the years to thinking up numbers that won the three-digit lottery, keeping quiet about which games Maxwell's high schoolers would lose, suggesting alternate vacation routes to avoid accidents and traffic tie-ups. The apparition of Luke was so much more than she ever dreamed she'd see.

She'd waited all her life, looking and listening for the perfect time to cross over the way Grandma said she could. From where she sat to what she'd dreamed and back, her gift had actually taken her somewhere.

Now that it finally happened, turns out I had no say-so in the how or why, but that's okay, too.

"We're open till five the rest of the week, or you can

just visit our Web site to complete your reservations." The travel agent rolled her chair backward and stood.

"I'm sorry," Vee apologized, turning to push the materials back across the desk. "I thought I saw an old friend."

"But there wasn't anybody out there where you were looking."

I'm psychic, not schizophrenic. "You must have missed him," she said.

Knowing that only she saw Luke, Vee kept her gaze and smile steady, reached into her purse, and produced an overstuffed wallet. "That'll be credit, thank you."

The agent sat, slowly, keeping her eyes riveted on Vee. She typed faster now, skipped the chitchat, and finished the transaction with curt, abrupt requests. "Number of passengers? Name? Smoking or nonsmoking hotel room? Anything else? Sign here. Enjoy your stay."

Vee wondered if she would.

The woman mirroring her face, haunting her dreams, sleeping with that fine-ass Luke, felt like a separate side of herself. Who she was and how they were bound worried Vee.

Rising to leave, she tried to focus, but couldn't. Distracted by the new world outside the window, she questioned Luke's presence here, worried that fate also had plans for her Mack on the other side.

Chapter Four

Wednesday, May 11
Detroit, Michigan

Maxwell dribbled downcourt, the moon glowing and growing in his grasp.

Navena waded in the front seat, watching him bob and weave through the rising pink water, feeling the tum-tump *of his nearing heartbeat in each moon-ball bounce.*

He rose from the water, arm arched for the layup.

Flew. Sailed. Missed.

And came crashing empty-handed through the backboard, now windshield, into her lap.

Mirrored shards exploded and sliced her skin. She opened her eyes.

Luke stood atop the moon.

Watching.

"Hello, beautiful."

Navena gasped.

"Babe, babe, it's me."

From the night sky to her bedroom, she slid through the dream's glass border, shattering it, and found herself falling into Luke's arms.

"How'd you get down . . . here?" The last word

slipped sheepishly from her lips as she felt for her comforter and found no shattered glass.

The burgeoning moon, now a wrought-iron wall sconce, softly lit Luke's rugged features, casting his ebony skin a mellower chocolate, his near-black eyes, cocoa. She slumped into his embrace. Safe. "What time is it?"

"Took the red-eye to surprise you. It's just after seven—in the morning." He leaned over to kiss her forehead while pulling the covers away from her body. "Time for a little lovin', I think."

"It's only been three days, you fiend." She felt hot and clammy, not moist and ready.

Undaunted, he rolled Navena onto her back, slid her sleep-damp chemise above her breasts, and straddled her body.

She blinked and saw Maxwell lying bloodied across her chest. In a surge of disoriented panic, she pushed Luke away and ran blindly into the bathroom.

Luke followed. "Navena! What the hell is wrong with you!"

Unable to close the door before he entered, Navena stared upward at his towering frame, which, until this moment, had never seemed quite so . . . insurmountable. Forcing herself to blink away the remnant dream, she refocused on his face and found the one she knew so well.

"Oh, it is you!" Wrapping her arms around his waist, she sank her face into his chest, inhaling the familiar—too familiar—smell of . . . what?

"Bad dream?" Even his softest voice managed to grate. "Is that really why you called the other night?"

"No. I *was* checking on you."

Totally true, yet Luke laughed in disbelief, as if she'd told a joke.

"I can tell when you're jonesing for me. I missed

you, too." He smiled the way he did when a new contract came through. "And I have"—he kissed the top of her head—"just the thing"—he reached into his pocket—"to keep you company when I'm gone." He opened his palm.

She looked and saw the sight she feared. Her heart sank. "Earrings!" she lied.

Luke released Navena and pulled back the box's felt-covered burgundy lid. Caught in a ray of sunlight, the diamond tucked inside sparkled like mirror shards.

"Will you marry me?" He bent to one knee.

Absolutely not. She took a deep breath before she spoke "I get a long engagement." She tried to soften the blow by placing her hands atop his shoulders.

"Six months," he countered.

"Two years."

"Then what's the purpose?"

His body bristled beneath her palms. Navena ran her hand across the low waves in his hair, trying to think of a new explanation. There was none, "Luke, we've talked about this."

She felt him freeze, then watched him rise, stepping back as he glowered at her.

"Damn it, Navena Larimore, I'm sick and tired of *talking* about this."

"I want more time, with the paper and my career."

"It's time for you to quit looking at the fact that your mama and grandmama lived alone and do for yourself." He sneered, the insult piercing Navena's gut. "Either you marry me this time or we're through."

He threw the open box into the sink and stormed out the door.

Navena watched as the ring swirled, slipped, and skidded around the porcelain basin, exhaling with relief once she heard Luke's Escalade roar away. He did have a point. She came from a long line of women without men in their lives. And they all seemed just fine—strong, smart, and sovereign. While she shied away from the powers they possessed, she appreciated the fact that the Larimore legacy encouraged her to live life on her own terms. And that meant unmarried, if she so chose.

Hesitating as she parted the shower curtain, Navena slowly turned the faucet. Real water—not moonbeams or shattered glass—flowed from the showerhead and warmed the cool stall. As her line between dream and reality blurred from night to night, she needed to confirm what she hoped to be true.

The day, so far, was real.

From the instant she said hello, Maxwell fought to steer his eyes from Navena, barely winning the battle moment by moment.

He loved her lashes, the way they brushed perilously close to the tinted lenses of her glasses. She didn't wear mascara and didn't need the soft black liner that arched her lids. But the shimmering gold that dusted her heart-drawn lips was a keeper. New, not the call-girl red she used to wear, this shade nearly blended into her powder-perfect skin except for the shimmer it cast under the fluorescent light.

In this age of sexual harassment sensitivity, he could not afford to have his intentions misread or, in this case, lingering affection uncovered.

His confidence surged, and he felt like he was standing in the free throw lane with the winning shot falling through the basket at the buzzer. Nothing but net, no time left on the clock. This situation was a surefire win. Career, love life, he saw it all falling in place.

Swish.

Sitting in his yet undecorated office, warmed by shimmering sunshine and a racing pulse, he reveled in imminent victory. He had scripted his entire reappearance in Navena's life: their introduction, the initial staff meeting, and soon, her promotion.

Assessing the staff's insecurities had been easy: They thought that he would "clean house," bring in his own staff, get rid of them all. But they'd be wrong. This was his first leadership position in publishing. He intended to make the *Dispatch* widely read and wildly profitable, certainly, but he would not destroy what Navena had worked so fervently to build.

Maxwell had read her first column inadvertently. He was in town for the Black Journalists' Society conference in '97 and had wandered into the Marriott gift shop for snacks and a newspaper before retiring to his room.

Someone had hurriedly dropped a copy of the *Dispatch* into the *Free Press* rack. Navena's picture smiled from a sidebar box beneath the week's headline. NEW COLUMNIST COMMENTS ON GUNS IN SCHOOLS. PAGE 1D. And boy, did she comment!

An avid reader, Maxwell devoured editorials as a daily ritual. He read the liberal writers he agreed with, writers whose viewpoints he despised, writers he thought were confused or bored—or both. Navena became a writer he liked. Week after week, she challenged him to check his conventional ideas, his comfortable existence, and his definition of the struggle. She seemed just as feisty as the twenty-year-old girl he'd debated with and fallen for years ago. Through her editorials and articles, he watched her grow into the woman who outshined his expectations.

Like her, Maxwell found, he believed that the struggle for justice must be conscious, must be more than politically correct, must transcend race. Her fight became his: demanding adequate health care, quality schools, decent housing, good jobs, clean parks, and accountable elected officials. Navena drew him to the *Dispatch*, not Richard Cullen.

Years spent sharpening his mind, rehabbing his body, and choosing his new "sport" readied him for this point in time, perfectly poised to capture Navena. Again.

Their breakup had left him bitter. The decade and a half separating them had not soothed the sting. He blamed it on her youth. What does a twenty-year-old know about what she wants in life and love? How could she appreciate what they'd had together? She hadn't even known what she'd wanted to be when she grew up.

But now their hour had finally arrived.

Pushing back from his desk, Maxwell walked toward the window. The day was beautiful, much more than he thought Detroit could muster up, even in spring. Pigeons perched on his sill and he tapped the dusty window in greeting. He felt incredible.

The last fourteen years spent learning to love women the right way would all be to Navena's benefit. Just like the old days, he'd be the intelligent man she craved, but with sensitivity only his divorce could have taught him. And, judging by her empty ring finger, time favored his hopes.

He turned to his computer and typed a simple e-mail:

If you can free your schedule for a luncheon meeting at one o'clock today, I'd like to review a few staff modifications with you.

He entered Navena's name in the TO line, clicked SEND, and smiled coyly.

Primed with a cola and a candy bar, Navena was entrenched in day-after-deadline duties by 8:15 AM. She skimmed her calendar and opened her in-box.

An e-mail appeared on the screen. Maxwell summoning her to lunch at one. *See you then,* she typed, firing off the reply and regretting her anxiousness the second she hit SEND.

Seemed she'd always been in a hurry to satisfy his whims. Fourteen years ago it was, "See you after class." "See you at the pool hall." And eventually, "See you next lifetime," when she walked away from the heartache.

They say be careful what you wish for. If this is our next lifetime, maybe I should've taken heed.

Her phone rang. Fern's name showed up on the caller ID.

"Hey, girl, what's up?" If Fern spent more time working and less time chitchatting, she'd be one helluva reporter.

"How's your day going?"

"Nothing to write home about." Navena stretched, recoiled, and finished sorting her remaining e-mails. "Had I known Luke was going to propose again, I probably would've stayed in bed."

Maybe she could survive without the spark they lacked, marry him, if she could convince herself that being a power couple was enough. "Our arrangement suits me and my career. Besides, we Larimores seem to repel marriage."

"Your daddy *died*. That was different."

"True. But Mama and Grandma did fine on their own. I probably could, too." *Since I'm so much like them all of a sudden.*

"If you don't want to be with Luke, you ought to start paying rent."

Navena frowned. "You know I try, but—"

"Yeah, yeah. He won't cash the checks." Fern paused. "So move out. Break up. Give yourself some space."

It had crossed her mind this week.

* * *

Maxwell escorted Navena into a new bistro on the fringes of downtown. She faced the window and could see the Detroit River and Canadian skyline beyond Maxwell's shoulders. Sun shone off the water. Freighters drifted by. Used to taking lunch at her desk, she took a moment to bask in being out of the fray of copy and deadlines.

The restaurant was packed, filled with what appeared to be regulars, ordering without menus and with no hesitation. Palm Pilots beeped, cell phones sang, and the conversation rivaled a casino floor's jangle. From the platters she could see the wait staff placing on other tables, this meal could also serve as tonight's dinner. For a newcomer, Maxwell had picked an excellent spot.

"So you've made a career of the *Dispatch*, haven't you, Larimore?" Maxwell jogged her daydream. He took a deliberate swig of his club soda, set it carefully on a small white napkin, folded his hands, and looked her in the eye.

"I've tried my best, *McKnight*." Navena peered over the top of her frameless Versace glasses, directly into Maxwell's half smile. She began to notice that he wore that look, that smirk thing, like a mask. Sculpted and haughty, not at all personal, like she first assumed.

"All right, all right, *Navena*," Maxwell said, hands thrown up in mock surrender. He chuckled. "Seriously, though, you're not bored with the black consciousness thing yet?"

"You mean why haven't I moved on to the dailies? Why haven't I given up this poverty pay scale for enough money to pay my car note and my rent out of one check instead of two?"

Navena lowered her eyes. Maxwell's gaze was too intense. She retossed her salad, stirring the crisp romaine leaves and softened croutons around and around in the puddle of vinaigrette swamping her plate.

They sat tucked into a corner table, elbow to elbow with a group of accountant-looking types. Maxwell was eagerly putting away a sixteen-ounce strip steak, the day's special, and most of the complimentary dinner rolls. Navena was wasting her Salad Nicoise and had already downed two glasses of cola. It seemed the "meeting" was beginning.

"I've been black all my life and writing just as long," Navena said. "One is just as natural as the other and I can't really change either fact. The *Dispatch* seemed like the right place to do both and sleep with a peaceful conscience."

"Still militant, I see," Maxwell quipped.

"Not at all," Navena replied. "Socially aware, I'd say, but not a social revolutionary. I possess the *wisdom to know the difference.*" She referred to the Serenity Prayer, most often used by twelve-steppers, but typed on a Post-it note hidden in her wallet behind her driver's license.

"Recovering?" Maxwell queried.

"From dope or booze, no," said Navena. "From commitment phobia, I'd say."

"Then you'll be getting married soon—to the guy in the picture on your desk, I presume?"

"No need to sound disappointed," Navena teased. "I'm not interested in marriage."

Maxwell raised his eyebrows. "You used to be."

"What? When I was with you? Youthful fantasy." She shook her head and rolled her eyes. "My experience shows that staying single works best. This way, Luke keeps his, I keep mine, we enjoy each other's company. That's plenty."

"What's he do anyway?"

"Architectural engineer. Runs his own company. Luke is a moneymaking machine."

"Sounds like he's got all the credentials. You'd feel differently about marriage if he was the one."

"You still believe in that?"

"More than ever."

Navena squirmed under Maxwell's unrelenting scrutiny. What was he trying to imply? *Something you're not trying to hear (again), girlfriend.*

"Yeah, right. The one." She smirked. "So, what were we talking about before you started grilling me like that steak?"

"I can take a hint. Just know that I'm more interested in your ideas for the paper than getting in your business, Navena," Maxwell laughed. "So, what does the *Dispatch* need that you and I can deliver?" He cut a sliver of steak, doused it with steak sauce, and tossed it in his mouth, giving Navena full view of his wonderfully white teeth.

"The *Dispatch* needs a new voice," said Navena. "We lack differentiation. We don't stand out anymore, we don't make the difference I think we should.

"Even so, Maxwell, the *Dispatch* has some great writers. Reporters. People who give a damn and dig, dig, dig." She paused to remove a stack of papers from the satchel beside her chair and handed the weighty document to Maxwell. "Fresh vision and a little cash would do wonders for morale—and circulation."

"Too bad you're going to miss all the action," Maxwell said, smirking and stabbing a parsley-covered potato. He flipped mockingly through the proposal she'd passed him and dropped it onto the floor with a thud. "Word is you're joining the very mainstream *Morning Star*. I guess this is where the black thing ends for you, huh?"

"There's always Black History Month." Navena laced the words with sarcasm. "How'd you hear?"

"The industry is a pretty small circle," said Maxwell. "The president of Detroit's Black Journalists' Society is night desk editor over there. I called for information on joining the society, told him I was headed over to the *Dispatch*, and he told me you'd just accepted an offer."

Navena tipped her head at his lie. The phone call with the offer came just before she ran out for lunch today. More importantly, she hadn't accepted the job. Yet.

"So much for confidential information." Navena played along. "Why?"

"I think I can convince you to reconsider."

More easily than you'd believe. "Try me."

"The *Dispatch* doesn't work because it projects an old-school image. We need new school, cutting-edge as opposed to the traditional canned news offering," said Maxwell.

"So you think the *Dispatch* takes the easy road, too?" Navena asked, agreeing with his assessment.

"No doubt," said Maxwell. "In fact, I think the community *depends* on us to present the black take on last week's mainstream headlines. And we have yet to let them down."

"But I think that even with sharper staff—not to say ours isn't sharp—and memberships to professional organizations, *better pay*, all that, none of it's going to make a difference if the higher-ups aren't behind us when a story's on the line," Navena countered and signaled the waiter for another glass of cola.

Curiosity pulled her deeper and deeper into what she knew was Maxwell's net. Yes, she'd considered another job. But only because she felt that, ultimately, the *Dispatch* had pushed her away with low pay and lack of respect. She desperately wanted to know where Maxwell was headed with all this.

"Bylines in the *Dispatch* don't mean diddley to Cullen," sneered Maxwell. "You have to know that by now." He leaned forward on his elbows, his face seductively nearing Navena's. "It's strictly money. And, truth is, the *Dispatch* is unprofitable. We don't make enough in two years to pay half the annual salaries around here."

"We're broke?" Navena was stunned.

"Technically," answered Maxwell. "But Cullen and Bartlett were buddies—"

"Old man Bartlett, the sales manager?"

"Yeah, him," Maxwell confirmed. "The deal was that Cullen kept the paper afloat so long as Bartlett kept it visible. Cullen felt he couldn't afford not to have presence in a city that's eighty percent black."

"What's the but?" Navena straightened in her chair, leaning nearer to Maxwell. She tried to ignore the smell of his cologne, heated in their nearness.

"Cullen's board of directors met last week." Maxwell lowered his eyes. Navena held her breath.

"They were prepared to shut down the *Dispatch* effective December thirty-first of this year. Liquidate and consolidate what they could. Offer staff positions at the other papers as they became available. But in short, vacate the *Dispatch* as efficiently as possible. Then I stepped in to save the day."

Maxwell leaned back in his seat and laced his fingers, smiling smugly.

Conflicting emotions pelted Navena. Anger tightened her throat as she fought back despair.

"Just like that." Navena snapped her fingers and rolled her neck. "They were ready to toss us out without another thought?" She took off her glasses and rubbed her temples to smooth away a brewing headache.

"So, what are you saying? That you've been sent here to get us fattened up for the slaughter. The inevitable sale? You've got a helluva lotta nerve." She accused.

"Hold up, Navena. I'm with you." He defended himself without hesitation. "If I wasn't, why would I invest now? You're not listening. I'm here to save the *Dispatch.*"

"So *you* can sell it when the price is right?" Navena challenged.

Taking a slow sip of club soda, Maxwell dove into his last piece of steak. He chewed thoughtfully and swallowed heavily. "Look, I know you have a talented team and I think there's a way we can prove Cullen and his crew wrong. You gonna fight this or help me out here?"

"What am I worth to you, McKnight?"

"Name your poison," he challenged.

"Sixty." Double her current salary.

"You know we can't afford that." Maxwell signaled for the server and asked for a dessert menu. "Guess that means I better find us some capital to cover your new paycheck."

For a moment, she thought he was telling her no. Then he smiled. Maxwell actually looked earnest. Navena's head exploded with ideas. Part of her contemplated the paper's future, while the other wondered if this explained why she hadn't married Luke yet.

"I've always given the *Dispatch* two hundred percent," Navena shared, wanting to stick to business. "The relationship hasn't been reciprocal. So, how do I know—"

"My word." He smiled.

She frowned.

"Okay! A contract," he laughed, shaking his head at her persistence. "Plus every name I know, every favor I can squeeze."

"Why not call your old ball-playing buddies and ask them to ante up?" Navena asked.

"I can get more money, but there's only one you." Maxwell hesitated. "In order to survive, this paper needs your gumption, your gall . . . your crazy faith. On my honor. I won't run out on you again." He held up the three-finger Boy Scout sign and crossed his heart with the other hand.

His obvious sincerity convinced her. "I suppose I'll stay," she said with a shrug. She would dare to take this chance, not so much for the paper, she knew, but for the changes it signaled in her future.

She'd have to call the *Morning Star*—which was hoping she could start in two weeks—and turn down their offer.

Her wandering mind would have to return its attention to the *Dispatch's* everyday struggle instead of front-page story worries she anticipated at the new job. If the paper folded she'd be out of work. Maxwell would become her lifeline.

He stared at her now, grasping her gaze and holding it tight, squeezing the promise from her with a smile. Navena laughed to break the stronghold and dropped her eyes. She was hungry, but the salad was inedible and the bread was gone. She sipped her cola and met Maxwell's eyes once more.

Remember, Navena, her heart whispered and a sly grin emerged. *Once a jerk, always a jerk.*

The dessert tray arrived. Maxwell lifted a flute of mousse in mock salute. Navena did likewise.

"Welcome to my world," she toasted. The words flooded her mouth without forethought, hung there with a familiar aftertaste.

"So glad to be in it," Maxwell said. "Now, let's put some *real* news on this week's front page."

They tapped glasses and locked eyes.

With the day's final meeting conquered and next week's editorial lineup assigned and in progress, Navena bounded out the *Dispatch* door at four-thirty sharp, without even waiting for her computer to shut down completely.

What a beautiful afternoon!

Late spring sun blazed through a cloudless sky, honeysuckle bushes perfumed the air, and just enough breeze stroked the worry lines from her forehead. She had to stop herself from skipping to the car. For a morning that started with her second nightmare, another fight with Luke, and uncertainty over Maxwell's plans for the paper, the hours had morphed into a day of promise.

Despite Mama's fantastic predictions, she had yet to intercept a stray thought, move traffic just by wishing, or bump into any ghosts since her supposed birthday "gifts" arrived. Their absence suited her just fine. In fact, she planned an extra-strenuous workout for tonight's aerobics students. By pushing the class, she hoped to wear herself out and, hopefully, wind up too sleepy to dream.

Fingers crossed.

Chances of Luke making his way downstairs to her flat (and bed) tonight were slim. He was livid. She felt pensive. Next to her memories of Maxwell—flaws and all—the life with Luke that had seemed perfectly acceptable three days ago suddenly fell below par.

"I *am* focused on my career. I *don't* see the sense in marriage. I *can't* keep this up," Navena admitted to herself at last. "Luke's threatening to leave anyway. Find somewhere else to live and just let him go."

Unlocking the Jeep door, she tossed her tote onto the passenger side, slid into the seat, and slammed the door with finality.

Yes, that's what I'll do.

Depositing her uncashed rent money into a savings account had proven wise. Now she could easily make the down payment on a small house in West Village, just outside downtown. That would shorten her commute and cut her fill-ups in half. She started the engine and reached absently for the radio dial, searching for a song to balance the sunshine outside and her brewing melancholy within.

Five years is a lot of time to leave behind. And what about the dream? If Mama's right, Luke could be in some kind of trouble. Should I just let that go, too?

The FM tuner settled on George Benson's "Masquerade." She turned up the music and sang along, lost in her decision and what it meant for the days ahead.

Chapter Five

Thursday, May 12
Detroit, Michigan

I gotta give it to him, Navena thought with guarded reverence, *he didn't lie.* She strolled through the newsroom taking note of each reporter's activity. It was early, but everybody was obviously working—not chitchatting, sipping coffee, or catching up on gossip.

Maxwell expected every reporter to work just as hard as he did. In the three days since his arrival, she'd even taken to getting in the building on time. His work ethic impressed her most, a trait she couldn't fully appreciate in a student-teacher relationship, yet all but worshipped as his colleague.

Judging by staff's sidelong glances at her entrance, she could tell that the admiration she held for Maxwell's management style hadn't trickled down to her staff.

They'll come around, she thought, settling into her desk and logging on to the computer. A lengthy list of e-mails popped onto the screen.

Among the spam selling erection cures and weight-loss wonders was her daily electronic dose of headline news from the city's daily papers and major broadcast stations. They all bore the same breaking local story:

WHO'LL SAVE THE SINKING DISPATCH? CITY'S BLACK PAPER STRUGGLING FOR SURVIVAL.

"Damn it, what is this?" Navena's out-of-character exclamation raised a ripple of heads around the newsroom. "So that's what's wrong with you all?" She met their accusing eyes, staring each person down until all gazes returned to their respective computer screens.

The headline atop the *Morning Star*'s business section screamed imminent disaster. Looking like he agreed, Cullen grinned from a 1980s black-and-white head shot. Just as bad, Maxwell's ancient NBA photo ran next to it, showing him airborne and dunking in short shorts and long socks. The picture was funny. The article was not.

This is the last thing we need right now. Maybe staff thought she knew all along. Navena stormed into Maxwell's office.

"Did you see the *Morning Star*?" she hissed at his back through clenched teeth.

As if awaiting her arrival, Maxwell turned slowly from the window he was staring out and looked at her warily. "Have a seat."

He motioned her forward as he walked toward his desk, stopping to offer her an apple-flavored Jolly Rancher as she took a seat.

My favorite. She fought off an encroaching smile as he watched her unwrap the sticky sweet and pop it into her mouth.

"You trying to tell me you didn't know until now?" Maxwell leaned back in his chair and laced his fingers behind his head. "It's been all over the news the whole morning."

Now I feel stupid.

No dream last night, as she hoped, but she awoke

just as groggy. By the time she stopped slamming the snooze button, there was only half an hour to shower, dress, and make it in on time. The TV didn't even come on this morning. And, of course, she only did CDs in the car. Never news. It felt too much like working all the time.

So now here she stood, facing Maxwell's soft lashing.

"I *am* managing editor." Admitting the fault left a bitter taste on her tongue. She swallowed and continued. "I should be up on what's happening at any given time."

There was nothing else to say.

"Don't feel bad." Maxwell leaned forward. "It's part of our strategy. I won't hold this slip against you. Just know that everybody else came in with the news flash written across their foreheads. I'd bet they've all got their résumés on their screens now."

"They probably think I knew."

"I would."

Navena exhaled with a heavy sigh. "Like I'm not having enough trouble convincing them nothing's going to change just because we're under new management. Ha!"

"Relax. Like I said, it's all part of my plan." Maxwell leaned forward. "I leaked the story."

Why stir up the very people you needed in your corner for survival? She frowned. "That doesn't make any sense to me. Why would—"

"Because I need to get black folks' attention in this city. Sad truth is we often rally around a cause." Maxwell returned to his lean-back position, tilting his chair enough to cross one long leg T-style across the other. "All my calls to 'do the right thing' won't get nearly as much response as the fear of losing Detroit's only real African-American voice. Betcha I have three new investors by week's end."

"Bet." Navena surprised herself by chirping up.

She loved the fact that he was willing to take such a huge chance with his reputation. Not so thrilled about him toying with her job, necessarily, but attracted in a very primal way to Maxwell in hunter mode.

His eyebrows rose. "Never knew you to be a gambler." He smiled. "You're on. The stakes?"

"I'll get back to you on that," she answered coyly. "Now, what about them?" She motioned over her shoulder toward the newsroom. "How much are *they* supposed to know?"

"Only what's in the paper." Maxwell's sudden sternness reminded her of the situation's true seriousness. They were in financial trouble. This "strategy" needed to work.

"Okay," she agreed. "Just that readership is down, the other papers in the chain are selling, and we need a new infusion of capital in order to stay afloat. What about the 'or else'?' "

"Leave that to me," he offered. "How about I address this in an e-mail and we—you and I—will take the team to lunch at Jamal's Shrimp and Seafood this afternoon? We'll do some morale boosting. What d'ya say?"

"That's a good idea." And it was, Navena had to admit. She just hoped he had one helluva sales pitch prepared. "I'll see you at lunch."

"So, Navena," Anderson said, smiling wryly, "do you think we'll go piece by piece to whoever asks . . . or lock, stock, and barrel to the highest bidder?"

Navena counted herself down to a speakable level of control before responding. "Neither, Anderson," she coolly replied. "Like Maxwell said in his e-mail, 'We can lie down and hand over the paper or we can stand up and give this community what it needs.' "

"Looks like a sucker punch to me," her colleague scoffed.

"How do you figure?"

"If he's on the up-and-up, why didn't he tell us what the deal was when he first came?" He threw Navena an accusing glare. "Bet he told you."

"I'm learning right along with you and everyone else." She lied and hoped she'd done it well, though Anderson's unflinching expression made her think otherwise. "What? You think we want the *Dispatch* to fold?" she continued. "Put everybody out of a job? Leave Detroit without this voice? No way."

"I just don't wanna be wasting my time. That's all." With a shrug, Anderson turned to greet the rest of the editorial team, assembling around the table by ones and twos.

Prodded by the heavy smells of shrimp, ribs, and homemade pound cake, the hungry group of reporters descended greedily upon the wobbly, makeshift table, quickly disguising its pocked vinyl surface with trays and napkins, silverware and beverages.

Navena wondered if Anderson's ambush hinted at an assault-in-waiting from her other reporters. She couldn't sort their emotions from those of the surrounding crowd. Hunger was the overwhelming vibe.

"Man, we won't last a year," Spence proclaimed as he took a seat.

"Yes, we will," Fern protested. "You-all don't have any faith." With a wave of her hand, she dismissed Spence, rounded the table, and plopped into the chair next to Navena. "What's up, girl? You order yet?"

"Nope. Waiting for you-all," Navena answered, relieved at the change in subject.

Lighthearted banter begun during the walk to lunch picked up as if it had not paused. Their conversation instinctively rose to compete with the raucous wall-to-wall crowd, the clatter of trays being collected and emptied, and an old-fashioned cash register clanging through brisk sales.

"Where's Maxwell?" Fern asked. A wisp of a girl, barely five feet tall, pecan brown from hair to toe, her trademark Cheshire Cat smile replaced, for the moment, by a set of pursed bronzed lips accented by a deeply furrowed brow.

"Stuck in a meeting," Navena answered absently.

"Are you disappointed or what?" Fern flashed a wide grin at Navena.

"Huh?" Wondering why she'd been misread, Navena turned her attention to the laminated menu in front of her. Though she'd memorized its offerings years before, today's lingering grease smears and corn bread crumbs allowed her to analyze her tone, choice of words, and facial expression away from Fern's piercing gaze.

A version of third-grade-crush embarrassment washed over her as she wondered if Fern could sense the fondness she held for Maxwell.

Is she suspicious . . . or just feeling me out? Navena decided to stay calm and not question her motives. "Disappointed? Hardly. I'm actually a little ticked off," she said in an attempt to save herself.

Raising the menu to hide her mouth from the group, Navena leaned toward Fern with a whisper. "He knew you guys would have a million questions. Now I'm stuck here by myself with no answers." Rolling her eyes, she sat upright and hoped that the disgust in her voice would cover the ambivalence she felt inside.

"That's messed up," Fern murmured with a shake of her head and a quick scan of the menu. "You'll be all right, though. We just need to eat."

"Absolutely." Knowing Fern probably wasn't finished with her, Navena accepted the reprieve and waved to signal their server.

Most of their midday meals were taken solo or in pairs in the building cafeteria or the *Dispatch*'s dungeon lounge. It was good to be out of the office, but it would have been better with Maxwell around to moderate.

"My name is Jolene. I'll be your waitress today." A plump, fair-skinned woman addressed them briskly. "Can I start you all with something to drink?"

"We'd like to go ahead and order." Navena took a quick glance around the table to confirm her statement. She was ready to get this over with.

Jolene got right to business, pointing at each reporter and committing all orders to memory, promising to return shortly with salads and water.

"Six months." Anderson spoke to no one in particular, making his statement a wager by tossing a dollar bill in the middle of the table.

"Unless we can find him something to make him wanna stay." Spence laughed disdainfully, and narrowed his eyes at Navena.

In response, she wondered if her nerves were overly sensitive. She wanted to give him the finger, but threw him a wry smile and sat silently instead. They all seemed to be giving up. The thought saddened her.

"Maybe if we find the brother a woman, all this sudden 'money trouble' will go away," Spence continued and turned to taunt Fern. "Any volunteers?"

"Not my type," she retorted.

"A woman? Hell naw." Anderson laughed and threw back half a glass of orange soda. He finished with a loud "aah," smacked his lips, and tipped his chair back cockily. "What Maxwell needs, hell, what we all need is some damn readers."

"Man, we got readers," Spence objected.

"Yeah, I get letters all the time from people who read my column," Fern offered.

"Uh . . . your prison fan club doesn't count, Fern."

They laughed. Navena frowned. She resisted the urge to chime in, afraid her response might stifle any budding discussion.

"My grandmama is the only person I know who reads the *Dispatch*," Anderson spat.

"Man, you crazy," countered Spence, tipping his plastic tumbler to suck down the last chips of his crushed ice. He chewed loudly, speaking between crunches. "Maybe nobody reads that crap you write, but everybody reads my business page."

"Uh-huh. One page. And a week late at that." Anderson sat forward as if challenging someone to disagree. The reporters hung their heads.

"Okay, Anderson." She couldn't silence herself any longer. "You're Maxwell McKnight. What do you do?"

"Tap into the top radio demographic. Get some new blood buying our stuff." Anderson looked like he was ready for a fight. "*That's* what we do."

Luckily, Jolene returned with appetizers, entrees, and drinks, immediately halting the conversation. Weary from all her pretense, Navena absently picked the shrimp from her jambalaya, tumbled her sausage through its rice, eating little. She took a long swig of cola and swallowed her swirling thoughts.

In just a few short hours, the team had lost faith. Maybe Maxwell knew this was coming. Perhaps this was the real reason he left her here alone: to get inside their thoughts and clue him in. The notion made her laugh.

Is this the feedback he's expecting? she wondered. *Then again, his arrogant behind could use a dose of reality.*

"All I'm saying is I think any one of us could've figured out what the *Dispatch* needs," said Anderson. "We didn't need some outsider with no experience trying to come in here and tell us what to do. That's all I'm saying." He reached for the hot sauce, doused his last jumbo shrimp, and swallowed it in one bite.

You're right about that, Navena agreed silently.

No doubt, she could handle Maxwell's job. Anderson probably could, too, though she preferred to picture herself as boss. Closing her Styrofoam dinner box and shutting out the ongoing chitchat, she cut her meal short and scooted her chair away from the table. "Fern, will you take care of the bill, please?"

"You got some money?" she asked with an outstretched palm.

Navena mentally tallied the damage and dropped three of Maxwell's twenty-dollar bills in Fern's hand. "And leave the right tip, girlfriend. Don't be stingy."

The group snickered as Navena stood and nodded a quick good-bye. She tossed her empty cup and crumpled napkins in the garbage can and resisted the urge to tell them lunch hour was over.

Stepping from the dim diner into the bright midday sun blinded her for a moment. She stopped, shutting her eyes against the light, to dig inside her purse, instinctively searching for her usually ready sunglasses.

Deep red dots circled inside her eyelids, bouncing against larger, brighter splotches. They swayed, drawing nearer, retreating, beckoning, retreating, in a surreal and heady waltz. She studied their frantic dance. Its growing frenzy chilled her spine, frightening in the eighty-degree afternoon.

Shades now in her grasp, she hurried to slide them onto her nose and flee the odd scene behind her lids. She opened her eyes with a sigh of relief to recognize the real world around her—only to see splatters of blood on her hands.

* * *

"Navena, you okay?"

Blocks past the blood dance, Maxwell shook Navena from her daze. Calling her from across the street, he hurriedly crossed to her side.

"I didn't think I left you any time for daydreaming," he joked, then paused. "What's the matter?" He turned up her palms and studied them, right, left, and right again. Holding both hands tightly, he queried her again. "Are you okay? I saw you shaking your wrists. Is something wrong?"

Navena pushed her mind to the present and pulled her hands from Maxwell's. "Fine, really. Bee sting."

"We should put something on it. Ice maybe." He reached for her as she stepped back.

"That's okay. It's not even swollen." She looked for blood smears on his hands and saw none. "Besides, I've got some Benadryl in my car. I'll grab it when we get back to the office." *Nothing on his means there's nothing on mine,* she thought. The chill returned. Navena shuddered.

"You aren't allergic, are you?" Maxwell asked.

"No. I'm fine, I told you. And you—you skipped a great little get-together. Don't think you're off the hook for dissing us common folk."

"It wasn't like that and you know it." He gave her a worried smile that let her know she wasn't off the hook either. "So, how did it go?" Maxwell turned and began walking.

Navena followed alongside, using her longest but most ladylike stride to keep pace. "There are those who feel like you're unnecessary."

"You one of those?"

"I could handle your job any day of the week."

"Don't think I'm unaware of that," he said with a wry smile.

"So why did they hire from the outside?"

"Knowing Cullen, I'd say presence, image. The appearance of really turning the corner on a new way of business." They stopped to await traffic at the intersection. "Personally, I think this opportunity presented itself for a reason. Nothing happens just because."

"True," Navena murmured, but hoped he was wrong. She glanced at her palms to reassure herself, double-checking her lengthy lifeline, and crossed the street behind Maxwell.

"Actually, since I bumped into you, how about we go back to my office and talk more?" Maxwell suggested. "I was on my way to the deli, till you distracted me." He smiled. "I'll eat at my desk."

"As usual," Navena replied with a disapproving shake of her dreadlocks. "You really should think about getting out of your cell sometime."

They stopped in a corner sandwich shop. Maxwell ordered a double stack of corned beef with a side of fries and a bottle of water. Navena grabbed another cola. They walked quietly the last two blocks to the *Dispatch*. Once inside, Maxwell ushered Navena into the office ahead of himself, quickly closing his door behind her.

"Let's sit at the table," he said. "More room to think over there."

Maxwell tossed his bag on a pile of papers and grabbed a stack of overloaded folders from his desk. He passed Navena a tablet. In turn, she hung her purse on an empty chair beside him and readied a clean page on the notepad.

They worked silently side by side for a moment, preparing for what felt like an increasingly important discussion. At last, their hurried movements slowed and they came to a stop seated directly across from each other.

Navena tried not to notice the way his white linen

shirt stood open at the collar, revealing a modest gold chain surrounded by thick curls of black chest hair. She pushed up her own shirtsleeves to match his—and give her eyes something else to do.

Her legs were crossed tightly at the knees and her foot swung nervously back and forth, dangerously close to Maxwell then retreating beneath her own chair. Maxwell tapped his felt-tip pen, flipping it quickly from lid to point, then point to lid.

He's as nervous as me.

The deli smells that had swallowed his cologne initially now cooled and revealed a lingering designer fragrance worn by some former lover Navena couldn't recall. Faraway flashbacks of candlelight and satin sheets filtered through her thoughts, hovering, then fading off.

She felt conspicuous, locked away with Maxwell. But she didn't rise to open the office blinds. The reporters weren't back yet. For the first time in fourteen years, they were alone together.

Navena's wandering thoughts drew warmth to her cheeks and moisture to her forehead. She scattered her thoughts with a toss of her dreadlocks and looked Maxwell directly in the eye. He met the challenge, holding Navena's gaze as if threatening to unmask her thoughts.

She scratched absently at her palms, floating out of her reverie into the comfort of his knowing smile.

Chapter Six

What's with her hands? Maxwell wondered. It was hard not to stare. She kept rubbing them, trying, but failing, to be discreet. *Definitely not a bee sting. A burn? Some other injury?*

The fact that she was lying bothered him most. And worried him. This was the first time he'd ever seen her so scattered, as if she was only half here. They had a lot to talk about and she was in no shape for strategizing this afternoon.

Guess everybody deserves a lapse, he thought. But it was so unlike her.

Seldom surprised, Maxwell found himself astounded by Navena's administrative insight and editorial instinct. She displayed a level of assertiveness that he admired. He guessed that she had been observing and analyzing the *Dispatch* for years, biding her time, collecting her thoughts, and lying in wait for someone to let her take charge.

Getting the staff behind Navena's leadership had been the easy part. Getting his own rules implemented had taken all the judiciousness he possessed. His first week among the reporters found him locked toe-to-toe in opinionated combat, making him feel like an interloper. More disappointing was that he hadn't regained Navena's trust.

He wanted to be her partner: his lead vision and finance; hers editorial, creative. He also wanted her love. But not witnessed by a bankrupt newsroom and her knucklehead boyfriend. Big-money knucklehead. And not with the mistakes of their past unresolved. He fought the urge to kiss her now and wander into that familiar place her eyes had drifted into only moments before.

"So, what's this about you-all not needing me?" Abruptly, he unwrapped the corned beef and took an athlete-sized bite. "What would you do without me?"

"Anderson suggested finding a different audience," Navena began, "although there was brief speculation about your love life—or lack thereof. Are you still sometimes separated or did you finally divorce and find someone to replace me?" Navena asked with a dig. "Someone to occupy your time besides the *Dispatch*?"

"Ooooh," laughed Maxwell. "Do I hear '*Do I have a life*?' "

"You said it. I didn't."

"Well, I guess I don't," said Maxwell. He'd come here to make her his life. Unfortunately, plans don't always work out.

Somber now, he gently placed the remains of his sandwich among the scattered fries that had accompanied it. He laced his fingers prayerlike and rested them under his chin.

"Jeez, Navena." He sighed into the tense air between them and fell back into his seat, arms flailing. "I have absorbed the life of this paper. It's mine. I have become the *Dispatch*. In my conversations, in my dreams, when I'm here, when I'm home, this paper is the only future I see."

"Until you came along, Maxwell, the *Dispatch* was

mine," said Navena. "I had the talent and the drive, but mostly the desire, to get the *Dispatch* to the place it ought to be—on every table or doorstep in the city every morning, every day. That was *my* charge. Now some outsider is running the ship."

"That's the tension?" Maxwell was genuinely surprised and leaned forward expectantly into Navena's nearness. "I just figured you thought I didn't know what I was doing. I had no idea this was a turf war."

Navena shrugged. "Basically it is. It makes us feel like Cullen doesn't trust our skills. Seems even Anderson would've appreciated a nod."

Concentration avoided him. Navena's words floated in a haze around his head. He tried to ignore her hands gently rubbing along her thighs.

He slowly consumed the last few bites of his burger, a one-by-one handful of fries, and a long, satiating drink of soda, all to swallow the apology he wanted so desperately to make. Less cocky, more thoughtful than he'd been earlier in the week, he avoided her gaze, even after his food was gone.

I'm sorry for everything I put you through, kiddo, he thought. *Sorry for Lila—it should've been you. Sorry about Luke—it ought to be me.*

He hung his head to gather his thoughts. Navena's perfume, softened by hours of wear, tugged at his manhood. It was the same scent he'd always known her to wear, Chanel No 5. Nothing else ever graced her skin. He pushed aside thoughts of him touching her skin.

"I can't change the things that have already happened." The carefully chosen words hung haltingly between them.

Maxwell leaned forward across the table and placed his hands as close to Navena's as he dared. "I can only fix the future. And I'd like your help to do it."

Navena blinked slowly, then met him eye-to-eye.

Silence filled the space between them. He began to wonder if his words were wrong. Digging into a nearby jar of M&M's for a peace offering, he searched his heart for clarification.

Business, he chided himself. *Dispatch only*.

"I've been on the phone day in, day out," Maxwell explained, "fielding calls from the faction that calls us sellouts, batting down the naysayers who keep saying good riddance, and shooing off the scavengers trying to hire my staff out from under me."

He shook his head and rolled several colored candies onto the tabletop like dice.

"Any other investors?" Navena asked quietly.

"A few." Maxwell shrugged his shoulders and thumped a candy her way. She picked it up and popped it into her mouth. He could see her palms, zigzags of red and beige where her long nails had irritated the tender skin.

"Well, we gotta do something, Maxwell. Morale is—there *is* no morale, Maxwell. Everybody's scared crazy about not having a job next month. They're all afraid you'll follow the industry practice of 'cleaning house' and bringing in your own staff. So nobody's doing a damn bit of work."

Laughter escaped him at the last statement, dispelling the seriousness shrouding them.

"You have an idea to get us out of this mess?" He raised an eyebrow.

"Anybody putting money into this sieve needs motivation," Navena began with a sentiment she might have used on Luke. "I can't see sinking a fortune into twenty pages of six-column headlines that recap last month's city council meeting. But we can change that."

Maxwell grabbed a green candy from the pile and slid it between his tongue and cheek.

Navena went on. "Anderson talked about targeting a

new audience. What if we convert the paper to a magazine, Maxwell? Showcase grassroots concerns, sharp political commentary, the inside scoop on entertainment. East Coast/West Coast attitude with Midwest flavor. Big pictures. Glossy. Serious design. Oversized." She took a breath. "Classy, like Motown back in the day. Like a brand-new Cadillac. *That's* worth an investment."

Possibilities took Maxwell away from Navena's eager explanation. She was right. A glossy magazine he could sell. He cast one last glance her way, eliciting a smug smile and that sexy gaze. "You think we can pull this off? Get the staff behind us?"

"Sure." Navena paused as if to convince herself. "We just have to make sure they feel like they own the change. Let them pick the title, the first cover story. You know, get them vested in our success."

"How much time do you think we need to put a plan together?"

"A week?"

"Three days?"

"Wow. Sure. If that's how you want it."

"Need it. I'm meeting with investors on May twenty-eighth, and now we'll have something to show them. We have to think this out and get staff on target by next Friday. Deal?"

"Can we push Monday's team meeting to Wednesday?"

"Sure. Whatever I can do to help."

Outside his door, he heard voices. Reporters returning from a very long lunch. He wouldn't call them on it, though. Their carelessness had given him time to simply sit and adore Navena.

Words escaped his mind. "This could be a whole new start."

"For the *Dispatch*?" she asked.

"Or more."

* * *

"Wasn't expecting to see you tonight." Navena opened the front door, hoping Luke wasn't here for a booty call. Then again, he could've used his key and crawled into bed beside her like he usually did. "Thanks for knocking."

"Thought you might miss me," Luke answered.

He ambled into the room, his bulky frame clothed in a loose-fitting pair of Guess jeans, Kenneth Cole slides, and a faded black Winans T-shirt, treasured souvenir from their first date. Hardened biceps peeked beneath the shrunken sleeves.

Navena's heart fluttered out of habit, betraying her inner conflict about turning his unannounced visit into a chance to break up.

"Oh, so now you're my man." She locked the door behind him and tightened the sash on her chenille robe, figuring he wore that shirt on purpose. "I haven't heard squat from you in two days."

He turned, blocking the hallway. "Don't think I got any messages from you either. If it bugs you so much, why'd you let me in?" He spoke with an edge that let her know the wound from her refusal to his proposal was still open.

"Because I was up watching the news." She wanted to get right to the point. "Look. Even though we're not talking, I have something to tell you."

"It's late. I don't want to talk about work right now, Navena."

Navena felt herself tense. While she wasn't fully convinced of Mama's directive, the dream *had* triggered some avalanche of consciousness that urged Navena not to tell Luke about the visions. Or about Maxwell.

"Can I at least get a brew?" he asked. "I promise I won't keep you up past bedtime."

"Then you wouldn't have come down this time of

night to begin with." Navena moved down the hallway, toward the kitchen. "Let's make it quick."

"Word is you-all are broke. Is that true?"

She really didn't want to discuss the *Dispatch* with Luke, but she also wanted to share her life with him. Although she knew she wouldn't marry him, they were still friends.

"The paper's turning upside down, is all," was the most she could truthfully muster.

"Well, aren't you glad you're headed for the *Morning Star*?" He placed his hands atop her shoulders and gave them a pulsing squeeze as they entered the kitchen. "You start when?"

Shrugging off his impromptu massage, she answered matter-of-factly, "I turned down the offer."

He spun her around and narrowed his eyes. "You're kidding, right?"

Navena averted his gaze, focusing instead on the grout between her ceramic tile, and searching for the right explanation.

"They need me at the *Dispatch* right now." Under Luke's scrutiny, the excuse sounded lame. She turned back toward the refrigerator and fumbled in the veggie drawer for a beer.

"Not after all that griping you did? After having a good interview and an offer for good money?" Luke continued, frowning. "What'd they do to make you stay all of a sudden?"

"You said you saw the news. Things are changing. Here." She thrust the bottle at Luke and leaned against the counter.

"They didn't say anything specific. What's going to be different?" Luke sat at the table, popped the top off his drink, and tipped it up for a long guzzle.

Not wanting to breathe Maxwell's name in front of Luke—convinced that remnants of affection from the affair would bleed through her words and betray her—she walked a tightrope of sharing his vision and justifying her job.

"McKnight thinks we can save the paper by restructuring it and bringing in some private money. Know anybody who'd be interested?"

"In putting money into that rag? Sorry, sweets, but there is no way in hell anybody with good sense would back that sinking ship," he scoffed. "Go ahead and hang around. That way when it goes under, the only place you can run is to me."

"I've told you before, Lucas Gabriel Benson, the *Dispatch* is a real paper, regardless of what you think. And I'll leave *you* before I let you coop me up in here barefoot and pregnant." She turned sharply toward the cabinet and took out a mug. Selecting a spiced tea bag from the rack, she filled the cup with hot water from the dispenser and walked to the table.

"You know what I meant." He attempted to clean up his bravado. "You're the one who keeps talking about needing a change and work being so hard. I'm just trying to give you a way out."

"It's been tough," Navena conceded. "But I have to be there to see this through. Otherwise, I'll go crazy."

"Looks to me like work is *making* you crazy," Luke accused. "But you're too damn stubborn to walk away from that drama and just let me spoil you."

"I don't want to be 'kept' like that." She stiffened as he approached and began massaging her shoulders. "It's all I can do to tolerate your garden parties and charity outings. Watching soap operas and painting my toenails all day does not appeal to me. At all."

"We'd be married" he argued. "You could volunteer. Work at the kids' school. You act like I'm trying to put you in prison." He gave up on her shoulders and sat across the table from Navena.

"Let's be fair, Luke. You got your shot, I need mine. I have worked way too hard to turn around and walk away from the *Dispatch*." She swallowed and sighed, and decided to tell him what was on her mind. "But I do think *we* should take some time apart."

"Oh, now *you're* trying to leave *me*?"

"It's not working with us and you know it."

Luke drained the rest of his beer and slammed the bottle on the table. "You've been acting funny all week. I think there's more to this."

"If you consider that we're trying to stretch this into something it isn't, then, yes." She wasn't going to let him bully her into staying. "We're screw buddies, not husband-wife candidates, Luke. See it for what it is. You want more. I just don't. I'm sorry."

"No, you're not, and that's too bad. See, my daddy taught me to appreciate a good woman: sweet, sexy, with a little bit of sass. You got all that." He leaned across the table toward her.

"Maybe I'm not the Mr. Perfect you dreamed up when you were little. I probably work too much and talk too little. Gifts might not be your thing, but that's the best I can do. Romance ain't me." He shrugged. "Besides, passion burns off ten, twenty years down the road. Then, what's important is what we have now. Good company, good sex, a good life. I can live with that."

Navena shook her head. "We don't want the same things. You need forever, so I'm bowing out."

Luke choked and wiped a dribble of beer from his chin with the back of his hand. "How 'bout I just give you a few days to reconsider?"

"No, Luke. Really." She dipped a forefinger into her cup and slowly stirred the tea. "I'll start looking for another place. This living arrangement won't work anymore."

"What about my PR for the Trentmoor Towers groundbreaking?"

"I'll finish the project out for you and then find somebody else to take over. That's all, Luke, okay?"

He stood and walked out of the room talking. "You'll change your mind is what you'll do."

The front door slammed.

Navena listened to Luke's heavy footsteps climb the outer hallway stairs that led to the upper flat. The sound moved upward and across the floor, stopping above her head. She froze, picturing him watching from afar.

Chapter Seven

Friday, May 13
St. Louis, Missouri

In the darkness next to Mack, Vee lay watching her dream twin's man. She studied Luke sitting astride the moon, commanding his lunar throne as if he owned the night.

Tree branches swayed behind him. Vee listened to their frantic chatter. Danger, *they warned.*

Half sleep, a slow, steady chill hummed through her veins while she waited for him to move, speak, at least hint at what he was up to.

In one deft motion, Luke stood, strung a rope of stars, and swung the lasso above his head.

He gave her the creeps. And that was hard to do.

"I don't trust him, and neither should you," she warned Navena.

Much more than Sunday's dream, this one alarmed Vee.

Luke tossed the ring, trying to snag Vee's wrists.

She writhed and hid her hands behind her back.

Luke grinned and reined in his rope. He slid the ends around his waist, belting his loose-fitting jeans.

"I can definitely see why she spends her nights with you." Despite Vee's better judgment, a smile escaped her lips.

He circled his hips and swung the lasso again.

A sensation reserved for Mack burned in her belly and trickled between her thighs. Her face flushed because her rising lust belonged to the man seducing her. He was tempting her in a primal, unfamiliar fashion that felt so good.

Vee dreamed she awoke, panting, perspiring, sex-wet as if she'd actually made love. She pulled her nightgown down around her hips, careful not to awaken Mack. Guilt nudged her heart. Fog settled over her mind like a blanket of amnesia.

"I have what I need," she said to herself

"Who, Mack?" he laughed. "Then why are you here?"

The lasso spun itself gold, the stars creating a ring more beautiful than her own wedding band.

"Marry me," he teased.

Mesmerized, Vee reached for the jewel.

Luke lunged out of the dream.

Detroit, Michigan

Navena hit the ground before realizing she'd fallen.

Strains of Jennifer Lopez continued "Waiting for Tonight" in the background as Navena's hip-hop aerobics class rippled to a halt.

Crumpled, pretzel-like, facedown on the padded workout mat, with the wireless microphone hooked around her ear now imprinted on one cheek, Navena wallowed in remnants of fatigue and fresh embarrassment.

"Damn. I think I broke my nose!"

Several of her health club students rushed to help, lifting Navena from the floor.

"Great leap. Tough landing," said the tallest of her

rescuers. Ponytailed, size six, no older than twenty-two, she tugged at Navena's arm in youthful overexuberance.

Five nights of poor sleep ganged up on Navena, challenging her effort to rise and restore her dignity. *That'll teach me to daydream in the middle of a move like that*, she thought.

Navena took pride in still fitting into her college leotards and keeping pace with her much younger students—boasted on teaching them. Perhaps not as limber, but certainly wiser, she knew better than to allow distractions in her dancing.

Faking a smile, she thanked the group gathered around, and shooed them back to their places. She allowed herself a quick glance in the wall-length mirror where she'd seen Luke charging from only moments before. A shiver rippled down her sweat-drenched back.

"Use these last ten minutes to get your money's worth and make me feel better." With a nod, Navena signaled a staffer to restart the music. "From the top. And five, six, seven, eight."

Her twenty-odd dancers launched full throttle into the Lopez remix with hip rolls and wide-legged stomps, and perfecting the leap that tripped up Navena.

"Great work!" She led a round of applause and a series of cool-down stretches before dismissing until next week.

Seven o'clock signaled salvation. Not just the end of class, but time for the rest she promised herself as she stared into the mirror. Nightmares, daydreams, and now hallucinations? Time to nip this stuff in the bud before it got any worse.

Rummaging through her dance bag, Navena found and slipped into her favorite jeans. Faded and wrinkled, the ten-year-old denims looked just like the latest styles. Balanced on one foot, then the other, Navena hopped gracefully while exchanging jazz shoes for mules and hoping Luke wouldn't be home.

What a vision. Navena reflected on the daydream of Luke on the moon with a lasso of stars that caused her tumble. *I'm not going to feel guilty about this breakup, if that's what you're hoping for, Luke.*

Still, her fall behind Luke's imaginary lunge made the week's dreams a little too real. *I need to figure out what's going on before I break my neck . . . or someone else gets hurt.*

She checked her watch and hoisted her dance bag, wincing as she rose. Her sore hip would provide the perfect excuse for canceling tomorrow's class. And since it was only five after seven, there was plenty of time left in the day for a short nap and a little sleuthing.

Outside the aerobics room, athletic, overweight, and ordinary people swapped places through a revolving health club door. Navena stepped out of the classroom into the hallway to join the waiting-to-leave line. Club members jostled her in their fray, bumping her body with insincere "excuse me's" and irritated glances.

Watching them circle in the revolving door in a seamless entrance/exit tango, Navena slid mindlessly into an open slot when her turn arrived. In autopilot motion, she placed one hand on the smudged glass, the other against the cool metal push bar, and pressed.

Instead of spinning forward, the door locked in place. Navena stood frozen, trapped in the transparent triangular prism of windows and doors. An airplane thundered overhead, shattering the glass of her makeshift prison. Dropping both bag and inhibitions, Navena reached into the rush of air surrounding her. The mysterious world she'd witnessed only at home appeared before her.

"I've crossed over. Awake. How?"

Before she could force herself further, a ball of fire fell from the sky. Her heart raced as she ran through space toward the apparition ahead. Within seconds, her nostrils swapped the smell of sweat for the stench of burning metal. Sounds of straining steel ricocheted from sky to earth and Navena's ears.

Wreckage materialized in the empty space. Twisted plane parts, melted tires, lifeless bodies littered the ground. A woman with Navena's face walked away from the carnage.

"Vee? You're here." Just like Mama said—I found you.

"Your dreams called me to your life. I had to answer."

"Mama said I needed you to 'complete my life.' But I'm fine. You can stay. I don't need you."

"We're better together. Trust me." Vee extended a matching half of the doll Mama had given Navena. "Trust me."

Not sure she wanted to take the toy, anxious about what it represented, Navena hesitated. "I still don't understand—"

"Unlike other Larimores, you were born with gifts. But like most children, you didn't have the patience or wisdom to control them. They ruled you, ultimately foreseeing Daddy's death."

"I thought Mama found him in the yard." Navena stood stunned as Vee rewrote her history.

"After it happened, you fainted from distress," Vee explained. "So between the time Daddy died and you awoke, the Mothers worked to preserve your gifts until your thirty-third Moon Year arrived."

"Mama locked them away." Navena thought back to their post-nightmare conversation. "That's what she meant. But how do you do that?"

"With her. She represents Larimore spirit." Vee thrust the doll half at Navena once more. "Mama used her—your spirit was split. I kept your essence safe—the part that will make you a true Larimore."

"What are they—my gifts?" Navena asked, not sure she wanted to know.

"Several abilities will touch your life—clairvoyance, telepathy, precognition, and psychokinesis." Vee beamed with excitement. "Some stay, others fade."

"Why bother, reuniting if I can't keep all the gifts?" Navena asked, disappointed.

Vee smiled. *"Think of them as your supporting cast. They all play an important part in your challenge, but they're not your lead. Let's start with the dreams. Your visions brought us together."*

Vee stepped closer. "The next visions bring signs that will map your journey from today to the next new moon. As random as they will seem, they tie directly to lives you must touch, activities you must affect, decisions you must make."

"You're saying that signs from my dreams will match something—a person, event, or choice—in my real life." Navena grappled with the idea of crossing realms and mixing realities.

"Match the pieces, solve the puzzle they create." Vee inched even closer.

"So once all these things have appeared and happened, I can undo the death I saw in my nightmare, right?" Navena stepped back.

Vee nodded and approached again. "You see, reunited, we form a Spinner, like Mama. You'll be able to manipulate pieces of time, space, and place."

"What about you, your realm?" Navena looked out at the smoldering airplane wreckage. "Can you recreate your reality?"

"No need to. Gramma told me one day I'd have to return. Now is that time." She hesitated. "But I'm not alone here. All I ask is that you take care of him for me."

"Her, you mean?" Navena studied the doll half, surprised at what she saw. "She has a heart."

"And now you will, too." Vee stood toe-to-toe with Navena. "Use it for him.*"*

Stumbling backward, Navena shouted, "I don't know how—"

"I won't leave you alone," Vee promised, then leaped into Navena's body with the strength of a boxer's jab.

Navena sucked in her breath and absorbed her sister-spirit as it filled her parched essence like monsoon after a drought. Replenished to overflowing, she marveled at the world from her new perspective, in full color rather than half shadow.

Vee rumbled and settled in. "You will never see life the same way again."

"Miss. You goin' or what? You're wasting my time."

Strange voices, urgent and edgy, pierced the vision, separating Navena from the white-hot plane crash and returning her to sweat-soaked gym companions awaiting their turn in the exiting line.

Doubled over, she straightened upright as a surge of energy washed over her, pulsing her muscles and tingling her joints. More than the extra pep she got from a great workout, Navena felt rejuvenated, as if waking from a good night's sleep and stepping into a promising day.

Her watch crept to 7:06 P.M. Only moments had passed in the other realm. Disoriented and disquieted, she pushed against the glass, spinning herself into an unusually scarlet sunset.

Chapter Eight

Saturday, May 14
St. Louis, Missouri

A red dawn weighted the clouds outside Vee's airplane window. Reaching for Mack's hand, she steeled herself against the sound of roaring engines by counting the puzzlelike pieces of neighborhoods below.

"You okay?" Mack squeezed her hand for reassurance, folded the complimentary airline magazine, and slid it into the seat-back pocket in front of him. "Were you able to set up any interviews before we left?"

Her husband's interest elicited a weak smile. Vee thrived on his always knowing what she needed and doing his best to provide it.

It was her first flight and the terrible turbulence called for the distraction he was trying to create. "I placed several calls and got time at two car companies," Vee answered. "And a reporter at the *Dispatch*—the black paper there—gave me the name of a multigenerational family of auto workers who expanded their personal profits into several successful public ventures. It's going to be a great story."

"Sounds like you've got it handled." He paused. "Didn't you say you'd been here before?"

"Once. When I was little." Vee played along with his attempt to change the topic, trying to take her mind off the shifting white masses outside her window. "My grandma brought me to visit relatives."

"We should've looked them up so we can visit."

"I don't remember them."

"They probably remember you." A bump spurred the plane's FASTEN SEATBELT light overhead. Flight attendants scurried down the aisle urging everyone to obey. Mack had never unbuckled.

As Vee gathered items she'd removed from her tote—Oprah's book of the month, her PalmPilot, a deck of tarot cards she used for solitaire instead of their intended purpose—the massive jet began to shudder through an onslaught of innocent-looking fluff. She wished Mack had agreed with her initial suggestion to drive. Take some time to enjoy the sights. See how many cities they could make love in between St. Louis and Detroit.

But he balked, and here she sat spending their condensed quality time fretting over bumps in the air and engine noises. The turbulence rattled her body and unhinged her fragile emotions. She slipped the book and PDA into a zippered leather slot and held on to the cards, shuffling them nervously in her lap.

"Stop, babe." Mack stroked the back of her hand.

Vee flipped the deck faster. "Told you I hate this. I knew . . ." She turned toward Mack and watched his face fall.

"What?"

Nothing. Irrationality ran rampant as her logic and psychic sense sat silent. Not so much as an inkling arose about the events ahead. Ordinarily, no signal meant good news. Instead, the absence of knowing began to fill her with blind foreboding.

The plane dipped to the left, sending up screams from its tilted passengers and flinging her loose cards onto the floor.

"Mack!"

Small yellow cups, rubber-banded to primitive breathing bags dropped from the ceiling in unison.

"Put it on, Vee!" Mack shouted directions through her disbelief. He held up two fingers, placed them on his heart and his lips—their courtside signal for "I love you"—and said, "Whatever happens . . ."

The jet began to plummet.

Detroit, Michigan

Navena felt herself swerve before she turned the wheel, saw the impact before she crashed. The premonition frightened her more than the actual collision.

Horns blared.

The cell phone flew from her hand as she tried to regain control. Instead, the Jeep bounced and whirled like a giant bumper car, slamming to a stop against the freeway median. The airbag deployed, punching the space between Navena's chest and the steering wheel, and wrestling her arms against the headrest.

She shrieked, snapping out of her cruise-induced daze and into a face full of hot, coarse cloth. Shards of glass rained around her. Straining metal quieted.

I saw this coming. I saw this coming. How? Her mind bounded across the possibilities. *Shouldn't have been on the phone. Daydreaming. It's like I wasn't even here.*

"Miss, are you all right?" A man's soothing tenor voice reached across her rising dreamscape, trying to pull her back across the border she'd seen before.

I can't breathe.

She felt a hand in her hair, rolling her face to one side and exposing her face to sunshine and warm air. Daring to breathe, Navena inhaled dust and fear, and exhaled gratitude.

"Hang in there, ma'am." The stranger spoke again.

She closed her eyes and took note of the sounds around her. Maxwell's static-smattered shouts echoed from her cell phone somewhere in the Jeep. Idling engines and audible song lyrics told her gawkers were slowing traffic. Sirens blared. She wanted to stand, stretch, and survey the damage, like everyone else.

Did this happen because I ignored the vision? Was I supposed to change something? Navena's mind flashed back to the heat-filled daydream she'd experienced in her birthday Lexus. But this glass was real. So were the cuts on her hand.

Darkness claimed her thoughts. *You win, Mama. I am a Larimore.*

"Glad to see you're awake, Ms. Larimore." A short, tan-skinned man in an expensive suit and regulation lab coat extended a hand to Navena. In the other, he held a clipboard stacked with multicolored sheets of paper and a navy blue Detroit Medical Center pen. "I'm Dr. Gupta. How are you feeling?"

"A little woozy." She lifted an achy palm to her forehead, wincing at the bruises circling her wrist and forearm.

"Be glad that's all. You are pretty lucky today." Withdrawing a narrow flashlight from his pocket, he scrunched his face and neared Navena's, shining the light in one eye, then the other. "Um-hmm. Looks good."

He clicked the light off, shoved it back into his pocket, and began to scribble on the clipboard. "Are you feeling any pain?"

"My head." She attempted to roll her shoulders forward and lift herself from the bed.

Dr. Gupta furrowed his eyebrows. "No, no. Not yet. Please rest."

Questions began to form, but her tongue seemed to lag behind her thoughts. "My mouth is dry."

"Ice chips. Get her some from down the hall, please." The doctor motioned toward the door and Luke emerged from behind him.

"Can I talk to her?"

A halo of light beaming from the hallway enshrined his shoulders. Luke looked like he did in the dream, atop the moon.

Steady drip-drop beeping from monitors beside Navena's bed hastened to pitter-patter speed as her heart lunged into her throat. Thursday's breakup and his refusal to accept it made her unsure of his intentions. She hadn't talked to Luke since and didn't welcome his sudden appearance.

"Your wife is thirsty." The scribbling doctor waved again. "Talk when you return. By then, I'll be finished with my exam."

I must still have him listed as my In Case of Emergency contact. Gotta change that to Fern.

Ignoring the doctor's directive, Luke continued standing in the doorway, arms folded.

Dr. Gupta lifted his head from the clipboard, studied Navena's frantic heart monitor, and then softened his expression. "You want me to get it myself?" he asked Luke over his shoulder, then waited.

Luke hesitated, frowned, and turned to walk down the hallway. "Back in a sec." The light attached to his shoulders followed him out the door, leaving an odd shadow in his wake.

"Relax. Your husband will only be gone for a minute." He patted her hand in misguided reassurance.

"Not my husband." Her chest tightened.

Dr. Gupta reached across Navena's head and pushed the red NURSE button on the wall. A sultry alto voice responded.

"Yes, Miss Larimore."

"This is Dr. Gupta. Please send her nurse. Stat." He looked at Navena. "Who is this man? What is the problem?"

Tell him what? About her dreams? The circle of light Luke carried into this room? That he shouldn't be here? "I'm tired. I just want to be alone."

The nurse entered at the tail end of Navena's weak explanation.

"Tall man with a cup of ice chips. Tell him we're giving her some pain medication and she's fallen asleep." He smiled at Navena. "Which I will do right after we finish talking. Be very still."

He lifted the stethoscope hanging around his neck and leaned over to listen to Navena's panicked heart.

Can he hear how crazy this sounds? That my mind foreshadowed my car accident so, suddenly, I think Wednesday's dream is telling me something about Luke.

Removing the miniature flashlight from his pocket again, he peeked into her ears, nostrils, and throat. Examined her eyes once more.

Can he see the visions I'm having?

As she drifted toward sleep, her eyes fluttered open long enough for her to see Luke hand over the ice chips and walk off as Maxwell entered the room.

Navena mustered a weak smile. "Howniceofyou," she slurred.

"She okay?" he asked Dr. Gupta through her haze.

"And who are you?" The doctor double-checked her pulse monitor, now back to its normal pace following Luke's departure.

"Her boss. An old friend."

"Eyes quite bruised from the airbag. Lacerations on

the cheek. I understand the windshield shattered. Strong girl here."

"Don't I know?" Maxwell said.

"You cannot stay. Please be quick." Dr. Gupta turned and walked from the room, leaving Navena and Maxwell under the watchful eye of her nurse.

"Navena, hey, I brought you something." Maxwell leaned in close.

Holding her eyes open was impossible. They fell shut, trudged upward as he spoke, and blurred the rectangle he held.

"Card game," he whispered. "One of those mind puzzles you like. Picked 'em up in the gift shop downstairs. This'll give you something to do until you go home." He placed the deck on her bedside table, patted her hand, and pulled up the sheet.

The game's silver-coated box reflected the circular room lights like moons. She didn't want them, but couldn't speak.

"Shhh." He placed a silencing finger to his lips. "Rest. You'll be out of here and back to normal in no time, I'm sure." He stood and rubbed her cheek. "Till then, I'll be checking on you."

Liquid from the bulging plastic sack above Navena's head dripped into her veins, chilling her arm and coaxing her to sleep. Weak, but aware, she fought the encroaching dream, beating at the familiar window that opened the space from here to there.

As Navena drifted up Mama's splintered porch steps, the worn screen door swung open to greet her. She slid through, squinting her eyes to peer into the darkened house. Rosewater and incense filled her lungs. Thoughts bellowed from a faraway room.

"Come in, Navena," Gramma Livia called to her from somewhere deep within the house. Navena obeyed, entered,

and floated toward the parlor, anxious to get help from the Mothers.

An arched doorway framed a girlhood scene. Three gold-rimmed teacups rested bottoms-up atop matching porcelain saucers, each separated from the walnut table beneath them by a frail yellowed doily. Behind one place setting sat Gramma, at the other sat Mama, facing each other across the short width of the table. Their eyes escorted Navena to the empty head chair.

At the opposite length of the table, her great-grandmother, MaDear, stood against a dusty wooden window lit by a moonless sky. She wore Gramma's silver wedding gown and a smile like Mama's. Rosewater scents and cicada songs swarmed in her midst, swaying on a gust of thought that fluttered the hem of her dress. Soft, soulful humming rose in the air.

The melody quickened steadily as MaDear smiled solemnly. With arms opened wide, she began to speak. "After your daddy died, your Mama knew fate was gonna catch up with you sooner or later."

"Your gift," MaDear declared. In her hand appeared a deck of cards.

Eagerly stretching her palms forward, Navena approached with curiosity and awe. MaDear fanned the stack, linked accordion style by a length of clear thread. No king, queen, or mystic icon, the cards revealed familiar silhouettes: a car, a cat, a smile, a barrel, and a rope. Navena folded her fingers around the treasure as the images began to fade.

"Welcome," the Mothers whispered.

St. Louis

"Breaking news tonight at County Metropolitan Airport, where we've just received word that a jetliner en route from St. Louis to Detroit has crashed only minutes from its destination. We're told by investigators on the scene in Michigan that there are no survivors of the devastating explosion. Believed to be among the one-hundred-plus passengers on board was one of St. Louis's favorite philanthropic couples. We'll bring you more on the story at eleven."

Chapter Nine

Sunday, May 15

Thunderous applause dragged Navena from the aromas and card decks of Larimore Manor into the antiseptic starkness of room 631 East. Sweat glued the striped cotton gown to her breasts and belly. Her left hand ached beneath layers of thick white tape that held the IV in place.

From the wall opposite her hospital bed, the Reverend Ernest Howell of Greater Peace Baptist Church fired up his worldwide television congregation. Ten thousand hands clapped approval of his message. Fighting to emerge fully into reality, she reached for the bedside remote and turned up the volume.

"And now let us bow our heads in prayer for the victims of yesterday's Midnight Airlines plane crash. We remember their friends and families and ask that their souls find peace. Amen."

The heart monitor above her pillow beeped faster as Navena's pulse began to race.

That plane crash was real? The unbandaged fingers on her right hand mashed fiercely at the unfamiliar remote control buttons, searching for evidence that what she'd seen two days before and heard just now was true.

On CNN, a similar report scrolled across the bottom of the screen. Local channels broke in with news of the same. The sports channel flashed a photo of a Mack Somebody, killed in the crash.

Navena's oxygen sensor blared in alarm as all breath caught in her throat.

"He looks just like Maxwell!"

Next channel, Mack and his wife at a charity gala.

"And she looks like me!"

Vee, the broadcaster commented, would be dearly missed by the community.

She smiled at Navena. "Take care of him."

The TV went blank.

Dreadlocks slid across the sweat on her nape. She heaved for air, mentally grasping for pieces that were starting to physically connect.

First there was Maxwell's arrival, then the dream, more visions, and finally the crash that returned Vee.

Now she was crossing over and bringing back not only warnings, but physical items, too. What else would explain that Maxwell's gift cards were identical to the ones MaDear gave her?

She glanced at the deck awaiting her on the table, then back at the empty TV.

"What else from your world crashed into mine?"

"Bam, baby!" Luke stepped into the room, laughing at the words she'd spoken aloud. "Told you I could show you how real love feels."

He strolled across the tiled floor and swept his hand across her damp forehead. Navena shrugged off his touch. "Stop. I'm hot." She flopped backward onto the pillow. A gardening show appeared on the television screen, midprogram as if it had been there all along.

"You all right?" Luke reached, then withdrew his hand as if remembering her rejection. "Saw Doc in the hallway. They're about to send you home."

Gray smoke seemed to swirl around Luke's head, settling on his shoulders.

Unsure of what she saw, Navena tried to bring him completely into focus. She blinked. The haze faded. She looked back at the TV.

Ignoring Luke's background chatter about calling the nurse and gathering her things, Navena began randomly pressing up/down arrows on the remote searching for more information about the airline crash.

"You hear about that plane crash last night?" She continued flicking from one channel to the next.

"Uh-uh. Where?" Luke answered.

"Here." The heart monitor began to beep as her frustration rose. "It's been all over the news. I saw it."

Snatching the remote, Luke searched the dial and quickly found CNN. Iraq was the morning topic, as usual. Likewise MSNBC. Local channels featured the latest candidate in upcoming Senate elections and the Detroit Lions football training camp. No air tragedy. Anywhere.

"Bad dream, darling." He ruffled her hair and tossed the remote onto the bed as Dr. Gupta entered the room wearing a green gauzy cloud around his head.

"Good news for you," the medic declared through his accent. "We'll send you home now if he promises to take good care of you."

The doctor threw Luke a wary glance before turning the page on his clipboard. He scribbled notes to the nurse, prescriptions for Navena, and nodded his head. "Take care."

"She's in good hands, Doc." Luke folded the papers and tucked them into his pocket. He closed the door as Dr. Gupta passed through it. The gray swirl reappeared around Luke as an amber-hued nurse entered the room. He stepped aside.

"I know you're glad to get out of here." Friendly chatter bubbled from the warm-spirited woman as she unhooked the monitors and untaped Navena's IV. "Hold this for me."

Before Navena could protest, the nurse had snatched the needle from her vein and replaced it with a cotton ball. With ritualistic quickness, she placed Navena's own finger atop the hidden hole in her opposite hand.

"There you go." She tossed the used materials in the trash. Scooting Navena's finger aside, she strapped on a bandage, turned toward the sink, and washed her hands using the touchless faucet. "Take care of yourself, now."

"That was quick. I didn't even have time to say ouch." She stretched, catlike, noting the quietness in the room now that the equipment was disconnected. The only movement came from the cloud drifting around Luke's head.

She'd never noticed these colors before. Auras, perhaps? She heard of them, of course. Not from Mama, mostly in the movies. Probably another gift from the Mothers. *If I'm going to be able to do everything they did, then, of course, I see the colors of people's spirits.*

Another glance at the deck of cards confirmed that the mysterious newscasts about the nonexistent crash she witnessed were all real somehow. Which meant the week's dreams were, too. She couldn't escape the danger. Navena closed and opened her eyelids with deliberate slowness, wiping away previous notions of the world around her. Shivering, she threw back the covers and hung her legs over the bed, not sure she wanted any more revelations today.

Nor did she want Luke to take her home. Being around him was too awkward. He was acting like nothing had changed between them, while she considered herself free.

"Luke, I appreciate you being here, but don't you have to pick up your mother from church soon?" She adjusted the pillow supporting her back. "I can call Fern. I'll be fine."

"So, it's like that, huh?" He shrugged. "All right. Just trying to be nice. Let me know if there's anything I can do—*friend*."

They stared at each other in silence for a moment before Luke turned and left.

Navena exhaled with relief.

"Thanks for picking me up on such short notice." Navena handed Fern the keys so that she could open the front door.

"I ought to kick your butt for not telling me about the accident," Fern snapped back playfully. She turned the key and stood aside to let Navena enter. "I know you want to take a shower. Go get changed, I'll make some tea. I brought my hair stuff, too."

Navena could see the flatirons, toiletries, and nail supplies poking out of her overstuffed tote. "Girl, you always know what to do. I won't be too long."

Fern kicked off her wide-strapped black sandals and abandoned them at the door. She scampered behind Navena's leggy strides with hurried half-sized steps, stopping every few seconds to shift her bundle. When they reached the den, she dropped her load beside the sofa and took a second to catch her breath before meeting Navena in the kitchen. "Get outta here. I know what to do."

Glad to be home and not alone, Navena attempted to stretch her sore muscles, but decided better. She tried to ignore Luke's gym shoes, work shirts, and colognes scattered around the bedroom. "Mental note. Pack this stuff up and set it on Luke's stairwell tomorrow."

After a quick shower, she slid into a well-worn pair of black velour jogging pants and an oversized white T-shirt. Food and pain relief beckoned. She half limped into the kitchen for her codeine tablets and some carryout.

"I know you're ready for these. Come on so we can eat." Fern had lined up Navena's supplies on the counter—a pain reliever, a muscle relaxant, and an antibiotic ointment. A pitcher of ice water and a new box of bandages stood ready. "What are we going to order?"

"Well, you know I can do Chinese every day, but let's go for barbecue. How's that sound?" Navena eased into a chair at the table, careful to avoid contact between her abdomen and any surface. Fern brought two pills and a glass of water to the table. Navena quickly downed both. "You are truly a lifesaver."

"Doing your man's job." She replaced the water glass with a cup of chamomile tea. "I called about your car, too. Not too bad—just the bumper and the airbag. You'll have it back sooner than you think."

Fern rummaged through the junk drawer beside the sink and pulled out a binder of restaurant menus. She flipped its pages, landing on Freddie's Fish and Ribs, and began mouthing the number as she walked toward the phone. "Where is he anyway?"

"Probably with his mother, the self-important Luvenia." She really didn't want to talk about Luke today, even with Fern. Nose buried in her near-empty teacup, she scoured its bottom for a few last drops of the relaxation it promised and more time to avoid Fern's interrogation.

"Right. One slab, one catfish dinner, a half pound of shrimp, a garden salad, and two pieces of pound cake. Forty-five minutes? Yes, that's fine. Thank you." Fern hung up the phone and made her way to the table.

"Now, you know I don't mind bringing you home. We're way overdue for girls' night, so I guess this'll have to do." Fern skewed her eyebrows so that one sat higher than the other. She grabbed the teacup from Navena and rose to refill it from a pot on the stove. "But he should've been there for you today."

"He was. I sent him home."

"Damn. He must have really been getting on your nerves. What did he do?" She hurried back to the table and handed Navena her fresh tea. She sat and leaned back in the chair.

Navena wished she could do the same. No position offered comfort. Not to mention that she was starving and sleepy. "Nothing. He just keeps pretending that I didn't break up with him Thursday."

"You're lying!"

"I wouldn't joke about that." Navena attempted to readjust her body in the narrow upright chair. "Besides you of all people know that split's been a long time coming. So now it's done."

"Well, you've had a helluva weekend. I should've been here for you. Why didn't you call?"

"Got a lot on my mind. Not just Luke. The job mostly." Navena definitely wasn't telling Fern about her recent rash of nightmares and daydreams. Or that every now and then, she knew just how her girlfriend was feeling. "All these transition issues are making me feel a little overwhelmed."

"That investor's party you mentioned at the meeting

Monday sounds like it should be nice," Fern said, changing the subject.

"It's not a party-party, Fern. Leave your video dance moves at home."

"Don't you try breaking out yours just because Luke won't be around."

The doorbell rang.

"I thought it would never get here." Navena pushed herself up from the chair. "Can you get that? I'm going to sit in the den so I can get comfortable."

Fern ran to the door to accept the delivery. Once situated in the den, they ate the steaming meal quickly and quietly, intermittently dousing portions with hot sauce and guzzling their half-chilled colas. They finished off the meal with oversized slices of pound cake and a moment of silence.

Fern fished through the tote at her side and pulled out cotton balls, nail polish, and remover. She drew up one knee and started giving herself a pedicure. "I know we're not here to talk about work, but what do you think of Maxwell McKnight so far?"

"Well, he's working me like a rented mule."

"Hmph. I'd like to work him, with his fine ass." Fern slathered lotion on her feet and shook her head. "Have mercy!"

Navena's don't-you-dare stare escaped before she could contain it.

Fern caught the look and its threat. "Is that why you broke up with Luke all of a sudden?"

"What? Because of McKnight? Please."

"Yeah. Try please being honest." She wagged her finger at Navena. "If you could've seen your expression just now. Hope Luke never saw that."

"I didn't even talk about him to Luke," Navena said, now defensive.

"Oh, now I know something's up. You can't hold hot

water. That has to be the only thing Luke doesn't know about you."

Not this week, she thought wryly. "What did you think of our magazine idea?" She hoped Fern would take the lead.

"Won't work. We're talking about your boy right now. Spill it."

"I know you won't say anything. To *anybody.*"

Fern brushed her fingers across her lips mock zipper style, then went back to painstakingly painting the last drops of chocolate fudge polish across her cotton-spread toenails.

Navena took a deep breath and blurted the secret. "Truth is we used to date."

"Get outta here!"

"Back when I was in college. He was an instructor. Separated from his wife. We were on totally different life tracks. I broke it off after a few months."

"You are good at kicking a brother to the curb, aren't you?" Fern laughed at a joke Navena didn't find funny. "Kinda weird that he would land here as your boss, huh? Small world."

"I can't believe this is a coincidence."

"He's not some kind of stalker, is he?" Fern asked, suddenly worried.

This time Navena laughed. "I didn't mean it like that. I've had a really *unusual* week. Bad dreams. I fell and hurt myself in aerobics class. I totaled my car."

"He took your job, too." Fern leaned forward like she'd uncovered some priceless secret. "Maybe he's bringing you all this bad luck."

"Hadn't thought of it that way." The notion distressed Navena. "As if I could do something about it," she dismissed the idea.

"Girl, if my mama was Lady-A-the-Psychic-Empress, my life would be perfect. Better ask her what to do."

"I try to keep my mother out of my man issues. You know that."

"And that's your problem. Gotta do everything yourself. And usually the hard way."

Chapter Ten

Monday, May 16

Morning, Navena decided, arrived much too fast. Ignoring the aches from her accident, she sat in Maxwell's office just after dawn, still tired, slightly irritable, wanting to lie down in his lap and go back to sleep.

Because they'd only been working on their approach since Thursday, she wondered if they were ready for an unveiling this afternoon. She also worried about how staff and readers would accept their changes. With his eyebrows furrowed, Maxwell's expression mirrored her thoughts.

"What's the matter?" she asked, rubbing her eyes and resisting a stretch.

"Nothing." He paused. "Ever see a shooting star?"

"Don't remember you being a sky gazer." Navena cocked her head in curiosity.

"Saw one for the first time the other night. The Eta Aquarids meteor shower."

Her heart stopped, yet her pulse raced. "What time?" Maybe there was a real-world explanation for the apparition—and it wasn't a far-off plane crash.

"Shortly before dark."

Relieved, she relaxed a bit. "Did you make a wish?"

"Um-hmm. But you know I can't tell."

He looks different, she thought. More than the far-off gaze, his manner—or her perception—had softened. A warm rush washed over her. Last week's what-if that she'd pondered and quickly dismissed suddenly seemed worth considering.

"It's the beard," she noted aloud.

"Like?" he asked, stroking the thin layer of well-groomed growth across his chin.

You know I do. That's how you used to look before. Navena tossed the thought through the wistful look in her eye, but refrained from speaking her mind.

His look-alike's picture on the hospital television flashed through her mind. What an incredible coincidence. She shook off the reverie, glad the victim wasn't Maxwell.

"So I see you spent your weekend primping and wishing." She ignored the college déjà vu and clicked her ink pen ready. "What's on the agenda for this morning?"

"Salvation for our *Dispatch*, of course." Maxwell smiled broadly and lifted his END AIDS mug for a swig of coffee. "They're going to love what we've put together."

Mood sure changed, she thought. Though mornings had never bothered him as far as she could remember, his switch from introspection to exuberance was jarring—especially this early.

"Can't wait to hear what you're up to," she offered, trying hard not to be snippy.

"What *I'm* up to?" he laughed. "Don't think I'm facing the wolves alone on this one . . . Miss Executive Editor."

She frowned in disbelief. "You're quitting? Already?" She didn't want his job *this* way.

He shook his head. "Think again."

She paused to clear the morning cobwebs from her head. "You're restructuring? And I'm being promoted?"

A big "huh" popped into her mouth, but she bit it and thought first. "You're promoting me?" Outward disbelief hid her inner excitement as Maxwell nodded yes. "So does this make me coconspirator or what?"

"More like co-getter-of-glory when we pull off this transformation."

"What else are you hiding behind that smile?" she teased, leaning forward.

He proudly passed her a sheet of paper. "Org chart."

She sat back and stared at the collection of rectangular boxes and attached lines that indicated staff positions and the team's reporting structure. At the top, Cullen, publisher emeritus. Then directly below, side by side, Maxwell as editor in chief and her name in the executive editor box. Wow.

"It's real."

"But it's not a gimme. You're already doing the work. The acknowledgment is long overdue. Plus, it'll match the raise I just gave you."

"Speaking of which, do you have enough investors yet?" she asked. "Anything I can do?"

"I've got this all under control. I'm asking investors to join me in order to build community rapport. The marketing and publicity benefits are invaluable." Maxwell oozed confidence. "And now it's not that I need the money. As a matter of fact, the contract is signed. My check has been cashed. I own the *Dispatch*."

"Wow! Congrats, then." His eagerness caught her off guard. She felt as if she'd insulted him by questioning his ability to get money. "So, what exactly comes with my new position?"

With a nod of his head to acknowledge the change in subject, he pushed a sheet of paper at her. This one was labeled *Job Description—Executive Editor.* Maxwell placed a similar set of papers in front of her on the table, each with titles matching boxes in the Org Chart. What she read disappointed her.

"So I'm still responsible for generating story ideas, assigning stories, making sure we hit deadline. So, what's new?" she huffed.

"Other duties as assigned." Maxwell gave her a coy smile. "All this is new. I want to give everyone the chance to show me their skills. You, I'd like to handle the budget and oversee a new part-time community relations position, which will be someone to keep us connected to the public." He pulled that job description from the pile for Navena's review.

"So basically my description is unwritten."

"I prefer to think that it's evolving," he finessed.

"And is everybody else making theirs up, too?"

"Staff duties are fully laid out. All the reporters will get their description this afternoon. I'll give them until Friday to review and revise and we'll finalize all of them by next Monday."

He paused to glance at his watch. "Let's wrap up. It's almost eight o'clock. Job duties will be most of my presentation for the meeting. Where are you with the magazine proposal?"

"I took your suggestion and closed in the concept to limit staff input to three areas—picking a name for the magazine, choosing a cover story, and determining a launch date. But I've defined the sections and assigned those. I have the layout concepts to share. And a mock e-zine that will replace our current Web site. I want to read through everything once more, make copies, and I'm set."

"How do you think they'll take it?"

"One minute, I think they're ready. The next minute,

I think they'll revolt. It is hard to tell. What's Cullen say about all this, by the way?"

"You didn't see *emeritus* at the top?" He shuffled the stack of papers and repositioned the Org Chart in front of her, pointing to Cullen's box. "He's retiring. Officially in ninety days. Unofficially, today."

"You're really going to make this happen." She was impressed with the obvious work he'd put into reshaping the *Dispatch*. And now she could understand his resentment over investors getting credit for his efforts. "I'm happy to help any way I can."

"So's your boyfriend apparently." He looked at Navena with thinly veiled jealousy.

She jerked to attention. "What are you talking about?"

"He called, you know. Didn't mention you, but said he was overnighting a check." Maxwell looked as surprised as she felt. "I thought you knew."

"Did you get it?"

"Saturday." He opened a folder and slid the check toward Navena. "Should I give you the honor of depositing it?"

"I don't have anything to do with this." She picked up the check to take a closer look. Her palms began to burn. "We split up Thursday."

Biting back a smile, he offered condolesences. "Sorry. Are you okay, though?"

Not when she saw all the zeros on that check. "Fifty thousand dollars!"

Based on Luke's reaction when she mentioned investing in the *Dispatch*, she had no idea he'd bother. She wondered if it was a ploy to win her back. Where the hell did he get *this* kind of money anyway?

"His business that good?" Maxwell asked.

"I guess so," she murmured, placing the check gingerly on the table and rubbing her hands together.

* * *

Navena welcomed three o'clock with a yawn. Alone in the conference room, she surveyed the stacks of paper placed in front of each seat, checked her watch, and smiled as Maxwell entered the room. This was their baby. He felt it, too. She saw it in his mellow confidence, the way he strolled casually to the front of the table and declined to take a seat. He was savoring his moment and sharing it with her.

Showtime, she thought, nervously clicking the top of her ballpoint pen, in and out, in and out. Reporters began to trickle into the room. Once everyone was assembled, the group's collective doubt clouded the room. No one spoke, so she could hear them all heavily, breathing, punctuated with long deep sighs as if air inside the usually ample space hung heavy and thick. Chairs creaked beneath the weight of squirming bodies until Maxwell broke the uncomfortable silence.

"Thanks for coming. I know you're all wondering what's going on around here these days, and I hope this meeting helps to ease your minds. I'm going to ask Navena to get us started." He stepped aside as she walked around the table to the front of the room. She wanted to strut, but the staff's somber gazes checked her enthusiasm.

Using a remote control, Navena turned on the PowerPoint projector in the center of the table to begin her slide presentation. She could feel jolts of excitement ripple through the staff as she laid out the magazine plan. By the time she finished, relieved smiles and quiet chitchat had replaced the sighs and silence that opened the meeting.

No longer nervous, she handed the remote to Maxwell and stepped aside as he explained the new staffing structure and applauded her promotion.

She finished the meeting with instructions to review

the new job descriptions and submit suggested changes no later than noon Friday. Ideas for magazine names, launch dates, and cover stories should also be submitted by then. All items would be finalized on Tuesday. As they finished, the reporters clapped. Navena looked at Maxwell with pride. *We did it*, she thought.

The team scattered, jubilant, full of conversation and questions, talking among themselves, grabbing Maxwell or Navena for congratulations or clarification. And then they were gone.

"Good job," Maxwell said. He walked toward the door and gently pushed it shut. "I think they got what they wanted. What do you think?" He sat next to her at the table and leaned back in the chair.

She turned to face him. Telling him he was a genius would sound so adolescent. Instead, she faked composure. "I think we have a lot to do this week."

"True. But, for now, let's celebrate."

"It's almost time to go home," she protested.

Maxwell threw her a chastising stare. "Since when do you turn down a big scoop of French vanilla on a waffle cone?"

Navena grinned, blushed, and giggled, finding it hard to believe he remembered her favorite flavor. "Fern drove me . . . well, let me grab my purse." She started to stand. Maxwell reached for her arm. The touch sent ripples through her belly. "What?" she asked softly.

"Friends?"

"Of course," she replied without thinking. The idea seemed natural, felt comfortable. Navena rose and Maxwell let his hand slide down her wrist as she stood. She eased past his seat, her hip brushing his shoulder as she moved toward the door. Maxwell dipped his head into his hands.

You do remember, she thought fondly. Once upon a

time, they lived for such stolen touches. Two or three would carry her through days of not seeing Maxwell. Now they ignited memories long tucked away.

"I'll meet you downstairs in ten minutes," Maxwell whispered as she left the room.

Navena hurried to her desk and checked the clock. Four-fifteen. Not a lot of time, but some. Shutting down the computer, she grabbed her satchel and pushed her chair up to the desk. She looked up to see Fern watching her from across the room with a smirk. Navena frowned in mock irritation, lifted her thumb and pinky to her ear like an imaginary phone, and mouthed "Call me" as she moved to the back of the newsroom. Taking the rear stairs would deter any further scrutiny from staff.

She eased down the stairwell, excited about being with Maxwell, though Luke's nagging presence popped in and out with every other step. Pushing it aside, she dug into her purse to find her sunglasses before opening the heavy steel exit door and emerging into the sunshine.

Maxwell pulled up to the curb in a red '65 Mustang. Navena opened the passenger-side door and climbed in. "You still drive this?" She was impressed.

"Not usually. But today I needed some luck," he replied. "A lot of memories with you over there in that seat." He moved deftly into traffic, hesitating at the corner. "Sure you want dessert or would you rather go for a drink?"

Liquor, flashed across her mind. "Ice cream," came out instead.

"Probably the smart choice," Maxwell laughed. He turned left down the one-way street that led to central downtown and the ice cream store. "So, how are you feeling about our new venture?"

"A little overwhelmed, I think. When are we going to review all the staff ideas?"

"Looks like we'll be working late. I've got a board meeting tonight, but the rest of the week is clear. How about your calendar?"

"Wednesdays, Fridays, and Saturdays, I teach a dance workout class. Other than that, I should be free."

"Wow, you still dance?"

"Hip-hop aerobics. Keeps me sane."

"Sounds good because I'd also appreciate your help with the investors party I'm planning first weekend in June. Can we start after work tomorrow?" He raised an eyebrow, but kept his tone matter-of-fact. "Is this a real breakup? I don't want to cause any problems on the home front."

"Done deal. It's fine."

Uneasy excitement washed over her, at the idea of spending alone time with her former Prince Charming. Palms simmering, gut twisting, Navena knew this was the career chance she'd been waiting for. No way was she going to blow it.

Maxwell parked at a meter and turned off the engine, leaving the radio on. *Car still purrs like a kitten. Maxwell still smells like heaven. I think I'm still hung up on him,* Navena thought. They sat in silence for a moment.

"When we make this happen, it'll be the best thing to hit Detroit in a long time," Maxwell said softly. "Don't be afraid."

"I'm not scared." True about the paper's fate, not so about everything else.

"I know you," Maxwell whispered. "You're worried about something. Success? Me, maybe?"

"That's more like it, I think." Navena sighed, glad to admit at least part of the truth.

"I'm not here to hurt you, gorgeous."

Ah, the old nickname despite the fading bruises and cuts. "So you say." Despite her resolve, she melted into his affection and the strains of Maxwell coming from the radio.

"I swear," he promised. "This time could be different for us, Navena. And I'm not trying to take advantage of your recent availability. I know you're going to need some time. But I didn't just land here by chance. It's—"

"What? Meant to be? That sounds *so* familiar, Maxwell." She turned to look out the side door window. "I believed you once."

"Try me again," he replied, running his fingers through her dreadlocks. "I guess you could say I've been marinating."

She closed her eyes, unable to face him. With a soft laugh, Maxwell pulled her chin toward him. Then he surprised her with a kiss—better than she remembered, even superior to Luke's. Unfortunately, he reeked of nostalgia that left a bitter taste on her tongue. Instead of returning his passion, she recoiled in frustration and slapped him.

Chapter Eleven

Tuesday, May 17

"I never would've thought she'd hit me," Maxwell mumbled to himself, rubbing his cheek, which had long since recovered. The only part of him that still stung was his ego, because she'd barely spoken to him all day. "All my cool points are shot."

He'd *intended* to kiss Navena yesterday. No question. Wooing her was his whole reason for seeking out the *Dispatch* and coming to Detroit. But he'd wanted to court her affection, make amends for his trifling ways, convince her first, conquer her later.

Meanwhile, he fought to keep from coming unglued every time she looked at him. And when she was close . . . he couldn't stand not taking her in his arms. Leaving her at the end of each day was so much harder than he imagined it could be. Fate, it seemed, had other designs on their lives.

Alone in the newsroom with only ceiling fans and CNN for company, he reviewed his game plan for the evening.

It'll be strictly business, he tried to convince himself.

But honestly, he didn't see how he could. With no one around . . . *What made me think working late—alone with her—would be a good idea? Hope her cologne has faded,* he thought miserably.

The building buzzer jarred him into reality. Navena stood on the sidewalk below the window he stared from, waving and buzzing, trying to get his attention. Maxwell smiled down at her, lifted his mug in greeting, and turned to go downstairs and let her in the building.

He found himself hurrying and deliberately slowed his pace, taking a second to loosen the top button of his shirt, smooth the crinkles in his khaki Dockers, and breathe. *Relax before you spill your coffee,* he chided himself. Moments later, he faced her and couldn't help but smile.

"That was quick."

"Party store's right down the block. I just ran in for snacks."

Her scowl made him feel stupid.

"Come on in." He ushered her inside with a sweeping gesture, mindful of his mug. "You ready? We've got a lot to do this evening."

"Deadline day. I should be headed home for a nap. But no. I'm fetching bottled water, Power Bars, and Twinkies for you."

"That's what I'm talking about!" Maxwell reached for the bags to free Navena's hands. *I didn't even ask for anything. She might be mad,* he thought, *but she remembers what I like.*

Closing the door behind her, he admonished himself to be professional. All night. Starting right now. "Lunchroom or conference room?"

"Might as well dive in."

Maxwell nodded approval, grateful for Navena's obvious self-control. They turned—at the same time, he noted—and walked slowly up to the newsroom.

"Where?" Navena asked, pausing at the landing to survey the surrounding workstations. "Conference room?" She crossed the floor without waiting for Maxwell's response. He followed closely, absorbing her perfume and fighting the growing stiffness in his jeans.

"Let me grab my files," he said, detouring to his office and a stack of waiting folders. "Meet you in there."

The diversion allowed him to get his pants straight and his mind focused. He could hear Navena through the surrounding silence, the paper bag crumbling and stretching as she apparently prepared to eat. Quickly surveying the neat stacks of paperwork he'd prepared for today, he selected a folder labeled EDITORIAL CALENDAR, another entitled STAFF ASSIGNMENTS, his pen, and a legal pad. With a quick tug at his crotch, he set off toward Navena.

"You remember how to get me started, I see," Maxwell joked, stopping to help her empty the paper bag, then taking a seat on the opposite side of the table. He spread papers and Post-it notes in the area between himself and Navena to minimize the distance.

Without responding to his comment, she reached into her leather tote and withdrew a similar stack of papers. "We got so many ideas from staff. I am really impressed with their participation."

"That's what we wanted, right? So, what looks good?"

"The best lead suggestions came from Anderson and Fern. He's pushing for 'Gangstas Gone Good.' It's a spin-off of the unsolved murder of Jesse Stiles, leader of the Castle Airs music group. The group stayed gold from '62 till '74 and when they filed suit against their record label, Stiles turned up dead."

"A real investigative opportunity," Maxwell said,

nodding with approval. "Think he can handle that kind of heat?"

"First time for everything." Navena shrugged. "If this is the work we're going to pursue, we have to start somewhere. Besides, Fern's story is more entertainment. 'Homespun Divas,' she's calling it."

"Work the divas piece for the first issue," Maxwell advised. "Take it from a bad-girl-makes-good angle. Then we can go with an out-of-the-life theme to tie it all together."

"You sure you want gang squad and murder all through the first issue? We might scare people off." Navena scribbled furiously in her steno pad as Maxwell chuckled.

"Yep. Let's start with a bang." He laughed harder.

"Oh, you've got jokes this evening," she said, trying to hide her amusement.

"Um-hmm. And one more for you. Sports. Whatever happened to—"

"Dennis Rodman!" they blurted in unison.

Maxwell loved the easy way they flowed. If he wasn't grayer and she wasn't more . . . womanly . . . he'd swear they were fourteen years back, sharing gossip in his apartment after class.

Even though he tried to avoid the comparison, his ex-wife wasn't half as smart as Navena. Lila was an academic, yes, but Navena had never feared a hunch. Now, she wouldn't call it instinct, but he knew that's what it was. And that's what the *Dispatch* needed in order to expand.

"Hey, what are we calling this thing?"

"Next order of business—name." Navena slid the previous stack of papers to Maxwell, grouped under a sticky note labeled ARTICLES. In its place, she withdrew a pile of printed e-mails paper-clipped under a sheet of looseleaf marked TITLES. "Got a whole slew of ideas from stupid to super. I took the liberty of narrowing it down to three. But here are the rest if you—"

Maxwell shook his head no. "I'll take your word."

"Our first contender—nominated by Anderson—*City Handbook*. Joining him in the ring is Fern's submission, *Our Scene*. And our final name for the ages, *Anthology*, the brainchild of yours truly."

Maxwell waved for the papers she read from. Navena passed them over. City Handbook could've stayed with the stupid group. He tossed its e-mail aside. At first hearing, he liked *Our Scene*. Within its glossy pages he could almost see the neon lights, the fast life, reporters connected to everything that mattered in Detroit.

"You know, I'm liking your idea, but . . ."

"Fern's is better, isn't it?" She snapped her fingers and smiled.

"So *Our Scene*'s the winner?"

Navena nodded. "Wow. That was easy."

Wish you were half as much, Maxwell thought playfully. "I think it highlights the history and tradition readers have come to know through the *Dispatch* and speaks to the higher-minded twenty-five-to-fifty-five-year-old demographic we want to pull for the magazine. Maybe we can subtitle it 'Detroit Today and Tomorrow.' With an ampersand. Good work, kiddo."

She stared at him quietly, her eyes seeming to look into his soul. "Means a lot to me, Maxwell—your support of this team."

"You don't need anybody to validate you. Especially me."

"Sometimes I do. When I don't hear it, I start to doubt myself, second-guess my decisions."

"Everything you've put together is right on track. Perfect. In fact, how about we develop the editorial calendar while we're hot and then break for dinner. Marketing strategy can wait until after we eat."

Navena glanced at the wall clock behind Maxwell's head. "Six-thirty already?"

With that, she placed a printout of June, July, and August calendars in the center of the table. They had decided to launch Labor Day week. From there, they back-timed through fifteen days of printing, three weeks of design, internal approvals, story development, and ad sales.

"Tight," Navena moaned.

"We should've started last month," Maxwell agreed.

"No way we can hold off the launch?"

"I'm afraid we'll lose our momentum. Election's coming up. The *Dispatch* would be out of sight until January. And that's just too long to wait." Using all ten fingers, he ticked off the timeline once more. "We're going to have to meet every day."

"With staff? They won't have time to write," Navena protested.

"No. Just you and me. I'll leave team oversight to you. Handle it however you wish."

"Fine. Does this mean we can eat now?"

Maxwell smiled, glad for the break. Besides, if Navena leaned any closer, he'd have to give up being strictly business. "Thai?"

She nodded yes, stood, and stretched. They decided to call ahead, pick it up, and eat in the conference room. That way they could keep working and try to bring the evening to a close.

Her favorite Thai restaurant was just four blocks over. At this hour, the usual bustle of midtown traffic slowed to a crawl. Navena and Maxwell encountered only a handful of cars and even fewer passersby. Afternoon air blew warm and windy with little humidity.

Both they and the world around them seemed quiet. Maxwell felt his chance to pry slipping away.

"So, what are you doing for Memorial Day?"

"We . . . Luke and I used to have an annual family barbecue. This year, I don't know."

"Again, I'm not trying to be pushy, but if you're still available by then, maybe we can get together."

"You're not going home?"

"To D.C.? No. Plenty to keep me busy here."

"*Our Scene* planning? We'll be done with the hard stuff by nine," Navena scoffed.

Self-pity, embarrassment, ego each kicked in. "Right. Thanks to you. But the investors' party is all in my head. No invitations, no caterer. Don't even have a location yet."

"May twenty-eight, you said?"

"Saturday before Memorial Day. Planned all this before I started so I didn't know about the city's other big coming-out party."

"You mean Trentmoor Towers?"

"Yeah. All the big shots are calling it a phoenix, like it's leading the city's rebirth. Hope I don't come off as some amateur competing with that kind of A-list publicity so soon."

"That's Luke's event," she confessed in a whisper.

"*Your* Luke?" He stopped walking. "You're kidding me, right?"

"I don't believe in luck, but if it existed, he'd have it." She shrugged. "He was strictly architectural engineering ten years ago, then hooked a few side projects—you know, restoring historic churches, renovating lofts, residential additions, that stuff—then he met this contractor who took a chance and gave him a deal. Voila. Now he's Detroit's reincarnator."

"No problem," Maxwell scoffed. "I'll take his leftovers for our shindig. Mayor Stewart, council members, any Detroit sports player I can scrounge."

The spring breezes picked up. They walked faster into the wind.

"Did you have to call in a lot of favors?"

"A few. Need one more, though."

"From . . ."

"You. Promise me you'll be there. Spotlight's on you just as much as it is on me."

"I've been handling Luke's PR. I'm committed to the event, but I'll see what I can do."

Is she trying to pacify me or is she telling the truth? Maxwell wondered as they entered Sala Thai. He gave his name and paid for the order, handing one bag to Navena and balancing the other two. They left the atmospheric Asian lobby and reentered the urban twilight retracing their steps. For a moment, he was tempted to leave well enough alone.

"Are you happy, Navena?"

"Maxwell, I am so glad you came along. I was starting to worry that the *Dispatch* was never going to leave an imprint on Detroit. Now—"

"What happened with Luke," Maxwell interrupted. "If I may ask?"

"Stuff happened," Navena struggled to find an explanation. "You know I'm kind of . . . complicated."

"Not you. You're special. Always remember that."

Silence accompanied them the remainder of the way, into the building and up the long stairway to the second floor. Back in the conference room, Navena doled out dinner from assorted white boxes, tossing him soy sauce and hot pepper packets, and stealing touches throughout.

The breakup must be real, Maxwell decided. *Or else she wouldn't be testing me.*

"You know what?" Navena began gathering the items she'd just laid out. "Let's move down to the end of the table, where we have more room."

Maxwell grabbed the white takeout containers and carried them to the new meal site. Navena brought the condiments and napkins and divided the items between them once more.

They settled into their seats on opposite sides of the table. Maxwell stretched his legs beneath the table and met Navena's halfway. He stopped. Jerking away would make it seem like he was afraid. Keeping his leg next to hers might come off as overly aggressive to her.

As he hesitated, Navena extended her leg as well—not away, but along the length of his calf. Head lowered over her food, she lifted her eyes and raised her brows with a smirk. She rubbed her leg back and forth. The friction ignited a fire in his loins. He wrapped his other leg around hers.

"You're being fast," Maxwell kidded.

"You didn't slow me down."

"I'm just trying to get comfortable." He teased her. "Can you pass me the hot pepper, please?"

Navena slid her hand across the table. Maxwell met her midway and found his hand atop hers, stroking her fingers, staring in her eyes.

"I shouldn't have done that," Navena whispered. She pulled away.

"Why are you here?"

"To work—"

"You were always a bad liar."

"True. But I can't do this yet."

"I know." He exhaled, then tipped his chin up. "I want you when you're ready for me. Not before."

"Bold assumption, don't you think? You're making it difficult for us to work together every day, Maxwell."

"Not if we stay on opposite sides of the building," he

joked. She smiled, but he knew he'd made her regretful. Again. Brought her more angst. Exactly what he didn't want to do.

No more guilty pleasures, he promised himself.

They untangled their legs, returned to their food, both stirring, neither one eating. Concentrating on work was now officially impossible. "Did you love him?"

"Luke wanted to marry me."

So do I, Maxwell thought. "You told me. I don't buy that 'too busy with my career' crap either."

"It's over and I really don't want to discuss it with you. Excuse me," Navena said abruptly, and left the room.

She stood and walked quickly from the room. Frustrated by his incredible desire for her and his unwillingness to wait, Maxwell leaned back in his chair and growled at himself. He felt just the way he did when they'd met. Swept. Totally. Instantly.

But things have obviously changed, he admitted. *Maybe I'm wrong about the looks, the smiles, those secret touches. I might really be history to her.* He slid his hands over his head. The very thought of being rejected pierced him.

Navena returned to the room and began clearing the table. He looked up at her, watched her blatantly trying to avoid his gaze, his touch, conversation. He needed to explain.

"I had to find you, Navena," he confessed aloud. "What you and I had might have been flawed, but it was real. I learned that from you. From being *without* you." He pushed himself back and brought a fist to his chest, forcefully. One, two, three times.

"Right here, gorgeous. Right here. You never left. I had to find you and see if there was still time for another chance." He turned toward the window. "I have always loved you, Navena. I have always loved *you.*"

Turning back to Navena, Maxwell thought he heard a sniffle.

"You crying?" he asked suddenly, rushing to her side. Her body began to tremble. He looked at her, held her so close.

No, I'm all right. She said nothing. Just cried quietly.

Maxwell knew she must be furious. Weakness was not her thing and these public tears had to be killing her inside. He hugged her tighter and dipped his nose into her hair. He felt her relax as she wrapped her arms around him, tears spilling onto his shirt. He fought his erection to no avail.

Navena lifted her head slightly and kissed his throat, exposed by his open-necked shirt. He pulled her hair back and brushed his lips across her forehead, down her nose, and stopped. She stood on tiptoe and kissed his lips. He tasted the saltiness of her tears and relished her sudden surrender.

Carefully, he laid her atop the table, his hands beneath her back to shield her from the hard wooden surface.

Impulsively straddling her atop the table, he leaned forward and looked into her eyes, trying to untangle the web of confusion that even he could see. He wanted to make love to her. Right there. Right now.

But she'll never forgive herself—or me for that matter. I can't have that.

He relented and stepped back. Lifting her hands, he placed a lingering kiss on each one.

"*I* can't. Not this way," Maxwell said. He pulled her toward him and hugged her once more. "You okay?"

She offered a weak smile. He gave her a hankerchief from his pants pocket to dry her face. "I think I'll work from my desk," she said softly.

"Good idea." He felt the sexual energy dissapate as she walked away. "I'll be in my office. Call if you need me. For anything."

Chapter Twelve

Wednesday, May 18

Less than three weeks until the murder.

Navena sat at the kitchen table dressed in beige slacks and a lightweight linen sweater. Ready for work, but stalled by the nagging thought that precious days until the next dark moon were quickly slipping away, she tried to figure out what she was supposed to do next.

So far the gifts Vee returned hadn't proven helpful to Navena. She said they'd come and go and that they did—plunging her into mentally overhearing staff conversations from rooms away, then cutting her off like a dropped cell phone call. At least the dreams, for now, had stopped.

Like every other woman she knew, Navena dreaded becoming her mother. While some bemoaned the family hips and others loathed the maternal nagging, Navena dreaded the Larimore Legacy. Since that mystical moment at the crash site with Vee, she felt like she was blindly moving puzzle pieces around, trying to create a coherent picture.

"This'll just take a minute," Navena told herself. She

hurried to the stove to pour herself another cup of tea, sat back down, and grabbed a napkin from its holder and a pen from her purse. "Here's what I know."

Much the way she'd develop an editorial calendar or a marketing plan, Navena divided the napkin into columns headed Dream, Sign, Gift, Results, and rows listing all weird occurrences since her birthday.

Confident that no Larimore had ever charted her gift quite this way, she thought the diagram would help get a hold of what was happening to her. She might not know what the next three weeks held in store, but she could at least plot her progress in this murder challenge the Mothers gave her.

Starting with Gifts seemed easiest. There were none. "I told Mama I'd pass on them and I think they passed on me."

Mentally eavesdropping on a few conversations and seeing rainbow auras around heads hardly deserved the esteemed Larimore Legacy tag.

Yet signs popped up all around her. Nearly every day her palms burned or she'd have déjà vu moments of things she'd seen in her dreams.

Like Luke walking overhead in the flat and stopping, standing the way he stood on top of the moon in her dream.

Her vision of a plane crash the night she connected with Vee and Maxwell mentioning the meteor shower he saw the same night.

The Jeep's over-heated steering wheel and exploding windshield.

And the cards MaDear gave her in the hospital dream that turned out to be the same ones Maxwell brought her from the gift shop.

She looked at her chart. The word "cards" tugged at her mind.

Dreams. Nightmares and visions ruled the first week after her birthday. And just as Mama said, they led her to Vee, her psychic half. But Mama didn't bother mentioning the heart detail—that Navena's was locked away with her family gifts. Power might have eluded her since her reunion with Vee, but the love bug bit hard.

"I can't believe I wasted so much time with Luke, content in that empty relationship." Navena smiled at her notes. "Now I see what I was missing."

The heart Vee returned immediately went to Maxwell. The fun of their college fling didn't compare to the fire consuming her now. Maybe their previous connection helped fate know who to place in her life. Or maybe Vee had spent the years aligning Navena's and Maxwell's stars all along.

Dreams were supposed to bring her other half, and Maxwell hitched a ride.

Coincidence?

With Luke out of her love life, did that now make Maxwell the dying man in her arms? Was this why Vee demanded that she take care of him?

She skimmed her chart entries and stopped on the word "cards" once more.

Concentration.

As if Vee flipped the light switch on the popular memory game, Navena began to search for matches to the cards MaDear presented.

Car. Cat. Smile. Barrel. Rope.

"Could it have something to do with the birthday car I gave back to Luke? Or is my Jeep finally going to quit on me? I don't have a cat. Don't feel much like smiling right now. And rope." She thought "noose" and shuddered.

Navena jotted her thoughts about the deck and what

it showed, disappointed that even on paper nothing made much sense.

"I wish I could tell somebody about all this." Tempted as she was to tell Fern last week, she decided that confessing Maxwell was plenty. No sense admitting that Lady-A-the-Psychic-Empress was a family business and Navena was its star junior executive.

She laughed and left for work.

May had selected a hazy, humid cloak from its late spring wardrobe. Detroit's usually mild air had suddenly decided to mimic Memphis, rendering the office's window air conditioner worthless and reducing the inept ceiling fans to a nuisance. Her dreadlocks, like her attitude, grew uncontrollable in the hot weather. She wiped the back of her hand across her sweaty forehead just in time to see Anderson heading her way.

"You and Maxwell have been talking an awful lot. Something must be up." Leaning his lanky frame over her low cubicle wall, he looked like Kanye West in a white button-down oxford and khaki slacks, but mimicked rap star 50 Cent's confrontational demeanor. "We gettin' laid off or what?"

"Is that what you think?" She shook her head at Anderson's assumption about her meetings with Maxwell. "I can tell you cutbacks aren't in the plan, but outside of that you have to wait until we see how the magazine sells, like everybody else."

"Let me guess. More work, same pay, right?" He frowned with exasperation.

"Anderson, believe me. We took your suggestions into consideration and I think you'll approve of our approach." Navena leaned back in her chair and contemplated the question he wasn't asking. "Something else on your mind?"

"Yeah. How can a brother get a few more dollars around here?"

"Everything okay? You having some problems?"

"Not yet. But you know I'm taking care of my moms now. Just moved back in with her because she needs someone with her. I'm working nights at the plant to make a little more cash since I just bought the house."

Navena leaned forward, "Tell you what. Watch your e-mail to see what we have planned and how you fit in. Then we can meet later with Maxwell to see if there's anything he can do."

Anderson's expression lifted, then fell. "Got another issue, too."

Navena's temples began to hum. "Spill it."

"Can we talk in the conference room?" Anderson responded with a furtive appraisal of bodies within earshot.

"Must be bad," she quickly assessed. "Let's go." She scooped up her PDA, notepad, and black felt-tip pen, forwarded her phone to voice mail, and rose to escort her frustrated associate to sanctuary. Anderson entered first, his suddenly frenetic energy carrying him to the other side of the room before Navena could even get the door closed behind her. She hastily took a seat at the end of the table opposite Maxwell's reserved seat. Sun shone in her eyes. She fumbled for a clean note page and tried to ignore the glare.

"Fern's getting a little too—familiar with me."

"Say what?" gasped Navena. She sat down and stared at him in disbelief.

"This is all about me not going out with her." He spoke in a shouted whisper and paced—stomped—menacingly just inches from Navena's seat. The room's sluggish air stirred in his wake. With each long-legged step, he seemed to measure Navena's reaction. "What, you telling me you don't know she asked me out?"

"When?"

"I don't know, three, four times." Anderson shrugged his shoulders. "The first time—was not too long after I started here a couple of years ago. I was still with my wife then, so you know, I turned her down. Gently. My wife didn't know.

"After that she came at me again, on the down low. I guess everybody had heard my home life was whack. But my head was kinda messed up and I told her *no, thanks* again.

"She asked me to the Christmas party last year, too. I was separated by then, but I just didn't think it was such a good idea." He paused to stuff his hands in his khaki pockets. "I know she's kinda shy and everything, so I tried to be real nice about telling her no. Maybe I was too nice 'cause she didn't get the hint."

"Lord have mercy." Navena shook her head.

Fern mentioned her attraction to him years ago, but Navena didn't take it seriously. Maybe the brother had her all strung out and she didn't want to admit it. The situation was almost funny, except that Anderson was genuinely exasperated.

"Me and Fern went to lunch together a few times, you know? But I started thinking that she might get the wrong idea about that. She doesn't just want to be friends. I don't want it to get too deep and ruin my career here."

Boy, I was about to throw you two together on the Our Scene cover story. Navena rammed her fingers into her hair, nails and rings catching on the thick twists. While her palms rested against her forehead, she took a deep breath and forced herself to think clearly.

"All right," she began. "What's happened lately?"

"She e-mailed me to say I'm missing a good thing."

"And how'd you respond?"

"I didn't." He shrugged his shoulders. "This morning I told her to leave me alone. I wasn't interested." He looked Navena in the eye. "Then she started to cry. I can't handle this now, Navena."

"Wow." Navena hitched one eyebrow and peered seriously at Anderson. Fern was her friend, the coworker privy to Navena's work woes, the faxes sneaked out on the company machine, long lunches with Luke disguised as lengthy interviews of this community leader or that, and now her past with the boss.

As a result, she was the employee Navena found most difficult to supervise. And, unfortunately, she was about to become Navena's first official disciplinary act since her promotion to executive editor. Anderson seemed to have legitimate grounds for sexual harassment.

"Everybody here knows I don't mind working hard," said Anderson. "So you understand that I wouldn't even bother with this if it wasn't so rough right now. Taking care of Moms and all, working this other gig, I'm not trying to fight off Fern, too," he sighed.

Navena assumed a serious tone in her voice and body movements. "I'll need some documentation, Anderson. Copies of your e-mails to and from Fern. Dates of voice or e-mail messages you've left. Whatever you can offer to support your allegation," advised Navena. "Can you get it to me by the end of the day tomorrow?"

Anderson nodded sullenly and slowly ceased his relentless pacing.

"That'll give me Friday morning to hammer out the details on my end and late afternoon to catch up with Fern for a sit-down with me and Maxwell." Navena thought her course of action aloud.

Anderson heaved a deep, whistling sigh.

"We value your dedication, Anderson," comforted Navena. "I can imagine how tough it was for you to come to me, but I'm glad you did. We'll get it straightened out."

She offered her hand and closed the meeting with a firm handshake. Anderson left her glued to the padded chair she'd planted herself in twenty minutes before.

Shouted music erupted from Anderson's hip as he opened the door. He smirked, then grabbed the cell phone to silence the sound.

"There she is now." He smiled.

Navena raised her eyebrows.

"Moms," he mouthed, pointing at the cell phone's receiver. Waving to excuse himself, he answered with a cheery greeting that raised goose bumps on Navena's skin. "Hey, Miss Kat. Whatcha need?"

Tiny beads of sweat speckled her forehead and dampened her dark roots. With no head wrap today, her dreads bounced freely with the slightest shift of her head. Their seemingly constant motion began to aggravate Navena. She slid her tailbone to the edge of the seat and lay her neck against the back of the chair. Stunned, she sat up.

Cat.

Never occurred to her that the card might symbolize a name. Like Kathleen. As in Anderson's mom.

Navena felt nauseated. Feverish. Afraid. Annoyed at her inability to put the puzzle together and wondering if Kat was indeed the card connected to the murder. Stress thumped at the back of her eyes, urging her to escape, clear her mind, maybe shuffle the pieces one more time.

Sure, Maxwell will understand. She picked up the phone and, instead of calling his extension, dialed directly into voice mail and left him a message. "Maxwell, I've got a headache and need some fresh air. I'm headed out for an early lunch. Got my cell phone if you have to reach me. Thanks."

Temporarily free, Navena hurried through the newsroom and out of the building. Nothing the Mothers gave her made sense. And what did Anderson's *mother* have to do with anything? By the time she reached the corner, Navena decided the cat-Kat connection was simple coincidence and that one had nothing to do with the other. She turned her thoughts to Maxwell.

While the initial shock of having him back in her life had passed, so had her good intentions of keeping him away from her heart. Vee's connection to Maxwell—of which he seemed unaware—acted like a magnet, forcing their eyes to lock at inappropriate moments, thoughts to cross in e-mail, and words to hang unspoken, but understood.

Until she received her "gifts," Navena steadfastly denied the sizzle in their reacquaintance and her rekindled attraction. Then last night, that kiss . . . having his body on top of hers . . . and her self-pitying tears, amounted to an admission she was mentally unprepared to make. Today hiding her feelings became all-consuming, distracting her from worrisome deadlines and dreary discussions of policy and personnel.

"Hey, stranger. Little early for you to be eating, isn't it?" Like magic, Maxwell emerged from a building shadow, shrouded in a bright red aura.

"Sunshine break, if that's okay, boss." Navena flashed a smile to match his disposition. "It's been a busy week."

"How are you feeling anyway? You were in a car accident, you know."

"My neck is a little stiff. I'm sore in a couple of places." She shrugged her achy shoulders and winced. "But I'm here, right?"

"Thank God for small favors," he said softly, searching her face as if to confirm its existence.

Their eyes caught for a moment. Her tongue tripped,

sputtered, and finally lay still. Grateful for her recovery, yet void of a witty response to express it, she could muster only another smile and a change of topic. "You coming from another meeting?"

Laughter tinted his aura orange. "Where else? Trying to do some one-to-ones for sponsorship and advertising—McClellan Corp and Umay Steel today. Urban Automotive Tech tomorrow."

"So, where are we on ad sales for *Our Scene*?"

"There's lots of available space. People aren't quite convinced."

"Then we should prepare a sample magazine for the investors party. Some people are more visual." Navena spoke quickly, excited by her idea. "We can include a list of committed investors and another list of advertisers that are already on board. The piece can serve as a thank-you and a sales tool."

"And you'll be doing this yourself since all your reporters are so busy?" Maxwell smirked. "Wonderful idea, though."

"Walked right into that one, didn't I?" Sun warmed her face and the mental receptors that had her thinking more about the way he kissed than the words he spoke. "That's a nice suit."

He smirked and raised an eyebrow. "Trying to weasel out of the work you just created for yourself?"

"As if I could."

"Anything's possible."

"Yeah. I'll remember that." Navena shook her head at the subtle seduction and furrowed her eyebrows. "Speaking of trouble, seems my girl Fern's got the hots for Anderson." She lowered her head and peered over her sunglasses to let Maxwell know she was serious.

"Fern? Really? What, she told you?"

"Unfortunately, no. Or else I could've steered her clear. Unfortunately, Anderson came to me this morning. She's been asking him out, sending him e-mails, that kind of stuff."

His voice dropped an octave. "You're telling me we've got a harassment issue here?"

"I think so." Part of her felt like she was betraying Fern. The other part felt that she was confiding in Maxwell and he'd help find a way out other than the obvious. "We don't have to fire her, do we?"

"That depends, but I can certainly see why you needed the fresh air." He rubbed a hand over his head, then glanced at his watch. "I have another meeting back at the office. Can we talk end of day?"

"Maybe." Pushing their professional boundaries, she wanted him to know she was still upset over his advances yesterday, though her instinct was to give in for old times' sake. "If you can behave."

"Don't I always?" He feigned innocence and stepped closer.

"You didn't yesterday." Returning the volley with sarcasm and a smile, she retreated half a step backward.

"But I *did* stop." Half apologizing, he advanced once more.

The world hummed past in silence, cars, pigeons, and panhandlers quieted by Navena's concentration. "What are you doing here? Why are you doing this?" she wondered aloud.

"I couldn't have found you if this wasn't meant to be."

"I'm on the rebound."

"How so? I don't think you even loved him." Glaring in defiance, Maxwell leaned toward Navena.

Pinned against the wall, she worried about staff happening by, getting her suit dirty, Maxwell still knowing her so well. "It wasn't like me and you. But that's where I am right now, Maxwell."

"Since when do you settle?"

"It's not that simple." She stomped in frustration.

He whispered into her ear, startling and arousing Navena. "Only if you complicate it."

"That seems to be *your* mission." His cologne filled her nostrils. A familiar throbbing drummed within her hips. Finding her resolve, she pushed him away.

"So I want to be with you. Is that wrong? We shouldn't have broken up to begin with. All that stuff with Lila . . . I was working that out. And you know it."

"Your loss, Maxwell. Life goes on."

With those words, Maxwell's face melted. Literally. Navena saw his mouth droop downward, the skin sag, and the eyes begin to hang from their sockets.

Loss. Maxwell. Life.

What she said, what she saw, was it more than déjà vu? It couldn't be. Panic suffocated her. She slid from his space and turned to run.

Loss. Maxwell. Life. The words reverberated against her skull. *But why would she send you here to die?*

He grabbed her arm and spun her into his. "What's the matter with you, Navena?" He shook her vehemently. "Why are you acting like you're afraid of me?"

"Not *of* you," she whispered. "*For* you."

Chapter Thirteen

Thursday, May 19

Larimore Manor glowed bright orange. Navena felt the Mothers' presence through the singing, first faint, then strong, the rhythm pulsing in time with a distant heartbeat. The whitewashed screen door creaked, paused, then opened as Mama and Fern emerged, dressed in short black dresses, calf-length and hip-hugging, with long black satin gloves and veiled black hats. Fern's gold earrings and Mama's pearl necklace glistened in the beaming light.

They descended the broad wooden stairs, fresh paint sticking to the soles of their square-toed pumps, leaving dainty footprints down the walkway in their wake. Knowingly, Mama reached for Fern's gloved hand and squeezed it tight as the hearse carrying Daddy pulled to the curb, followed by a black Escalade filled with Dispatch *staff.*

Chapter Fourteen

Friday, May 20

"Woman fatally wounded in apparent robbery attempt on Detroit's East Side. Kathleen Cole, sixty-eight, found by her son, died of her injuries en route to Detroit Receiving Hospital. Police are investigating. More on the story at noon."

Missing the headline on the *Dispatch*'s demise taught Navena to pay attention. Even when she was deep in sleep, the news flash slipped between realms to awaken her. Eyes wide, she sat up in bed searching for the remote. Finding it and flipping the flat screen TV to the local Fox news channel, she watched the words spoken to her moments before. Capitalized small print crawling across the screen finally linked the real world to her nightmare.

Kathleen. Kat. Cat. Murdered.

Anderson's mother was dead. Navena grabbed her chest as if she'd been shot herself. Guilt and shock choked the air from her lungs. She coughed and gasped in disbelief. *This is beyond real.*

Her mind's eye drew a lipstick-red X through the cat card. It floated from her vision, leaving a black hole in the line of puzzle pictures. The feeling of danger, daggers, and imminent death that greeted her as she rejected Luke's marriage proposal returned, thick and heavy as the early morning air. Coincidence, like dominoes, had begun to fall into fate's design. She counted to ten, claimed her composure, and stood beside the bed, refusing to tumble on cue.

"Yep. I'm right around the corner, Maxwell. See you in a minute."

Navena flipped her cell phone shut and wheeled the Jeep onto Anderson's street. The need for concern about his mother's safety was obvious with every cracked patch of concrete she rolled over—worry rendered moot now that Kat had been killed. Luke's city renaissance hadn't reached this neighborhood. Abandoned houses, thigh-high lawns, garbage-strewn alleys ruled this block.

Used-to-be beauty haunted grand porches, vaulted roofs, and wrought-iron railings. A forty-year-old snapshot would reveal homes owned by proud autoworkers with stay-at-home wives. Their pristine yards would boast neat, obedient children at play. Now grandparents, those former kids who remained at home stayed inside behind barred windows afraid of the new kids on the block. Navena feared them, too. Resisting the urge to take cover, she pulled over to the curb and parked just beyond the caution-tape police barricade.

Unbelievable.

Squad cars, TV crews, and nosy neighbors quelled any lingering doubt she harbored. The scene beckoned and she obeyed, exiting the SUV in search of Maxwell's car and the next puzzle piece. A wave from the crowd's edge caught her eye.

She returned the gesture with an instinctive smile,

linking the unseen face behind the motion with her vibrating cell phone. "Hey, I'm right here," she said without looking at the caller I.D.

"Well, you're supposed to be *here*. At my office. So, where are you?"

Luke. "I am so sorry, Luke! Anderson's mother was killed last night. I'm at his house."

"Sorry to hear that, but you could've called, Navena."

True, except that nothing had mattered from the moment the newscast awoke her two hours ago. Navena's mind wrapped itself around the "why" and "what next" of her emerging reality, determined to prevent whatever future tragedy the Fates concocted. That meant talking to Anderson and uncovering Kat's connection to her life. Luke had fallen off today's to-do list.

"How about I just e-mail you the new brochure layout? There's no way I can get out of here any time soon. Please, Luke?" Navena sugared the plea with a singsong voice she hoped would soothe his ego and avert the inevitable *Dispatch* griping. "You'll still have it today. Promise."

"We can't get together at all?" Agitation edged the rhetorical question.

"Probably not. This looks like a pretty big police investigation. I'm sure we'll be tied up awhile."

"We?"

"Maxwell's here, too." She paused to assess the muted suspicion in Luke's tone. "As a reporter and Anderson's longtime-colleague-now-supervisor, this is the least I can do, Luke."

"So, what's *he* doing?"

"Same thing, I guess. Plus a little face time since he's still an unknown in these circles."

"Whatever you say. And yeah, I'll watch my e-mail." He hung up without a good-bye, his way of letting Navena know how furious he was.

Be mad. I've got a mystery to solve and seventeen days left to do it. She flipped the phone shut and maneuvered through the crowd to the waving hand she assumed was Maxwell's.

"You're just in time." Maxwell grabbed her elbow and led her away from the throng. "They're about to shut down the scene. Neighbors keep whispering about drugs and some gang war in the area. Cops don't want anybody else hurt. Come on."

Stumbling along beside him until she regained her balance, Navena noted the houses, cars, and absence of residents. Though many of them might be gathered at the crime scene, the street felt vacant, like a movie set occupied for the moment by actors and extras pretending to be real. Everything felt fake.

Anderson's mother's house sat between two empty lots. The redbrick bungalow rose above neatly trimmed grass and a budding vegetable garden, shaded by an overgrown oak tree sprinkled with baby acorns. Anderson's old Mercedes sat near the curb.

Free of Maxwell's grasp, Navena allowed him to take the lead up the walk, flashing his press credentials at the officers gathered around. Crime lab photographers ignored them as they dodged camera clicks. Weepy relatives shared their unabashed anger and grief with local media and each other. Anderson met them at the porch.

"Wow. Thanks for coming through. Here." He turned back toward the house and shepherded them around a corner laced with rosebushes and bees to the side door.

The tiny A-frame was immaculate, in stark contrast to the world beyond its lawn and Anderson's disheveled persona. Navena resisted the urge to act the part of dumb reporter and silenced the "how are you feeling?" that hung on her lips.

"I am so sorry, Anderson." She approached him with open arms and embraced him in a heartfelt hug. Life without his mother would be tough. "Anything I can do. Really."

"Same here, man." Maxwell spoke with brotherly reassurance and an outstretched palm.

Anderson released Navena and accepted the handshake. They performed the one-two-three, clasp-grasp-fist-bump ritual that men used to talk with when words weren't available.

"Moms is gone. Can't believe this bull." He shook his head violently. Muddy red light circled a mustard-colored sea that swam in his wake. Anger and sadness seemed ready to consume him.

She thought of her father's sudden death and empathized fully with Anderson's tormented state. "What happened? Do you know?"

"I was supposed to be here." He kicked a weathered screen door, bouncing it open. Maxwell grabbed its handle and allowed the distracted Anderson and Navena to pass under his arm. They paused for a moment in the minifoyer that led downward to the basement and up a short flight into the kitchen.

Anderson started upward, toward the sound of voices. Just past his shoulder, Navena could see dimness and dark-suited bodies. In a house structured like this, it would be the dining room and those would be cops.

"I stopped at the store after I left the gym instead of coming straight home." He dug his toe into the linoleum, connecting with a metal dinette chair and moving it several inches across the well-waxed floor.

Navena pictured Kat frowning at her son for scuffing the shine.

"Robbery?" Maxwell asked.

Anderson shrugged. "Nothing's missing as far as I

can tell. They just killed her. How can you shoot an old lady, man?" Tears streamed down his clenched jaws.

Navena reached for his hand and squeezed it tight. Her heart raced. Street noise clashed with the home's stillness, creating a gear-grinding click that mimicked her churning thoughts. "You're always home at the same time?"

"Pretty much. She kinda depended on me that way."

"Somebody could've been casing the place." Maxwell hopped aboard Navena's train of thought. "But if they weren't thieves . . ."

"What did they want?" Navena completed the sentence as Anderson, incredulous, plopped onto the displaced chair.

"Me," he said, head in hands and sobbing. "They came to take my ass out and got Moms instead."

Navena scanned the area for evidence of a sordid youth—bandanas, missing school photos, needle tracks in his exposed forearms. Something that showed he wasn't all polish and professionalism. Maybe his character ran deeper than she knew.

"You in trouble, Anderson?" Maxwell pulled up a matching chair and sat next to him. The brotherly tone had grown patriarchal—as if the wrong answer would demand a good butt-whipping—then softened with empathy as he asked, "What can we do to help?"

"I brought it on myself, man. Fired off my mouth at these young cats. They been—were—harassing my mother. Had her scared to leave the house, let alone stand at the bus stop. So I moved in here and tried to muscle them out." He shook his head in disbelief, like he couldn't believe his own naïveté.

Maxwell frowned. Navena bit her lip. Anderson obviously crossed the wrong crew and they wanted him to know it. Probably wouldn't help much to pat him on the back for taking a stand.

"So, where are you staying tonight?" she asked, hoping he wasn't planning to push the fight any further.

"You're welcome to crash with me," Maxwell offered. "My door is open as long as you need it."

Surprise lit Anderson's eyes. He spoke with deliberateness, slightly hoarse, but undeterred. "Sounds stupid now, but I ain't no punk. They killed her, man. And I can't walk away from that." Tears welled and spilled.

Navena wrapped her arms around his shoulders. "You can't do anything if you let them kill you, too." She turned his chin to face her. "Be smart. We can nail their asses to the wall if we play this right. Come on, now."

"True. We can keep pressure on the Detroit Police Department. Make sure your mother's murderer goes down—"

Anderson nodded in reluctant agreement.

A fake cough pierced the conversation as a uniformed officer peeked into the room. "Mr. Cole. We'd like to talk to you now if we could."

Without awaiting his response, the policeman entered the cramped space, followed by a woman in a lab coat and what Navena assumed to be a couple of undercover narcs. They placed themselves strategically around the cabinets—for intimidation or interrogation purposes, Navena wasn't sure. But instinctively, she scooted closer to Anderson, as if to protect him from the coming onslaught.

"Thank you for the statement you gave earlier, Mr. Cole. But we do have a few more questions and we're hoping you have answers."

"Please, have a seat." Maxwell stood, making his seat available for the lead officer, and gestured at remaining chairs for others. He raised his eyebrows at Anderson and nodded his head to signal his support, then moved to the back of the room to watch the proceedings.

"I got this," Anderson told Navena, shrugging off

her nearness. "Let me do what I gotta do. You and Maxwell can wait downstairs. I'll holler."

Navena rose, waited for Maxwell to join her, and then turned from the huddled group to make her way through the crowded kitchen toward the side door. Ahead of her, Maxwell turned right, hit the wall switch, and hunched to avoid bumping his head on the old bungalow's low basement ceiling. Mere steps away, they spied a full-sized dining room table amid a second kitchen setup. Range, refrigerator, and countertops adorned a corner of the remodeled room.

"Isn't this something?" Maxwell remarked.

"Cooler for summer cooking," Navena answered. Rows of bundt pans and serving trays gave away Kat's fondness for food. They plopped down at the dining table, set with place mats and napkins, always ready for company.

But not under these circumstances, Navena thought.

Their side-by-side seating forced their faces kissably close. She could smell his breath, not toothpaste fresh, but ordinary and familiar. Maxwell's cologne was still midday strong. His aura was turning a passionate red.

"How could you think of kissing me at a time like this?" Navena fussed as if reading his mind.

"Trying damn hard to concentrate on this craziness, but you're all up on me. A brother's only human." He tried to smile through the tragedy of the day. Navena heard it and felt exactly the same way.

"Gotta be something we can do."

"We'll figure it out. Give the cops a chance to do their jobs first."

"I don't know, in this part of the hood they might write this off, Maxwell. I've seen it before. Folks lock up their houses and their lips. Witnesses disappear. And poof, the bad guys are right back at it."

"Looks like our work's cut out for us."

"Thanks for letting him stay with you." Navena raised her eyes. "That was sweet."

Maxwell's aura continued to swell with heat, blistering the curiosity bordering Navena's temptation. "We better go check on Anderson," she said, attempting to break up the vibe.

After a last mischievous glance, they rose in unison to rejoin the interrogation. Navena was surprised to see that the officers had apparently completed their questioning and were now searching the house for additional clues.

"Who's this?" asked the lab technician, peeking into the kitchen with a color photo of a young woman in hand. The picture contrasted a row of old-fashioned black-and-white images on the hallway wall behind her.

"Ex-wife." Displeasure was evident in Anderson's tone. "She was Mom's favorite of all my girlfriends. No kids, so we don't keep in touch."

The white coat made a note on a tablet, turned, and left.

"So the ex must be the rumor mill target. Spence's fiancée" Navena whispered to Maxwell.

"Woman as pretty as her probably doesn't spend much time without a man," he remarked with a hush.

Navena kicked him in the ankle before approaching Anderson to ask if there was anything else they could do. "All you have to do is call," she reminded him.

"Here, man, let me give you my home number." Maxwell rummaged in his pocket for a business card. He recited the digits aloud as he wrote. Navena memorized each one.

He handed the card to Anderson. "I'll swing by here around seven to pick you up. That okay?"

With a nod and another fist shake, Maxwell left Anderson standing in front of the photographs, grieving his mother through bleary eyes and clenched jaws.

Navena took Maxwell's hand and led him through the door. Midafternoon sun arched above them, not yet its warmest of the day, but hotter than they'd left just a few hours before.

Maxwell's pulse throbbed through his palm, surging through Navena's skin, up her veins, directly into her heart. His raw emotion wedged there between Vee's leftover affection and Navena's smoldering fire.

Like everything else unfolding in her life, she figured the surge in affection for a man she'd once run from must tie into the dream murder. Just as Kat's killing held a clue, so did this man who tried to claim her heart. Still, she hung back, remembering their past.

She released her grasp. "Heading back to the office?"

He looked surprised as she wriggled free and spoke as if trying to hang on. "Want to grab some lunch first?"

"Probably not a good idea." Honesty felt like the proper, though tough, tactic to take. She smiled to soften the rejection. "Got a lot of work. We're trying to put out a magazine and all."

"Can I bring you something back?" he asked, taking another tack.

Well, he's persistent if nothing else. "No, thanks, Maxwell. I'll grab something on the way. You'll be in to meet with Fern shortly?"

"Sure. I'll catch you then. We can do a status check at the end of the day."

With a nod and a wave, Navena trotted through the thinning crowd back to her Jeep at the end of the block. Safely out of Maxwell's sights, she leaned against the car and fanned herself with her hand.

That man's got me all hot.

The newsroom clamored with competing emotions. Navena sensed them even from the bottom of the stairway. Some happy, others hostile, exchanges flew faster than she could catch them. The sound escalated, then exploded as she climbed the steps and walked into the commotion.

Only, no one was speaking.

Dang it. What was that Mama said about sensing feelings? Clairvoyance makes its appearance.

She walked slowly past the desks, overwhelmed by the onslaught of every reporter's mood. Her staff seemed more unsettled than usual this afternoon, looking at her to see if she was looking at them as she headed toward her cubicle.

Aside from being a little obtrusive, this piece of her supposed gift wasn't so bad. At the moment, she appreciated the insight. It felt like sneaking a peek at your best friend's diary. Today the pages revealed a mix of excitement and dread as staff awaited a progress report on the paper's transition.

Per the team's Monday meeting, they assembled in the conference room at three o'clock sharp.

"First of all, I'm missing confidentiality statements from two of you," Maxwell began. "Can I get those before we begin?"

Spence and Fern slid their contracts across the table toward Navena. She took a brief look at each sheet to be sure the signatures were in place and all appropriate boxes had been checked that swore employees to secrecy regarding the *Dispatch*'s impending changes.

"Thanks. Now, as you all know, we're going from a weekly paper to a monthly magazine," she began. "We're looking at sixty-four pages, lots of photos, a solid cover story, and three secondary features. Is anyone interested in penning the commentary every issue?" Three hands went up.

"I'll meet with each of you this week to set up tryouts. We'll make this as fair as possible. Questions so far?"

"How much advertising space are we talking about to support this thing?" Spence asked.

"More than we're providing now, but no more than twenty percent of the magazine, we hope. Maxwell is in the process of interviewing sales execs to help out on that end."

"What we want to do is increase ad value and guarantee competitive pricing in the market," Maxwell interjected. "I'm also beating the streets looking for new funding sources and potential revenue opportunities."

"How do we know this is going to work?" asked Fern.

"Because we've done our homework," said Navena. "Our ad agency has recently completed a household readership survey telling us that newspaper readership is down, but targeted magazines command loyal audiences. People are starved to read about, learn from, and see themselves in print.

"We're aiming for a similar readership as the current *Dispatch*. But our entertainment needs to be *Vibe* for the eighteen-to-twenty-five segment. Business pages need to be *Emerge* to the professional crowd. News features should be as hard-hitting as *Time* from a black point of view.

"Our job is to recreate our approach to journalism. We have to energize our writing and satisfy those hungry readers. They're just waiting for something like this," Navena concluded.

"What's happening with our story lines for the first issue?" asked Maxwell.

Navena looked quickly at Fern. In Anderson's absence, she hadn't had any time between her conversation with him and this meeting to talk to Fern about the duo's work-to-date.

"Well, he does have a lead on the gang-related piece." Spence offered the information as if to reel Navena to safety. "We have a mutual friend who has a cousin that works gang squad over in the Western District. The stuff that's going on down there makes that *Cops* TV show look like kiddie cops and robbers." He shook his head.

"So, what's the hook?" asked Maxwell.

"Rehab. They got a program down there pulling some of these young cats out of trouble, turning them around, and getting them to help clean up the streets. That's some dangerous stuff, man."

"Is the source safe?"

"Of course. We all get along," he said defensively, everyone in the room understanding that the "mutual friend" was Anderson's ex. "He also did an interview with some old man who got himself out of the life back in the eighties. And he's about to interview the gang squad cop who brought the crime ring down."

"Thanks for the update, Spence." Maxwell nodded as a compliment. "That's good stuff."

Navena followed the discussion with increasing concern. Was it the *story* that caused the tragedy? Was that what she should stop? Suddenly she thought perhaps they should change their cover article. Try something . . . safer.

"Fern, where are we with the *Homespun Divas*?" She looked at her for some acknowledgment only to find her smiling in another direction.

I hope she's not daydreaming about Anderson. Navena shook her head in pity. *We really need to handle that situation.* "Fern, your story."

"Oh yeah. I went to the Motown Museum and talked to the tour coordinator. He put me in touch with the executive director, who maintains contact with a lot of those sixties stars. The story'll be just fine."

Fern flashed a sarcastic smile and returned to her distraction.

"Sounds great, Fern. Let's wrap this up. I just want

to thank everybody for their hard work," said Maxwell. "You've been fantastic and I want you to know that your dedication has not gone unnoticed. Keep it up and we'll make *Our Scene* a reality."

Chapter Fifteen

Saturday, May 21

Detroit's tepid May finally turned pleasant, which boded well for next week's holiday. Today even promised scattered glimpses of sunshine. Navena accepted the seventy-degree day with gratitude as she sped toward Anderson's East Side home.

The faster she drove, the more the windshield crackled and the hotter the steering wheel got. A cheetah-print cover helped protect her hands as she drove, but if the breaks crept across the entire windshield she wouldn't be able to see.

"I'll have this taken care of by then."

Waving arms from the roadside caught her eye. A short distance ahead, a tall black man signaled for help.

Her first instinct was to stop. After all, how often did a black man admit he was in trouble? On second thought, she decided instead to phone his license plate and car make in to the courtesy assistance center. As she approached and slowed down, paper fluttered from his open hood.

Litter? No. Playing cards. Their metallic backs glistened in the sunlight as five of them wafted toward the freeway and laid themselves end to end on the pavement's dividing line. She rolled past them in slow motion.

The first two, featuring a car and a cat, flittered away in the gust of her engine's passing. A woman rose from the third card. Tall, brown-skinned, and wrapped in a faded gray 1980s duster, her shoulder-length hair hung unkempt, weighted with glistening scalp oil and sponge roller curls. She stepped in Navena's path, trying to flag her down. The smile gave her away.

It was the woman on Anderson's wall.

His ex-wife, straight from the long ago photo, pushed a wooden barrel across the road, trying to stop a car in full motion. The last card twisted itself into a rope, formed a noose, and lassoed the wayward barrel.

Panicked, Navena pounded her horn. "Stupid—"

No one.

"Of course." Embarrassed, she gestured in apology to the frightened driver on her left. The steering wheel simmered beneath its protective cover. Not realizing she'd already reached her exit, Navena veered from the middle lane, to the right, and onto the ramp.

She bounced her hands in an attempt to distribute the rising heat. This was real. As real as the woman in the road whom she knew nothing about. As real as Anderson's dead mother. Kat. Card number one. Dreams invaded her reality once more. Navena swallowed her trepidation and turned onto Anderson's street.

The house appeared vacant. Not a car in the driveway or on the street out front. No sign of Anderson, Maxwell, or a single neighbor.

"What the hell?" Navena double-checked her phone's in-box. The text message that summoned her here no longer existed. "I know I didn't delete it."

Dialing the number she'd memorized here days before, Navena called Maxwell hoping the mix-up was a technical glitch.

"Were we meeting at Anderson's this morning?" She backed into the question in case she'd jumped up, gotten dressed, and flown over here in vain. He didn't need to know she was losing her mind.

"If you want to see me, all you have to do is ask." Maxwell laughed. "But no, hanging out at Anderson's is not what I'd suggest."

"Just checking." But she wondered if Maxwell was free. "Has he heard anything else about the case?"

"No leads yet. I'm taking him to the basketball game tonight to help get his mind off everything."

"That's nice of you." Visiting him while Anderson was staying there wasn't a good idea anyway. And no way she'd have company with Luke lurking upstairs. "You guys have fun. I'll be house-hunting today."

"See you Monday, then."

Navena hung up feeling stupid. *I can't believe I did that.* A final check of her text log still showed no messages this morning. *But since I'm up, I'll stop by home to grab my vacancy listing and find myself a new place.*

"Can't wait to invite you over."

Listening to the Isley Brothers all the way home only underscored the sentiment. Soon she could sit down with Maxwell in privacy, hash out their unresolved issues, and see if taking care of him meant keeping him as well.

Getting the electronic editions of area papers brought not only news to her desk, but classified ads, too. Yesterday she searched the listings and found a house for sale in West Village, just as she hoped. Instead of putting the info in her PDA, she wrote it on a Post-it note and shoved it in her tote.

"I'll just grab that and head back out." Do some shopping, catch a movie. Just be out of the flat and away from Luke. Looking forward to the day, Navena turned the corner toward home.

Cars lined both sides of the street. Even her driveway was full. Her temples began to throb. Luke obviously had company. A bunch.

"Hopefully I can get in and out without running into anybody I know from our couple days."

She parked at the end of the block and pulled up the hood on her jacket as a minimal disguise. Music and loud voices flooded the hallway that branched to the upstairs and downstairs apartments.

If I didn't know better . . . Navena turned the key in her lock and opened the door.

"Surprise, baby!"

Stunned by anger and embarrassment, Navena froze. Luke swaggered over, beer in hand, and attempted to kiss her. She ducked and looked around the room.

Benson Construction staff, his mother, *Fern,* and several other people she knew sat on her couch, leaned against her walls, and acted as if she'd invited them.

"What is this, Luke?"

"Keep your voice down or people will think you're ungrateful." He flashed a sly grin that suited his ever-murky aura. "This is your belated-birthday, congratulations-on-your-promotion, glad-you're-feeling-better party. They're all here just for you."

"Have you lost your mind?" Obviously no one knew they'd split up. Except Fern. Navena spied her in the crowd and motioned her forward.

Fern breezed over on a cloud of floral designer perfume. Her formfitting denim sundress and strappy high-heeled sandals were in stark contrast to Navena's jeans and gym shoes. She started explaining herself from three feet away. "Girl, he called talking about a surprise party last night. I thought maybe y'all got back together."

Navena rolled her eyes.

"What did you want me to do?" Fern shrugged and

chugged her beer. "Call you up to see if it was legit and ruin the surprise if it was?"

"Yes." Navena grabbed Fern's arm and pulled her out of Luke's earshot. "You're supposed to be my girl. If he ever calls you for anything related to me, you let me know. Please."

Luke sauntered over. "Don't be rude. You have other guests."

He'd gone too far. Frighteningly so. *I gotta get out of this place.*

"Glad you're up and about." Mrs. Luvenia Benson sashayed toward Navena. "Luke told me you two had a little tiff. I knew you'd work it out. This is so nice, what he did for you."

"And how are you, Mrs. Benson?" Navena smiled broadly. "Anything I can get you?"

"No, honey. My baby has taken care of everything. *You* must be awfully tired," she began. "I mean with everything you've been through . . . and Luke tells me you've been working mighty hard at that little job of yours." She took a longer sip of her drink and raised her eyebrows at Navena, who in turn took a visibly deep breath.

"Yes, ma'am. I am a hard worker." Navena spoke cautiously, measuring her words at a slower than normal pace. "I believe in working hard to get what I want."

"Um-hmm, well, once me and Henry moved up from Memphis, I had Luke right away and never worked outside the home for one day." She placed her empty iced tea glass deliberately on the table. "What are your plans?"

"Why, my girl's gonna rule the world one day," interrupted Fern. She haughtily shook her freshly unwrapped hair and hugged Navena before nodding hello to Mrs. Benson. "Didn't you get bored?"

"Not hardly, chile." Luvenia hmphed at the very idea.

"Why, I made my own money making candles and selling crafts. Perfumed goods and whatnot. But my husband always came first. Men like that, you know."

A brisk discussion ensued about the merits of motherhood and the evils of working—according to Luvenia Benson—and the untamable spirit of independence Navena's friend preferred. Luke broke up the battle.

"Food's here," he injected into the room's hot air. Luvenia and Fern retreated to invisible corners, each eyeing her supporter for empathy.

"You'll excuse me." Navena nodded at Mrs. Benson and went to see who was in her kitchen with what food.

During the years she dated Luke, she catered to his mother. Mostly because the woman carried herself like someone who gets star treatment.

They were strong people, influential, opinionated, confident, risk-takers, and smart. An invincible character combination that served them well in their business, social, and personal lives. Strangers were magnetically drawn to them, seemingly forced to agree with whatever they suggested and left spent and limp. Today, however, mother and son rated the D list.

Fern showed up at her side. "Girl, they got greens, barbecue, shrimp, and seafood—your favorite—all kinds of desserts."

"Stop it." Navena scowled. "You're supposed to be on *my* side."

Waitstaff in short white coats and black pants filed through the kitchen to refill the drink fountain and food trays.

Navena moaned. "I just cleaned this place up. I had plans for today."

"Ooh, girl, with Maxwell?"

"Shh! Of course not. And why are you trying to talk about this right now? You know he's right in the den," Navena hissed between her teeth.

"You should invite him. Bet that'll shut Luke up."
"Oh, please, girl. You're just trying to start some mess." Navena waved her hand at Fern to shut her up. "I want to get out in one piece. I'm not trying to annoy that man."
"How is he taking it?" Sarcasm tinged Fern's question. She glanced around the room for emphasis.
"You couldn't have convinced me that he would trip out like this. I figured he'd walk away and have somebody new in a day or so."
"Like you?"
Navena looked around for Luke and whispered, "Not the same. This was before Luke. And it's better."
"What's better? You sleeping with him already?"
"Shh! Come here." Navena led Fern out the patio door, through a small crowd on the deck, to an empty table in the center of the yard.
"Maxwell just got here. How do you figure we're having sex already?"
"Because you are lit up like a Christmas tree."
They giggled and Navena relaxed. "No nookie, but he did kiss me the other day."
"So you gonna get back together with him?"
"We'll see." She fought not to tell Fern any more about Maxwell. "Until he showed up, I was okay living without that deep-bellied-mad-love. Now I know what I've been missing."
"I'll be right here when you need me."
"Good, because first I have to get away from this. You can go house-hunting with me."
"But hey, are you going to mingle? This is your party."
I shouldn't. But she did. They rose and returned to the house. Fern took a seat in the den with another beer. Navena wound through the house saying hello.
Acting was tough. She had entertained all these peo-

ple over the years. Most of them would've been here in two weeks for the Memorial Day bash.

She spent a few minutes talking to the executive team of Benson Construction—guys Luke had come up side by side with through the construction business. From summers spent laying asphalt, they formed an alliance that led them to become the city's primary minority subcontractor.

Their wives and children ebbed and flowed through the house. Unattached acquaintances from Luke and Navena's pre-couple lives strategically filled empty yard chairs between couple-friends from church choir and usher board who were the last to arrive.

When dusk approached, Navena and Fern lit the torches and citronella candles while Luke put Michael Jackson's *Off the Wall* CD on the stereo and cranked the volume. The yard swayed with the rhythm of "Rock With You" as guests took to dancing, children chased lightning bugs.

I'll miss this, she thought, which was probably Luke's whole line of attack.

The sound of tapping glass broke through her revelry. Luke was beckoning her forward. She shook her head no. He called for her over the guests, silencing the crowd.

Oh no, she thought, walking cautiously across the yard to stand at his side on the deck's top stair.

"A toast," Luke declared, pouring her a glass of champagne as guests speedily followed suit. "To the best woman in the world, the best friends a couple could have, and a family we couldn't live without."

They raised their glasses amid cheers of "Hear, hear!" Fern stood wide-eyed a few feet in front of them and shook her head in disbelief.

"And me and my partners would like to formally

thank everyone here for making this year the best one of my life." Loud cheering filled the yard. "Now we're just waiting for tenants to move in to Trentmoor Towers so we can get started on the next headache. I'm about to become a major partner in the *Detroit Dispatch*."

Enraged, Navena shook Luke loose and stormed off the deck toward Fern. "I'm staying with you tonight. Let's go."

Chapter Sixteen

Sunday, May 22

"The drama queen arises." Fern bowed.

"I overreacted, didn't I?" Navena kicked the blanket off her legs and over the sofa edge.

"No, you were absolutely right. Luke was tripping." Fern folded her arms. "But no way would I have left my ex-boyfriend in my house with a bunch of strangers. No telling what you'll have when you get back. If anything."

"Luke wouldn't do anything crazy." Navena hoped more than believed.

"Oh, you're right." Fern eased into a pair of ultra-tight jeans. She zipped them closed and shook her head. "Just like he wouldn't pretend you two were still together in front of all his family and friends."

"You were right to try and talk me into staying, but thanks for taking me in anyway." Navena stood beside the sofa and stretched. "Let me get back over there."

"Uh-uh. Get your trouble's worth. Let him wonder where you went."

Maxwell's place would've been nice. She warmed at the idea. "Hey, where are you going?"

"*We.*" Fern slipped a gauzy peasant top over her head scarf, then shook out her hair.
"The reception for Dr. Zumbaki starts at two. We have three hours to get cute, full, and over to the museum."
"I hear that new African art installation is breathtaking, but I didn't get anything done yesterday." Navena thought of how violated she felt by Luke taking over her space without her knowing. The surprise party went beyond denial. It bordered on obsession. "Finding a new house is top priority today."
"Oh, come on. Don't make me go by myself." Fern pouted. "You just want to see Luke."
"Not hardly." Navena grimaced and plopped her hands on her hips. "Tell me I don't need to get out of there."
"So true." Fern imitated Navena's stance. "Put your clothes on, we'll grab some burgers at the drive-through, and go house-hunting now."
Navena appreciated the quick thinking. As much as she wanted to see how her place fared after the party, she dreaded running into Luke. "Let's stop at the hardware store while we're out. I need to change my locks."
"Gotcha covered, girlfriend." Fern disappeared through the doorway and returned with a packaged lock set. She walked across the room and set it with Navena's clothes, piled in the settee. "One who attracts crazy men must always be prepared."
They laughed. Navena relaxed in the comfort of Fern's rainbow aura. *I feel better, too.* "Thanks, Fern."
"No problem. Get dressed so we can get out of here." She left the room again.
Moments later, Navena heard her banging cabinet doors and clinking ceramic mugs, no doubt preparing to microwave her morning coffee. Navena ruffled her

dreadlocks and adjusted her attitude about putting yesterday's clothes back on for another whole day.

"Your chair looks great," Navena shouted, rubbing her toe along the faded edge of the settee.

"I was watching one of those antique shows on the House and Home Channel and they had one like it. That settee's an antique." She sat on the sofa sipping her almond-scented brew. Even if it's not worth much, I can't just give it to charity for someone to trash."

"I'm sure your grandmother would appreciate the way you've taken care of her favorite piece of furniture all these years."

Navena reached into her black jogging suit jacket and pulled the sleeve right side out. She slipped it on without zipping it up and hopped into the coordinating pants.

"Speaking of losing people you love, what time are services tomorrow?"

Pausing to retie her cotton headband, Navena exhaled the answer in a gust of sorrow. "Family hour is at ten. Funeral's at noon."

No doubt this would be a big, old-fashioned Church Mother homegoing. Last time she'd attended one of those was when Daddy died. The whole town came. "You going?"

"Absolutely. He's going to have to be so strong." She set her empty cup on the wooden end table at her elbow. "Can we leave already?"

"As soon I grab a wash towel to wash my face and brush my teeth." Navena scurried around the corner to the tiny apartment's bathroom.

She turned her thoughts to Kat's good-bye. It would be like her memories of funerals down South. She remembered the Wright Brothers Funeral Home fans with the curvy wooden stick stapled to the back. Women would wave them so hard that Navena always thought their pretty pictures would shake loose and fall. Tears of long ago flooded the faded pews, spilling from then to now.

Sorrow never seemed to change. She hid the new heartache in a series of swallows that stung her eyes and seared her throat.

"Here I come," she called.

Grabbing her purse and sunglasses, Navena stepped into her gym shoes and followed Fern outside. She paused to look up at the sky. *Today marks my fresh start.*

They drove their own cars—Navena her Jeep and Fern her decade-old Volvo—keeping tabs on each other by cell phone the entire ride.

Freeway turned to surface street as they cruised through downtown Detroit. Crossing intersections until strolling couples and flocks of teens thinned to specialty markets and strip malls, Navena led Fern into an obscure neighborhood called West Village.

Known to residents and envious outsiders, the area boasted well-crafted houses with brick, hardwood, and wrought iron that hinted at Detroit's artisan history when automakers reigned as urban royalty and their accountants, doctors, and lawyers lived here, enjoying the spoils.

"I love this neighborhood." Navena felt magical driving these streets where turn-of-the-century Tudor- and Victorian-style homes stood side by side with similar-era apartment buildings and flats-turned-condos. Trying to remember the address by heart, she wove past the eclectic buildings hoping one would shout the numbers she sought.

"Do you know where you're going?" asked Fern across the line.

"Almost," Navena half answered, still searching for

her perfect house. "This is the street. Just looking for a—"

"Vacancy? Like that one across the street?"

Maybe. No sign in the yard or window helped keep petty criminals from knowing the home was empty. Navena pulled closer. "Yes. We're here."

She tried not to drool. People who moved here seldom left, which meant that rentals and sales were rare. Whatever the tidy Victorian house looked like on the inside, she knew it would be wonderful.

And it's going to be mine.

Parking spots in the bustling neighborhood were also sparse. She found a spot two blocks away and Fern parked even farther over. Navena waited for her outside on the sidewalk.

Is that my phone? She fished her cell from the bottom of her purse and caught the last notes of her Alicia Keys ring tone. "Are you lost that quick?" she answered, assuming it was Fern.

"Without you?" Maxwell's rich bass erupted in laughter. "Yes."

"Well, what a surprise." Nerves flip-flopped her stomach from excitement to anxiety and back. "Is everything okay with Anderson?"

"He's better today. Ditched me for some babe on the other side of town." He paused. "I don't think he'll be back."

Maxwell created the perfect opening, leaving her plenty of room to dive headfirst into his convenient scenario. She didn't budge.

"As in tonight?"

"More like she's back from an out-of-town visit to her family and that's where he'll be until further notice."

You're alone. I'm available. The stars / realms / ancestors—something—were manipulating their lives again.

"At the moment I'm house-hunting."

Fern caught up and they crossed the street together. She hung back as Navena approached the door and rang the bell.

"Hold on a sec," she said, covering the receiver with one hand. "Hello. I'm here to see a rental."

"You have an appointment?" A pale white woman with big hips and cropped hair surveyed Navena.

Her heart thudded with disappointment. "No, the ad didn't ask for one."

"I'm the agent. This home was just listed today. You're quick." The woman opened the door farther, revealing bright red toenail polish and an ankle tattoo. "Come in. Let's take a look around."

Navena smiled at her bright yellow aura as she stepped inside. The agent was anxious to unload the place and open to negotiation. Fern followed with an audible gasp.

Parquet floors, a tile fireplace, and arched doorways told Navena all she needed to know. She signaled to the agent with a forefinger and a grin to please wait one moment and turned her back to finish the phone call.

"Wow. This is it. I just hope I can get it," Navena whispered. She mentally calculated the home's square footage, amenities, and probable asking price. "It's beautiful. And available."

"How about you? Got any plans afterward?"

Her heartbeat quickened. "It's Sunday night. I have to get ready for work tomorrow. This has been a crazy weekend."

"You talk like it's over." Maxwell acted hurt. "There's plenty of time for dinner."

Her breathing grew shallow. "I promised Fern I'd go to a reception at the museum with her."

"That is this afternoon, isn't it?" Silence.

Her pelvis began to throb. "But the event ends at five."

"So I'll see you when?"

She squeezed her thighs to stop the pulsing between her legs. "Seven-thirty."

"Great. Take my address."

Navena scrounged through her purse for a pen and pulled out an old grocery receipt to write on. She scribbled as fast as he spoke, her hand trembling with anticipation.

"See you when you get here."

Exhaling quiet, she hung up and tried to compose herself before turning around.

Fern leaned over and whispered, "I know that wasn't Luke."

The goofy grin she flashed said it all. She toned it down and continued the tour, her mind racing her pulse.

"This house was built in 1912. It is twenty-four hundred square feet and has central air, forced heating, and new appliances. The basement is unfinished. If you like—"

"How much?" Navena held her breath for the bad news.

"We're asking a hundred and forty-nine thousand or lease-to-own at nine hundred a month."

Fern's and Navena's eyes widened. Fern squared her body with Navena's and crossed her arms as if to say, "You better!"

Thank you for the otherworldly meddling. Finding a lease-to-own property was almost too good to be true. "Can I write you a check for the deposit?"

"Certainly." The agent's eyes sparkled with excitement. "We'll hold it pending a credit and reference check. I'll get you an application from the kitchen. You can complete it here and we'll notify you with a decision by the end of the week."

Navena searched her archive of dreams, signs, and apparitions to be sure a house hadn't appeared in any of them.

The gilded dome of Detroit's Museum of African-American History sparkled majestically beneath the cloudless sky. Overbearing sunshine masked the afternoon's true coolness. Navena appreciated the deception.

"We should be ashamed for not coming here more often."

"You've always got something going on at this place," Fern chided. "This art show. That photographer. Some gallery opening. What are you talking about?"

"That's what I mean. We have the largest black history museum in the country and we only come when we 'have' to."

"It's usually not my thing. I'm not into ancient art. But this is supposed to be more modern." Fern looked genuine, but her aura betrayed her. "Besides, it's free food and drinks and Anderson's supposed to be here."

"You need to leave that man alone, Fern, before you lose your job." Navena mustered the most stern look she could to meet her friend's dismay. "Anderson's ready to take steps . . ."

"Don't I know you?" An unfamiliar female voice injected itself in their conversation.

Navena stopped and turned, coming nearly nose-to-nose with the heavyset woman—tall, stunningly made up with Beyoncé-blond hair. Her unexpected appearance zapped the planned retort from Navena's lips. She finally managed a demure hello and offered her hand in greeting.

"No. I don't believe we've met. I'm Navena Larimore."

"Pleased to meet you. Rachel." Barely acknowledging Navena's gesture, she remarked, "You're in the paper."

"Every week. Thanks for reading it." Navena withdrew her attempted handshake. "We appreciate your support."

"Whatever I can do. Nice to meet you." The woman walked away under a muddy brown aura Navena couldn't interpret. She studied the stranger's profile until she moved out of sight.

"So weird." Fern shook her head.

"So you have your prison pen pals and I have—"

"A stalker probably."

They entered the building in preoccupied silence. For the second time in an hour, Navena flipped through the vision's cards. This time to see if the woman's face was among them.

Maxwell lived in a two-story riverfront condo facing downtown Detroit on one side and the Canadian border on the other. Navena sat in his S-shaped driveway hiding behind her Gucci shades, her eyes tracing the home's shadowy silhouette against the sunlit skyline. She turned the ignition key, silencing the Jeep's humming motor and an old Lauryn Hill CD. True, nothing mattered but the moment.

"Calm down," Navena demanded of herself. She took a deep breath and leaned awkwardly against the window. "You will not walk into that man's house and make a fool of yourself."

She'd gone home after the museum reception and found Luke away and her apartment immaculate. The cleanliness made her wonder if he snooped while she was out.

Worried that he might appear at any second, she took a quick shower and slid on some shea butter and a sundress that played peekaboo with her toned body.

She snuck out of her own place, driving off as Luke rounded the opposite corner.

Now, as the seconds ticked slowly away, she began to feel *very* foolish. Even in the closed sun-warmed car, a nervous coolness settled around her bare shoulders and chilled her. The length of leg exposed by her dress didn't feel sexy at all. Just cold.

She was afraid of being alone at Maxwell's, afraid of reconciling—that taking him back might bring Vee's words to life and put the dream's prophesy in full motion.

"Why are you here?" she asked herself aloud.

As if sensing her heart's reply, Maxwell's door opened. He leaned casually against the backlit entry, looking like a beacon, tall and slender. He smiled knowingly. Had he seen her sulking there all along?

With less than ten feet between them, Navena took careful notice of his casual sexiness: a beige, banded-collar shirt—open at the neck, sleeves loosely rolled to show off the Rolex and the thick gold bracelet on his wrist. Matching slacks draped sensually from his hips and fell softly onto a pair of brown patent leather slip-ons.

It was difficult to distinguish where the clothing ended and his skin began, the creamy scheme making him nearly nude before her. She closed her eyes and groaned. Once long ago, on a very similar night, Maxwell had looked just this way. And she had come to him just as needy as she was tonight.

Not wanting to miss any hint his face might reveal about his intentions for the evening, Navena fixed her gaze on Maxwell's eyes and prepared to meet her former lover.

On cue, Maxwell stepped back against the door and motioned in a sweeping gesture to usher Navena into the house. A smile escaped her lips as she freed herself from the car to accept his invitation.

Her cell phone chirped.

Just a text message, she thought. *Ignore it.*

It chirped twice more in rapid succession.

Oh, jeez. Aggravated at the interruption, but wondering if there might be an emergency somewhere, she tapped out the word "READ" on her PDA and opened the messaging menu.

Luke. Luke. Luke.

Only the first line of each text was visible for preview. And all three started the same way. *I'm sorry. I love you. Where—*

She had barely arrived and already Luke had called, apologizing and asking questions. Navena pressed the END button and watched the phone power off. She slid her cell phone back into her purse and continued up the walkway where Maxwell stood watching her. At the door, Maxwell moved close enough to smother her in cologne, preventing her from further entering the house or backing out.

"Hey, gorgeous." He replayed the favorite nickname, greeting her without any hint of pretense that this was professional.

"Hi, handsome," Navena mumbled, retreating to her pet name for him. She tilted her head back to search his eyes for permission to fall all over again.

"You look guilty as hell," Maxwell said, smirking. "So, are you going to chicken out or stay here, like you know you want to?" He leaned close to her face. She could feel his breath on her skin.

A shiver ran down her spine. Conflicting feelings of mistrust from their past and pent-up desire from waiting so long knotted in her stomach.

"I'm staying," she answered with desperate determination, shifting nervously in her strappy high-heeled sandals.

"Of course you are," Maxwell answered confidently, kissing her. She knew it was coming and didn't fight it this time. She gave in and returned his passion, opening her mouth and reaching up to hold him urgently. For her, he was like cotton candy to a kid. Her tongue searched for every single piece of sugar he held. Eyes closed, she lingered before finally pulling away.

"You got some wine?" she asked, spellbound.

"Merlot all right?" he whispered into her lips.

"How about Piesporter, for old times' sake?" Navena teased.

Leaning back to look at her, Maxwell slid his index finger tenderly down her nose beyond her glasses and suspended it atop her lips. He looked like he wanted to kiss her again. His body hinted that he wanted more. Navena stepped away, purposely putting space between their heated hips. She was reeling. The good-as-it-used-to-be taste of Maxwell nearly toppled her off her heels. She pushed at him playfully.

"The wine, please." She smiled sweetly. Maxwell turned to walk away.

Navena followed behind him for a step or two, leaving the ceramic-tiled foyer and entering the parquet-floored living room. She detoured midroom toward skyline views provided through floor-to-ceiling windows clad in lush burgundy velour drapes. The fabric was drawn halfway across the glass to ward off the day's blazing sun.

Impressed by his décor, she scrutinized the luxurious space, noting the surround sound of Luther and the burning candles on the mantel. Italian leather love seats, a big-screen TV, and a walnut entertainment center spoke clearly of Maxwell's excellent taste.

"You can sit down, you know. I don't bite." Looking

back before exiting the room, Maxwell spoke teasingly. "Yet."

She eased onto the couch and set her purse on the marble coffee table. Maxwell returned with her wine and a goblet of his own.

"Can we toast?" He leaned forward with his glass. "Your choice."

New beginnings? Second chances? she thought. "How about now? Just this."

"I'll take it." Maxwell rubbed his goblet against hers. Condensation covered its surface. Droplets began to form.

Navena shifted her hips as her own body began to moisten. He was so close. Smelled so good. The throbbing between her legs returned, stronger and more urgent than before. Now she had ambience, nearness, and no reason not to have him.

He slid his knuckles across the back of her hand and down her arm. "You look incredible."

Taking her wineglass, he placed it on the table next to his own and scooted beside her.

Afraid that if she opened her mouth, a growing moan would escape, she said nothing. Just lowered her lids and tried to catch her breath.

Fingering her dreads, he whispered into her ear, "Thank you for coming." He kissed her cheek. Turned her mouth toward his and nibbled her lips.

Her body throbbed so hard it hurt. She traced his mouth with her tongue, tasting wine, coolness, heat.

Maxwell's tongue danced with hers as he leaned her back against the arm of the couch and placed his hand inside her dress.

The moan escaped. She arched her back. His hand disappeared inside her panties, fingers inside her wet, ready body.

Navena gasped for air. "Oh, Maxwell." She threw

her head back and forced herself upright. "Too much."

"I'll slow it down." He nuzzled closer as she inched into the couch.

"No. Stop. Please." Her body dripped with passion and uncertainty. Anger she recognized as frustration began to cool. Navena knew it was wrong—to take him to the brink of satisfaction, at last, and change her mind.

But jumping into bed with Maxwell wouldn't give her the break she needed after Luke or answer her questions about what Maxwell truly wanted. Most of all, she couldn't help but think that tangling their lives might bring dire consequences. "I'm sorry, Maxwell."

"It's sooner than I thought it would be, but I wasn't going to turn you down." He teased and kissed her nose. "Are you all right?"

Head bowed, eyes closed, she nodded.

Maxwell brushed his palm against her cheek.

Navena kissed his hand and struggled to her feet. A younger Maxwell would have thrown a tantrum and tried again. She appreciated that this version of the man knew they were rushing things.

He stood and faced her, so close again.

"We'll talk tomorrow?" she asked, gathering her purse and straightening her dress.

"You know it, gorgeous." He lifted her chin and kissed her on the forehead. "Don't worry. I'm not going anywhere this time. Promise."

Chapter Seventeen

Monday, May 23

Just weeks away from Labor Day and the launch edition of Our Scene, *Anderson receives a call from Fern. Across the newsroom he watches her mouth move in slow motion as her words spin through his phone receiver.*

"There's a break in the case," she exclaims. "I just heard it on the police scanner."

"They found our boy?" Anderson asks in disbelief. Despite his complaint against her, after his mother's death, he needed her help.

"On their way to the place right now," Fern confirms. "We gotta be there."

"I know that's right," echoes Anderson. "I'll drive. Let's go."

He hangs up the phone, shaking his head, astonished at their incredible luck. For months he's been working on Our Scene's *cover story with Fern. Once Navena got her organized, Fern was pretty cool to work with. A potential* Dispatch *investor connected her with Neal Raines, the brother who ran Detroit's Pit Bull Boyz back in the eighties.*

Two jail terms, bachelor's, master's, and doctorate degrees later, Raines was now working in the psychology depart-

ment at Wayne State University teaching "Street Mind 101" to area police departments. He was also trying to pull his nephew off the same streets that brought him down twenty-five years before.

Nephew, as he lovingly referred to him, could only be traced through surveillance tape and informant leads. Raines pursued the young man relentlessly, determined to reel him in before the cops or a paid hit felled him. It looked like tonight was going to be their night.

Navena watches Fern eye Anderson oddly from across the room. She watches Anderson shudder as if a sudden wind has chilled him. Almost in unison, the pair turns from their parallel spaces to eye each other suspiciously. Navena wants to warn them. Warn him. But instead, the duo scoop notebooks and ink pens into purses and pockets, hurriedly tell Navena they're chasing a break in the story, and dart out the door.

Navena sighs from her dream perch, awaiting her next opportunity to warn them.

Night falls. Time, space, and distance blur, thrusting Anderson's car onto a darkened, tree-laden street of dilapidated houses and undercover SUVs. The scene screams "Halloween" in a bad B-movie.

Shuddering under a down comforter and quilted duvet, Navena reached blindly for more covers. Finding none, she tumbled deeper into her dream.

Anderson drives slowly as Fern ticks off the odd-numbered addresses. "Twenty-one, twenty-five, twenty-seven, next block," she announces with authority. "Should be . . . right there. Over there, 62855. This is Whitlock, right? That's it up there." She places a hand gently on Anderson's arm as if to brake the car. He stops. They hold their breath.

"Yeah, that's it." Navena hears the fear welling in Ander-

son's chest as he speaks, strongly, calmly, not knowing he faces death. He exhales. Fern drops her hand, picks up her purse, and slowly slides the bag beneath her seat. "Ready?" they ask each other.

"Maybe." Fern reaches for Anderson's arm again. "Isn't that Maxwell's truck across the street?" The space around Anderson's head turns in dark watercolors, leaving ripples of black hair and cocoa skin in an opposite space.

"Damn," he says. "How could he beat us here?"

"Forget that," shouts Fern. "He ain't gettin' my story." She opens the door and bolts from the car. She floats up the uneven sidewalk, broken in patches by tree roots and old age, toward a car she thinks is Maxwell's.

"No. That's Luke's truck," Navena whimpers with shock into a vicious wind.

Anderson freezes, as if he hears her. Bodies arise from the crumbling concrete stoop next door to house number 855, from behind the SUVs, and from shadows in the block ahead. Guns drawn, they shout a warning. The cops' irate exclamations draw panic from within the target's house. Hooded gangsters emerge ready for war and begin the battle.

Bullets fly.

Fern dives.

A shadow in Luke's Escalade falls. The truck's lights flash as the alarm blares and the horn shrieks.

She awakened at exactly three o'clock, terrified, frantic. Lips clamped shut by fear and dryness, Navena hadn't opened her mouth. Her street lay silent. A crescent moon grinned through the thin Roman shades guarding her from the outside world and the dream-to-be.

"What is going on?" she asked aloud. "And where are you in all of this, Maxwell McKnight?" How, she wondered, could he be so absent from such an important moment?

Navena turned from back to side, wishing he was here, safe in her arms. She did not sleep.

Only two cars sat in the *Dispatch*'s staff parking lot. Maxwell had given employees the morning off to attend Katherine Cole's services. Navena stood a measured twelve inches from the Jeep, avoiding its heat and watching him approach. Despite the shelter of her oversized sunglasses, his eyes bored straight through hers. She turned her head to avoid his direct gaze.

"Are you going to be okay?" Maxwell asked.

I don't know.

"It's a nice gesture, but you don't have to do this." He held Navena's hands. "Maybe you should reconsider."

His body felt good against hers, but still she stiffened, trying to avoid touching him.

"Can I ride with you?" She pushed away from the car as she asked.

Maxwell smiled and kissed her on the forehead, leaving a moist spot on her skin that warmed in the sun. Navena wanted to wrap her arms around him and put her head on his chest. He always smelled so good. She closed her eyes and inhaled, remembering yesterday's nearness and hoping for more in the days ahead.

"Gonna get me in trouble out here, gorgeous." He laughed.

She shook off her fantasy as they strolled to the car in silence.

Less than a mile away, the route to the church was filled with cars. Not a parking space in sight for six blocks.

"We could've left the car and walked," Maxwell grumbled.

Once inside the church—filled with family, friends, neighbors, and outraged citizens—Navena felt like she was suffocating. Mourners trailed up the aisle, cried at the casket, and turned to Anderson with condolences.

Yet, her eyes saw Daddy in his only Sunday suit—gray—with matching shoes beside his body. The Mothers stood shoulder to shoulder weeping silently the way strong women did. All Mama's heartache lay strangled in the fisted glove wrapped around Navena's pulsing hand.

Too young to be so stoic, Navena noted of herself, seeing herself in a vision from the past. She stood afraid and confused then, wanting to hug Daddy, wondering why Mama couldn't conjure him back. She didn't dare complain. Couldn't even tell them how much she missed him.

Over the years his absence festered inside until now, when she could see how his death had misshaped her heart: Strong enough to survive and too hard to love, she gave up Maxwell to avoid anything resembling a struggle and settled for Luke the same way. In days, she knew one of those men would die.

Overwhelmed by the thought, Navena excused herself from the pew, saying she needed air, and scurried down the side aisle to escape.

Outside the massive stone structure, she walked toward midtown amid a throng of hungry lunchtimers. They walked quickly, conversing with colleagues, politely acknowledging strangers, minding their own business. Amid their mass, she disappeared to be alone with her thoughts.

Ahead, she could hear paces quickening and voices rising. A news crew in the next block—WDTR-TV Channel 8—was conducting man-on-the-street interviews. There seemed to be a breaking story. About what, she didn't care.

As she walked, worried, and worked to avoid the

gathering crowd, a police cruiser breezed by, intermittently blaring its siren, forcing a part in the bumper-to-bumper traffic as it crept through the street-side gridlock. The sound froze her footsteps in déjà vu slow motion.

The reporter, the cops, and the smell of Maxwell's cologne wafting from her skin in the muggy afternoon air converged. This wasn't the intersection or the time of day, but the scene mimicked her birthday nightmare.

Without sunglasses, her vision blurred. She tried to continue to walk away to clear her head. One block, two, but by the third, she decided to retreat into Einstein's Deli for relief. Sandwiched between a copy shop and a small CPA firm, the eatery might be her only haven for another half mile.

The sickening pulse of a mounting migraine settled deep into her skull. Her throat went dry. Her stomach rolled. She stepped delicately out of the doorway, avoiding too much movement, and dropped her head dejectedly into her hands. Navena stomped her foot in aggravation. A designer-suited businessman stopped to ask if she needed help.

"No, I'll be all right, thanks." She tried to wave him off, but he hesitated and asked her once again before relenting to her wishes. Walking deliberately into the deli and through increasingly bleary eyes, she reached for the purse that waited in Maxwell's car. Without money or credit cards, she resorted to ordering a glass of water, and retreated with her drink to a dark corner booth.

Meanwhile, the headache began to eclipse her senses. Quiet banter from neighboring tables seemed deafening. The soft diner lights became blinding. Water sloshed sickeningly in her belly. Walking back to the office was out of the question.

No cell phone.

She asked a woman at the next table if she could make an emergency phone call and dialed Fern. No answer.

Desperately, Navena dialed Maxwell. Service probably wasn't over, but she'd leave a message. His voice resonated deeply through the phone, telling her to leave a message. Hesitating, feeling more than foolish, Navena measured her words, not wanting to sound as weak as she felt.

"Maxwell, I need you come get me, please." She spoke evenly. "I'm sick. I'm at Einstein's. Please."

Turning off the phone, Navena returned it to the kind stranger. A damsel-in-distress contentment washed over her. Maxwell, her knight, would save her. She laughed at the thought.

Notions of Prince Charming died with Daddy's funeral and were resurrected with this one. So did her migraine. The last headache kept her in bed for days, with Mama and Grandma Livia making poultices and murmuring promises she couldn't comprehend.

It makes more sense now. She thought of Vee's revised personal history lesson. How Mama had separated Navena from her gifts. *They stripped the essence of my soul and I suffered for it.* Now the pain appeared in reverse, as the heart and soul once taken were now being restored.

As if some mental wall had rolled away, she felt Maxwell's tension. She liked this sudden feeling, this power, this Knowing. She liked eliminating the element of surprise. She did not want to think of where it came from or why it emerged from a headache. For now, she'd accept it as another part of the Larimore gift.

In her mind she saw Maxwell park his car, jog up the sidewalk, and enter the building that housed the deli. She heard his footsteps tapping strong and swift across the tiled floor. His long legs carried him through the doorway and across the crowded diner in four strides. When he reached her table, Navena knew. She smirked and struggled upright.

"Navena. Hey, hon, you all right?" Worry haunted his eyes.

"Migraine, that's all." She shrugged her shoulders to mock the situation and lighten the mood. "Haven't had one in years. Can't say I've missed them."

"I think you might need a couple of days off." Navena spied what he didn't say. Rustling through the air like dry leaves on an autumn gust, crisp and lazy, friendly and welcoming, Maxwell's relief at being there for her eased his disappointment over last night's events. His feelings nearly found their way into his words.

"I'll be fine, handsome," she mouthed.

"C'mon, babe. Let me get you home." Maxwell helped Navena rise from her seat. She steadied herself by gripping the crook of his elbow as they inched away from the table.

He tenderly stroked Navena's face, pausing to smooth her eyebrows with his thumb and stare deeply into her eyes.

His quiet caresses soothed and aroused her. She sighed and submitted to their tumbling emotions as he leaned forward to kiss her heavily on the lips.

"You ought to go home." He paused long enough for Navena to spy his hurt at the idea of leaving her. "I'll drive you."

"Thank you," she whispered.

Waves of nausea pelted Navena, spilling into her throat and forcing her to swallow deep and hard against their assault. Maxwell was right, of course. She couldn't drive. Even walking was painful. Slowly, she lifted her head against the weighty pain, wanting to see who was staring at them and gauge how much of a spectacle she'd become.

Oblivious, Maxwell lumbered onward, her crutch through the crowded deli, down the sidewalk and into the Mustang. He started the engine as his worry trounced through Navena's mind in violent, frightening gusts.

Thunder escorted the Mustang onto I-75, toward Navena's house and yet another setback in Maxwell's attempt to win her back. Maybe it was selfish, but he resented having to be apart from her this way. After yesterday's near miss, he planned to regain his momentum today by reassuring her that this time he was playing for keeps.

Soft splatters of rain began to polka-dot the windshield, splicing his view with crisscrossed smears of city grime. Downtown was just around the bend in the freeway. He turned on the wipers and headlights and merged into the exit lane. At the traffic light, he watched the raindrops drizzle helter-skelter across the glass, becoming larger and larger, then splitting up and running off. They mirrored his mood; his mind tying unrelated thoughts into threads of imaginary hope that wound him tighter and tighter until now he thought he'd explode.

He couldn't put this off to coincidence—Navena being enraptured one moment, then gone the next. The sudden headache as they sat together at the funeral. He worried that the tiny opening he'd wedged in her heart these past few weeks was closing. As he pulled into traffic, Maxwell wondered if Navena's reluctance was fate's way of keeping them apart for good.

Navena's cell phone vibrated in tune with the thump-thump in her head. She slowly lifted the phone to her ears.

"I had a dream about you last night." Mama spoke before Navena could say hello.

"Later, Mama. I don't feel so good." The headache exploded.

"Be careful."

"I know, Mama. I am."

The phone went silent. A drop of blood fell from the receiver onto her lap. She opened her palm to find a sewing needle piercing her hand's lifeline. A clear thread slipped from the needle's eye.

Shadows fell across the sky as they rolled down the freeway. Navena shuddered and shivered, trying to shake the worsening thud in her head and warm away a sudden chill. She took off her glasses and rubbed her eyes, trying to fight the sleep that beckoned her.

Five minutes, she promised. *That's all.* Her head fell back against the headrest.

Before she dreamed, she smelled him in her arms, from a forgotten place she wanted to revisit. Once, he smiled loudly and made her laugh. Now he weakened moment by moment, his scent fading as the sirens blared. She awoke with his voice in her ear, softly offering to take her home.

She opened her eyes to see him melt. She opened her mouth for a long, silent scream. A flurry of conflicting images and emotions cluttered her pounding head. She groaned.

"That bad, huh." Maxwell tried to soothe her headache, having no idea what he'd awakened.

"What's that cologne?" Navena asked groggily.

"It's called soap 'n skin by now," Maxwell answered lightly. "I haven't put on any more smell-good since this morning."

But that was it indeed. More than cologne, a collision of morning shower, faded fragrance, and a full day's work added up to the scent that had driven her crazy for the last three weeks. She inhaled Maxwell's nearness once more to double-check her discovery.

"That must be some slammer . . . making you worry about how I smell," Maxwell joked quietly.

She wanted to smile, bathe in his tenderness, rest in his warmth.

"I'll take good care of you." Maxwell spoke from far off, a whisper Navena overheard. She squirmed against the onslaught of his words, clenched her eyes against the now unwelcome Knowing, and drifted into a deep and fitful sleep.

Chapter Eighteen

Wednesday, May 25

Sunk deep into his sofa's butter-soft leather, Maxwell sat motionless, in the same space Navena had occupied days before, hunched over, head in hands, wishing for a do-over.

"Maybe I came on too strong," he chided himself. "I knew she wasn't ready."

Evening had long since turned to night and would soon cross into morning. Three AM found him wide awake, watching the digital clock on the DVD player turning one moment into the next, each one taking him further from Navena.

The only thing worse than watching her walk away still in pain Sunday night, was leaving her alone in her bed Monday night.

"I don't care what you say. You are not fine." But he obeyed her wishes, worried that his attempt to stay might be misinterpreted as trying to take advantage of her. He came home feeling powerless and resentful.

He could only imagine how awkward her housing arrangements must be. Who'd want to be under the constant surveillance of their ex? Maxwell vowed not to complicate her life again.

It'll work out, he told himself. Besides, growing up aside, she'd changed in unexpected ways. *I imagined a lot of scenarios over the years. Paranoia was not one of them.*

But, really, as much as he loved her, he swore Navena had become a bit touched. Maybe Luke was driving her crazy. Literally.

She seemed fine when he first arrived. Friendly. A little distant, but he attributed that to the I-got-a-man thing. Since the breakup, though, he'd noticed a new edginess, a different distance. Sometimes he caught her looking at him like he'd grown a third eye.

He could deal with the palm scratching. Maybe she'd developed eczema. Freaking out in his office? Probably saw a bug and didn't want to admit she was scared. But running off in the heat of passion? No one but a nutcase would do that.

"Not with what I had planned," Maxwell fretted. Being alone with his thoughts angered him even more. Call it ego, but he figured they'd reached the point of making love. Not the way he wanted—with her having business and household ties to some other man—but it could only get better once she finished this last project and moved out. Sunday would've been one hell of an appetizer for the smorgasbord to come.

But then Monday, she'd suddenly gotten sick again. So he couldn't even bring up the idea of another visit.

Instead, here he sat, alone with Luther Vandross and Alicia Keys reminding him of how bad he felt. *She didn't even stay long enough to finish her drink.* He hadn't been this irate since she broke off their affair.

It worried him. The change in Navena wasn't natural. Yes, fourteen years had passed, but from what he *thought* he knew of her heart and soul, something was wrong.

She spooked him.

She told me more than once that she's afraid for me. "Makes no sense," Maxwell muttered aloud. Deciding he'd had enough pity time, he stood, stretched, and walked out onto the patio. A cool river breeze overpowered the evening heat. The predawn air was downright chilly. "Like Navena," he grumbled.

"I will win you back," he declared. An eerie hush settled over the sky. He headed inside to the kitchen for a drink and an escape.

Maybe fear kept Navena with him. *If she's worried about* me . . . *maybe it's because of Luke.*

"Does he know about what we had, Navena?" He poured a glass of Merlot, downed it, and poured one more. He could feel the first serving coursing through his veins, raising his ire.

What am I up against? he wondered. *Who is this Benson cat—really?*

One thing Maxwell had learned from buddies who'd lost all their signing bonuses and capital ventures in shaky deals, was to know your investors before they signed anything. He was about to get the lowdown on Luke. What was his relationship with Navena really? What was his true interest in *Our Scene*?

Where does his money really come from? That was the million-dollar question. Maxwell did the mental math: Brother drives a sixty-thousand-dollar Escalade. Fern tattled that he bought Navena a Lexus she refused to drive. That's a forty-thousand-dollar car. They lived in University District. Houses there ran, what, two hundred and fifty thousand or so? Then there's the matter of that fifty-thousand-dollar check for a slice of *Our Scene*.

"I made a million a year and even I don't live like that." He shook his head. "Nope. No way business is that good in this economy." He threw back the last swallow of wine and placed the goblet gingerly on the counter.

"As busy as I am with the paper's transition and Saturday night's investors' reception, I think it's time for a little investigative journalism of my own." Property deeds, bank accounts, business partners, tax records could all be uncovered. "I know people, too, Luke."

When she finally crawled out of bed, her head exploded with thoughts that weren't her own. Only two people's this time—Luke's and Maxwell's—but their conversations Ping-Ponged relentlessly between her ears, strangling her brain in the ceaseless banter.

Instinctively, Navena stood, to shake off the particles of her dreams. Then she quickly dropped to the side of the bed in disbelief. She looked anxiously around the room to convince herself that she was alone. She cupped her hands gingerly over her ears to hush the din of voices. Then pressed them tight against the clamoring, to no avail. The voices carried on as if she were watching some avante-garde theatrical piece—all sound and no pictures. With a slump, she submitted to the chatter.

Luke, she quickly surmised, was on his way home from the cleaner's. Apparently he still didn't believe the breakup was real.

She laughed aloud.

While Luke tussled with being dumped, Maxwell's thoughts were far more scattered. From the maid's failure to carefully clean the baseboards, to raccoons in the garbage, to the van driving too slowly in front of him (and the restraint it took him not to honk), and, finally, to work. Navena. Work.

He did not settle on her and she found herself disappointed. He was more worried about the magazine's success and the intentions of various tentative partners, including Luke.

Wondering about their musings was nearly impossible. She literally couldn't hear herself think. The two trains of thought mingled and parted, jostled and wove until she wanted to scream. Instead, she stood next to the bed feeling wobbly-kneed and faint. No recent meal came to mind as she reached for the footboard to steady her gait. She took a deep breath against the men in her head and desperately started to sing.

The Isley Brothers' "Summer Breeze" poured out soulful and strong and for the first time in twenty minutes, she felt quieted and, well, normal. Still, it was hard to sing and think. If the music lulled even a moment, Maxwell or Luke ambushed the silence.

Fear crept into her throat and warbled her melody. Tears scratched at the backs of her eyes as she made her way slowly across the thick Persian carpet to the bathroom door on the opposite wall. She didn't dare stop singing to tell herself not to cry and soon she welled up and over with the weight of confusion and exhaustion.

Once in the bathroom, Navena sobbed openly and heavily to a pitifully hummed refrain. Sliding the crinkled satin gown from her shoulders, she stepped into the cold, dry tub and pulled the curtain liner around her. Habit took over. Twisting the twin gold knobs to create just the right warmth, she reached above her head and pushed the On button of her shower radio as the water hit her face. And that's when she heard only her own voice for the first time that afternoon.

Amid the strains of Evelyn Champagne King's "Shame," there was no Maxwell and no Luke. She smiled and eagerly rinsed away tears that continued to flow. Navena abandoned the remains of "Summer Breeze" and swayed cautiously to the sound that had saved her sanity. She dared to wonder just what the migraine had conjured up and how on earth she was going to live with it. She couldn't go around singing all day to clear her head. And, according to the dreams and signs promised by Mama and Vee, *this* was her latest "gift."

Why?

Luke operated like clockwork. Saturdays were for dry cleaners, but the DJ said it was Wednesday. How long ago did he alter his schedule and why didn't she know? Maybe that's why the Mothers had graced her with glimpses of his aura. Still, maybe they weren't enough to tell her all she needed to know.

The phone began to chirp, startling Navena. She jumped and nearly lost her footing, grabbing on to the slippery liner for balance.

"Whoops!" she shouted aloud. By the time she regained her composure, the answering machine had kicked in.

"Good afternoon, Ms. Larimore. I'm calling from Realtor Properties regarding the house in West Village."

Navena's heart skipped a beat. She didn't want to pick up the handset, just in case the owners had denied her application. Anonymity allowed her to pray while the woman was talking.

"We are pleased to inform you that your credit and reference checks were great and we would love to offer you the property in a lease-to-buy agreement. Please call me at 555-1108 as soon as possible so that we can complete the process including your two-thousand-dollar down payment, purchase agreement, and selecting a move-in date. I look forward to talking with you soon."

"Thank you, thank you, thank you," she squealed. The news brought instant relief on several levels. She could go home, sleep, and hang out without Luke overhead, in the hallway or at her door. Saturday's Trentmoor Towers groundbreaking signaled the end of her work for Luke.

That was also the night of Maxwell's investors' reception. Maybe they could celebrate. She could allow herself to see where the relationship was going. Sunday and Monday she could move.

Overly excited, she exhaled heavily to calm herself and scrubbed zealously across her belly with the loofah. The tingling of the coarse netting distracted her from her racing thoughts, the radio, and Luke's mental chitchat.

Dead air seized the radio. Apparently the DJ got hung up in the bathroom, or hadn't changed the disc in time, or just wasn't paying attention. And in slipped Luke.

Don't even worry about it. That brother is locked up for good, she heard him think. *The place is flipped and the money's in the bank. Next.* He laughed.

Luke's words stopped Navena's scrubbing. An ad for a local car dealership cluttered the dead air and disconnected her from the rest of his conversation.

Who was he talking about? In all their years together, she had never heard him talk about buying or selling property. Certainly not making purchases for quick sale. When did he start this flipping? And what prisoner was he tangling with? She didn't know what to make of it.

She pictured Luke speeding down the freeway, intimidating cautious drivers in his always-shining Escalade. Wireless headset flashing, he'd be talking business on the phone while on his way to drum up business elsewhere. He was busier than she thought.

Was it sunny? Rainy? Hot? She didn't know. She thought, hummed, and scrubbed. Hummed and scrubbed, pouring the last of her lilac-scented body wash down her shins, then pausing to listen as Big Tony signed off the radio and brought on the three o'clock Old School Show to the strains of Parliament Funkadelic.

Wanting to hear Luke, wanting to know what he was up to and why, Navena turned down the radio. But, instead, she intercepted Maxwell mentally applauding Tiger Woods's latest win. She closed her eyes and focused on his words, as if she were watching him speak face-to-face.

As she concentrated, murmurings of Luke faded into the background and eventually disappeared. It was like being far outside the city on a lone stretch of road searching the radio for a *good* song. Her mind was straight highway and Maxwell was an old Temptations tune that suddenly broke through. She clung to the station, fighting off the static of Luke's thoughts and punctuating Maxwell's ramblings like a playful DJ.

I wonder if Navena golfs, he thought.

No, she responded, surprised. *Does he?*

Maybe I could take her to the Buick Open, Maxwell continued. Navena wrinkled her nose.

"I don't think so," she scoffed aloud. But Maxwell carried on.

Um-hmm. No. We could cover *the Buick Open for the sports section.* He paused. *No. Then Anderson would have to go. And I couldn't have a special incentive for the magazine partners . . . Luke would want to come. Damn.*

"Oh, I see what you're scheming up," Navena laughed. This was scary, but she had to admit that—right now anyway—this mental eavesdropping thing was more fun than simple clairvoyance.

When it first appeared in the newsroom last Friday, she could only sense emotions. Today she had mental TV, feelings, words, and glimmers of images. She rotated the showerhead to massage and turned her back to the pulsing water.

When had Maxwell taken up golf? Or had he? She was amused, flattered, and aroused at the notion that he was trying to get her alone. Alone and far away. But, without the radio, Luke static began to interrupt her thoughts and she fought to retune Maxwell.

Oh yeah. That'll work. Navena could almost hear him laughing at some idea she'd missed. He was obviously confident that he'd found the perfect way to get her to himself. Flattered by his cockiness, she wondered about his plans.

So, you think you got it like that, huh? Her heart fluttered and, distracted, Luke crept into the mind waves, jolting her with with his intrusion.

At some point, the water had grown cold, yet she hadn't even noticed. She shivered, turned to rinse her breasts and underarms, and sharply cut the faucet off. Bubbling with happiness, Navena nudged the radio's volume to a level that drowned out Luke and Maxwell, and stepped from the shower.

Draping a thick navy blue body wrap around herself, she pulled the ruffled shower cap loose from her limp dreadlocks. She shook like a puppy, wiggling off the weirdness, her fear of this Knowing, her intrigue with Maxwell's interest, her worry of Luke's business dealings. She traded them for a slathering of shea butter across her water-wrinkled skin and a spritz of Chanel.

The garage door rumbled as Luke pulled up. She slipped into a comfy pair of boy-cut panties, faded Levi's, and a sweatshirt that would hide her bralessness. Outside the French doors, the sun beat down on her jumbled feelings.

Navena had Maxwell now. And the Knowing. She'd gone into a headache-induced sleep confused and insecure, but awakened clear, with an empowering advantage that boosted her confidence.

Staring out her bedroom window through the blinds, she watched Luke struggle to hang on to the overstuffed bags he carried to his apartment. She didn't budge. No artificial need to seek his affection or share hers. "Thanks for that lock," she murmured, thinking of Fern and the Sunday night quick change she'd performed after returning from Maxwell's.

The men's voices fought to reemerge. Momentarily distracted by them, she eyed the stereo in the corner of the den and moved quickly toward it.

Stereo blasting to ward off unwelcome mental conversations, Navena admitted she was hungry, and sauntered into the kitchen to find something to eat.

Luther cascaded from the surround-sound speakers in the corners of the ceiling. Navena breathed a sigh of relief and remembrance. It was the same song Maxwell had been playing the night she *almost* gave in to passion.

Luke's footsteps marched above her lusty thoughts.

"I have missed you, Maxwell." Fantasies beckoned but hunger won the battle for her attention. Besides, no sense pretending. She was very much alone and determined not to let Maxwell in her dream. She started the teapot brewing, grabbed a diet frozen meal from the freezer, opened the container, and popped it in the microwave.

When it beeped, she poured her tea, grabbed her meal, turned, and left the room. As she walked, the music faded away behind her and a voice flooded in. Luke was talking, she surmised, so his thoughts weren't free for interception.

Maxwell, it seemed, was cementing the plot he'd hatched earlier to have her to himself. His thoughts jumbled in a mood of excitement and mischief as she strolled through the kitchen en route to fresh air. Again, she'd missed the train of thought that revealed his exact plan.

"How'd I do that?" she wondered, annoyed and unnerved.

The blanks in Maxwell's mental connection left her uneasy. She opened the French doors and stepped onto the deck, inhaling and exhaling deeply. An entire day had passed since she'd stood in a breeze. Navena descended the redwood stairs, strolling toward an old-fashioned cushioned glider in the far corner of the yard. She sat yoga-style and rocked. Meanwhile, her thoughts collected, assembling like a swarm of bees poised to strike.

Already, she noticed, the power to overhear was more pliable than when she first awoke. Navena felt more control over what she discerned and found that, like lifting the lid on a boiling pot, she could prevent the external thoughts from spilling into her own. Music served as today's intervention. Tomorrow would surely bring yet more skills.

The wind caught her dreadlocks and tossed them over her shoulder. The moon sat beside the sun awaiting its turn to command the sky. Cicadas sang. Leaves rustled. Legs crossed, waiting, she tipped up her last swallow of cola.

The cicadas' humming rhythm reminded her of the melody in the Mothers' dream. The Larimores had shared their gifts and their grief. What did the singing insects bring? Navena listened.

Signs. Matches. Answers. Signs. Matches. Answers. Signs. Matches. Answers.

She replayed the chant in her head. Signs had arrived. Matches between the dream life and reality had begun to emerge. But answers? None yet. The puzzle remained unsolved.

How much time will I have once the last sign-reality match is made until the murder nightmare unfolds? The answer, she knew, would tell her how to keep a man from being murdered. And she had ten days to do it.

The migraine was worth her Knowing—the strongest gift yet. She had a feeling answers were finally close.

The cicadas hushed.

Wait a minute. She calmed herself. *This Knowing has to be good for more than wiretapping.* Her eyes fell closed. *Has to be.*

"Is," she demanded aloud. Staring into the moon, she gave her mind a push.

Maxwell jumped, startled from his train of thoughts.

"Damn," he muttered under his breath, looking for the stream of consciousness seemingly snatched from his head. Not finding it, he threw his mechanical pencil at the cluttered table, breaking the lead and leaving a dark streak across a worn newspaper page.

Most of his time at home was spent here in his simple home study. One day, if he and Navena got married, this could be a nursery. For now, it was four beige walls, a rectangular oak dining table that provided the legroom he needed in a desk, matching chairs, plush black carpet, and a 1980s stereo in one corner. A laptop, albums, and 8-Track tapes neatly shared the table's far end.

An old Isley Brothers song hung in the air while he sat admiring several old photos of Navena from her years at Hillstone College. In one faded Polaroid, she reclined on a leather love seat wrapped in Maxwell's arms. They were in his apartment. Some unremembered friend had taken the picture. He stroked her frozen smile. In other photos, she was alone, he the reverent photographer. In each of them, she stared lovingly at him. Across the miles, through all this time, from a photo or in the newsroom, she adored him.

He believed she still did.

His confidence surged as his thoughts returned to the place they started: making Navena his again. Admittedly, he hadn't counted on Luke. Sure, he knew there could be a man. She was a beautiful woman. No way she'd be alone. But the breakup was a dream come true for him.

All he needed to do was explain. He scratched his head at the thought and rubbed his hands quickly across his jeans, the coarse surface soothing a sudden irritation.

Palm's itching, he thought mindlessly, then laughed. *Someone must be talking about me.* Once soothed, his hands returned to the clutter before him.

Mixed in the photographs Maxwell brooded over were newspaper clippings of his favorite Navena columns, architectural trade journals, and travel magazines paper-clipped open to ads for golf getaways, three-day cruises, and spa weekends. He was about to send Navena on a press junket. He smiled at his genius.

The assignment would take her around the country for three-day stops in select cities. She'd be researching a sidebar to their *Our Scene* cover story. He'd arranged with colleagues in New Orleans, Chicago, and Miami to share their gang tragedies and triumphs, introduce her to local adults who'd overcome the streets, and help her infuse a global feel into the new publication.

According to the trade magazines, Luke would be featured at the HomeBuilders of America national convention. As their presession presenter and midweek keynoter, he'd be gone for a week, probably traveling to Philadelphia Monday night for Tuesday's workshops.

"That gives me four days with Navena—without Luke breathing down her neck. She probably can't even think straight with him around."

If everything went as planned, she would depart next Thursday for Miami. He would join her Friday night. They would return together Sunday night.

Meanwhile, Navena would hit the road again the following Tuesday, staying in Chicago until Friday morning, then flying directly on to New Orleans for the weekend. Maxwell planned to fly out that Wednesday afternoon, return Thursday morning, and spend the entire weekend with her in the bayou. He figured he had just these next ten days to regain her trust.

Maxwell stood and stretched, extremely proud of himself. He began to clear his mess. He tossed the clippings into a fireproof box at his feet and gathered the architectural magazines, stacking them neatly for future reference.

"Let me go ahead and call her." Tired of trying to distract himself with old memories, he decided the only way to know if she felt better was to call.

With a sigh and a smile, he scooped his Smartphone off the table and dialed Navena's number. Music met his ear after the first ring. She shouted, "Hold on" into the receiver, and then he heard the sounds dim.

"Hey, you," she breathed happily into the receiver.

"Ah, there's my girl." She laughed as he flashed back two days ago when her weak condition left her struggling to speak or walk, debilitated by a pain he likened to the torn ligaments and stress fractures of his NBA days. "So the headache's gone?"

"Think so. But I'm still a little groggy."

"Take tomorrow off if you need to." He offered the option even though he hated the idea of not seeing her for another day.

"Rest. There's a novel idea." She paused. "Did you know that I haven't taken any time off this year? The migraine is probably from stress."

"What, am I working you too hard?" Maxwell tried to joke, but wondered if he *was* pushing *Dispatch* staff too hard with this accelerated timeline. Maybe his aspiration was unreasonable. "How about if I redeem my tyranny by getting you out of town for a while?"

"When, where?"

Got your attention now. "New Orleans, Chicago, and Miami." He listened for dissent, then continued. "My colleagues at the leading black newspapers in those areas have agreed to help us expand our 'Gangstas Gone Good' notion by coauthoring stories of their own turnarounds."

"That'll take our credibility beyond the southeast Michigan region. We get exposure throughout the Midwest and the South and East Coasts."

"Do I hear a yes, then?"

"Depends on the timing. With so much going on right now—"

"A week from tomorrow you'd leave for Miami. Tuesday you head to Chicago and New Orleans. Interviews are being set up in advance, so two or three days in each city should suffice."

"You had me worried. I'm planning to move Sunday and Monday. I thought you were trying to get rid of me this Friday or something."

"Why would I want to get rid of you? I'm hoping you'll let me tag along. I'll even sweeten the deal by helping you move." He paused to keep from stumbling over his racing thoughts.

Moving on with her life told him she might not be ready for a renewed relationship with him, but her life as Luke's woman was done. *Then if that's where her head really is, why is she fending me off?*

"You're coming from all angles today, huh?"

He wasn't sure how to interpret Navena's chuckle

and wondered if, once again, he'd stepped over the line and fouled her.

"Will we be in separate rooms or are you offering to help out by keeping me warm, too?"

"Your call." He sighed with relief. Humor meant she wasn't mad. Might even be interested in his proposition. "No pressure."

"Not from you."

Her deep exhale prompted an obvious question. "How's Luke handling the breakup? Does he know you're moving out?"

Another sigh launched a story about the surprise party, changing locks, persistent text messages, and forlorn voice mails. "I had no idea he'd react this way," she said.

"So, what's the deal with you two? He didn't know you wanted out?"

"I don't think anybody's ever turned Luke down for anything—especially not a woman. He's used to having his pick of the litter and females responding like puppies from the time they're hooked up."

Maxwell laughed. "As in you're to be submissive and all that?"

"Oh yeah. He's proposed several times . . . but honestly, I never felt that way about him. We started as landlord-tenant, then business colleagues, then, well, you know. Our being in the same house for all intents and purposes, stuff happened."

"But not enough stuff for you to see things his way."

"No. And now I think he's mad more than hurt. So I got that place I was looking at Sunday. It's a house, lease-to-own, in West Village."

"Right around the corner from me?" *Knew she couldn't stay away.* Maxwell's doubts about possibilities with Navena melted away.

"Closer to work, and, yes, you, too."

He could almost hear her smile.

"So, when can I take you to dinner and celebrate?" His voice lifted to reflect his own lightened mood. "How about Memorial Day, since neither of us have any plans?"

"Sure. I have to meet with Luke in the morning to close out my work on his groundbreaking ceremony. After that, there's just the move and all my loose ends will be tied up."

"That's cool." He couldn't keep from grinning. "Look, I know it's getting late and you need your rest. Can I call you tomorrow . . . to see how you're doing?"

"I'll be here." She shooed him off and hung up the phone.

Maxwell *thought* he scripted their reunion. But fate played a heavier hand in this deal than he realized. That the *Dispatch*—the place Navena worked at—would wind up for sale. That she'd break up with her boyfriend a week after he arrived. And now that the perfect house, just minutes away from his own, was hers for the taking.

"They say be careful what you ask for. Yeah, right. Everything I've ever wanted just fell into my lap."

Chapter Nineteen

Thursday, May 26

For the first time since her birthday, Navena slept soundly through the night. Protected by the Knowing, she could hear if Luke continued trying to win her back and if Maxwell was in danger.

The noon news ended and rolled right into her favorite soap opera. It was a show she seldom saw unless a late night allowed her to watch its replay on cable. She turned up the volume and sipped her tea.

Sleeping in was a treat she indulged in today, rising midday after a long night of sweet talk with Maxwell. She hugged herself in his absence, longing for the smile in his eyes and the smell of his heat.

Soon, she thought with pause. *Please don't let the puzzle say he isn't really mine or something.*

Maxwell, the breakup, her move—life pieces she hadn't even thought about a month ago—fit so smoothly . . . *This has to be right.*

Just as the soap's lead female was about to reveal her baby's true father, Navena felt Luke enter the house. Without seeing him she knew he was ecstatic and standing at her door.

"Baby!" he called through the thick, chained wood. "You are not gonna believe this! Navena, open up!"

Well, you have to talk to him about the project anyway. Let him in. Maybe being nice will keep him from suspecting you're on your way out of here.

Pulling her robe tighter, wishing she was dressed, Navena called to Luke to hang on a second. "He will definitely get the wrong message if you answer the door like this," she advised herself.

Navena hurried down the hall to her bedroom and slipped into jeans and a sweater. The jogging suit would've been her choice for lounging, but she wanted to look like she might have somewhere to go.

"Here I come." She opened the door a few inches, keeping her foot braced against its base to prevent Luke from barging in. "What's up?"

"We just got some great news." He pushed his way in and walked down the lengthy hallway toward the bedroom, stopping to peer in the two spare rooms and guest bath along the way.

Even though the television interrupted what the Knowing would ordinarily interpret, had she gauged animosity in his demeanor, she would've have said something to him about his nosiness. He wasn't angry, just superpsyched about something.

But she did note the "we" in his opening statement.

"C'mon, Luke, I've got stuff to do." She turned back toward the living room and caught a few snatches of her soap opera.

Luke approached her from behind and swayed along with her to a beat she couldn't hear. He blew into her ear.

She wriggled away.

"Stop it, Luke." Annoyed, watching for aura changes, and listening for any thoughts that might break through, she demanded once more, "Do you need something?"

"Guess what, sweetheart?" Luke cooed. "They're giving me the Frontiers Under Forty Award at the conference!"

"You're kidding!" exclaimed Navena. "That is so incredible, Luke. Congratulations." She was genuinely happy for him.

"I want you to come with me," he gushed. "I don't have to be there till Tuesday morning, but I'd planned to leave early Sunday and spend Memorial Day with a few partners of mine up there. We'd have a great time."

Here we go. Silence mounted as she searched her mind for a response that wouldn't aggravate his already bruised ego. *I just want to get out of this—away from here—as cleanly as possible.*

Granted, the Frontiers Under Forty was a tremendous honor. The National Architectural & Engineering Association presented the award annually to a young professional who "demonstrated a commitment to the Association's beliefs, practices, and standards of excellence with zest, innovation, and uncompromising success." Luke practically salivated year after year awaiting a call that took six years to arrive.

Next year he'd be ineligible and all the near-misses would have been too much for him to bear. He deserved the nod and her support.

"Yoo-hoo . . . Earth to Navena . . . Where'd you go?" Luke's singsong words propelled Navena into the present. He stared intently into her eyes, then leaned forward to lick lightly at her earlobe. She felt herself stiffen, only momentarily but just enough for Luke to notice. Luke looked wounded.

Stupid ego, Navena fretted.

"You don't want me to touch you?" Luke asked with an edge of bruised pride. Gray dust began to float above his shoulders. "You're taking this breakup thing a little too far, don't you think?"

What do you want me to say?

"I'm tired. I've been home sick for two days. And I'm serious about being by myself right now, Luke." Navena rebuffed him sympathetically. "You know good and well I can't take this trip with you."

"What about the PR support you still owe me? I already paid you for the whole month." He sounded smug, as if she couldn't think of a comeback.

"The groundbreaking is Saturday. Everything's done." Navena noted each accomplishment on her fingers as she spoke. "You signed off on the new brochure. The printer will deliver it to your office this afternoon. Your secretary can do what she wants with them. All your memorabilia items will be delivered to your office by tomorrow morning."

She continued ticking off her final obligations. "The press advisory went out two weeks ago and the press release is ready to be distributed tomorrow. I'll send the e-mail list to Eunice and she can get that out for you. I'll find someone else to handle the Frontiers Under Forty Award press."

"I can't believe you'd pull this at the most important time in my life," Luke muttered. He spun on his heel and marched toward the door, slamming it behind him.

"You'll get over it." Navena spoke to herself with a smirk. She locked the door, happy to have him gone. But the exchange had made her tired.

Clicking power on the remote to turn off the TV, she strolled to the bedroom, yawning, and looked at herself in the oversized dresser mirror. Her dreads were a mess, loose, crinkled waywardly, some framing her face, others cocked to the side and pointing to midair. Dark circles ringed her eyes; a small pimple dotted her forehead.

"Oh, I don't think so," she chided the blemish. "I'll take care of you tomorrow."

Pulling a headband from her top drawer, she wrapped her hair, deftly taming the disheveled locks. Primping cleared her mind and soothed her spirit. The moment reassured her that she was in control of what lay ahead, which, according to Vee was taking care of him.

What better man than Maxwell?

Navena was no less drawn to him now than she was the first day of her last chance at college. Sophomore year. His class—the History of Afro-American Business—would provide the easy grade she needed to free herself from academic probation and reclaim her ruined scholarship—penance for a freshman year spent discovering sex, taste-testing Mad Dog, or mixing the two.

Three minutes late for the 8:40 class, she arrived to find the lecture already under way. Her instructor, McKnight, halted midthought to visually warn her. She wasn't late again.

Every class he eyed her, his gaze softening as the months rolled by. Each stare, look, glance, and, finally, smile, prefacing a compliment too intentional to be casual.

She considered his advances, despite the Jeri Curl and his barely beige complexion. He was cute. Taller and thinner than she preferred and he walked with a slight limp on rainy days—the sole evidence of a pro basketball career derailed by a knee injury.

Though jocks didn't interest her and instructors were taboo, Maxwell seemed enough of an intellectual to make her think he was interesting. He aroused her curiosity. He was well groomed and smelled wonderful. But her life was too bogged with men in varying stages of emotional disarray to add McKnight's affection to her list. Reason overrode her sense of adventure. She chose to ignore him.

She took her A in the class and her reinstated scholarship with a heaven-sent "Thank you" and walked out of his class, only to bump into him at the pool hall the Friday before break. He challenged her, lost, and paid with four drinks she downed until laughter was the only answer she could muster to anything he said. He took her home. She slept with him. She did not go home for that Christmas fourteen years before.

With a couple of family gifts and the right life clue, they'd spend this Christmas together as well.

To ensure that would happen, Navena decided to spend the afternoon listening to old CDs and studying her dream chart. She grabbed her headphones and headed for the kitchen table.

Time to see how many clues she'd collected and whether the car, cat, smile, barrel, and rope were matching—or not matching—life the way she thought: to Kat's death, her car crash, Rachel's smile, and events yet to be.

Floating down the freeway on remnants of last night's conversation with Navena, Maxwell didn't even let his lateness destroy the mood. Managing the office was hectic without her. She deserved every cent of the raise he gave her and then some. Even with the delays at the office, he'd only be five or ten minutes late for this interview with the county executive.

Weaving in and out of city-to-suburb traffic, Maxwell effortlessly steered the candy-apple-colored Mustang through sluggish spots on the freeway, breezing past cars strolling along at sixty-five miles an hour, into the fast lane and a comfortable clip of eighty. He tapped his nondriving foot in time to an old-school O'Jays tune, singing along, four beats behind, very distracted and slightly annoyed. The time 2:52 beamed from the dashboard clock.

"Maybe I should stop by the investigator's office. See what they've turned up on Luke so far. Gotta be something."

Maxwell's gut liked the idea, but his brain stepped in, knowing he was already pushing his on-time arrival for his three o'clock appointment. "Business before pleasure," he decided, pressing the steering wheel's hand controls to reluctantly turn down the radio. He dialed Navena's phone number and waited through several rings for the voice mail to kick in.

This'll get her, he thought as her message ended. "Hey, hope you're even better today. Just wanted to let you know that I really enjoyed talking to you last night. Call me if you need anything. Later."

A candy-apple-colored Cougar swerved out of Maxwell's rearview mirror and into the center lane to pass him. Temporarily slowed by the phone call, he regained his road edge and played tag with the daring sports car in front of him, mashing the accelerator until he'd returned to a comfortable eighty-mile-an-hour pace. He peered into his right-side mirror to watch the Cougar fall behind.

He was, admittedly, impressed and a little bit proud that the *Dispatch* staff seemed to think so highly of Navena. Maybe that explained why she was so attached to the place. It proved that her talents would be fully utilized with *Our Scene*. Maxwell felt confident they could take on the world. If their relationship evolved, *Our Scene* could even become a family-run operation.

"Almost there," he murmured, changing lanes to approach his exit one mile up the road. Unexpected construction barrels shifted him back into the far lane and slowing traffic. He saw the car quickly approaching in his rearview mirror.

Maxwell flicked his turn signal and moved to ease

into the reduced traffic lane. He checked the rearview once more to find the Cougar had disappeared into his blind spot and the SUV behind him hadn't slowed yet.

"Damn!" He swerved into the left lane, hoping the Cougar had eased by. Instead, the SUV slammed Maxwell's rear bumper and he swerved and crashed into the other candy-apple car. They skidded, tangled, into the concrete median.

Chapter Twenty

Friday, May 27

"Welcome back, gorgeous. How are you feeling?" Maxwell startled Navena as she stepped into the *Dispatch*'s tiny lunchroom.

"What happened?" Although he showed outward perfection, she could tell something was amiss. "I just talked to you—"

"How did you—? Little fender bender in that new I-75 construction zone." Maxwell tried to make light of the incident. "Doggone Cougar trying to outgun a Mustang. Ain't gonna happen."

"Oh, I had it all wrong!" Cat—*Cougar*. Car—*Maxwell's*. Barrel—*Construction*. She didn't like the way the clues now matched up. They blatantly drew Maxwell into the puzzle and tied him directly to its resolution. "But it makes more sense this way—that all the clues revolve around the man who's going to be killed."

Maxwell stood speechless, watching Navena talk to herself. "Hey, I'm right here. What are you talking about . . . clues, killing? Is this what you meant when you said you were afraid for me?"

"Yes, exactly, Maxwell." Navena felt nauseated.

"It was an accident. Unless you can see into the future, there's nothing you could have done to prevent it."

"Speaking of which," she murmured, "we need to talk."

"Good. Seems like you've had something on your mind for a while. In fact, maybe you should've stayed home until Monday."

"No. I'm glad I didn't."

"I missed you. I've been so worried about you, Navena." Maxwell stood in the narrow doorway, nervously tapping his Cross pen on the reporter's notebook he carried. He dropped his eyes for a moment before raising his pensive gaze to meet hers. "I feel like we've been apart forever."

She couldn't remember ever seeing him so . . . vulnerable? Or sexy? Any uncertainty she felt vanished as all her pent-up adoration spilled into the space between them.

He leaned forward to kiss her. Fervently. She wrapped her arms around him and returned the affection without care or concern for where they were and what could happen. Thoughts of losing him rushed into her mind and she kissed him harder, thrusting her tongue into his mouth. He kissed her back, then released her to brush his lips along her chin and down her neck. He nuzzled beneath her suit jacket and nibbled at her shoulder, then returned to kiss her once more.

"I love you," he whispered. "I love you, Navena. And I will not let you go again."

"No, not this time, Maxwell." *Not if I can help it.* She smiled, so happy to be in his arms. Grateful for another chance.

He pulled her closer and dipped his nose into her hair. Navena closed her eyes and rested her head on his chest.

She inhaled his cologne and stirred the frightening

undercurrent of her vision; she could lose Maxwell again, this time forever.

"Can I see you tonight?" she asked, suddenly afraid to leave him alone.

"No question. You just made this the first Friday night worth looking forward to in about fourteen years."

Maxwell answered evenly, but Navena felt his heart race with the response. She sneaked one last embrace, then released him quickly as footsteps clicked closer in the outside hallway. He lovingly brushed her hair from her eyes and rubbed his thumb along her mouth to smooth her lipstick. She quickly reciprocated the cleanup favor and scooted backward, away from him, as Fern entered the room.

Navena glanced guiltily her way. Fern smirked and bounced her eyes between the pair.

"'Scuze me," she muttered, making her way between them, toward the vending machine. "Hope I didn't disturb you-all." Navena smiled at Maxwell behind Fern's back.

"Eight o'clock," he mouthed with a grin.

Navena puckered her lips in response as Fern bent to pull her powdered donuts from the machine. Maxwell turned and briskly left the room. Navena swore his gait was lighter. Hers certainly was as she walked with Fern back to the newsroom.

She tried not to think about how much work awaited her. E-mail surely swamped her mailbox after so many days. Voice mail was certainly full. And although she knew Maxwell was editing copy last night, her in-box probably overflowed. She wanted to focus on eight o'clock tonight, but duty called yet this morning.

"Hey, you. You in the pinstripes." Fern mocked Navena's distraction.

"Huh? Oh, what'd you say?" she stammered.

"I wanna know what you two were doing back

there," Fern accused playfully as she lifted Navena's hand to peer at the nonexistent engagement ring. "Freedom seems to be agreeing with you."

"Quit, Fern." Navena snatched her hand away in a failed attempt to act indignant.

"Oh, you've got it bad all right." Fern shook her head and turned toward the vending machine.

"Navena Larimore. Navena Larimore, you have a guest in the lobby." The loudspeaker shook Navena from her thoughts and saved her from Fern's interrogation.

"Hey, Fern, I'll call you later, okay?" She hastily begged out of the conversation and trotted ahead, her heels echoing down the hall toward the lobby.

One of the reasons she kept an empty calendar on Friday mornings was that readers, promoters, and hopeful interviewees were prone to placing ads on payday. These assorted irregulars added an element of surprise to Navena's week that she'd come to enjoy. She wondered who was leading off today.

Arriving in the reception area slightly out of breath from anticipation and exertion, Navena instinctively frowned and pursed her lips at the sight of Rachel posing in the corner under the pretense of examining one of Navena's many publication awards hanging on the wall.

The woman from the museum? Why would she be here? Remembering that the stranger knew who she was, Navena fussed silently, then tried to tune in to her thoughts just to glimpse her intentions.

So far, she'd only been able to read Luke and Maxwell and believed she must need an emotional connection to scan anyone else's mind. Could she capture Rachel's wavelengths in the few seconds available?

"Apparently so," she whispered softly as Rachel's singular concentration spewed forth. Luke, of course.

What did he see in Navena? She didn't deserve him. He couldn't possibly love her. She works here? At that, Rachel snickered aloud.

So she knows Luke? Is she a past girlfriend, chick on the side, what? Regardless, she seems to think Luke and I are still an item. Navena launched her offensive, approaching with an outstretched hand and speaking assertively.

"Good morning. Rachel, is it? How can I help you?" Her glaring confidence summoned the hoped-for response, apparently catching Miss Thing off guard and disrupting her mental rampage. Rachel turned quickly to face Navena.

"Oh, hello, Navena," she stammered and motioned her palm forward to offer a limp handshake. Navena squeezed her hand tightly, using her strongest authoritative grip while cockily staring Rachel in the eye. Obviously surprised at Navena's assertiveness, Rachel belatedly tightened her clasp and quickly freed her hand. "I'd like to run an ad in this week's paper."

"Then you'll need to talk to someone in sales," Navena explained smugly. "I'm over the editorial department."

"Well, I did. I told them I wanted to run a full page ad with information about my new dermatology practice and they told me to ask for you." Rachel had overcome her initial surprise and now spoke with poise and confidence. "I'm opening an office in Trentmoor Towers. Luke didn't mention it?" At this she smiled.

"No. It must have slipped his mind," Navena retorted smoothly. "But congratulations. So you want to run an advertorial, then—a paid page of copy?"

"Yes, that's it," Rachel answered. "Can I make Wednesday's edition?"

Navena didn't have a clue what the paper looked like this week. She'd only stopped by her desk long enough to log on to her computer and grab change for the vending machine. By now, the paper should be full.

But as badly as the *Dispatch* needed money, Navena figured they could find space.

"I'll have to check to see what's available. I've been out of the office for a few days—"

"Oh yes, forgive me. How are you feeling?" Rachel interrupted coyly.

So you knew I was sick and wanted to make sure I know you're informed. Navena kept her cool.

"I'm fine, Doctor, thanks. Bad migraine was all." Navena changed the subject. "If you have a few minutes we can go upstairs and I can pull this week's layout to see if we have any space available. This way please."

As Navena turned to climb the stairs, she replaced her show-stopping smile with a frown. She needed a moment to calm down. The woman seemed intent on annoying her and she didn't know why. What was her purpose anyway?

"So, Navena, how's Luke treating you?"

Rachel's misplaced taunt pushed Navena's patience. She stopped midstep and spun around to face the arrogant stranger.

"Fine, considering we're not together. So, what's your deal? You had him or want him? Either way, he's yours." She flung the words evenly, but coldly into Rachel's smirking face.

In that instant, Maxwell floated by Navena, descending the stair on the opposite handrail. She paused as he passed, her breath audibly catching in her throat. He didn't speak. She wouldn't dare. Rachel raised a curious eyebrow at the unspoken exchange.

"I used to be engaged to Luke," she offered. "Then you came along."

Stunned, Navena nearly stammered. "He didn't tell me he was involved—"

Rachel waved off the apology. "We ended long before you came along. By then I was in Ghana with the peace corps."

"Thanks for the Memory Lane trip, Rachel. But I'm working right now. Let's talk about—"

"Why'd you break up?"

"None of your business but I'll simply say it wasn't working."

"So that means *you* broke it off. Bet he didn't take that too well, did he?"

"He'll be fine. Men and their egos. You know."

"He'll think there's another reason. Like my man on the steps." Rachel tipped her head toward the doorway. "If I can tell, Luke could, too, you know." Rachel's accusation landed squarely between the two women as Rachel reached the top step.

"What are you talking about?" Navena tossed over her shoulder, spewing the words despite her best effort to not hiss. She didn't want anyone to overhear such a personal conversation.

Besides, she hated letting Rachel rattle her nerves. She turned toward her desk, walking hard, certain that Rachel would follow closely even without prompting. Nervously she wondered what Rachel saw in the moment that Maxwell strolled by. Was their affection so obvious?

"I've known Luke for twenty years if you count grade school. I understand him better than you ever will. And I taught him things I wish he hadn't learned."

Annoyed, but curious, Navena turned into her cubicle and ushered Rachel toward a guest chair facing her desk. She did not need this woman here, talking about the man she'd just left. Or did she? Rachel seemed so insistent.

"Things like what?" Navena muttered, plopping into her chair and rolling herself tightly against the desk. She glanced at her computer clock—9:17.

"Like how to spot a wandering heart."

Okay, she's toying with me. Fishing for info to use against me. She's probably trying to get back with Luke by convincing him that I was fooling around. Navena scoffed inwardly. *I will not give her the pleasure.* But Rachel had piqued her reporter's instinct. "What? You cheated on Luke or something?"

"Yes."

Stunned by her honesty, Navena glared at Rachel, her skepticism demanding details.

"There was a time in college when me and Luke decided to give each other some space. We wanted to date other people . . . well . . . I wanted to go out with someone else. And he let me." She smiled wistfully at the recollection. Then frowned as she continued. "I married my A.J. Ran off and eloped on New Year's Eve." She dropped her head. "It broke Luke's heart."

Wow. Navena couldn't believe someone had gotten the upper hand on Luke. He seemed the type who'd had a life plan since kindergarten.

"You married someone else. *Right*. For how long?" *And why should I care?*

"A year," she continued. "Me and A.J. never told our parents. We were going to wait until we graduated."

Beneath the bravado, Navena caught a glimpse of shadowy desperation in Rachel's eyes. She softened her tone. "You asked me, so there must be a reason. How'd Luke take that?"

"Let's just say that as much as I loved A.J., I found leaving Luke not an option." Her eyes clouded over. The overly confident doctor twisted her ankles and twirled her fingers. "The whole thing infuriated him." She dropped her voice an octave to mimic Luke's angry voice. " 'I give you a little space and you lose your mind.'

"He insisted on getting back together anyway, that

we go home for weekends and holidays together, just like we'd always done. I split summer between campus with A.J. and Detroit with Luke." A wry smile escaped. "It was crazy."

"And your husband went along with this?"

"Of course not." Rachel grinned slyly. "A.J. was chasing his master's and working two jobs. He never knew I was still seeing Luke."

"Get outta here. There's no way—"

"Yeah, there is. And that's what Luke learned from me"—she exhaled like she was exhausted—"how a woman cheats."

Oh.

Suddenly Luke trying to buy the *Dispatch*, throwing that ridiculous party, sending text messages and voice mails like nothing had changed, asking her to accompany him to Philly for the award—it all made sense. The hound dog smelled a fox.

"So who is Mr. Handsome on the steps?" Rachel asked.

"No one."

"Wrong answer." Rachel leaned forward, invisibly pushing Navena back as she neared. "I didn't ask who he was to *you*, which is how you answered. Obviously he works here. *That's* what you should have said."

Navena froze, her brain scurrying frantically for an excuse. Something to erase whatever Rachel thought she saw.

"You need to get your no one in check." A condescending laugh erupted from Rachel's throat, loose and uninhibited. Slumping casually back into the chair, she winked and smirked. "So, can I run my ad this week or what?"

"Let me check later. I have a meeting now." She lied to make Rachel go away. "I'm actually late. Is there anything else I can do for you?"

"For yourself, really. My sister Eunice says he's been uptight lately. Impatient, short-tempered, forgetful. She figures either business is bad or you are."

"Thanks for the tip." Navena had spent enough time with Rachel and her strange confession. "I'll leave a packet with the receptionist for you. It'll be ready after one o'clock."

Rachel looked down her nose at Navena and laughed. "Nice talking to you, too." Rising haughtily, she sauntered out of the newsroom. "Don't say I didn't warn you."

Navena fought the urge to run Rachel down and stomp her. Right there in the newsroom. Anger and guilt ebbed, flowed, through her veins. That Luke thought she'd been sneaking around, well, that was scary. She now regretted not being woman enough to break things off sooner.

In a dark corner of her mind, sounds—gunfire, shouting—escaped from her dream, riled by Rachel's weird visit. The flash of fear and recollection left her skin cold and her mind racing.

The computer clock flashed 9:40. The time paused her for a moment while she tried to remember why it felt familiar. She shrugged off the déjà vu, realizing the time in reality.

Reaching across her desk to grab a pen and notepad, she hurried off toward Maxwell's office, slid quietly through the door, and sat at the table, mind still swirling.

Maxwell strolled to the seat across from her, eyeing her as he crossed the room.

"What's wrong, babe?" He approached her hesitantly, earnestly. "Are you feeling bad again? What?" He rounded the table to squat beside her chair and wrapped her in his arms.

Why can't I just love you? First your ex-wife-to-be kept

us apart, and now signs and clues are threatening your life, and Luke won't let me go.

"Take the rest of the day off," Maxwell suggested. "Start fresh after the holiday."

"No. I'm fine." She stroked his bruised face and kissed the top of his head. "Besides, you need help getting ready for tomorrow and I could use the distraction of work."

He raised his eyebrows, quizzing her silently for more information.

She shook her head. "Eight o'clock, remember? Until then, please take better care of yourself."

Chapter Twenty-one

Friday, May 27, 8:00 PM

"Technically, it's a first date, no matter how long you've known him. No sex. Besides, I don't want an Anderson/Fern situation."

Trying to calm her neglected hormones proved harder than Navena thought as she cruised downtown toward Maxwell's house. A quick finger tally of the days since she'd made love left her at about two months. As her relationship with Luke deteriorated, the intimacy disappeared. Part of his frustration had to be related to the fact that she had refused him for so long.

"That might give a man reason to think there's someone else." While she hadn't considered that before, it didn't matter at the moment. Her mind was on Maxwell.

Tonight's self-control wasn't about dating etiquette or morals. Navena worried that her affection was drawing Maxwell toward the nightmare's murder scene.

"We kissed and nothing seemed to worsen with the dreams and clues. But once I admitted to falling in love again—to myself, anyway—he crashes his car. What happens if I tell him? Or if we make love?

"Keep it business. Flirting's fine. Just resist the urge to tackle him at the door and have your way with him." A silly smile still covered her face as she wheeled into his driveway picturing him splayed beneath her, helpless.

In a déjà vu of the first attempted tryst, he met her at the door, too sexy in a pair of baggy jeans and a black linen shirt.

"Mmmm, you smell so good," she remarked, reminding herself once more to behave. "Look nice, too."

"Trying to keep you from running out on me again," he teased, then ushered her inside. That smile, the one matching her memories, crept across his face.

She returned his humor. "What, with cheap beer and a good line?"

"Me? Never! But I'm not above trying pricey wine and a little sweet talk." With a reassuring squeeze of her hand, he promised, "I'm going to take very good care of you."

"No need for the hard sell, handsome." Noting his shoes beside the entryway, she slipped off her sandals and let him lead her through the foyer and into the living room. "I'm definitely staying."

"Then have a seat." He nudged her gently toward the sofa and headed for the kitchen. "I've been saving your glass of wine all this time."

"I didn't mean to hurt you, Maxwell." Smooth jazz flowed from the stereo and helped ease her tension. The scene looked identical to the one she'd run from Sunday night. Swallowing jitters, nerves, and the thud in her heart, she asked inwardly for his forgiveness. No. Tonight she wouldn't be running. "I just wanted it to be . . . right."

"Actually, I respect your resolve," he conceded, returning to her side. "Makes me think you're truly ready to give me a chance."

She accepted the drink he offered and the toast that came with it. "To us." Glasses clinked, twinkling in the last rays of setting sun. Maxwell leaned to kiss her.

"Wait," she whispered, placing her hand over his lips. "Before we do this . . . I . . . need to know if anything . . . unusual . . . has happened to you lately—besides the accident."

There, she'd said it, feeling dumb now under the weight of Maxwell's scrutinizing gaze.

"I knew something was going on." He stood above her. "Tell me the truth."

Was that fear beneath the urgency of his demand? No. Worry. The CD player paused to switch discs, just long enough for Luke's voice to creep into her head, bobbing and weaving with static . . . and anger.

"Shhh!" Eyes closed, she held up a finger to silence Maxwell and listen.

I need you to track her down. Now!

Luke's command blared through Navena's senses. Dropping her goblet, she slammed her hands over her ears and doubled forward. *Why is he so angry?*

When thoughts of Rachel's visit chimed in—her words about letting go not being an option—Navena's unseen dread spilled into her reality. *Leave me alone!* she screamed.

She snapped out of her reverie with Maxwell shaking her furiously, grasping her arms, panicked. "Navena! Baby, talk to me. Tell me what's wrong!"

"Stop it!" she shouted, wiggling free of his clutch. "I'm not sick, Maxwell." She sat back further and inhaled deeply before speaking again." I'm . . . I'm psychic. Seeing things. Having visions."

His handprint echoed the strength of his grip even after he'd let go. She rubbed her arms absently, studying Maxwell's reaction. Splatters of red wine wasted on her thigh seeped into her dark jeans; others beaded on the leather sofa and ran beneath her leg. She held her breath, waiting for Maxwell to say something, anything.

Once, in fifth grade, she'd shared her family secret with a "best friend" only to be ridiculed and ostracized for the remainder of elementary school. Hope pressed her to believe that the man she loved would react better.

Instead, he stood and backed away, his eyelids half cast in fear and suspicion. "You *are* crazy."

She patted the space beside her. "A little. But sit."

No movement.

"Please, Maxwell. I'll explain."

He shook his head and began circling the room, his hand atop his low-slung jeans. "I see you looking at me strange, and I tell myself you're daydreaming. Watched you scratch your palms, constantly some days, and it's like you don't even realize what you're doing. You screamed that day in my office like you saw a ghost—"

"I did."

"Are you high?" He crossed his arms across his chest. This, she realized, was his idea of an intervention.

"I swear to you, Maxwell McKnight, no booze, no dope. Walk through this with me, then ask questions. Okay?"

No response.

She continued carefully, selecting her words for maximum effect. He needed to catch on quick. He had to lose the fear.

"Seems that I can do things other people can't. I dream visions that materialize. See signs of things to come. Hear voices from other people's heads." She paused to digest his mixed look of incredulity and suspicion. "What, Maxwell?"

"You've got problems, Navena." With a dubious sneer, he began pacing, careful not to turn his back on her.

"So do you. You just don't know it." *I'm losing him,* she thought desperately. *I need you to believe, Maxwell.* "Think something."

He threw his head back in mock exasperation. "If you don't want to be with me, you don't have to try and scare me off. I'd rather you just leave."

"Like hell. For a flash, you thought about how the lamb chops Dijon you prepared for me will go to waste. How you spent all that time online until you found the perfect recipe, one from Julien Durand, the chef you met in Baton Rouge during your last season in the NBA. Mostly, though, and now, you think I must still be sick."

"How can you do that?" Wide-eyed, Maxwell downed the remainder of his wine in a single swallow.

"It's a family thing. My mother, my grandmother, all of us can do . . . stuff." She scoffed and stared at him hard, wanting him to understand. "They call it a *gift*."

"That explains why you did so well at Hillstone." He stopped pacing and smirked.

"No. I'm just smart, thank you very much." She laughed softly and patted his vacated space beside her, beckoning him forward. "Could be I'm not fully recovered from the migraine. You're probably right. But I don't think I'll ever be who I was before." She searched his eyes for empathy. Finding a hint, she continued. "So, while it seems I'm *not* myself, I actually am for the first time."

He returned to the sofa and plopped down beside her. "Back up."

She laid his head in her lap and stroked his face. "I never wanted this. I'd forgotten it. Thought I was defying my inheritance by living my own life, not my ancestors'." She sighed and shuddered.

"You *all* have this—inkling?"

"Kind of. We're each different. Mama does cards, fortunes, tea leaves, that type of thing. Gramma Livia, her mother, prophesied. I get more."

"Since when? I mean, how come you're so different lately? Fourteen years or forever, I know a few things about your personality, Navena, and you are *not* the same."

"Everything changed on my birthday," she sat up and looked into his eyes. "According to my mother, I'm at the age when I receive my gift. But apparently, I was born with those abilities. As I got older, my mother worried that certain experiences I was exposed to would cause me irreversible trauma. For lack of a better explanation, they put my gift, my heart, essentially my life, on hold until about two weeks ago."

"They can do that? Control you that way?"

"If I can read your mind, why wouldn't they be just as capable?"

"So, like, what have you ever *inkled* that came true?"

"My daddy's death."

Maxwell sat upright, mouth agape, the half-cast fear crossing through his vision again. "You're kidding me."

"I wish." Eyes closed, she shook her head slowly. "It was so awful. My eighteenth birthday. Daddy was cutting the grass, Mama sent me out to call him in for cake and ice cream. I saw him, plain as day, fall and die. But it was a prophasy. I ran inside to tell my mother. When she went to see about him, he was dead. Dead, Maxwell."

Tears spilled onto her cheeks. She cupped her hands to hide her face. "For years they hid that from me." Bitterness edged her voice. She leaned onto Maxwell's shoulder.

He lovingly stroked her arms. "That's a lot for any kid to bear, Navena. Your mother was probably right doing whatever she did. You might not be the woman you are now if you had to carry that knowledge all these years."

"I can only imagine, because I've been out of my mind with worry these last few weeks.

"So this happened right around the time—"

"You arrived."

Brow furrowed, Maxwell interrogated her. "And at work that day, when you said you were afraid for me. What else haven't you told me?"

"Depends." She sat upright and looked deeply into his eyes. Fear subsiding, doubt persisting, she had hoped faith would kick in sooner. "You still don't believe me?"

He sat silently for a moment, then shrugged. "Maybe I told you about the chef a long time ago. You can certainly smell the lamb chops." He leaned back against the sofa cushions. "You were pretty convincing, but it might've been luck."

"Test me. Think about your favorite birthday party as a kid." Navena closed her eyes and concentrated on the musk in his scent, the rise and fall of his breathing, then channeled his mind's eye.

Confetti and pony rides filled her head. Sun shone on an elderly black man in clown attire who twisted balloon animals and performed magic tricks. A two-tier cake wearing white icing and streamers burned bright with a circle of seven candles. Stevie Wonder boomed behind a little boy in a Superman birthday hat. Finally, Maxwell, standing between a beautiful woman and a girl of about ten.

"Your mother is there next to you?" she whispered.

"Yes."

"And that must be your sister. She's tall?"

"We both are," he laughed.

"Clown, ponies, that huge cake. What did you wish for?" She smiled and opened her eyes.

"My father," admitted Maxwell. "He was at work, like always. He gave me the party. I just wanted *him* there."

To Navena at that moment, he looked like the little boy she'd envisioned. Same soft lashes, same broken heart.

"Why didn't you tell me before?" At last the fear in his voice dissipated, replaced with the understanding she hoped for.

She took a deep breath. "Maxwell, I was young. Embarrassed. Glad as hell to be away from Sikeston and all those people who thought me, Mama, Gramma were all . . . witches. I've never told anybody." She shook her head briskly back and forth.

"Hard to say how I might have responded. Honestly. Obviously, the time is right for you to let me in." He kissed her nose, then narrowed his eyes. "Does *he* know?"

"I said *nobody*. So, even though he teased me about Mama's 'job' from time to time, I never let on." She shrugged. "Besides, if he knew, he'd be looking for a way to make money from it. Otherwise, the information wouldn't have been any good to him."

"How could you spend so much time with someone who doesn't really know you?"

"Let's say I wasn't myself during my relationship with Luke. Part of the family legacy I received on my birthday involved using my heart to take care of *you*." Navena looked Maxwell in the eye. "Turns out *this* is what I've been waiting for. Life with Luke is over."

"So I had a lot more to do with this sudden ending than I would've thought?" Hope flowed through the question and peeked through his smile.

"Everything." She paused. "Thank you. For giving me my life back."

Confusion rushed through his mind as the CD player paused. Pride, lust, fear, denial fought for dominance among his thoughts as he tried to sort his feelings about what Navena had told him.

"Okay, I need a break. Another drink, some food. You've got to give me some time to get my mind right about this." He stood and turned toward the kitchen without waiting. "You hungry? Come on."

The music resumed, a soft slow ballad that made Navena crave the days after the new moon when everything would be right between them. *By then I will have collected my clues, solved the murder mystery, and kept you safe. We can move on with our life the way Vee would want it.*

She'd always been able to talk to Maxwell. It's what they did best. Whether it was dishing over politics or venting about Lila, conversation was definitely their strong suit. Even recently, the way they had the same ideas for the paper's future. How they could oversee daily work at the *Dispatch* while executing the plan for *Our Scene*. Feeling their way back into love.

"I know it's a lot to deal with, Maxwell, but I only told you because I'm ready to be with you. I need to know that you can love me as I am."

"The question of *we* really doesn't have anything to do with your newfound gift," Maxwell responded curtly as he moved between stove and countertop preparing their plates.

Her hands flailed in frustration. "How do you figure that? We've been doing this dance since you got here—"

Maxwell turned to face her again. They stood less than a foot apart. "No. We've been playing this game for fourteen years. Before I make this fantastic leap of faith, I at least need to know if you love me, Navena."

Prodded by the wine and fueled by her physical longing, she forgot about the dangers the dream might hold if she told him the truth. Her eyes fell closed. His cologne invaded her sensibilities and blurred all the good intentions she had arrived with. She swallowed and looked away.

"Of course I love you, Maxwell McKnight." The words escaped her mouth as if poised for release, like they knew their moment would come. She sensed his heat and tried to fill her mind with the clues she'd collected and how she wanted Maxwell in her arms alive, not dead like the man in her dreams.

Maybe the accident was a coincidence. I have to believe that giving in to my heart isn't handing you over to a killer. The notion blazed across her mind and tumbled outward through a teasing gaze before she could remind her body to behave.

"Your turn," she teased.

Instead of answering, he leaned against the counter and motioned her forward with a finger.

She tried to escape, without success. Sweat trickled down the center of her back. The slit in her long denim skirt opened and closed as she eased toward him, offering peekaboo glimpses of her long shapely legs.

"Food's ready." Maxwell's gaze traveled down her body and rose to greet her eyes. He met her halfway across the kitchen, wrapped her in his arms, and began backing Navena up until she reached the refrigerator. "How about a hot snack?"

"Now that you mention it, I am a little hungry," she murmured. Arching away from the steel door's chill into Maxwell's warmth ignited a throb through her hips.

"I made your favorite dish," Maxwell whispered, completing his come-on by straddling her legs and pinning her into place with a deep, ravenous kiss.

This was not the kiss she remembered. It was not the hasty kiss of someone with ten minutes to get busy before class began. It was not the embrace of a desperate coed unable to have the man she held. Now it was deliberate and free.

The big man was gentle, but firm. He pressed his body against hers and raised her arms above her head, holding them captive with his left hand as his right hand slid down her body, tracing its shape with his fingertips.

His urgent passion burned from her belly to her thighs, like he'd been waiting forever for this perfect moment. Want tugged at the fabric constraining her.

Giving up the notion of resistance, she closed her eyes and submitted. Navena kissed him back, picking up where she'd left off this morning in the *Dispatch* lunchroom. Her tongue entered his mouth, this time finding the solace she'd sought five nights ago. She squeezed his arms and inhaled.

Thoughts of dolls, cards, and nightmares disappeared into the mingled scents of manliness and soap, heated by the sudden onslaught of her desire. She licked the warmth of his mouth, then withdrew to taste the fullness of his lips—sweet with the wine from hers—caress the soft stubble of his beard, laced bitter by a splash of cologne, teasingly nip the ticklish spot beneath his ear. He exhaled heavily into her hair.

Rising to tiptoe, Navena slid her hands into the gap between their bodies and groped for his zipper and the present within. Maxwell answered by lifting her blouse and unbuttoning her skirt. It slithered to the floor as he plunged his fingers into the dampness inside her. She gasped and released his hardness to remove his jeans.

He entered her roughly. She screamed with pleasure.

The refrigerator struggled to support them as they

sent car keys and junk mail perched atop crashing onto the tile. Navena embraced Maxwell, scratching him coarsely, trying to grab hold of their future in this moment.

He groaned, gripped her shoulders, pummeled her faster, faster and faster until her head flew back and his passion exploded inside her body and down her legs. They fell to the floor.

Navena smiled and rolled on top of him. He rubbed his hands down her sides, circling her bottom, and returning to her arms, caressing the shivers of fear and longing that rumbled through her body.

She kissed his forehead, his eyes, his ears, his neck. Their bodies remained locked, writhing in silence, as she returned to his lips.

Brushing her dreads aside, Maxwell placed his lips skillfully below her ear, right in Navena's kill spot, tonguing playfully, mercilessly as she squirmed atop him. He ran his tongue down her neck, slid the fabric of her blouse aside, and nibbled deeply into the back of her shoulder.

"Take it off, Maxwell."

Obediently, he loosened the drawstring neck of her gauzy blouse and lifted it over her head. The air's chill against her skin electrified Navena, flooding the curls between her legs with a new wave of steamy wetness. She pressed his face between her palms, found his mouth, and rammed her tongue inside, not caring what he thought, just getting what she wanted.

Maxwell filled his hands with her breasts and tore angrily at the front closure of her bra. She felt it explode loose as he tore his mouth away from hers and sucked thirstily at both breasts. She felt for his chest. She bit at his nipples as his hands rummaged over her nakedness.

Pushing her away, he laid her on his back and dived

inside her warmth. She swung her knees upward and he placed them over his shoulders and entered her again. He was like thunder. He was so filling, so, so good. Again and again he pulsed, making her arch and scratch and moan uncontrollably. She came twice before he finished, each time shuddering harder than the time before, nearly losing consciousness, calling his name "maxwellmaxwellmaxwell" loud enough to rouse the sleeping boats docked in the marina half a mile away.

When Maxwell's frenzied thrusting brought Navena to her last climax, she sank her teeth into his chest and her nails into his thighs. He spilled into her and onto her and all over his shiny ceramic tile.

She kissed his forehead, mouthing the salty evidence of what they had shared. "Feels like it's been forever."

"Fourteen years is just as long." He sighed and freed her legs to fall softly to the floor, cradling his body between them. He carefully shifted his weight, rose, and lifted Navena from the floor.

Smiling that smile she loved, he offered a look of resigned understanding. "So I still love you, okay? Now what?"

Gathering her clothes, starting to dress, trying to find words to underscore her feelings and her fear, Navena wound up blurting the truth before she overthought the issue and said nothing at all.

"The night before you came to the paper I had a dream. I saw someone dead in my arms. At first I thought it was Luke. Then I had the little chat with Mama and a week of weird dreams. In the end I found myself." Itching burned her palms. She looked down and saw that her lifeline zigzagged from her index finger to her wrist in a blazing streak. She tried to stay calm and scratched. "I discovered that I belong to you, but only if I can make sense of the signs I'm being given."

All the passion had drained from Maxwell's face once more. He finished dressing, walked to the counter, and put their plates into the microwave one at a time. As they finished heating, he poured them each a glass of ice water. He extended a hand.

She followed it to a bar stool at the kitchen's center island. "For example, the cards you gave me in the hospital are the exact same cards I dreamed about after you visited. They were covered in symbols—car, cat, smile, barrel, and a rope. I was looking for things in life that the cards represented. And I thought I'd found most of them—until your accident."

Maxwell raised his glass and took a long, quiet sip. "You're saying you predicted my car crash."

"I hope not. But is it coincidence that you had a car accident—not a mishap in the house or at work—involving a Cougar-slash-cat in a construction zone filled with barrels?"

"Damn. Better be, huh? Or else what, Navena? I'm going to die?"

She hung her head. "Not if I can help it."

"Why? When? What's going to happen?" Masked panic ebbed between his words. Jumping up, he crossed the room in long, quick strides, running his hands over his head.

"Next new moon. June fourth. Eight days from now." Navena hated to tell him, but maybe knowing would help prepare him for the worst. "By then, I'm supposed to have matched all the clues to real-life elements. Once that happens I'll be able to solve the puzzle and prevent the murder."

"So you're playing *Wheel of Fortune* with my life?" With his hands on his hips, skepticism crept into his voice once more. "How do you know it's me?"

"Just a feeling." She smiled meekly. "I promised to take care of you. I think that means I may have to save you from . . . something."

"You always had a dramatic flair and I think your family just feeds into that. Remember—I came to Detroit solely to be with Miss Navena Larimore. If nothing is coincidence, maybe fate sent me here to save *you*."

The idea that she might be in danger had never crossed her mind. *Could Maxwell be right?* She considered the notion.

"Listen. When you thought I was sick earlier, I was *hearing* Luke. He was furious. I think he's looking for me."

"What does he want and why would he be mad?"

"He hasn't taken the breakup very well. I didn't want to mention it because I'm moving in two days. It's all cleared with the real estate company. He leaves town Sunday morning, I'm packed and out by Monday night."

"No man likes to be dumped." Maxwell chuckled and furrowed his brow. "Is he harassing you?"

"If you call throwing me a bogus surprise party and asking me to go out of town with him harassment, then yes. But I can handle clingy guys." Navena took a long sip of the chilled water and watched her ice cubes float in the glass. "What really unnerved me was a visit from his former fiancée this morning."

"When was this? What did she want with you?"

"Still not sure, but she said he'd been acting weird lately—her sister's his secretary—and she was worried. Seems that when she tried to break up with him, he didn't give her that option."

"What the hell does that mean?"

Navena shrugged. "And now from the thoughts I'm overhearing, he's tripping more than I thought."

"Is he the vengeful type?"
She thought a moment. "Unforgiving, I'd say. Doesn't believe in benefit of the doubt. That's what I know of him personally. I'm even more detached on the business side."
"Lucky for you, I'm not." Maxwell leaned across the table. "Now, don't get mad at me, Navena."
"What did you do?"
"Standard procedure for any investor. I had him checked out." He leaned back.
Not sure what to think, Navena let Maxwell's news sink in. Whether an investigation was good or bad depended entirely on the outcome. What she didn't want was for Maxwell to discover that Luke was some disreputable creep she should have uncovered herself long ago.
"Are you aware that he took on a new business partner recently?"
"Of course. I just finished the press kit for the merger." Navena resented Maxwell trying to treat her like an old-fashioned wife in the dark about her husband's affairs. "He plans to announce it at the groundbreaking tomorrow night."
"So you're well versed in this Edmonton Holdings Group?"
"I admit. With all that's going on at work, I didn't conduct my own research into the company." Once she said it, she instantly felt uncomfortable, wondering if some pertinent detail had been left out of their public files. She continued in her defense. "They provided me with ample information—history, employees, finance, sales and marketing reports—everything. I developed Luke's material based on what they gave me.
"You found something, didn't you?"
"Weird link. One of the guys who invested heavily in the company back in the seventies is related to one

of Anderson's interviewees for the 'Gangstas Gone Good' story." Smugness she hadn't seen since Maxwell's first week returned to his face.

"So there's no problem as long as everybody's really dealing straight these days, right?"

"And that's what remains to be seen." Maxwell grabbed her glass and stood. "All this business talk is killing the mood. Didn't we come in here to eat?"

What-ifs had taken over, prompting Navena to wonder if Luke's anger was bigger than the breakup. "Who are you talking to in this investigation?"

"Old friends in the business." He returned to the table with their plates. "They're professional. Discreet. Don't worry. Luke will never know."

"Yeah, but if these Edmonton players have been entrenched in the underground for thirty years, they could have eyes and ears anywhere." Goose pimples rose on her skin. "Just be careful, Maxwell."

"You're the one with the super skills. Excuse me, gifts," he corrected, raising his eyebrows. "You trust him?"

"He's never done anything to hurt me." The air between them swirled with nervous energy. "Why wouldn't I?"

"He trust you?"

"Rachel got me thinking that maybe he had some crazy notion about me seeing someone else." She toyed with her food. "Do you think he knows about our past?"

"Maybe he has inklings, too." Again Maxwell laughed, this time tossing up his hand to punctuate the bad joke.

"That's not funny." She frowned and pushed at his chest. "Rachel told me all this stuff about her and Luke. How she cheated on him and how, now, he 'knows what to look for.' "

"You changed your locks, right? Does he know you're moving?"
"Based on the way he's been acting since the breakup, I figured it would be best to move out quietly." She put down the fork and drank some more water. Her appetite ebbed. "It'll be easy to let him know from afar since he'll be out of town when it happens."
"Think he'd try to keep tabs on you while he's away?" Maxwell asked seriously.
His line of questioning was beginning to scare her. She thought of how easily he had entered her space for the surprise party. When they were together he had unrestricted access to her place and her belongings. Though she'd never caught him tiptoeing around in there, he knew her schedule well enough to get in, snoop, and get out if he needed.
Now, not only had she locked him out of her life, she'd locked him out of the place, too. Suddenly chilled, Navena folded her arms across her chest for warmth. "You think I'm safe?"
"You mean are *we* safe?" He shook his head back and forth, and prepped a forkful of lamb chops for swallowing. "Originally you thought your nightmare was about Luke. Are you sure he's not a part of it?"
"No." By not being with him day in and day out anymore, she had no idea if clues were matching up with his life as well. *But I'm going to find out*. She wanted Maxwell by her side.
"I know you love me, but I'm not assuming you can still be with me—now that you know." She edged her voice with sternness to hide the fear that he might say no.
I wonder if Daddy really knew. Maybe that's why Larimore Manor has always been ours, the women's. The reason we're always widows or husbandless mothers. Maybe men can't handle the Knowing.

"I'll admit. Brother's a little shaky. But I'm not going to leave you in this all alone. You promised to take care of me, that's the least I can do for you."

You didn't answer the question, but I'll give you time to adjust and decide. "So, can we start over?"

"Sure you're ready?" he asked, barely a whisper.

"You're what I want, Maxwell. The man I love."

"Then let's do this." He grinned and reached for her hand across the table.

Whatever "this" might be. Navena smiled and began to eat.

Chapter Twenty-two

Saturday, May 28

Nights like the one that left Maxwell and Navena bedridden until Saturday noon used to make regular appearances in their first courtship. In their grown-up world of too little time and too many duties, today's sleep-in made a welcome appearance.

Tipsier than she'd been in a year, she and Maxwell savored his gourmet meal and then headed to the living room for more wine and uninterrupted mood music. Much of the night they talked, but for even more of it they danced like kids—slower perhaps, but no less enthusiastic, rocking hips on the fast songs and locking lips on the slow tunes, reeling themselves into a sexual frenzy from living room to shower to bedroom. They kept each other awake until four.

The aftermath of competing colognes, unwashed sex, and seared scented candles hovered in the air. Navena awoke first, unable and unwilling to fall back to sleep. Carefully, trying not to disturb Maxwell, she gathered the wet sheets around her nakedness as if to shield herself from the eyes of the crowd in her dream.

Instinctively, Maxwell reached from his own sleep to

lovingly wrap her in his long arms and pull her into his heat. "Good morning, gorgeous. Tell me something wonderful."

"Actions speak louder," Navena whispered, stroking his hand as it caressed her breast. Behind her, he stretched and stiffened, and slid his way between her sticky thighs, damp from the dew of their predawn lovemaking. Taking his body's cue, she writhed rhythmically in submission to his gentle thrusts.

Rocking steadily, Navena closed her eyes to freeze the moment. She absorbed the sound of his tender groans, the bass resounding crisply through space and time into her head and heart where it curled tightly in her chest and gripped her breath until it exploded as a moan, her passion quenched as Maxwell's finally peaked.

"I love you, Navena," he whispered. She arched into his air kisses at the nape of her neck, and basked in the pureness of his affection.

"Always and forever." She agreed to the promise though the phrase sat unsettled on her lips as she found herself suddenly uncertain about their life in the days ahead.

"Since we're not going to be together until late tonight, why don't we hop up and go have brunch?" Maxwell suggested, not a question, more a decision. He spoke suddenly, stirring Navena from her drifting thoughts.

"Can't. Remember I was sick two days. I didn't have a chance to get shoes and jewelry for tonight. And I have to pick up the dress. Spending the day apart will give you something to look forward to." She turned to face him. "Do you need anything else for tonight?"

"You know I need help, but if anything's undone at this point it's a little late." He smiled. "Is there something else you *want* to do for me?"

Soft-voiced and seductive, his plea unleashed a vision of moist nearness, bare-shouldered teasing, strong fingers tangling her hair, frosted lip prints dusting his chest. "Whatever it takes."

"I am never going to make it!" Navena fussed at herself aloud. By the time she got to the West Side, it would be one o'clock. She still had to shower, buy stockings, shoes, everything. No way did she have time to shop, clean herself up, and be back at Maxwell's in three hours. She had hoped to sneak in time with him before the guests arrived.

"No way," she declared, reaching for her purse on the seat beside her.

With a quick twist of her wrist, she dumped its contents and felt for the cell phone. Finding it, she pressed the number 5.

"Oh, Miss Kay, you're there." Navena breathed a sigh of relief. Her Knowing told her Kyra would be at the boutique personally taking calls, even in the middle of her shop's busiest day. She worked way too hard and today Navena was thankful. "I need a huge favor. *Huge.*"

"I figured I'd see you last week sometime . . . even with your last-minute-shopping self," Kyra laughed, deep and throaty. "You run your panty hose getting ready for the party?"

"Worse. First of all, I'm not seeing Luke anymore. Wrong party."

"Sounds like a story you need to share. Come on with it."

Customers called and chatted over Kyra's shoulder. Navena didn't want to keep her from business. "Got a different event. And, yes, I need a dress."

"For tonight?" Kyra shouted into the phone.

Navena pressed the accelerator and took stock of the

clock once more. Four o'clock was approaching much too fast.

"I hate to ask, but can you do it?" pleaded Navena.

"Honey, you know I can. Matter of fact, I got an early shipment this morning. Haven't even opened it up. But I suspect the perfect dress is inside. How about red?"

Laughter escaped Navena's heart and skipped away on the brisk wind blowing through the car. It sure helped to have friends. She rolled up the windows and turned off the vents.

"I'm not even at home." She hushed Kyra before she spoke. "Ah. Don't ask. I'll be there in two hours."

"Yeah, yeah, yeah," Kyra teased. "Try not to get a ticket on the way. See ya when ya get here, honey."

Maxwell knew he had no business inviting Navena to brunch. At least she had sense enough to decline. He watched Navena drive away, then hurried into the house to check his Smartphone.

"We should have been up hours ago." True. But he didn't want to let her leave. His body tensed at the realization that he'd finally held her, made love to her again.

Tonight, however, was one of the most important in his life. Right up there with his Rookie of the Year honor was this investors' reception he was hosting for the *Dispatch*. He turned off his libido and ticked through a list of text messages and voice mails.

It was twelve thirty, the meeting planner was due any minute, and had called to say she was en route. The cleaners should be right behind her with his suit.

Florist and caterer would be here at two o'clock, followed by the band for setup at three. The invitations told guests that drinks and hors d'oeuvres would be served at five and dinner promptly at six o'clock.

Luke's gala activities were slated to start one hour

later. Maxwell felt badly about Navena's dress situation and hoped that Luke wasn't playing mind games with her today.

With everything she was juggling in her life, he knew she wouldn't arrive worry-free, but he wanted her to have a fun, forget-your-troubles kind of evening. Luke's antics would definitely put a damper on the day.

The event planner sent an instant message. *Made a stop. Be there in ten.* Maxwell launched into gear, locking the front door and running upstairs for a quick shower.

Maxwell had negotiated the NBA's grueling eighty-game schedule, grading college exams for two-hundred-plus students, divorcing Lila with his sanity intact. But the *Dispatch*'s swift reinvention continued to challenge him physically, financially, and emotionally, costing more than he expected with salary and equipment upgrades and barely keeping up with its four-month transition goal.

But right now, all that drama felt like someone else's story. Tonight the world would find out what was really in store for Detroit's best black newspaper.

Four hours till showtime, he thought proudly, shaking off his sweatpants and stepping into the cool shower. "This should calm me down, for a while anyway."

Lathering and rinsing quickly, he replayed the mental pictures from last night, her sitting on top of him, swept away in ecstasy. He turned down the hot water faucet and shivered beneath the water. "That should do it," he told himself, knowing that as soon as he saw her, all the shower's hard work would come undone.

The doorbell rang as he dressed. He bounded down the stairs as the first vendors of the day arrived to transform his condo for an unforgettable night.

* * *

So glad that Luke's Escalade wasn't in the garage when she pulled into the driveway, Navena felt like her excitement conjured him up as the phone rang. She only debated answering for a second, deciding it was best to maintain the appearance of normalcy until he left town and she moved out.

"Hello?" she answered haltingly, determined to keep the peace with Luke. She heard music in the background. Frantic commands by a female voice faded in and out.

"Navena?" Luke asked. He sounded surprised to hear her voice and not her message.

"What's up?" she answered abruptly, stepping out of the car and walking briskly toward the front door.

While she couldn't tap his thoughts with all the music on both ends of the conversation, she sensed the hurt and anger beneath the surface of his cordial greeting. Navena fumbled for her keys and opened both locks on the outer door, then smiled and keyed the new locks guarding her flat.

"Everything all right?" Luke asked pointedly.

"Great. You should be, too." She wanted to balance the conversation between his big night and her not being there. "Got everything you need on the PR end? Eunice isn't having any problems, is she?"

That would be all I'd need right now. She dropped her purse on the couch, locked the door, and started turning off lamps she'd left on the night before.

"I wish you were here," he said simply. "You *should* be here. I could really use your support right now."

"You're surrounded by talent, Luke. Your team can pull this off blindfolded. Trust them."

"Right. Look where trust got me with you." His tone became edgy, betraying his inner aggravation.

Navena decided to end the conversation as quickly and kindly as possible. She headed for the kitchen and a much-needed cup of tea. "It's probably just nerves. Even for a rock-steady man like you, this is a big deal. But everything's going to be just fine. Watch."

"Where were you last night?"

"At Fern's." *I should've called and asked her to cover for me. Damn.*

"Funny. I ran into her at the gym this morning and she was looking for you."

Navena's gut clenched though she was about ninety-nine percent certain that under the girlfriends' code of breakup behavior, Fern wouldn't dare ask Luke anything.

"Well, you know Fern's a kidder." She paused. "Look, I gotta go, Luke. Good luck tonight. Take care, okay?"

"I love you, Navena."

"It's better this way, Luke, really." She hung up without waiting for a response and scrolled through her messages from the previous night.

Call after call from Luke, with voice mails interspersed among them. The brother was not giving up.

She tossed the PDA on the couch, double-checked her door locks, and went back to shower. Tomorrow she'd escape this apartment-turned-cage.

Maxwell walked into the backyard and checked his Rolex. One hour until showtime.

Throughout the afternoon's brief span, experts worked to transform the house and yard. Japanese lanterns had been strung across the expanse from house to boardwalk. Food stations featuring seafood, prime rib, pasta, fruits and vegetables, dessert, and bayou delicacies filled the corners.

Soft jazz filled the spaces conversation would soon occupy, tuxedoed wait staff replaced apron-clad caterers, and the valet team was perched for action.

Maxwell stopped to sniff and admire the head table's daffodil centerpiece. He then lifted a pair of crystal goblets to the evening light to check for water spots and potential embarrassment. Everything seemed perfect, making him wish that much harder for Navena.

"She'll be here soon." He could hardly contain his excitement. It was almost too much good for one night.

Flashing his sexiest all-charm, I'm-in-charge-here grin, Maxwell ambled confidently into the yard, ready to greet his guests.

"Wow." Navena exhaled with delighted surprise. "You did say red, but, Miss Kay, you outdid yourself this time. I look incredible."

"Almost, Miss Thang," Kyra laughed and coughed. Ironically, Navena read the cough as a barometer of her stylist's excitement. The happier Kyra was, the more her two-pack-a-day cigarette habit betrayed her. Smoking was banned in the shop, out of kindness for the clothes, but an ashtray stood ready at the back door for quick escapes into the alley.

"You all right?" Navena asked. "Need a break? I know I didn't have an appointment."

"Don't you worry about me, sugar," Kyra reassured her. She buzzed from one side of the shop to the other, picking up earrings from one rack, a bottle of perfume from the counter, and a chiffon scarf from the neck of a window mannequin. "Once I get shoes on your feet and perfume in all the right places, then I can take a break. I want you to turn that party upside down."

Three thirty-four.

Kyra passed her basket of scented lotions and creams. No wonder the boutique smelled more like a flower shop than a couture clothes store. Navena chose an exotic-smelling body butter to slather on her skin, topping it with a glittering body lotion. Silky smooth, she slid into a pair of sheer gold stockings—courtesy of Kyra—and forced her frame into a tummy-flattening, bosom-boosting body shaper she'd brought along. Kyra took it from there.

Her expertise was obvious. The deep red satin sheath, hemmed just below the knee, reminded Navena of 1940s movie star dresses. Maybe she wasn't quite as buxom, but the dress was all sultry. She wished for a little less tummy at the moment, but Kyra knew her figure flaws and made sure the piece played up her exercise-toned arms, boyish hips, and long, shapely legs.

Kyra had even planned the makeup, accenting Navena's wide eyes with a charcoal liner, a swoosh of chestnut shadow across the lids, and a couple of strategically placed false lashes at the outer corners. Chestnut-colored contour cream was smudged just below her cheekbones for depth and together they chose a coppery frost and nutmeg liner for her lips.

Dusted with an all-over poof of glittering powder to set the look, Kyra was ready for finishing touches: an inch-wide tennis bracelet on the left wrist, a two-carat emerald-cut topaz ring on the right hand, dangling pearl-drop earrings, and a pair of red open-toed pumps that shone sunset gold under the light. She fluffed Navena's dreadlocks, sprinkled gold powder at the roots, and fluffed again to disperse the shimmer.

Navena couldn't believe her eyes. The ninety-minute transformation was worth her last-minute request. Kyra stepped back and admired her work, then burst into action once more.

"You're beautiful, doll, but you know that." She thrust a red satin clutch into Navena's hand. "Now get outta here so the folks who need to ogle you can get started."

They hugged tightly. Navena was nearly moved to

tears at her friend's generosity. She should have been home relaxing by now.

"You're welcome to come, you know," Navena offered belatedly. She suddenly felt bad for not inviting Kyra.

"I know, honey. No need to worry about me taking the afterthought personally. I figure there's a real good story in the breakup with Luke and that glow on your face." Kyra grinned suspiciously. "We'll have a real good chat about it next week."

"Oh, I love you, Kyra!" Navena beamed with excitement, the kind of joy that makes people cry. She could only hope that the evening would turn out as wonderful as she felt.

"You ruin that mascara I'll kill you!" Kyra shouted playfully. "Now, hurry up. Shoo!"

The reception was about to begin, and Maxwell's place was twenty minutes away. Navena scurried carefully out of the shop and headed for the Jeep. Moonlight revealed the need for a car wash. Hopefully no one would notice the road grime.

No. They'd better not notice anything but me once I walk through that door.

Sliding carefully into place, Navena tossed the clutch into the passenger seat and hastily started the car. She peered into the rearview mirror to check her look. Habit. She had no doubt that she looked gorgeous. A smile crossed her lips at Maxwell's pet name.

With a deep breath and a tap on the CD changer, Navena pulled into traffic, on her way at last. She woke up in Maxwell's arms, kept Luke at bay, and lucked up on an incredible outfit. It seemed that Maxwell and Navena, the star-crossed lovers, were finally going to have their day.

Flashing lights in her rearview mirror snatched Navena from the trance. An ambulance nearly swallowed her as she daydreamed. But the interruption did more than steer her to the right lane of the freeway. She pulled jerkily off the road altogether. Once there, she sat with her hands clenching the blazing steering wheel, knuckles pale, watching the apparition.

She panted, distressed, watching twilight approach through shattered glass. Maxwell lay next to her, bleeding and unconscious, face bloodied, distorted from . . . what? She lifted her hands to peer at her bloody palms in the moonlight. And screamed.

Four Lauryn Hill songs later, she found herself just as she'd started. The vision dissolved, she released the steering wheel, stretched her fingers, and put the SUV in drive, easing cautiously back into traffic. Downtown lay at the foot of the road ahead. In the setting sun, it glowed, but not enough to erase the swirling red lights from her mind.

Navena trembled the remaining two miles. Warming up and calming down only when surrounded by the reality of the night ahead.

Maxwell's complex stood out from its neighboring condos. Floodlights in the front yard wove ribbons around the sky ahead of her, announcing the celebration and guiding drivers to the festivities.

Twenty minutes had grown to forty and her eventual arrival was exaggerated by a long line of Jaguars, Benzes, and Lexuses vying for valet attention. Navena cut jaggedly through the line, forcing her way ahead by angering the patient drivers and challenging the aggressive ones.

"The *Dispatch* is VIP tonight," she mused. "And I'm the head woman in charge."

She banged the horn and forced a final front-end passage to the door. Pleased with her assertiveness and certain of her allure, she eased herself from the buttery soft leather seat, careful not to tug at the sequins beneath her, and allowed the valet manager to escort her inside.

"You must be Miss Larimore," he remarked. Navena raised her eyebrows. "Oh, Mr. McKnight asked that I look out for you."

A smile of mixed pleasure graced her face.

"Thank you. I appreciate the special attention."

He bowed jokingly and opened the door to allow her through.

Navena swore that a hush fell over the room. The band missed a beat. Someone dropped a platter. Rice paper lanterns rustled eerily in the sudden quiet. Maxwell, standing near the center of the room, turned in slow motion and smiled broadly as she entered. For a moment, no one moved. Or so it seemed. And then she breathed.

Music resumed, muted, but upbeat. Scattered laughter peppered the air. Maxwell beamed as he crossed the room in three long strides, catching up to her before she'd taken more than one or two graceful steps into the room.

"Sorry I'm late," she whispered.

Maxwell leaned over and whispered with a smile, "Surprised you made it this soon . . . lying in bed all day."

"How's it going so far?" Navena asked. Judging by the vibrant ambience, outside traffic, and constant chatter, it was a silly question.

"This is incredible. I can't believe everybody's on time, too."

"You might want to back up dinner from six to six thirty," Navena suggested. "It's only twenty minutes away and there are that many cars awaiting a valet."

"Seems the nontransferable invite got passed along anyway, huh?" Maxwell shook his head. "I guess that as long as we have enough food, it's all good."

"Looks like we'll make enough money to cover the

bill," said Navena. "I believe this is what they call 'the time of your life.' "

"And I believe they're right," Maxwell responded.

Pure pride, unmasked pleasure, and boylike joy shone in his voice. He and Navena spent the remainder of the evening introducing each other to Detroit's local celebrities—rising wannabes, teetotalling politicians, used-to-be singers, past and present star athletes, and a host of others.

Navena knew the mayor and city council president through interviews she'd conducted with them both. Maxwell seemed impressed to meet them. She was likewise awestruck to shake hands with the Detroit Pistons' latest rookie star and a local dancer who was opening a Broadway show at the Fisher Theatre the following week. Of course, there were the familiar faces; Dispatch faithfuls who'd followed the paper through all its ups and downs, waiting for a day like this.

Hugs and handshakes flowed throughout the evening. Everyone they met seemed genuinely happy for the *Dispatch* and its team. This was unquestionably their shining hour. For the first time in weeks, Navena felt totally in control.

Chapter Twenty-three

Sunday, May 29

Luke paced all night, walking the floor above her head as if he hoped his distant tirade might force her to confront him.

Navena stayed focused on the bathroom mirror, wrapping her dreads in a large satin head scarf. Kyra's save-the-day makeup looked as fresh as it did eight hours ago—the last evidence of how stunning she looked at the party. She hated to wash it off.

"Eyes on the prize, girlfriend, eyes on the prize." Pressing up and down on her pump dispenser until her hand held a golf ball's worth of light foam cleanser, she stroked the tiny bubbles on her face, smearing, then removing the glitter and glam from her skin. A brief scrub with a hot wash towel followed, finished off by a dutiful application of moisturizer.

"Good genes, yes, but no sense taking it for granted." Navena smiled at herself and brushed her teeth. She glanced in the mirror at the retired ensemble behind her. The scarlet dress and its matching wrap hung from the shower rod on a padded hanger, while her shimmery panty hose and the unforgiving body shaper lay draped over the tub ready for hand washing. Wouldn't happen in the wee hours of this Sunday morning, though. She tossed the undergarments in a tote bag and would take care of them at the new house.

Eyes on the prize.

Even another night with Maxwell couldn't draw her from the day's mission. He understood her single-minded need to go home and pack rather than hang out with him and offered to come as soon as she signaled. So far, it was all she could do to drown out her Knowing and ignore Luke's overhead attempt at Chinese water torture. No drip, drip, drip for hours on end. It was walk, walk, walk, with stomps thrown in for effect every few minutes or so.

The moving team was scheduled to arrive at 8:00 AM. By that time Luke would be well above the Midwest on his flight to Philly. She couldn't wait for the quiet to return. That would mean she was closer to being out.

Thanks to Maxwell, this would be one of her easiest moves ever. No manual-transmission U-Haul, bribed male friends who always bowed out after the beer arrived, or even a broken fingernail from shuttling boxes from room to truck to room. This company would send three movers and *they'd* pack the place. She'd stay out of their way, offer water, and direct work flow if they needed her to.

Until then, a steady stack of CDs and memories of Maxwell's reception helped her relax. Navena was amazed at how vendors had converted the condo from bachelor pad to an internationally themed gala within just hours. Must've cost a fortune—but it was worth every dollar.

"They're probably still cleaning up." Talking aloud to keep herself company and drown out Luke, she felt a twinge of guilt picturing Maxwell managing the exodus of rented tables, chairs, and lanterns. The DJ and caterers had to break down their own setups and Maxwell said his event planner was handling the disposal of floral arrangements and the return of other items. "If I thought you'd be left alone to do all that, I would have stayed. But I'll just be in the way with all that after-party efficiency going on."

Tonight's plan was to stay awake long enough to pack all her toiletries and knickknacks. Before she got home from the party, she also had grand notions of packing her clothes and CDs herself, too. Now, with sleep tugging at her lids and reminding herself that Maxwell was footing the bill so she could relax, she decided to do just that.

Slipping out of her robe en route to the bedroom, she changed into a pair of sweats and an old acrylic sweater. Navena lotioned her feet and shoved them into a pair of thick gym socks. With a glance at the trembling ceiling and the invisible giant above it, she decided to move her pillow and linens into the living room to sleep.

"He probably figures he's going to keep me awake all night." If she'd been trying to rest, he would've been right. And he seemed to be convinced that she was indeed at the far end of the house, in the bedroom. "Please don't follow me," she begged, dragging her sleeping items into the living room and hunkering down on the couch.

Seamlessly transported into the vision she watches, Navena sees herself round the corner of Whitlock Street, pocked only by flashes of gunfire. Speeding into the fray, she searches for Maxwell and finds instead Luke's bullet-riddled truck. She screeches to a halt beside the Escalade, ducks into her front seat, and crawls toward the passenger-side door.

Slowly, she opens the door and shouts Maxwell's name.

Luke's bloody face appears, waterlike in the window. "Run, run as fast as you can, witch girl," he taunts, then falls forward.

Marked police cars turn the corner behind her, blaring their horns. Navena's truck blocks their way. Terrified, she slips out the passenger door and scurries, hunches to hide behind the Escalade. A man appears behind her, shielding her body and dragging her to safety in a squad car farther back. She screams for Maxwell, still sees Luke's face. She cries for Luke and falls limply into a cold, caged backseat.

Peering cautiously through the windshield, she sees police in riot gear charging house number 62855 with a battering ram. Positioned on neighboring rooftops, other officers hoist rifles on their shoulders, poised and ready. An undercover cop, badge swinging around his neck, runs toward her carrying Fern in his arms. Navena throws open the car door and the officer quickly drops a hysterical Fern beside her. He slams the door and returns to the melee.

"Where's Anderson?" mouths Navena. Fern continues to sob, but eventually sputters that she thinks he's still in the car. "What about Maxwell?"

"In that truck." Fern speaks in slow motion, pointing shakily at Luke's Escalade. "There."

Navena rises from the car, floating quickly and effortlessly in her dream state, to look inside the truck. Luke sits slumped against the driver's-side window, Maxwell leans against the opposite door. Both bloody and unconscious, neither hears Navena scream as the front door of the house falls inward and gunfire erupts.

Interspersed among the shoot-out, Navena didn't hear the doorbell when it rang. Instead the ballad attached to Maxwell's cell phone number caught her ear and pulled her out of the frightening realm.

"What a dream." She spoke into her PDA's receiver,

yawning, half-listening to the voice on the other end. This time, the doorbell chimed through loud and clear.

Maxwell responded, "They're at the door."

Silence from upstairs was the first thing she noticed as she stumbled off the couch and toward the flat's outer door. With an eight-thirty flight, he was long gone. She opened the door and let the movers in. They walked from room to room as she talked to Maxwell.

"If you're ready, you can come on through." *Even if we do sit for the next few hours as they pack.*

Which is exactly what they did. He arrived as the movers carried the last of Navena's belongings out to the van. Not in the mood for board games, and with the television unplugged, they sat inside the house chatting about tomorrow and another new beginning.

"What should we do to celebrate?" Maxwell asked.

"Clean, unpack, and eat. Somewhere nice."

"It's a date."

Sadness stabbed at Navena as she looked around the empty rooms. But anticipation pushed her out the door, toward her new life.

Navena stood in the driveway humming an empty tune to drown out Luke's mental tirade and her own jumbled thoughts. She solemnly surveyed her haul: the mountain bike, the CD collection, the good china, and a handful of bulky sweaters and hipless jeans that she had decided to pack herself after all. The hatch and backseat of her Jeep were crammed with evidence of her material world. Prodded by bad vibes and a brisk early afternoon breeze, she moved swiftly from box to bag, checking that everything was present and secured.

"Can you do this for me?" she asked, handing Maxwell her key ring with the flat's new keys separated out.

"You're just determined to spare your nails in this move, aren't you?" He laughed and took the jangling ring, quickly sliding the two selected keys off and placing them in her palm.

"This is it, darling." Wistful, but so ready, she strolled back inside to lock her flat's door. She climbed the stairs to Luke's flat, fighting off memories of how often she'd made this trek for entirely different reasons. She slid the keys under his doormat, took out her PDA, and called to leave him a message.

"Hey, Luke. It's Navena. I'm moving out today and wanted to let you know I left the keys under your front doormat. The original locks and keys are in the kitchen pantry if you need them." She paused to think, trying to avoid making another call for something she forgot to say. "Well, I guess that's it. Take care of yourself, Luke."

Done.

When she pressed END and exhaled, a thousand pounds of pressure lifted from her shoulders. She bounded down the stairs to Maxwell.

"Funny, isn't it? That you don't realize how stressed you are sometimes until the stress is gone?"

"What'd you do up there? Get some crazy miracle makeover? You're like a new woman." Maxwell marveled at her happy mood.

"I should've done this years ago. Maybe never should've started." She shrugged.

"Ready to put it in the past?"

"Yep." Navena nodded. "Let's go."

Maxwell headed toward his Benz as she climbed into the Jeep's driver side and put the SUV in gear. Hazard lights flashing, she led the moving van, Maxwell followed behind. She'd forgotten how slow the big trucks moved and agonized not being able to speed down the freeway during the entire forty-five-minute trip—twice the time it usually took.

When they turned the corner to her street and pulled

up in front of her house, she saw the value in every melodramatic moment spent with Luke, the years of carrying empty space in her heart, the timing of Maxwell's return, and being a Larimore. Each piece of her life fit in a way that placed her at this point in time.

She wanted to scream with excitement. "And if you do, your new neighbors will promptly put you out," she laughed.

Their small caravan peeled off. Navena pulled into the garage as the movers waited in the middle of the street. Maxwell turned in next, parking his car beside hers.

This is so cool.

An older structure than the two-family flat she left, this garage wasn't connected to the house. They left its shade and walked across a gravel footpath that led to the side door. Crocuses and daffodils that hadn't bloomed when she paid her first visit here, now stretched for drops of dappled sunlight that fell from the maple tree above.

Even cooler than I thought.

The van began to beep and back into the driveway. She unlocked the door and wove through the kitchen, breakfast nook, and dining room en route to the front door. Maxwell unlocked and pulled back the heavy wooden door, then propped open the screen door in preparation for the movers.

"We might as well empty your car, too," he said. "What's your plan of attack? I know you have one."

"To unpack the bathrooms first, starting with the one downstairs. Then the kitchen. And then—"

"It'll be time to eat."

Paper bags rustled and dipped as Maxwell moved across the empty dining room toward Navena. His long, muscular legs covered the short distance in two swift strides. He sat down behind her as she sorted boxes of books, straddling her in the center of his leggy V. He leaned over her shoulder and placed the bags of sub sandwiches and chips in front of her.

Talking as he opened napkins, Maxwell examined the sandwiches and counted out the chips, unzipped the straw wrappers, and dunked one straw into a cola and the other into a supersized cherry slush. He pushed the soda her way and took a long, slow sip of the frozen treat.

"Aw." She pouted in disappointment. "I thought that was mine."

Maxwell released the straw in surprise. "Since when?" he asked. "You *always* drink cola. But you want some?"

"Not now," she teased. She leaned over her straw and took a long, loud, slurping sip of her cola in mock imitation of Maxwell. They laughed. He hugged her closer and grabbed half of his Italian sausage sub. She took a lingering sip of the cola.

He talked between swallows, finished the second half, and searched the table for his chips. "Want the rest of mine?" she asked, too anxious to be as hungry as she originally thought.

"Yeah, I'll take it." He pushed her drink away and wrapped his arms around her waist. She felt his breath on her neck, followed by soft, soft kisses across her collarbone and shoulder.

"Did I miss anything last night?" she asked quietly.

"This," he answered, nuzzling deeper and more persistently.

"You got the house back in order?" She fought the urge to succumb to the pulsing behind her and within her. Maxwell paused just long enough to answer.

"Yep. And I'm never doing anything like that in my home again." He lifted her dreadlocks and kissed the nape of her neck. "Too many people in my stuff, especially since the invitation was passed around so freely." Another kiss. "What did you think?" A nibble. "Did a brother do all right last night?" He tipped her chin back toward him and dipped his tongue into her ear. That was more than she could stand.

She leaned into Maxwell and slid out of her shirt. The skin on her breasts tingled. He touched them and turned her gently around. She kissed him, undressed him, and slid out of her sweatpants. They made love quickly, almost frantically, Maxwell pressing her into the smooth, cool hardwood, finishing almost as soon as he'd started. She stared up into his glistening face.

"Good and quick," Navena whispered, running her nails up and down his bare back.

He surprised her with the onslaught of affection. Perhaps it surprised him, too.

"Couldn't help myself." He smirked, pulled out gently, stood, and stretched naked above her. Early evening sun shone through the lead glass windows at the top of the wall. The sweat on Maxwell's chest, caught in the rays, twinkled like a kaleidoscope. He looked like Atlas—except that she was the one carrying the weight of the world.

A ragged hum broke the wonder of the moment. Maxwell's cell phone buzzed in his jeans pocket somewhere on the floor.

"Your phone, hon," she urged, figuring it was an *Our Scene* supporter, but not wanting to turn down the stereo and mentally eavesdrop.

Maxwell reached a little higher to finish off the stretch, then turned briskly toward his piled clothing. With one toss, he sorted shirt from jeans, and grabbed his phone from the pocket. As he glanced at the caller ID on the cellular's face, his expression went from casual to concerned. He flipped open the handset and dove into an intense discussion.

"McKnight here. What'd they say?"

Ignoring his apparent crisis-of-the-day, Navena rose from the floor, gathered her clothing, and started to dress. Watching Maxwell stand in the center of the room talking serious business butt-naked brought on a cascade of giggles. She tied the drawstring in her pants and began carting books to the room's built-in bookshelves.

"Guess we should hang some blinds in here before the neighbors get an eyeful," Navena joked.

"Fine time to think about that now," laughed Maxwell as he shut the cell phone and slid into his jeans and fleece sweatshirt. He checked over his shoulder to ensure that all the window coverings were indeed in place. "Ha, ha."

Darkness would take over soon. Maxwell would leave. Or not. "Can you stay with me tonight?

"If you keep feeding me all that good loving, I might not ever go."

"I'm nervous. Had a really bad dream last night and all this space is going to take some getting used to."

"You'll adjust. And you know I'll be here whenever you need me." He walked up and swatted her behind. "Let's take it easy tomorrow. Sleep in. Unpack what we can. Explore the house . . . and each other."

"So you figure we're just going to lie around all day? It's a holiday."

"What better way to spend it before we hit the ground running on Tuesday?"

"Gotta point there." She walked away, swinging her hips in a way that would've made Gramma furious. "Sounds like a plan to me."

Chapter Twenty-four

Tuesday, May 31

Navena falls from her hovering space above Maxwell and Luke. She tumbles to the ground as police exit house 855 with handcuffed young men dressed in varying degrees of hip-hop-inspired denim and jewelry. One by one they parade down the porch steps, across the adjoining lawns, into the waiting line of police cars and transport vans. Fifteen fellas in all, including "Nephew," the tipster who drew Dispatch staff to this now tragic scene.

Shouting for help, she waves her arms to attract an officer. A female SWAT team member jogs over and radios for assistance in removing the two sizable men from the car and getting them medical attention. Bloody-handed, Navena sits on the grass until the ambulance arrives.

She awoke on the couch, edgy and unsettled, in the darkness of her new house. The linen dress she'd worn to work was crumpled and spotted with patches of perspiration. Using the sofa cushions for support, she pushed herself upright, pulled the clinging fabric from between her breasts with her forefinger and thumb, and fanned the dampness with her other hand.

Her purse, keys, and beige leather mules were tossed carelessly atop a box marked BOOKS. Last thing she remembered was collapsing on the nearest soft surface free of plastic and packing peanuts, turning on the stereo, and closing her eyes to think. Now she wished for daylight and Maxwell to erase the nightmare that invaded her rest.

Her watch beeped nine o'clock.

Asleep for hours, she craved a glass of water, with lots of ice cubes, like Mama used to make her when she was little. On cue, the phone rang. Somewhere.

Jumping up to look behind boxes and picture frames that blocked her view of the den's baseboards, she turned up the phone jack and the nearby socket where the handset base was plugged. The handset itself was missing and continued to ring nearby. Navena stood, hands on the hips of her wrinkled dress, and scanned the room once more.

The ringing stopped, then started again. *Hold on, Mama, it's gotta be here.* She moved the jacket to her dress—discarded before she napped—from on top of a box of candles and uncovered the cordless handset. She scrambled toward the comfort of Mama's voice.

"I'm really afraid," Navena whispered to her mother. So fresh from dozing off, she realized the nightmare didn't reveal Luke's and Maxwell's fates. Whether they lived or died, she didn't know. "I'm getting impatient with all these visions and signs. How many more blanks do I have to fill in before I can solve this puzzle?"

She thought of Maxwell's *Wheel of Fortune* comparison and stumbled on, frustrated. "I can't just lie here and dream, Mama. There must be something I can do now."

"If it was time, your answer would have been revealed." Mama explained.

"Based on the dream I just had, things are getting worse. It looks like they both died."

"That means they've both become part of the answer you have to find," said Mama.

"Great," Navena thought aloud. Frustration set in. She walked from the den to find the kitchen and cold water. Navena flicked light switches and tapped dimmer buttons along the way to mark her path. "I've only promised to save Maxwell. So what do I do with Luke?"

"Maxwell has your heart, but you'll need to balance that emotion on many levels in order to fully use your gifts and find the right answer," Mama answered. "You can't deal with Luke as coldly as you did before the reunification. You are above that type of personal disconnect now."

"I have to play nice with Luke?" Entering the kitchen, Navena rebuffed her mother as respectfully as she could, then snatched a tumbler from the cabinet. She sidled to the refrigerator, pushed the glass against the door-front dispenser, and filled it with crushed ice and cold water. Frustrated, she leaned against the counter. "He's bound to misinterpret any kindness I extend. You know that."

"Depends on your timing."

Mama's responses irritated Navena. She wanted direction. Answers. Guilt about Luke's fate washed over her throbbing concern for Maxwell. Their safety, their lives, her life, her love seemed crisscrossed, about to collide and explode.

"Who holds the last sign's match?" Navena blurted. "What will bring this to life, Mama?"

"Navena, it's just not time yet," Mama responded with even-toned patience. "What choices have you made based on what you know so far?"

Navena paused. She pushed herself away from the counter, walked to the breakfast bar, and took a straddling seat on a tall stool. "I left Luke."

"That was before Vee. What since?" Mama asked casually and in the following silence pushed Navena for details.

"Well, I promised to take care of Maxwell. Being in love makes it easier. I moved—"

Mama interrupted, "Navena, what *one* thing has been most important?" Mama posed the question for effect. Navena knew her tactics. Mama wanted to make her think. That's the way she taught Navena to read. "If a-t is 'at,' then c-a-t must be 'cat,' right?" Sound it out, she used to say. Navena began to do just that.

"Believing," Navena realized, picturing the two men wounded and unconscious in the front seat of the Escalade. "Trusting that I really am a part of the Larimore Legacy and when I need to, I'll be able to do something to undo the death."

"Then trust that the answer will unfold in its time."

"So there's no sense worrying myself, trying to get ahead of the clues."

"None at all." Mama sighed as if relieved. "Conserve your energy and keep dreaming, sweetheart. I know it's hard on you, but it's the only way. Really."

I can do that, Navena thought. *Now that I know I just have to wait.*

"Okay, Mama." Navena exhaled deeply. "Thank you. For everything."

"That's what I'm here for. Call me tomorrow, love."

"Love you, too, Mama. Night." Navena pressed the phone's Off button, feeling stronger, certain she'd be able to do whatever she was meant to in the days ahead.

The phone rang again, Maxwell's voice replacing Mama's.

"You finally left the office?" Navena continued to admire Maxwell's dedication to making *Our Scene* a success.

They got the *Dispatch* to press on time, then met to debrief over the past week and make adjustments to next week's plan. Navena left him at the office waiting to meet with new investors generated through Saturday's event.

"Am I coming that way tonight?" Maxwell asked.

"If we stay here, I'll spend all our time unpacking. I need a break. Mind if I stay with you instead?"

"As soon as you can get here. Drive safe."

Chapter Twenty-five

Wednesday, June 1

Sunrise replaced moonbeams. Diffused through the window's sheer curtains, hazy light greeted Navena as she stirred to find Maxwell watching her waken.

A self-conscious smile tipped the corners of his mouth. "Feel like a kid in a candy store," he murmured, eyeing her lustfully. "Don't know what to eat first."

"Too much sugar is bad for your health," she admonished with mixed embarrassment and pride.

"Yeah, but yours is great for my heart." He pushed aside a stray dreadlock, lovingly fingering its twist before tucking the hair into place.

"I still can't believe we're here." She took a moment to absorb this new reality, his presence beside her, the dampness left behind from last night.

Rising to one elbow and propping his head on his palm, Maxwell lifted the sheet to peek at her nakedness beneath.

"Look, love, but don't touch." She jerked herself upright, shoving the sheet beneath her arms. "If we get started again, we'll be late for work."

"Oh, come on," Maxwell teased, sneaking his hand under the sheet and creeping his fingers up her thigh.

Navena hit him with a pillow, knocking him onto his back. Shifting her position to straddle his hips, she playfully rapped him on the forehead. "That's all you want!"

"Fine, then." He faked a pout and raised a quizzical eyebrow. "How'd you sleep?"

"Dreamlessly. Almost too quiet for days riddled with the kind of visions I've been having." *Was the emptiness a clue of its own? A fork in the road between signs?*

"Did you hear from Luke yesterday?"

Boy, you're full of questions this morning. "You know I did. I debated telling him, but legally, he's my landlord. I broke my lease.

"So what's he talking about now?"

" 'Have a nice life.' 'Don't expect me to be here when you come to your senses.' Same old man stuff." Navena shook her head. "I can't believe all this hostility is just about me, though. Rachel and Eunice think business is involved somehow. I'll bet that's true." She paused.

"Please be extra careful, Maxwell."

"Why? I'm still going to get mysteriously knocked off?" He dipped his finger playfully in her navel gun-style and pretended to fire.

Navena frowned and pulled the sheet up to her shoulders, knocking his hand out of the way. "Yes. If we don't pull the cover story for *Our Scene*. There's something about that gangster . . . Anderson's connection . . . this cagey nephew. Too many loose ends." She paused to emphasize the gravity of the situation. "I don't want you hurt."

"Maybe you're misinterpreting this inkling thing, Navena. Regardless, we are going to print on Friday.

Canceling now means we can't launch until December. It'll ruin my reputation and totally discredit the *Dispatch*."

"Get yourself killed, then." Navena snatched off the sheets and flung them at Maxwell. Like her grade school best friend, he obviously wasn't to be trusted with her secret either.

She stood, saddened by the revelation, backing away as Maxwell reached for her.

"I'll be late for work," she stated flatly, stopping to gather her clothes and walking out the bedroom door.

Navena exited the condo in her most theatrical, half-dressed huff, leaving Maxwell's shouts to come back unanswered. She tossed her sandals and handbag into the Jeep's passenger seat, slid behind the steering wheel, slipped on her sunglasses, and sped out of the driveway.

"You big jerk." She sniffed.

Just yesterday, Maxwell was bringing her fantasies to life. Now he'd dropped her squarely in the ugly reality of his ridicule. *What made me think he would understand?* A pout pulled at her lip. *He did, of course.*

That he could accept her visions the way he supported her daydreams seemed only natural. Though now, because he taunted her, she knew her assumption was wrong. "Looks like I'm alone in facing this challenge."

Recalling Luke's anger barely hidden beneath the surface of his voice mails and Maxwell's speculation that she might be followed made Navena thankful for the move. If she had to drive all the way to the West Side right now, she would be *very* late for work.

As long as the visions and signs align the way fate aligned to get me this house, we'll be just fine.

Her eyes darted from one side of the street to the

other, seeking strange cars or "lost" men wandering the block. Seeing none, she raised the garage door and wheeled quickly inside. The sudden memory of Luke's hulking Escalade beside her SUV each night gave her the willies. She shuddered, lowered the garage door, and walked toward the house.

"Anybody here?" she called as she entered.

Silly woman.

But shouting into the stillness did bring her comfort. So did not getting a response. Reassured, she bolted up the stairs to call Mama before bathing and changing for work.

Watching herself in the master bath mirror, she undressed to her bra and panties, speed-dialed her mother on the wall-mounted speakerphone, and began lathering her face with cleanser.

"Navena, baby? What's going on?"

Of course she knew something was up. "Mama, what do I do if someone won't listen?" She splashed her masked face, then paused. "If they're affected by the signs but won't believe? What happens?"

"You told Maxwell, didn't you?"

"Luke always thought you were a witch. Telling *him* probably would've been easier." With a cotton ball, she applied toner to her forehead, nose, and chin, then surveyed her work closely in the mirror. "So I let Maxwell in on the Larimore Legacy."

"Did he run or laugh?"

"I thought he was okay with it, until today."

Big jerk, she thought miserably, dabbing on another dose of toner and choosing not to answer.

"Even good Larimore lovin' can't keep a man once he knows, Navena." Mama paused. "I had to let you find that out on your own."

"Actually, I stumbled on that notion in my dream—

the first night of my headache." She tipped a bottle of moisturizer into her palm, releasing a dime-sized puddle. "But I guess I learned it this morning."

Using the tip of her middle finger, Navena dotted her face in five spots, then smoothed them all together. She put the stopper into the tub, turned on a warm stream of water, and slid out of her underwear. Thoughts of Maxwell's mouth . . . everywhere . . . brushed across her mind, making her quiver. A slow blink brought her back to the present and her mother's questioning.

"Which cards are left?"

"The rope. And in the beginning there was lots of glass. Never on the cards, but in the dream and in the car. The last two cards are blank."

"Might not be a literal rope," Mama offered, a lilt of hope in her voice. "They're symbolic. You saw that. So the rope is probably just a line that ties things together."

"That could be anything—a telephone cord, gas pump, fishing line—anything." Matching the final sign suddenly seemed impossible. Navena turned off the water running into the bath and plucked her loofah sponge from the towel rack.

"Where's your hope chest?" her mother asked.

"I put it upstairs in the guest bedroom." Beautiful, but antique, filled, Navena assumed, with knickknacks of bygone days that had nothing to do with her. She'd cast it aside years ago, never even sifting its contents for relevance or value.

In simplest terms, the cherry-wood Lane chest didn't match her décor at the other place or seem to have a purpose outside of storing family memories. But more truthfully, the heirloom represented the past she'd shied away from until recently.

Here it fit with the crown-molded ceilings and hardwood floors and her acceptance of who she was.

"After my bath, I'll go find the cards and call you back."

"Not the cards. Look for a sewing kit. You'll need it in case of emergency."

With that, Mama hung up.

That's why I hate calling you sometimes. Irritation washed over Navena as she finally stepped into the tub.

Wrestling with the appearance and understanding of her newfound gifts had consumed Navena. That, and connecting the signs she believed would move her toward resolving the mystery of her dream.

Disappointment over Maxwell's skepticism still pierced her heart. He let her down. And topping off her dismay was that she needed Mama's help in deciphering her life. Navena felt childlike rushing through her bath so that she could do her mother's bidding.

She scrubbed in quick, broad strokes, racing the loofah up and down her soapy skin. Five minutes later she emerged reddened but invigorated, determined to unearth . . . whatever . . . and make it to the *Dispatch* in an hour. She lotioned herself, tossed on a robe, and hurried into the box-filled room across the hall.

You are in control here, Navena Larimore.

As she squeezed past boxed past editions of the *Dispatch*, high school journals, and notebooks of poetry en route to the hope chest, Navena decided to check in on Luke. She pushed her thoughts toward him. "What are you up to, Lucas Benson?"

Not a trace? she heard him ask. *All you had to do was follow the moving van! What do you think I'm paying you for? Don't call me until you can tell me what I want to hear!*

"Apparently, I'm two or three steps ahead of whoever you hired." She smirked. "But are you watching Maxwell, too?"

Despite being annoyed at his nonchalance this morning, which she interpreted as a lack of support, she wouldn't dare abandon Maxwell. *I love him and he deserves my protection,* she conceded. *Though from what?*

Hopefully, this Mama-directed search held another clue.

Navena found a red box near the bottom of her dust-covered chest, looking like it had fallen from her dream of the Mothers and landed carefully in the corner. She wrestled it free from layers of family photographs and Gramma's girlhood Bible, opened it, and removed the contents.

Inside, waited a well-worn assortment of items to which Navena had no personal attachment—needle and thread, scissors, an eraser, pencils, and old-fashioned paste glue. Her Mother had never seemed the craft type.

But Mama called it a sewing *kit—for emergencies, no less.*

Navena could see mending as a common theme among the mementos, and maybe that's what made it first aid. But for what kind of emergency?

I guess that depends on what I'll need to fix.

By now, the dawn she'd left at Maxwell's was long gone. She'd spent much longer than she'd planned on the phone with Mama and, according to the VCR clock, she was already half an hour late for work. Even with quick makeup and her simplest summer work dress, no way she'd be there before ten. But she'd try. Navena picked up the handset and dialed Maxwell.

"McKnight speaking."

"It's me." Her heart pounded at the sound of his voice, despite her attempt to control it. "Had something to do after I left."

"Are you still mad at me?"

She could see him grinning, pegging her for the same forgiving girl she used to be. Hmph. "Yep. Still ticked." A fib, but she wanted him to squirm. "Be there in an hour."

"No problem. I'm holding an editorial meeting just for you. See you when you get here."

Taking one last glance at the box as she hung up the phone, she gasped to find each item looking brand-new. A voice inside assured her they were now ready for use.

An hour later, Navena left for work, amazed at how much smoother the move made her commute. Snippets of Luke's thoughts slipped in during a radio talk show. Mired in static, his agitation lured her through mid-morning traffic, weaving a checkered plot.

Finally exhausted by the mental chase, she wheeled her Jeep into the *Dispatch* lot at a quarter to eleven, tense and defensive. *Has he found out about our first affair?* She shuddered and shut off the last of his thoughts by popping in her Jill Scott CD.

Anxious for Maxwell's comfort and confidence, Navena stepped from the SUV's air-conditioned interior onto the unshaded asphalt lot. The smell of simmering tar filled her nostrils. A siren wailed.

Navena closed her eyes and listened to the blood rush through Luke's pulsing forehead. He was angry all right, ranting about how she cared more about the *Dispatch* than she did about him. That he didn't like the way that Maxwell brother would always be hovering around her when he called the office. How could he just happen to be at her desk, or Navena just happen to be in his office every time?

The combination of Luke's accusations and Motor City humidity made Navena woozy. She felt herself sway in the heat and held tight to the car door for balance. "Get it together! Luke's smart, but you're powerful, too. Just keep watching and wait, like Mama said. Everything will be fine."

She walked steadily, inwardly marching to her own directive, *stay steady, stay focused*. Across the parking lot, *stay steady, stay focused*. Through the building lobby and scattered hellos, *stay steady, stay focused*, until she reached her desk.

Her phone rang the moment she plopped into the chair. Maxwell, she knew. Luke's words still echoing, nerves hung in her throat, she answered breathlessly. "What time are we meeting?"

"Now, unless you need a minute."

"Let's get it over with," she urged, wanting but unable to focus her Knowing. "Five minutes." Gripped by sudden indecision, Navena sat frozen. *I really don't have time for work today*, she thought. So many other things needed her attention: outwitting Luke, convincing Maxwell to cancel their *Out of the Life* cover story, and getting the blood off her hands came to mind.

"Where've you been?" Fern snapped Navena to attention. "It's your fault we're meeting at lunchtime."

"Shouldn't be long," Navena answered absently, ferreting her pen and steno pad from her tote. "Let me log in right quick. I'll meet you in there."

User name and password entered into the computer, she scanned her e-mail for a link to the only remaining clue, a key word or phrase that would settle the ticking in her head. *What's the thread that weaves all this together?*

The red box floated to mind and faded away. None of the other clues' real-life matches were revealed by the Mothers; why would the rope be revealed so easily?

Time, she felt, was running out. Luke's words tumbled in and out of static, bouncing from his displeasure with the breakup to new thoughts about Maxwell's assets to trying to figure out where she'd moved to.

"Wait a minute! How does he know what Maxwell owns?" The belated realization made her feel stupid. "Duh, he's checking up on *both* of us."

Talking to the computer as her mind unraveled the morning's disjointed Knowing, she clicked on the Internet icon and typed in Fico.com. She hadn't checked her credit report in months, but maybe Luke had. And Maxwell's, too.

"Navena! We're starting," Maxwell called from across the newsroom. Softness had replaced the stern edge such a reminder would usually carry. Navena smiled and temporarily abandoned her investigation. Surely Luke couldn't do much damage in the short time they'd be meeting.

"What's this about?" Anderson asked.

"I realize everybody's hard at work on next week's *Dispatch* and the paper's transition." Maxwell held up his hand as if to quell the inquiry and quiet the remaining whisperers. "There's been a change in plan." He looked directly at Navena. "We are postponing the launch of *Our Scene* until January."

Muffled exclamations rippled through the room.

Thank you, Navena sighed, pushing her appreciation across the room into Maxwell's mind.

"You're welcome," he mouthed, then turned his attention to the group. "Hey, folks. Let me explain. We are very much on track with our investment plan. But the Michigan economy is lagging behind most of the country and we want to be sure we can sustain what we start. Adding four months to the timeline is going to enable us to secure a broader advertising base, boost our marketing efforts, and have two issues in the hopper when we launch. That's going to save us time and money during the last phase of this transition."

"And I'm supposed to do *what* now?" Anderson asked bitterly.

"Let me talk to you after the meeting," Maxwell answered. "The rest of you should continue as you have been. Good work getting the paper out yesterday. We'll continue the weekly until further notice and regroup on Friday. If you have questions, come by my office, call, or e-mail. Thanks." He motioned for Navena to wait while reporters filed from the conference room.

"Anderson, I've gotten wind that one of your sources may not be on the up-and-up. I want to call in a few favors and see if we can get a better idea of what's going on."

"You're full of it, McKnight," he spat, leaning forward to challenge Maxwell. "You just don't want me to get the glory when my story breaks. This is the best story the *Dispatch* has ever had and you know it."

Navena raised an eyebrow at Maxwell, trying to signal him to let her speak. He nodded in agreement.

"Anderson, we're responsible for your safety," she gently explained. "Last week gang squad busted three associates of this Nephew guy—"

"I know about that. So what?" Anderson continued to defy Navena's good intentions.

"Then you know that one of those cops remains in the hospital. It's getting messy and we don't want you hurt," she declared.

"Precisely," Maxwell interjected. "I'm telling you to drop the piece until things cool off. You'll still get the cover when *Our Scene* launches."

"Guaranteed," Navena added.

"No! I'm not backing off now." Knocking over the chair as he stood, Anderson marched out of the conference room without an apology.

Maxwell followed slowly and closed the door behind him. He thrust his hands into his pockets and leaned against the wall. "That went well, I'd say." A wry, but loving smile crossed his lips. *Only for you, gorgeous.* Navena snatched the fleeting thought.

"I know. I know. Thank you. Again." *Guess you believe me after all.*

"Lunch?"

"I'm thinking that's a bad idea."

Pulling his hands out of his pockets and folding his arms across his chest, Maxwell threw Navena a "what are you up to?" glare.

Being able to confide in Maxwell provided Navena with perspective. Assured her she wasn't as crazy as she'd begun to think in those days after the headache. "Luke's on a rampage. Having me followed, I think. Checking up on you, too."

"How?"

"Not sure. How would he know what car you drive and how many houses you own?"

"DMV. Registrar of Deeds."

"What about out-of-state property?"

Maxwell frowned. "He pulled my credit report?"

"That's what I'm thinking. I was going to check mine before I came in for the meeting. Ran out of time."

Before she'd finished the sentence, Maxwell had opened the door and turned briskly down the hallway. Unsure of what he planned, Navena scurried out of her seat and ran behind him. Anger swirled around him in hot gusts that sucked away her breath as she passed through them. Once he reached his office, Maxwell motioned her inside and firmly shut the door.

"What else did you hear?" he asked.

"That he's going to 'get the truth out of me' when he gets back from Philly." She hesitated, afraid of upsetting Maxwell further. "You can't believe Luke would try to kill me over some imaginary affair—do you?"

Maxwell's unexpected laughter startled Navena. *Still skeptical, after all?* "We really are seeing each other now. He won't know when that started."

"Point taken. But who the hell does Luke think he is?" Maxwell sat down at his computer. "Come here."

Navena walked around the desk and stood behind his seat. Now that the anger had dissipated, she wanted to rub his shoulders, kiss his neck. Make love in his high-backed leather chair, hidden from view in case someone opened the door. The idea made her tingle.

Visiting the same credit Web site Navena had pulled up minutes before, Maxwell typed in his credit card number and ordered reports from all three bureaus. "Want yours, too?" he asked, scooting aside to free up the keyboard. She entered her payment info and printed both their reports.

"LJL Enterprises on yours?" he asked.

"Regularly for the last three months." Unnerved, she looked for other strange entries. "Who's that?"

Maxwell unhooked his cell phone from its waistband holster and speed-dialed a number. "Hey, man. Got anything on an LJL Enterprises? . . . Uh-huh. Yep. Thanks."

"Don't know anything about it, do you?"

"Maybe . . ." Maxwell said, frustration marking his words.

"That's a subsidiary of Benson Construction. But it's in his mother's name. Offices on the East Side. Real estate, it seems."

Word of Luke's expansion didn't surprise Navena. Ambition fueled his existence. He wanted to be like the rap stars who had reinvented their personas and diversified their businesses to become global contenders in several economic arenas.

"So, what else has your investigation turned up?" Navena cocked an eyebrow.

"Very high property turnover since the merger with Edmonton Holdings."

"Probably because he's flipping houses. I overheard him talking about it." She pointed to her head. "That's not illegal, though."

"No, but the IRS will hunt you down if there's any drug money involved. And with what we found in the Edmonton history, that's quite likely."

"Think maybe he checked you out before he put his money in the paper?"

"Logical course of action." Maxwell nodded. "Except that he wrote the check before he pulled my report. Sorry, gorgeous."

Chapter Twenty-six

Thursday, June 2

Questions surrounding LJL Enterprises distracted Navena from headlines needing edits, Rachel's waiting ad, and Anderson's new assignment. Instead, she turned to her computer and began an Internet search for the company that she suspected was "Luke-Joshua-Luvenia" Enterprises—named for Luke, his brother, and their mother.

Real Estate, huh?

True enough, she found a Web site listing Luke as the agent on a four-hundred-thousand-dollar property. And a 2002 newsletter listing him as top seller with a now-defunct Realtor. *He's been at this for years, right under my nose. So why wouldn't he tell me?*

Between inputting keywords and following links, she reminisced on her time with Maxwell. Trembling at the very thought of his touch, she sensed new ripples of desire building, pulsing in anticipation of their next moments together. Navena smiled, ready to enjoy the fullness of her new man. At last he was back in her life, arms, heart, reassuring her that he was what she'd been missing all along.

The wait's been worth it. She smiled, tapping on the keyboard. Each new screen layered revelations about Luke. Web page after Web page told her Luke had been hiding his whole life from her. His mother, it seemed, hid a business genius behind her southern charm. Real estate, Laundromats, and the city's largest car wash chain. Even do-nothing Joshua owned property and, at least on paper, ran two automotive parts companies. Again, why the secrets?

He couldn't possibly think I was after him for his money—especially when he gave it away so freely, She thought, thinking of the money he invested in the *Dispatch*.

Funny thing was, she'd looked up Luke before and searched on his whole Christian name. But never his initials, or Joshua's, especially combined with their mother's name. In an LJL search, their individual names were buried so deep in the Web sites that turned up, she would have to read through hundreds of pages to come across Luke's name. How clever.

What's done in the dark will come to the light, Navena mused.

More importantly, the question of purpose remained. What did Luke plan to do what with this financial information about her and Maxwell?

He probably just wanted to see if I'd purchased a house with someone else.

I've been assuming Maxwell is his intended target, she thought suddenly. *What if he thinks I'm involved with someone else?*

Navena reviewed her Knowing session with Luke, carefully sorting words from nuances, or to use Maxwell's word, "inkling," from actuality. A Benz and a house. She assumed that would be Maxwell. And indeed, LJL Enterprises was on his report.

But wouldn't Luke have checked him out anyway—

even after writing the check? Then that inquiry would be so out of place. So, for all she knew, Luke could be checking out anybody she talked to or worked with.

But who else fits the description of what I overheard?

The answer came as a bolt of lightning. Anderson.

He bought that old Mercedes last year, she remembered. Kept it at home, "pimping it out" when he got money to work on it. And just a few months ago, he finally bought his mother's house on the East Side, not far from LJL's offices.

Creepy, but laughable, Luke's hunch was way off. No wonder he couldn't find her last night. She snickered aloud and signed off the Internet, not quite certain, but willing to accept, that his hound dogs were suitably lost.

"Where are you?" Maxwell's anxiety crackled through Navena's cell phone, over Luther's latest jam and the buzz of evening traffic.

"It took me longer to unpack the den than I planned," she apologized. "And I needed a few minutes to decompress."

"Long day, true," he agreed. "Sounds like a good excuse for a massage."

"You're on. Be there shortly." She blew a kiss into the receiver and ended the call grinning contentedly.

Glad that *Our Scene* was off the docket for another four months, that Maxwell had asked her back for the evening and no shadowing cars appeared in her rearview mirror, Navena floored the gas pedal en route to her rendezvous. Tomorrow night they'd stay at her place so she could finish unpacking and start getting used to being in that big house. Maxwell wouldn't be there every night.

Air gusted through her open windows, cooled by the descending twilight. She loved summer's long days, though a month from now the daylight would begin to shrink. Perfect excuse for making the most of her nights with Maxwell. New moon, new man, new life.

Soon, she promised herself, *all the pieces will be in order, I'll guess the winning game show phrase, and we'll all live happily ever after. I wish.*

Maxwell wasn't aware that Luke indeed had someone tailing her. She refused to worry him further by confirming his suspicions. On the other hand, the misguided chase certainly allowed her to relax and anticipate the upcoming hours. After all, if the spy had gotten his task right, she wouldn't be seeing Maxwell at all.

Navena steered onto the private road leading toward Maxwell's development, dialing his number to tell him she was near.

"Park inside the garage. The door will be open. You can come in through the kitchen."

His insight impressed her. *Either he figures Luke's next move would be tracking me down or he's just thinking like a man.* Then again, perhaps he discovered new information after they talked this morning.

Clouds passed over the moon. Her Jeep rolled onto the driveway and into the garage. The metal door lowered behind her. Maxwell appeared in the kitchen doorway, smiling, but seemingly worried. He reached forward and led her inside, toward the stainless steel island centering his kitchen.

"Finally," he whispered, hugging her tightly and exhaling relief. "You're here. Safe."

"I'm fine, silly." She freed herself from his embrace. "What's the matter with you?"

"I don't think you should go back home."

"That's a pitiful seduction, Mr. McKnight." To no avail, she tried to lighten the mood and suppress her rising fear.

"This is serious, Navena. I'm not sure exactly what's

going down, but someone's been back and forth by your place all day. Have you noticed anything strange? Phone calls? Visitors? How about at work?"

"Nothing. Why? You found out that Luke really is following me?"

"Well, he's out of town. But, yes, somebody's on your tail. Tough."

"So are you apparently." Miffed. Unsettled. Not sure who to be upset with, she flopped onto a counter stool. "I thought you were just checking out Luke. What are you doing at my place?"

"Convergence, darling." Maxwell walked closer, uncrossed her legs, and hooked them around his own. "First of all, my hunch has grown into good ol'-fashioned follow-your-nose journalism. And *you* are right in the middle of it." He wrapped her in his arms and kissed her on the forehead. "*I'm* investigating Luke and *he's* shadowing you."

"Probably because he thinks I'm messing around."

"No man likes the idea of his woman giving herself to someone else. Most men don't even like past loves to move on." Maxwell lifted her chin with his forefinger and searched her eyes. "But what's important is how Luke handles it. Do you think he'll confront you? Or will he wait out his revenge?"

Navena shrugged. "To my knowledge, Luke has never been this angry. I have no idea how he'll react."

"From what I've uncovered, he seems to have changed quite a bit *recently*." He furrowed his brows. "Like you and everybody else, I'm starting to think it's more than jealousy."

Maxwell strolled to the corner walnut cabinetry and pulled out a box of Ritz crackers. He opened a long roll, placed a handful of the round snacks on a nearby napkin, and returned the box to its shelf. "Are you aware that Benson Construction is only a front?"

"Well," Navena stammered defensively, "you told me about the LJL connection and I found some other side companies on the Internet."

"I didn't want to spring it on you like this, but the side companies are his business. The construction facade makes it all appear legit." He sauntered to the center island and straddled a stool. Motioning for Navena to return to her stool, he placed the cracker-filled napkin between them. "He makes more money this way. I can appreciate a brother trying to make a living, but I think he's tangled with the wrong people in this Edmonton merger. You could be in real danger."

"Me?" she laughed. "*You* maybe. Luke probably. *I'm* the one person who's getting out of this craziness alive."

"Yeah, so you say." Maxwell popped a cracker in his mouth. "Do you know a Matthias Benson?" he asked through the chewing.

She halted. "Joshua's middle name is Matthias. Nobody calls him that, though. And there's a cousin." Exasperated now. Hands on hips. "It's a family name, I think.

"To outsiders, Matthias appears to be a personal assistant. On the real deal, though, they're not even sure Matthias Benson is his name." Visibly annoyed, he spun away from her, busily retrieving glasses and cola from the cupboards and ice from the refrigerator door. "Can't you use that inkling of yours to conjure up some background on this guy?"

"My gift is not some preprogrammed eight ball," Navena retorted. "Even if it was, all the answers would point to saving you right now."

He placed the glasses between them and took a seat on an opposite stool. "Can't your mother help you out? Clue us in to what's going on?"

She frowned. "I was on the phone with her this

morning for half an hour. She helped me find a first-aid kit. What's that tell you?"

Surprise, sprang into Navena's head, jolting her from Maxwell's anxious scrutiny. Quick as they came, the words floated away, making Navena wonder if she'd heard them at all. "He's up to something."

Maxwell jumped into action. "Let's go." He grabbed her hand, dragging her from the counter stool toward the garage door. "You're sure you weren't followed?"

"Positive."

"Because he could be on to us by now. You stay in the garage. Let me go out, circle the block, see if I pick up a tail. If not, I'll swing back by. You hop in and we're out of here."

"To . . . ?"

"Somewhere we can think." He led her out the same way he'd brought her in just an hour before, squeezed her hands, and kissed her forehead as if to say "now stay put."

Despite the fear it stirred, Maxwell's I'm-in-charge attitude excited her, too. Relinquishing control brought unexpected relief, time to digest all that was happening, a moment to realize she was clearly on the path to fulfilling the dream . . . and dragging the man she loved deeper into the abyss. *God, please keep him safe*, she prayed as he entered the car. Rising slowly, the heavy garage door revealed bits and pieces of the darkening late summer sky. Ribbons of scarlet and gold dipped in and out of lumpy clouds and shadowed light. Navena shivered.

Maxwell backed into the driveway, turned onto the street, and sped away. She quickly pressed the automatic garage control on the wall beside her, mentally hurrying the door downward.

With no windows to peek through, she peered instead into Maxwell's thoughts, racing from one worried idea to another: fear that Luke might try to hurt her—and what he'd do if that happened, wondering if Navena was really psychic and whether she'd figure out that puzzle in time to save him.

Her heart ached for him, this man she'd swept into chaos. Closing her eyes, she pictured his face, raised her hands, and massaged lines she imagined in his forehead. She cupped the make-believe chin in her palms and stroked his stubbled cheeks. Air-kissed his lips and felt him relax.

At last he honked. She opened her eyes and raised the garage door, scurrying under when it was halfway. When she reached the Benz, it began to lower once again.

Inside, seated beside Maxwell, Navena could sense that his nervousness had eased. Navena missed the Mustang, totaled in his accident. While the Benz exuded luxury and class, the Mustang had character and memories that could not be replaced. They'd have to fill this interior with new moments to treasure.

"There's a cute little bed-and-breakfast on the way to Ann Arbor. We could go there." She hesitated. "Pay cash. So we can't be tracked." She watched his lips curve at the suggestion.

"Sounds good. There's about forty-five minutes between here and there, right? That's far enough away for us to relax and make a full evening of it."

He steered the Benz onto the private road leading out, its streetlights coming to life, late commuters rushing past. "Meanwhile, you got any new info?"

"I think Rachel's joining him at the convention."

"Do I detect a hint of displeasure?"

Too late to disguise it now, she chastised herself. "Can't stand that woman."

"How well do you know her?"

"Not very," Navena admitted. "Just enough to not trust her. Bad, very bad vibe I get when she's around. I've come to think she wants Luke back and me out of the way."

"You're the expert here, but that's a pretty big leap, isn't it?" Maxwell raised his eyebrows.

"She shows up on my job. Tells me she's opening an office in the building Luke just built. Then she says I looked at you funny when we passed you by."

"You did." Frowning. "Think she'll tell Luke what she saw?"

"If she hasn't already," Navena murmured. "In which case—"

"He'll have proof, however bogus."

"Which is probably just what he's been waiting for." She turned her head to look out the side-door window and watched the scenery speed by. Luke emitted incredible anger. Had for days now. All his suspicions would be confirmed if Rachel shared her observation.

"He said he was going to kill me if he found anything out."

Navena felt the car lurch as Maxwell unwittingly pressed the accelerator. "I'd probably feel just as angry," he said. "Whether or not I'd act on it is entirely different. I know what his business partners have reportedly done. You have no feel for what Luke is capable of?"

"With all that I've discovered in the last twenty-four hours, my gut says he's for real. After all, cornered animals are always more vicious," Navena sighed. "I'm so glad I moved when I did."

"Me, too, gorgeous." Tension lowered Maxwell's voice. "But I'll be damned if I run from Luke."

Chapter Twenty-seven

Friday, June 3

Navena dreamt Maxwell's funeral. She viewed herself, grieving, unrequited and guilty of getting him killed. Luke smirked in the distance of her mind. She awoke naked. Alone.

She was panicked to find Maxwell gone and the sun long risen. Calming down, she heard paper rustling as she sat up and pulled the sheet around her chest.

> *Hey, love,* he'd scrawled on a piece of hotel stationery. *It's two o'clock and I'm going home. I'll be back by three. You sleep as late as you want—I didn't ask for a wake-up call. Me being there and you being here will throw Luke off, I think. Don't go home. Brochure in the room says there's a boutique down the street. Go buy yourself an outfit and meet me at the office. Get something to eat, take an airport limo to the deli, walk to the office. Money's on the desk for anything you need. Call me.—M*

The note, though sweet, did not excuse his absence. How could he leave her with things the way they were? What happened to their plan? *Looks like you're still on your own, girlfriend.* Navena pouted, deliberating Maxwell's suggestion to shop, dine, and stroll in at her leisure. She tossed off the sheets and rose, bare-bodied and charged, prepared for the unexpected. "I sure don't have time to be lying around, acting kept. That's for sure."

Two nights until the new moon. What happened to Luke and Maxwell in the next forty-eight hours weighed heavily—especially since Mama said she had to be nice to Luke. Postponing *Our Scene* should eliminate the story's connection to the dream—if it wasn't already too late.

Anderson needed a new project so he wouldn't feel like he'd been overlooked and outsourced—again. The atmosphere of her dream state hung heavy, felt real.

If it seems close enough to touch, the signs' influences must be converging. She studied herself in the mirror as she dressed, thinking, *I'll be glad when this is over.*

One final reassurance and she set out, stuffing a handful of Maxwell's twenty-dollar bills in her purse. At the desk, she found he'd settled the bill when he left. Directly across the street stood This 'N That, an overpriced dress shop selling trendy tops, designer jeans, and fabulous shoes. Resisting the urge to treat her feet, she stopped in and purchased a red silk blouse and khaki-colored denims for work. Ten minutes later her cab arrived for the long ride back to Detroit.

En route she replayed her nightmare. Each darkened frame felt familiar now, every street committed to memory, the missing ending needing one of her gifts to materialize. Navena built an uneasy alliance with the visions. She relied on the scenes and signs for understanding; they needed her to become real.

By the time she reached the *Dispatch*, most of the team would be out for lunch. *Maxwell's smarter than he looks*, she laughed to herself. *I'll be able to creep in pretty much unnoticed and act like I've been there all day. No idea what the paper looks like, what's going on in the city. So focused on averting my unknown disaster, I've lost touch with work*. She never thought that would happen.

"Wonder what next week's headline will be."

"Excuse me, miss. Where you going?"

"Midtown. Just off Delmar. Know the area?"

"Sure thing. Have you there in five minutes."

Navena stiffened at the reality of arriving. Seeing Maxwell, cajoling Anderson, confronting Luke . . . who was probably on his way home at this very moment.

"You can stop here. Thanks." She dug the last of Maxwell's crumpled bills from her purse and handed the cabbie seventy dollars and a ten-dollar tip. "Keep the change." She smiled and stepped out into the bustling post-lunch crowd. Excited about seeing Maxwell, she fished for her cell phone and dialed his direct line.

"Finally," he answered.

"I'm coming from the deli now. Anything going on?"

"I've scheduled a sit-down for you, me, and Anderson at three o'clock. He's furious. Sent a two-page e-mail to both of us." Pause. "We may have to let him go. I can't have this type of unprofessionalism and insubordination. Not on my ship. Destroys morale."

"Well, Maxwell, you have to understand where he's coming from." Navena wanted Maxwell calm before they met. "He's looking for a creative outlet. Just like the rest of us. And, unfortunately, it seems like each time an opportunity arises, we snatch it away. First by going outside to hire you instead of promoting staff from the inside. Now we've taken his cover story on the best thing to hit Detroit. Then Fern. His mother . . ."

"I see your point, Navena. His, too, but he's going about it all wrong."

"Breathe. I'll be there in a minute." She stopped to

survey the intersection before crossing. "We can chat more then."

"Enough talking. How'd you sleep, gorgeous?"

"Bad dreams. And nobody to hold when I woke up."

"My hunch paid off, though. I drove past your street. There was a silver Denali parked a few doors down. When I got to my place, there was a Yukon down the block. I parked the Benz in the driveway, didn't raise the door because your car is inside. The Yukon was still there when I left for work."

"So how am I getting home?"

"All taken care of." Maxwell spoke with a sense of pride. "I rented a look-alike for you. Brought in your plates and made the switch when it was delivered a couple hours ago. It's just temporary, of course. We'll swap back when you turn in the rental. At some point. For now, just get here safe, okay?"

"Promise. In a minute, babe." She blew a kiss into the receiver and disconnected the call.

No sun spots behind the shades today, but an ill breeze nudged her shoulder. Afraid to turn, knowing what she'd find, Navena picked up her pace and dug inside her purse for a compact mirror. By holding it in front of her mouth and pretending to apply a layer of lipstick, she could see a silver Denali creeping through traffic half a block behind her.

Panic swept through. *Call Maxwell,* she thought. Then as quickly, *No. He's done enough today. I'm supposed to be saving him.*

Only one block from work, she sensed the Denali behind her still. "On top of it, now I'm being followed."

Think, Navena. What's the link between Luke and your dream?

She flipped through the mental frames. Plot. Scenes. Actors.

Anderson?

He'd been there all along, blatantly canvassing for attention, at work and in the nightmare. She rang the building buzzer, once, twice, a long, third time.

"It's Navena," she breathed into the intercom when the receptionist graciously answered. Sprinting across the lobby, skipping stairs to reach the second floor, she ran to Maxwell's office, noting Anderson's empty desk along the way.

"Where is he?" she demanded, breathing hard, thinking faster.

"Lunch?"

"You better hope, Maxwell." She pointed at the window, directing his attention to the outside view. "See if it's there."

He looked at her deliberately, offering a plaintive half smile. With an even slower stride, he walked to the window and peered carefully through the blinds. The slump in his shoulders cemented her suspicion.

"Same one, isn't it?"

"I'd say yes. You recognize the car? The guy inside?"

"Not especially. All Luke's partners drive very nice rides." She shrugged. "Business is booming at Benson Construction."

"Maybe he works for LJL. Whatever they do there." Disgusted, he turned from the window and returned to her side. "Most everyday employees can't afford the gas for a fifty-thousand-dollar SUV. Forget the car note."

She allowed herself the distraction of Maxwell's voice, his scent, the memory of twelve hours before. Concentrating would mean acknowledging his unspoken accusation and her growing wariness of Anderson. Uncharacteristically muddled and weak in his presence, she fought the urge to melt into his arms and send Luke and Anderson to their vision-told ends.

"In the dream, he's chasing a story," she calculated

aloud. "It's the end of the day. There's a new lead. And Fern."

"But we killed the story."

"Yeah, but what if he won't drop it?" Navena shot Maxwell a "he was really serious about not giving up" look.

"Wow! Because if we don't want the exclusive, he can always sell it to someone else, huh?"

"Yeah. It would finally be the career break he's looking for. But why would Luke care?"

"Maybe Luke doesn't care. About Anderson anyway." He looked sympathetic, as if apologizing for the idea.

"So if this Matthias is the connecting piece between Benson Construction and Anderson's story, you can bet Luke does not want that article to run," Navena surmised.

"What about Rachel? How do you think she loops into this?" Maxwell asked.

Navena huffed, then quickly recanted her sarcasm. "She was awfully familiar with the way we work. Knew the departments. Who to talk to . . . Think she knows our Anderson?"

"If so, that ties her to your dream and its male characters, as well as the paper and you."

But why? She can't hate me that much. We don't even know each other. "Think he'll stand us up for our meeting? I need that time to stall."

Maxwell looked bewildered at her change in focus.

"I'm going down to pull some property deeds."

Navena drove away from the *Dispatch* carrying the feeling she wouldn't return. *Melodramatic,* she laughed, *but isn't all this a bit over the top?*

Deciding that wading through county archives would take too much time, she detoured downtown instead, headed for the Detroit Public Library's newspaper files. The *Legal News* published all public filings—contract bids, city real estate purchases, marriage, divorce, bankruptcy. Knowing the name of Luke's other company made those files easier to narrow down. She checked her rearview mirror to ensure that the Denali was close behind. *Besides, following me into the library will definitely blow your cover.*

Out of curiosity, she speed-dialed Luke. With airlines requiring early arrival, she envisioned him at the gate, antsy to return. Still, the phone rang three times before he answered. She pictured the look of anger and angst that crossed his face when he saw her number on the caller ID.

"Change your mind? Moving back?" he laughed.

"Just wanted to say congratulations." Her pulse raced as the "I'm trying to be nice here" lie slid off her tongue.

"Sure you did. Where are you anyway?"

His arrogance strengthened her conviction to undo the death and keep being civil to him. "Working. Trying to shake your tail."

"Done pretty good so far."

"You ain't seen nothing yet." She hung up the call, her heart caught in her throat, fear and bitterness choking back rationality. *How in the world did we wind up here?* she wondered, pondering the quiet life she'd lived with Luke just three months ago. No dreams. No *Our Scene.* No car-cat-smile-barrel-rope signs. Goose bumps pimpled her skin. *Funny how it all fell apart the moment Maxwell arrived.*

She stared in her rearview mirror. With forced composure, she drove slowly, pretending to be totally unaware of the Denali's presence. Then she turned suddenly and waved at the driver. He grinned. *Perfect.*

Making mental eye contact with him, Navena

pushed, her mind commanding the driver to U-turn and speed off. No one she recognized, but she knew the spell was broken, game over. No telling what they might do now. *Maybe I'm not a mind-reader, but I'll take what I can get.* She smirked.

Able to relax now, she drove past the library searching for an empty parking meter. Found one two blocks away and pumped it full of coins. Then she called Maxwell.

"Yeah, I'm at the library. Car followed me all the way here."

"Navena, don't do anything stupid. We need all the time you can buy."

A little late, she conceded. "I'm desperate, not crazy." Silence. "Anderson show up?"

"Not yet." He sighed.

Navena detected a thinness in his he-man act of the last several days. Fatigue, uncertainty, or a desperation mimicking her own? "I'll call when I'm on my way back."

"Please be careful."

Turning to glance over her shoulder, she entered the library. At the information desk sat a solid woman whose sackcloth dress matched the worn, cotton-covered chair, her spine glued mercilessly to its high-backed seat. Seemingly melded with the fixture, she might have been born into the chair she occupied, holding the yellowed book she waved, bellowing the directions she shared. "Microfiche room. Upstairs. Third floor. All the way in the back."

"Thank you," Navena whispered, respectful of her surroundings, glad to be free of her Denali shadow.

Cryptic signage pointed her to the elevator, its old-fashioned doors closing slowly as it lifted her to the library's top level. *Never been in here.* She surveyed her surroundings, deciphered the back from the front of the expansive floor, found an old-fashioned viewing machine, and set to work.

Whether hunch, Inkling, or Knowing, they signaled that Rachel, Anderson, and Luke were tied before the days of Web sites and online databases. Something in the past kept them bound. Page after page of old news flipped past, until, on July 2, 1992, she found it. The legal briefing simply announced that Anderson Jeremy Cole and Rachel Nicole Patrick had applied for a marriage license. According to the paper, they married three days later.

"Bingo!" The word bounced from stone wall to tile floor. "That's why you called your husband *A.J.* Why you know the paper so well. Obviously you keep in close touch."

Meanwhile, she found that Luke held the deed to land on the city's East Side, just as Maxwell had said. Owned by LJL Enterprises, the property kept company with a host of houses, two Koney Islands, and a scattering of other local lots. All hidden from her view. Navena mentally eavesdropped on Luke and heard him admiring sights below the clouds. Realizing that he'd soon be home from his business up East, she hurried into action.

"I guess I owe Maxwell an apology." Now she could admit that she'd second-guessed his information. Deep inside she felt he was out to destroy Luke without cause—though she should know him so much better than that. "Please don't doubt me the way I've doubted you," she pleaded, gathering her tablet and tote bag.

The stairs, she figured, would be faster than the elevators. Taking them two at a time, she leapfrogged down the broad flights, past the sentry, and out into a darkening afternoon. Beyond the city skyline, sun shadows grew long. With no sign of the banished Denali, she ran to the Jeep, fumbling with the unfamiliar rental keys, let herself in, and started the engine. *Definitely not mine. No shattered glass. Or fiery steering wheel.* She drove off with a sigh of relief.

Moments later her calm evaporated as she pulled into the *Dispatch* parking lot and saw no sign of Anderson's car.

Maxwell waited in his Benz, engine purring, frustration obvious, even through the window. He opened the door and stepped out as Navena swung the Jeep beside him.

"First of all . . . you're okay?" He strolled to her, holding the door open as she descended.

I'm in trouble, I think. "Fine." Navena halted him by talking quickly, before he could assault her. "It just took longer than I thought." Then, hesitating, "You're right about everything, Maxwell." She looked him in the eye. "I'm sorry."

"He worked real hard to make sure nobody caught on. And, like I said before, I think until just last month with this Edmonton merger, Luke was honest, just greedy." Maxwell's eyes caressed her hurt. "How could you know?"

She shrugged. "Just seems I should've been smarter. I mean, he even figured *us* out."

"You didn't have your gifts yet, remember?" With a mischievous smile, Maxwell glanced furtively around, as if checking for staff or spies. "But since we've been exposed, can I get a hug?"

"You better." Having frightened off the Denali, she eased into his embrace. Pidgeons flew overhead, drifters caroused on the corner. Luke crouched in the dredges of her mind. Maxwell held her tighter, like he sensed her apprehension.

"It's going to be all right, gorgeous."

"Maybe." She pulled back to frame him in her view. "In addition to proving you right, guess what else I found out at the library?"
"Surprise me."
"Anderson used to be married to Rachel."
"Now, that's a wild one!"
"They were young. We all do dumb things when we're young." She lightly pinched Maxwell's nose and kissed him on the cheek. "Speaking of which, he didn't show, huh?"
"Unfortunately." Maxwell stepped away and leaned against the roof of his Benz. "Got any idea where he is?"
"Fern should have an address. I believe Anderson is with his source."
"This 'Nephew' character?" Maxwell unhitched his Smartphone without waiting for a reply and dialed quickly. "Yes, this is Maxwell. Can you page Fern for me, please?"
So far, so good, sighed Navena. At the moment, nothing looked the way it did in the dream. She didn't have her own car. Luke wasn't even in town. Fern and Anderson hadn't left together. And there were still hours left until nightfall.
"Hey, Fern. Need a favor." He took a deep breath. "I have to ask you for an address, phone number, all your contact information for Nephew."
Navena pictured Fern, undoubtedly belligerent on the other end.
"Don't bother coming down. Just e-mail me. I'll pick it up in my phone." He paused. "Anderson? No, actually I don't. Did he mention where he was headed? . . . Well, lunch was a long time ago, wasn't it? Okay, Fern. Thanks."
"That was easy." Navena sometimes envied Maxwell's charm. Seemed he could finagle anything out of anybody.

"Gotta know how to handle people." He smiled. "Let's take my car. I'll feel better knowing you're right beside me."

With deliberate pacing—in contemplation of what lay ahead—Navena retrieved her tote bag and flat shoes from the rental. Maxwell opened his car door for her, waited patiently as she loaded her bundle and changed her shoes, then swung it firmly shut, locking her inside. She only hoped Fern's information indeed led to Anderson. And that they weren't too late.

Shadows deepened in the eastern sky. "Looks like rain," Maxwell observed, following her gaze. "Fifty percent chance, they say."

"We should be there before then . . . What are we going over there to do anyway?"

"Break up whatever's going down if we can." Maxwell started the car and lay on the accelerator. "Call the cops for backup if we have to."

Clouds swirled in the distance, pitching eerie light patterns around them. She turned to study Maxwell and bask in his energy, hoping to conjure a protective shield around him. *Will you be here tomorrow?* she wondered. They exited the parking lot as Maxwell's windshield shattered into a mist of invisible pieces.

Navena watched the city stumble past through the "shattered" windshield.

"Is the steering wheel hot?" she asked Maxwell.

He lifted a quizzical eyebrow, but didn't turn his head to look at her. "Only from the heat of being in the sun earlier."

Good. I've spared you my angst. The car's closed-in summer warmth made Navena drowsy, but, afraid of what sleep would reveal, she fought the urge to drift into her dream. Instead, she chose to focus on enjoying this time alone with Maxwell. It might be their last.

"I used to pray for a day when we could ride down the street together like this." She loosened his grip on the gearshift and caressed his hand in hers. "No staring students or lonely Lila . . ."

"Just us." He laced his fingers through hers.

"I love you, Maxwell." She lifted his hand and kissed it longingly. "Promise me you'll take care of yourself tonight."

"Of course. And you, too."

Giving her fingers a quick squeeze, he slid his hand free and unhitched his phone from its waist clip. "We're approaching unfamiliar territory here. What's the map say?"

Navena took the phone he offered and arrowed down through the shorthand directions. "According to this, there's no good freeway route, it's all surface streets." She read her watch and performed the calculation. "Let's take Woodward Avenue. With another forty minutes to travel, we should be there by four thirty."

Shoving the phone into the console between their seats, she turned to stare out her passenger-side window. Skies that were darkening when they left now hung heavy with gray-green clouds. No sun in sight. A brisk breeze in the air. Raindrops began to splatter all around them. Maxwell switched on the wipers and headlights.

"I wonder if I've been leading us astray." Navena spoke barely above a whisper.

"What? Did I make a wrong turn that fast?"

"No. But I think I did." She thought of her recent conversations with Mama. "Once the Knowing came and I could read minds . . . a little anyway . . . I thought that was it. That everything would be taken care of because I have this 'psychic edge.'"

"It worked on me. . . ."

"Oh, it's real all right." She furrowed her eyebrows

and studied the rain. "But Mama says it's like a *map* key. Not the *answer* key I was trying to use it as."

"Makes sense to me." Maxwell shrugged. "It'll get you where you need to be, but the rest is on you."

"Like a diagnosis only gets you so far. It's what the doctor does with that information that really affects your life." The light went on. Navena finally appreciated the sign collecting, the waiting, the unfolding dream with no ending.

"They're all part of the diagnosis. The death is like a disease. I am the doctor who will take all the tests—visions and signs—and decide whether to remove the elements, alter the elements, or ignore the elements that can cure the disease—undo the death."

"So, in our game plan, that leaves us where?" he asked.

"Due for a surprise from Luke."

"And you've probably had enough of those." Maxwell deftly wheeled the Benz across a merge lane and onto Eight Mile Road. "Please don't think the worst of me here, but would you be offended if we . . . pulled over . . . for a while?"

Aahhh, so you are afraid. "At a time like this, food is all you can think of?" she joked, trying to ease his mind. She knew he couldn't help but laugh. And he did, with a fullness that calmed them both and brought a flush to her cheeks.

"You know what I meant, Navena." His chuckle faded away.

"Yeah, I did. Can I ask you a question, though?"

"Shoot."

She shivered at the euphemism. "Would it be 'just in case' sex?"

He turned up the radio and drove half a mile before answering, "Absolutely."

"Then, no. We just promised to take care of each other. If we mean it, let's make a date for tomorrow night."

"You're right. Eight o'clock."

Maxwell didn't sound convinced, but Navena refused to make love under such potentially sad circumstances.

Vibrations shook her feet. *My phone*, she thought, Knowing Luke was on the other end. She dug for it and surveyed the caller ID. "It's him, Maxwell. Think I should answer?"

"Sure. Maybe he'll spoil the surprise."

"What?" she snipped at Luke.

"Let's be grown-ups about this, Navena." Pretentiousness dripped from his words. "How about dinner? Pick up where we left off before your breakup. Sweet Georgia Brown at seven?"

Navena glanced at her watch, estimating his arrival time and wondering if she and Maxwell would have rescued Anderson by then.

"So you won't be home to greet me?"

She refused to answer.

"Too bad," he continued. "I was counting on that crotchless-panty lap dance you welcome me home with—"

Blushing, she hoped Maxwell couldn't hear Luke's words. "What do you want?"

"To protect my interests."

"I'm not your property, Luke." She softened her tone. "It wasn't working with us. Admit it."

"Was till Mr. McKnight arrived. Don't you think?"

He just heralded the changes that were due in my life. "You know better than that, Luke."

"Not only were you screwing around, Navena, you and that damned paper are trying to mess with my money, too."

"No, we're not. What are you talking about?"

"Like you didn't know." His anger seared her ear. She switched the phone to the other side and listened, wide-eyed. "Why would you sic Anderson on me?" he ranted. "Of all people? Stirring up stuff with him and Rachel. Got the feds all in my business. What are you trying to prove?"

"Luke, whatever trouble you're in, cooperate with the authorities. You've worked too hard to go down like this. If you're involved, turn yourself in." She halted. "I've got a bad feeling about all this."

"Did your mother tell you something? What?"

Navena chose not to elaborate on who knew what. "Someone could end up dead, Luke. These new partners of yours—"

"What do you know about them? How?" he demanded.

"We have our sources."

With that, Maxwell vehemently shook his head. "Don't tell him that!" he mouthed.

"I won't let you do this to me," snarled Luke.

Click.

The phone's display went blank. Navena grew numb. "Maxwell, do you think Luke could be Anderson's 'Nephew'?"

"He hasn't done any prison time recently, has he?"

"No. . . ." She considered the idea for a moment. "Can't certain people 'convince' somebody in their crew to take the fall for them?"

"Hmm." Maxwell thought aloud. "Maybe we need to look into the charges this Nephew went up on. Talk to the prosecutor and see how they got their man."

"We don't have time for all that. It's already after four." *City offices are closed. Anderson's probably knee deep in trouble by now. Luke's on his way home. . . .*

"Bad guys aren't the only ones with connections."

Maxwell grinned. "Do me a favor? Search my address book and get Thad Levy's number, please."

Navena delved into Maxwell's phone and scrolled through an extensive list of alphabetized friends, family, colleagues, and business acquaintances. *Old lovers?* she wondered, as she anxiously looked for her own name among the many. She smiled as it rolled past just before stopping at Levy. Taking the liberty of making the call for him, she pressed SEND and then handed over the phone.

"Thaddeus Levy," he bellowed into the phone. "Maxwell McKnight here . . . Yes, it's been a while. Thanks, I'm good. And you? The family? . . . Great. Hey, Thad, you always said I was good for one favor—and I pulled that one the other day. But I need a follow-up if you can. Right. That . . . This cat 'Nephew.' Who locked him up? Anything suspicious about the case? . . . Circumstantial, huh? Never got the kingpin?" He shot Navena a cold glance. "Think you've told me everything I need to know, Thad. I appreciate your time and the information . . . You do the same. Thanks."

He tossed his phone into the console with a heavy sigh. "Thad's office handled the case. It was Nephew who went to jail, but Nephew's boss was the one they wanted. And they never got to him. But the press was all over the story—money laundering, tax evasion, drug trafficking—somebody had to go down, so they settled for the flunky and five years. He's out as we speak."

"And that's probably Matthias, Edmonton's mysterious employee." Navena slammed a fist against the car door, angered that Luke had fallen victim to his own ambition, too greedy to see the company he merged with was backed by thugs.

"I just figured he knew where his new partner's

money came from. He grew up in the money game and he's been around the players long enough to know better." She hunched forward in momentary resignation. "But as the principal who signs the checks and runs Benson Construction, he'll be the one held responsible."

"If he chooses to take the fall, yes." Maxwell reached over and rubbed her back. "It's not your fight anymore, Navena."

She laid her head in his lap.

"You hungry?" He twirled her hair.

"At a time like this? First sex, now food." She sat upright. "Sure, we can probably squeeze in a drive-through meal. Should be something along this stretch of road."

Hungrier than she realized, Navena skipped the salad, figuring she'd need the calories to fuel whatever work her gifts had to perform tonight.

They ordered double cheeseburgers, fries, and chocolate shakes—promising to eat better tomorrow—and were back en route within fifteen minutes.

"When I left Ann Arbor this morning, I felt really good," she told Maxwell between sips. "None of the day's events had fallen into place according to the dream. I thought I'd altered the course we were on. Guess I was wrong about that, too."

"Everything's the same?"

"Except that Fern isn't with Anderson. Otherwise, yes."

"We're going to win," Maxwell reassured her, reaching across the table to stroke her fingers. "In the end, the story will still be a great one and you and I will finally get our second chance."

They continued in silence, Navena assuming Maxwell was as deep in thought as she was.

"Do you know any undercover cops?" she asked

suddenly, scooping up the last of her fries. "I think we should go *in* with police backup instead of waiting until something happens."

"I've got a friend named Darryl. I'll have to tell him about the story," Maxwell said through a mouthful of burger. He looked at her intently. "Luke will probably end up in jail."

"I tried to be nice." The words belied her mixed emotions. She wanted to be free of Luke—but not like that.

"I'll make the call when I finish eating. As long as you're sure you can handle watching your ex being carted off to prison."

The address on Whitlock was now just fifteen minutes away. By the time they arrived, the rain had departed, but left the sky looking like midnight. A dewy chill hung in the air.

Just as the dream said, Whitlock was laden with trees. Lining both sides of the street, they blocked lamplight and moonlight and dumped droplets onto Maxwell's car as he slowly cruised along. His windshield remained shattered—at least in Navena's view. And since the phone call with Luke, her seat had grown progressively hotter. She rubbed her thighs together and felt a layer of sweat sticking to the panty hose beneath her slacks.

"There's Anderson's car!" exclaimed Navena, pointing across Maxwell's line of vision. "I think he's inside."

"We can't make a move until Darryl and the rest of the squad arrive."

"Tell him when he gets promoted, he owes you half his raise," Navena laughed.

"You got that right." Maxwell shut off the engine and turned down the radio. "Darryl couldn't believe his luck when I called. The Detroit Police Department has been chasing this urban legend around for years, waiting for a break. And we gave it to them. Unfortunately, Luke's right in the middle of this. It's too bad. He seemed like a good guy."

Maybe he'll choose not to show, Navena thought. *That is his choice to make.*

Navena turned to watch a couple of teenagers strutting down the broken sidewalk, hitching their pants as they moved forward with gangster bravado. A matching pair strolled down the opposite sidewalk as well. She noted that there were no raggedy cars on the entire block. Unnerving in a neighborhood where the median income couldn't be more than thirty thousand a year for a family of four. The mix of new-looking SUVs, sports cars, and restored lowriders lining both sides of the street totally contrasted their surroundings. *We certainly don't look out of place,* she thought ruefully. "Are all these houses empty?"

"I doubt it. Dealers probably just ran all the good folks out." Maxwell finally parked the Benz, choosing to operate from the far end of the block. "I don't see anybody but these baby gangstas. Must be keeping watch."

"Think we're on their list?"

"Oh, I'd say so." He shut off the car's lights.

Thunder boomed above them. The artificial darkness that accompanies summer storms settled around them like fog as the sky unleashed its fury, catapulting leaves, small branches, and trash gathered beside the curb. Navena sat mesmerized as her dream unfurled in fullness.

So what good have you done? she asked herself. Fighting panic, she double-checked and analyzed the path that led her here. *I did what Mama said. Followed the dreams: Met Vee. Matched the car-cat-smile-barrel signs. All except the rope. Made my choices: Staying at the* Dispatch. *Breaking up with Luke. Loving Maxwell again. Al-*

lowing Anderson to follow his gut on the Nephew story, then taking the article away. Trying to interpret the nightmare before it was time. Listening in. Getting it wrong. Now here we sit.

"Something feels wrong," Navena muttered aloud. She turned to look at Maxwell.

Dappled moonlight seeped through the "shattered" windshield and fell on his face. Through her mind's lens, his features contorted, becoming misshapen and grotesque. Just as he had that afternoon in his office, Maxwell looked like he was melting. She gasped, throwing both hands over her mouth and falling back against the passenger-side door. "Drive!" she shouted.

"What?" he said in slow motion, turning to face her.

"Now!" she screamed, reaching to turn the ignition key. "Get out of here!" *How,* she thought frantically, *can I save his life if I've led him to the slaughter?*

Maxwell obeyed, wheeling the car into the street with Nascar control.

"Reverse!" Navena screamed. Headlights raced toward them. "Back up, Maxwell. Back up and turn right!" She held on to the door and braced herself, back against the seat.

As Maxwell spun the car, the approaching vehicle slammed into his rear fender, pushing them fully around the corner. He floored the accelerator. "Luke or one of his henchmen?" Maxwell asked rhetorically, turning onto the next block as Navena had instructed.

"Luke." She wondered if she could redirect him, the way she'd handled the Denali at the library. "Next block turn left. We're about to shake him."

Hard to impress, Navena marveled at Maxwell's driving. These were city streets in an old established neighborhood without driveways or garages. Everybody parked on the roadside. That left one center lane to maneuver through, topped with new rainfall and little lamplight. Their escape would be a miracle. *But it's going to happen*, she commanded.

She leaned forward to look into the passenger-side rearview mirror. "Adjust this mirror outward." Maxwell complied, bringing Luke's hulking Escalade into full view. She closed her eyes and pushed. *Stop*. He jerked the SUV, hitting a car parked alongside. Its alarm bellowed in the darkness, but Luke's pursuit continued.

"Go back to the office," she hissed aloud.

Maxwell looked over his shoulder at her. "Turn around?"

"Not you. Luke. I'm telling Luke. You pull over and cut the lights." She stared into the outside mirror once again and closed her eyes. *Go back to the office. Protect your interests,* her mind radioed to Luke.

She opened her eyes as Maxwell drifted onto the next block, pulled aside, and silenced the car. He looked at her like she was crazy. But she knew he was clinging to hope. *Yes, we'll have our tomorrow night*, she assured him.

In the rearview, distance had grown between their car and Luke's. He appeared to be slowing down. *The cops are coming*, she jeered. At this he stopped. Moments later, the Escalade began moving forward again, driving right past them on the shadowy street. She slumped back into her seat and exhaled all the tension of the past three months.

"Call Darryl. Tell him Luke's on his way," she sighed. "They'll need to prepare for battle."

Her own weariness released, she felt the air lighten around Maxwell. Not everyone would make it out of the fray tonight. He knew that and so did she. Anderson would. Luke would not.

Maxwell leaned over and hugged her tightly. She could scarcely breathe, and it felt wonderful. They kissed. She fought back tears. Happiness at saving Maxwell, that they would really have a future. Sadness, that Luke didn't heed her warning. A mixture of anger and appreciation for the gift she possessed.

"There's nothing else we can do here, babe." She reached and gave his hand a reassuring squeeze. "Let's go home."

Chapter Twenty-eight

I promised to take care of him, she consoled herself as Maxwell steered free of the neighborhood. Meanwhile, unbeknownst to Maxwell, Navena focused her mind's eye on the scene fading behind them, watching her dream unravel.

"Where the hell did they go?" Luke growled. He sped past their hiding place. Furious. Out of control. Two, three, four times more, he slammed cars jutting just-so into his path, backed up, then continued in his maniacal pursuit. "I'll kill him. I'll kill him. I'll kill him." Car alarms honked and wailed up and down his narrow route.

Within seconds, he was headed back to Whitlock Street, making a hard right at the end of the block, and another one a hundred yards later. He lurched down Whitlock, searching for his lookouts, trying to find Navena and Maxwell. Angry, he jerked the Escalade's nose into half an available space. Leaving the remainder of the vehicle in the center of the street, he jumped from the SUV and vaulted the steps in front of his headquarters, shouting "Open the damn door. Now!"

At his command, the front door opened, casting light onto the darkened walkway, and signaling undercover officers hidden in backyards, on rooftops, and in lowriders a few houses down. They emerged, guns drawn.

"Luke Benson! Stop right there! Get your hands up! Get 'em up!"

The lookouts quickly obeyed. A set of DEA officers pushed them to the ground at gunpoint, cuffed their hands and feet, and led them to approaching vehicles. Rights were being read up and down the street. Luke, meanwhile, continued sprinting toward the house.

"Stop or we'll shoot!"

She studied Luke, straddling the crossroads of earth and eternity. Had she expected joy at this moment? Some semblance of satisfaction? When she broke up with him, did she really believe she'd never see him again? Of course not.

A gunman opened the door for Luke and began targeting officers gathered at the yard's edge. A sniper on the roof next door took him down with a single bullet. Shots rang out from cops and crooks alike. Even in her mind, the barrage was deafening.

Luke grabbed his shoulder and screamed. It was the same piercing shout she'd heard the first night of the vision. Again, the sound left her chilled. Just like her daddy succumbed sixteen years before, Luke hunched forward.

Navena's conscience churned. She flipped her palms upward and stared at the "blood-tinged" skin. Rapidly opening and closing them, she willed her hands clean. "There will be no blood here," she whispered. "I can save you both." Concentrating on the space between bullets and Luke's body, she closed her eyes and pushed.

Luke's massive frame hit the concrete walkway with a thud that shook Navena.

She stared onto the road ahead, holding her breath as the windshield repaired itself. "He's alive," she sighed with unexpected relief. A glance at her now clear palms confirmed her intervention.

SWAT team members and undercover cops surrounded Luke's writhing body, weapons drawn, reading rights. Rachel emerged from the shadows with a smug smirk, arms crossed at her waist, swaggering toward the house under siege.

"What's she doing there?" Navena asked, confused. "And why does she look so pleased with herself?" She sat up in her seat as if to get a closer look.

"Who? Should we go back?" Maxwell asked, pressing the brake in anticipation. He swerved left, crossing two lanes to make a U-turn in the busy thoroughfare, and narrowly avoided the oncoming traffic. Cars honked, fists emerged from windows rolled down in anger. "Talk to me, gorgeous." He raced back to the scene of the crime.

Navena sensed his anxiety rising, thinking, no doubt, that they were still in danger. "Relax, babe. I'm certain that Luke is taken care of. But how unlikely is it that Rachel would show up as the police gun him down?"

"What? You were . . . watching . . . the whole thing?"

He shuddered, then placed his hand lovingly on her thigh. "Are you okay? Is Luke . . . dead?"

She found the motion of his hand comforting and took strength in Knowing that they would see the end of her dream together.

"Pretty hurt, I think. But alive." She shook her head in empathy. "Ought to be on his way to the hospital by now. Then jail, I imagine."

"And his ex just happens to be in the neighborhood?" He scoffed. "I'm with you on this one." He paused and gave her his best boss expression. "Got your credentials?"

She did, of course, and produced them from the bottom of her purse.

"Think you can handle the aftermath?" He raised his stroking to her wrist.

"You're with me." She smiled weakly. "I'll be okay." *Though I never expected to be the one covering this headliner.* She kissed her forefinger and placed it on his cheek. "Thank you, Maxwell McKnight."

He furrowed his brow. "For?"

"Coming back." *And taking care of me.*

The car slowed two blocks before the Whitlock Street turn. Already, yellow caution tape outlined the crime area perimeter.

"Looks like we'll have to walk from here." Maxwell pulled onto a side street and turned off the car. "Ready?"

"Yes." She felt the dream's finale and her own happy ending were long overdue. Credentials in hand, she shoved her purse under the seat for safekeeping. "Notebook?"

"Digital recorder." He reached into the glove box and withdrew a pocket-sized machine, showing it to her as if for approval. "Let's go."

Navena took a deep breath and stepped into the late evening coolness. A surge of power jolted her veins. *I succeeded in my Larimore challenge. I can do anything.* Everything around her appeared clearer. The air smelled fresher. Maybe it was the rain. Maybe it was her psyche, free of fear for the first time in weeks.

Or perhaps, she thought solemnly, *it's my heart free of bogus obligations.*

She hesitated for a moment and allowed Maxwell to walk ahead.

Obligations.

Beyond her promise to Vee, did she feel indebted to Maxwell's determination for reconciliation? If he (or Vee) hadn't shown up, wouldn't she have been content to live her life without him?

And Luke. The convenience she clung to in their relationship made her ashamed to admit they were together five years.

Truth peppered the edges of her mind the way twilight now hung on the fringes of rooftops. Ordinarily, eight thirty would be the day's first darkness.

Today it brings me dawn, she thought.

Maxwell shook his head, perusing the chaos in front of them. Then he paused, turned, and reached back for her hand, gently squeezing it as they approached a DPD squad car guarding the scene. She stepped in front of him as they drew close, offering only the word "Press" and her *Dispatch* ID badge for entry. Maxwell followed suit and the officer stepped grudgingly aside.

They walked to Whitlock, once again hand in hand, hers trembling slightly. News vans from local networks lined the block. Reporters stood at odd intervals, taping "stand-ups" and sending live feeds to their stations. Navena gleaned nothing new as she passed each camera crew and microphone.

Farther ahead, she could see the makeshift lighting rigs from DPD evidence trucks and county forensic teams. Latex-gloved men swarmed, plucking bullets from the grass and dropping them into plastic sandwich-style bags. They were close enough to the house to see others inside dusting for prints.

Luke lay on a stretcher being loaded into a crowded ambulance. Navena swallowed her rising nausea and clenched Maxwell's fingers. Rachel stood at the rear of the EMS vehicle, talking with officers and medical personnel, her M.D. badge in plain sight on her white lab jacket.

No blood, she didn't touch Luke. She's obviously not here for emergency support.

Elsewhere, bodies splayed in outline were strewn up

and down the street. Maxwell stepped in front of her, blocking the agonizing view.

"I think this was a bad idea." He grasped her shoulders and stared into her eyes. "I had no idea this was so gruesome. It's too much for you."

"No, I just need to know what she's doing here." Navena spat the sentence into the confusion, hoping Rachel heard.

"I thought he'd be dead." Rachel hurried toward Navena, embracing her wildly. "I'm so glad you're all right!"

Shocked, Navena writhed free. "What do you care?"

"I tried to warn you, remember?" Rachel's eyes were mere slits. She spoke through clenched teeth and a trembling jaw. "Luke got mixed up with some awful man. They're furious about your story. You're lucky they didn't have you killed." The "you" she tossed at Maxwell.

I know this, but how could you? "The breakup was worse than you let on?"

"Not me and Luke's, but me and A.J.'s." She turned her head, pointing her gaze across the street, where Anderson stood taking notes from a DPD detective. "They've been at odds ever since because their paths continue to cross."

Navena's gaze vollied between Rachel and Anderson.

With that tidbit, a closer look at Rachel let Navena see the woman Luke and A.J. fought for—sans the blond and a hundred-plus pounds. The revelation seemed so obvious that Navena shielded her naïveté behind nonchalance.

"Why are we talking about twenty-year-old news?"

"Because with Luke it's new fuel for the Anderson fire." Rachel turned to face her once more. "You know about Anderson's mother's murder?"

Maxwell pulled Navena close protectively as she

spoke. "Of course. We've been trying to keep it in the news."

"Wasn't a robbery. It was one of Luke's guys after Anderson. Word of that Nephew story leaked out pretty quick. The Edmonton crew didn't want Luke—or anybody else—to learn about their criminal ties."

"Edmonton had Anderson's mother killed?"

"No. He'd never dirty his hands. But that place"—she nodded toward the house—"is crawling with thugs waiting to earn their stripes in his army. One of them broke in and shot her in the dark, trying to set Luke up. Then he did himself in by panicking over the story, thinking Anderson was out to get him and making himself look too guilty."

Rachel shook her head in a way that told Navena she still cared. "I thought hooking him up with Anderson would give him a chance to tell his side before this kind of thing happened. In the end, he thought everybody was after his empire, even you."

"Rachel, look at all this trouble you caused," Navena hissed, lunging forward. "All of us could have been killed."

Not intimidated, Rachel leaned into Navena's attack. "I tried to warn you." Standing back, she crossed her arms. "My only purpose was to *save your life*. They would have killed you, too, Navena. And still might . . . since Luke managed to live."

"How do I know I won't end up like Lila?" Now that he was hers, Navena struggled to balance the unresolved issues in their previous relationship with her obligation—and desire—to care for him. She scooted backward, locking her nakedness with his.

"Because I love you more." Maxwell tiptoed his fingers up her back, then ran them over her shoulder and down into her hand.

"So you'll be faithful to me?"
"Always. I swear." He wrapped her tightly and kissed the back of her neck. "Can I ask the same about you?"
She rolled her eyes and frowned. "Of course I'll be faithful."
"You won't get tired of me like before? Or like Luke?"
"I'm *in love* with you," she insisted, her body stiffening in response to the conflict. "Yes, I was somewhat detached before, focused on school. But you weren't available anyway. And it's almost like Luke was holding your place."
"And Lila yours." His breathing pulsed warm, then cool on her skin, rising and falling in rhythm with Eric Benet's sensual singing from a CD across the room.
Outside the wall-length window, stars emerged as the day's lingering clouds finally subsided. Scenes from the shoot-out bounced through her head. Maxwell was safe. She had to believe that the Mothers aligned their fates so that everything would now be okay. Even if Luke was alive.
"I'll Know if you're lying to me, Maxwell." She wouldn't, because that gift faded once it was no longer needed. But Navena teased Maxwell anyway.
"So I'll have to stay honest," he laughed. "Haven't caught me deceiving you yet. Right?"
"True." *Even when you were scheming to get me out of town, you told me about your plans the next day.* She rolled over to face him.
"Maybe we've both grown up in the last fourteen years. You think?" He kissed her on the nose.
Navena closed her eyes and murmured, "In more ways than one."
"This is a WSFT-FM breaking news bulletin," blared from the radio, accompanied by military-style horn play and the nighttime air personality. Maxwell sat up

in the bed, pulling Navena with him. He wrapped the sheet around their shoulders and held her close, stroking her hair.

"We've just received word that prominent businessman Lucas Benson of Benson and Associates has been arrested this evening on Detroit's East Side. Benson, most recently noted for constructing Trentmoor Towers, was wounded in an undercover sting operation after attempting to enter a well-known drug den. Police have refused comment on the situation. Stay tuned to your sophisticated station for all the news that matters."

A melancholy Janet Jackson tune replaced the interruption.

"You need a couple days off?" Maxwell rubbed her back slowly. "That's the least I can do."

"Thanks anyway, babe." She shrugged. "It's going to be everywhere for a while. Might as well work my way through it."

Maxwell reached for the TV remote atop his night table. "I can watch this in the other room if you'd prefer."

"No, stay. But can I use your phone?"

He nodded yes, reaching again to hand her the cordless. Navena yawned, stretched, and rose from the bed. Dragging the sheet with her, she stepped into the adjacent master bathroom and called her mother.

"Mama . . . I beat the dream." Navena's reflection looked to her as worn as the antique mirror she stared into. "I saved them both."

"But how . . . ?" Her voice trailed.

The hesitation seemed to speak for itself. Nervous about Mama's reaction, she rubbed at her mascara-streaked eyes and lipstick-smudged mouth.

"I told Maxwell about the nightmare. I tried to warn Luke to be careful. Maybe that communication opened them up to being pushed in this situation, regardless of what the visions and signs said. Or maybe it's just because you told me I had the power to change *anything*."

"But you did dream it. It should have come true."

I hope not.

"I don't believe that murder belongs in our legacy." Navena frowned at her reflection. "How long did it take you to learn your gift, Mama?"

"Not long. But I have the kind of gift that gets used. Yours is a little tougher."

"What good is this legacy of ours?" she sneered.

"I believe the answer is real close by," Mama soothed.

Mother was always right. Navena smiled, thinking of Maxwell in the next room. "Thank you for seeing me through, Mama."

"Oh, don't worry. We'll have plenty more times ahead." Her laughter sparked across the distance and lightened Navena's mood.

"I love you."

"And I'll talk to you later. Go tend to your man."

Mama blew an air kiss across the miles and hung up the phone. A drop of blood fell from the receiver. Navena opened her palm to find a sewing needle piercing her hand's lifeline. Clear, "invisible" thread slipped from the needle's eye.

Oh no, it's not finished.

With all the chaos they left behind this evening, Navena felt certain she'd met the obligations of her challenge by saving both men. Now, as she shook her hand to clear the vision, she wondered.

When she reentered the room, the television newscaster was wrapping up Luke's story.

"They put it in the second block," Maxwell observed as he flipped the station.

"Not at the top?" The decision to downplay the arrest surprised her. But, then again, they didn't know the whole story. "What we need to do—"

"Is a special edition."

"Better yet, let's get *Our Scene* back on track." Adrenaline coursed through her veins. "Forgive me if I sound crass, but we've got the inside story. Even if the dailies run it front page tomorrow, we have the reporter in the middle *and* the informant."

"This could put your personal life under the microscope, bring you a lot of anguish." Concern etched Maxwell's face. "You're sure?"

"We're only a few days off the old magazine schedule. The whole team will pull together on this one. Besides, it'll be therapeutic."

"And so will this." Snatching the sheet from around her, Maxwell opened his arms and invited her back to bed.

Chapter Twenty-nine

Saturday, June 4

He's not out of danger, you know. Navena stared at Maxwell's spine, listening to him snore. For seven nights in a row the *snurgley* sound of his slumber had lulled her to sleep. At dawn, she lay awake, again contemplating ways to save his life.

This will be the final battle, she decided, *the one that wins the war.* She ran her index finger across his shoulder, outlining its shape against the sunrise. He stirred with a moan.

"Do you love me?" she whispered. The break in his breathing told her he'd awakened.

"Navena, hon, we've talked about this." Rolling slowly, Maxwell turned to face her, heavy with sleep, bristling with irritation.

The Knowing had left her after Luke's near-miss, but she sensed dismay. Muscles tensed beneath his skin. His breathing quickened.

Yes, but—

"This is not about love." He rubbed his eyes and ran his hand over his head with a sigh. "You still don't trust me. Why not?" He seemed to wait for the truth.

"It's been a long time, Maxwell. You can't just come in here and expect me to drop everything. I did that once." With that she glowered momentarily, eliciting a sympathetic frown.

"Don't tell me you haven't moved past 'go,'" he teased. "Or haven't you forgiven me yet?"

"*I* broke up with *you*, remember?"

"What I mean is that, in the great sisterhood sorority, I think you're still feeling bad for Lila."

Moonlight cast his coffee-cream skin in half shadow. The man was too fine for words. She smiled. "No, Maxwell, this is all about me. My love, my heart." *And the consequences of a promise.*

"You could've told me this before instead of stringing me along all this time." His annoyance spilled into anger. "If you cared anything about me, it would have been better if you'd just ignored me from the beginning."

Navena sat upright to brace herself against the onslaught.

Nothing.

A sigh. "I knew things would be incredible once we were back together." He spoke softly. "But I didn't expect . . ."

"Second thoughts?" She finished his sentence with words from her own struggle. "Now that Lila and Luke are out of our way—"

"It's like we wanted to be together because we couldn't." Maxwell sat up and pulled her close.

Maybe she'd come full circle: from being alone and empty to being a couple and incomplete to having Maxwell and understanding what true love really is. She had the dreams to thank for that realization.

Those same visions also reminded her that the nightmare continued to lurk. If she did nothing—remained in Maxwell's life as if everything was fine—her promise would be broken by tomorrow night's new moon. She would have failed her challenge to undo the death.

"I pictured us here in this house, married and making babies," he confessed. "I can't believe I came all this way . . . that you fell for me the way you did just to pitch me aside again. You must have no heart at all in there."

"You know that's not true, Maxwell. I will always love you." Tears stung the corners of her eyes.

"Don't think I like your kind of love."

"I'm sorry, handsome," she said.

Knowing no explanation would ease his hurt, she offered nothing more. He didn't need to know why she was leaving or that she didn't want to go. Navena dipped her head into his shoulder. Inhaled his presence. To remember. "What about the paper?"

"You are all work, aren't you?" He shook his head and shrugged. "We'll launch *Our Scene.* Like I promised. Then I think I'll take off for my next venture. I can't stay here now.

"You want my job?" Maxwell shifted his position, rustling the sheets and stroking her hair.

She looked up at him through bleary eyes. *Me in charge? Not like this.* "Oh, Maxwell. I don't know . . ."

Odd that life was so clear before he arrived. *Why would the Mothers bring him here if he isn't really mine?*

Maybe I can realign . . .

Navena tipped her head, the way puzzled puppies do. "Tell me. Where would you be if you hadn't come to Detroit?"

"Coaching college basketball probably. Maybe teaching, put my degrees to good use. Somewhere down South." He pulled away and lifted her chin. "That's a weird question. What made you think of that?"

My life has taken a twisted turn from vision to reality to surreal since you arrived, she thought, *but you did bring me power*. "If I can alter the future, think I can change the past?"

"I'd rather you didn't. I've had enough heartache from you, thanks." A familiar touch of fear tinged his voice. The one Navena had heard the night she told him about her Knowing.

"The past is all we'll have after today, right?" She swallowed past the lump rising in her throat. "Because we're breaking up?"

Beyond Maxwell's shoulder, sunrise peeked through the window.

"Can we say moving forward instead?"

"Okay." Didn't matter to her. Right now she wished for a simple escape. One that would find them in very different places tomorrow.

And then the answer came to her.

Navena glanced quickly around the room, wanting to remember all the pieces of Maxwell that she was about to forget. Including his kiss. She rose to her knees and straddled him, pushing him down onto the bed. Leaning forward, she pressed her breasts against his skin and kissed his face. Cheeks, eyes, ears, chin. His lips. Deeply. He writhed beneath her. She allowed him to enter. One last time before closing the door.

"How are they treating you?"

"How do you expect?" Luke snarled.

Glad they were separated by Plexiglas and surrounded by guards, Navena tried to push into Luke's mind. To no avail. As quickly as it appeared, the Knowing had indeed vanished, leaving her to find new ways of outsmarting her ex-man.

On her right sat a mother, dressed in Sunday hat and high-heeled shoes, assuring her son that she was doing all she could to get him freed. At her left, a girl (too young to be visiting a prison alone, Navena tsk-

tsked) promised her young fella she'd find bail money. Somehow.

You get neither, thought Navena, looking directly in Luke's eyes. "I just came to . . . apologize," she blurted at last. "I should've been a bigger woman and broken things off a long time ago."

"It's my bad . . . for not taking care of that McKnight and his big ideas when he showed up." Luke rose to his feet, roaring, "Watch your back, Navena!"

Convinced now of what she had to do, she stumbled over her chair to escape as guards ran to subdue Luke and lead him back to custody.

This memory she did not want to keep.

Chapter Thirty

Sunday, June 5

Navena rummaged through the assorted items in her red Mothers' Box. She smiled at the memory of finding it and not understanding its scattered contents: needle and clear thread, scissors, an eraser, pencils, and a jar of paste glue—as fresh as the day it was left for her. Sunday seemed odd for such a drastic shift, but tomorrow it wouldn't matter what today had been.

She sat cross-legged on the bedroom floor, blank cards, box items, and photographs spread before her. Lovingly, she selected a photo of her and Maxwell and began to cut herself from the picture. When finished, she rubbed a thin layer of thick glue on the back of each photo half and pasted them on separate white cards. Next, she found a photo of herself with Luke and performed the same task.

With a sigh, Navena laid the remaining white cards in a straight row, mimicking the dividing line on a one-way road. She placed her card at the beginning of the trail, Maxwell's next, and Luke's last. Taking a pencil from the box, she wrote *No, thank you* on two other white cards. She placed one under Maxwell's photo card and one under Luke's.

Carefully, she threaded the needle and began to connect the white cards with a single stitch in each. Navena wove through her pictures and the *No, thank you* cards, but not Maxwell's and Luke's photo cards. When all cards were loosely connected, she tied a knot in the end of the thread.

Taking a deep breath and wiping a stray tear, she took the eraser from the box and began to rub it across Luke's face. Starting slowly, then moving faster, he began to disintegrate before her. Likewise Maxwell. Until nothing was left of either photo card. When she was finished, all that remained was a shadow embossed with *No, thank you* in their places.

Night enveloped her bare window and cast her in starlight. She lifted the string of cards—segments of her existence thoughtfully assembled across a timeline—and carried them to the bed. Laying them one atop another, strung to preserve her life's continuity, she placed them gently beneath her pillow.

Navena showered. Her bath favorites were boxed downstairs, awaiting their permanent home tomorrow. No need to unpack. Content to use a sliver of soap she'd left behind, she scrubbed and prayed, uncertain, but unafraid of tomorrow. She toweled off slowly and slipped on a T-shirt and panties. Exhausted and anxious, she tucked herself into bed to dream.

Navena couldn't wait to head home for the holidays. She hadn't seen Mama during the entire fall semester. She walked out of her last exam with a bounce in her step and a smile on her face.

"Miss Larimore," echoed a familiar voice. "Good work this term."

"Thanks for all your help, Mr. McKnight."

"My pleasure. You're an extremely promising student. Glad I could help." He paused. "Are you heading home for the holidays?"

"Yeah. I'm kinda in a hurry. Gotta pack."

"Mind if I walk with you a ways?"

"Oh, that's okay, Mr. McKnight. No, thank you."

Chapter Thirty-one

"The sports world counts itself lucky tonight with news that former NBA All Star and community activist Mack McKnight has emerged from a lengthy coma in a Detroit area nursing home. A spokesperson for the unnamed facility reports that McKnight was admitted several weeks ago after being found unconscious in a local neighborhood park.

"With no identification and suffering from severe internal injuries, McKnight had been thought indigent and without family. It was the sixty-five-year-old night shift janitor who recently recognized the ailing athlete as 'that boy with the half court jumper.' He shared his suspicions with staff and they were able to confirm who he was.

"However, sources are telling us that initial test results indicate the onetime power forward suffers from amnesia, which doctors think may be trauma-induced.

"Even authorities declared McKnight's reappearance as a miracle. Along with his wife, he was pronounced among the dead of a Midnight Air flight that crashed outside Detroit last month, leaving no recognizable remains."

Chapter Thirty-two

A brisk wind fluttered Navena's short, wispy hair. Her breath hung cloudlike in the twilight mist. Fading tulips withered among throngs of yellow daylilies in oversized concrete planters. The flowers bowed and waved as she walked. Lights along the thoroughfare stuttered and glowed, one by one, timing their appearance with her footsteps. She warmed beneath their watch.

Until now, she'd been chilly, hurrying down Woodward in search of her car and a blast of heat. As she passed the windows along the front of a bookstore, something on the other side of the glass pecked at her mind, tapping like a forgotten grocery list item. Telling her to come in. She stopped to stare at the empty store's neat periodical stacks and unfamiliar DVDs.

"Do I need something from here?" Her words fogged the window.

I don't think so.

Our Scene's debut issue graced all the newsstands. With enough copies to supply a school, she didn't need to buy any more.

But I can check on sales.

With a quick push, Navena spun through the revolving door and entered the other world she loved so much. Here, imagination ruled. Perhaps became certainty. Dreams came true.

The lights flickered. People appeared. One sand-colored man in particular seemed to come from nowhere. He stood beside her thumbing through a men's magazine.

"Oh my," she murmured, straightening her shawl, smoothing her hair, and wishing she had changed out of her work suit. She felt overdressed next to his open-necked cotton shirt and wide-legged jeans.

"You look fine." He smiled, but didn't take his eyes from the glossy fashion spread in front of him. Opening the magazine wider, he asked, "Do you know anybody who dresses like this?"

Instead of looking at the page, Navena let her gaze land on the near side of his boldly sculptured face. A precision shave accented his square jaw and broad nose. If she didn't know better, she'd say a barber hidden in the back had just touched up his fade. Sprinkles of gray strands peeked from his beard and above his ears; distinguished, like the man modeling the suit she was supposed to be studying.

"I believe that was made for you," she offered, glancing up and down his frame. "Takes a tall man to pull that off."

"Know your Italian designers, do you . . . ?" He offered his hand, motioning for her name.

"Navena Larimore. Great ads, not clothes, happen to be a weakness. . . ." She grasped his palm and tilted her head, listening for his name.

"They tell me I'm Mack McKnight. Maybe back in the day, I would've worn this." He closed the magazine and returned it to the shelf.

"You disagree with what they tell you or don't know . . ." She stopped. "Oh. I am so sorry. I didn't realize."

Navena wanted to kick herself. Of course, she should have known who he was right away. His face had been plastered on every newscast and front page in the city for days. How stupid could she be?

"Not your fault." He shrugged, searching the shelf for another quick read. "Just tells me you're not a news junkie. And that's nice."

"Boy, I have to apologize again." Leaving seemed like a good idea about now.

He paused. "Why? What? You're really a Jerry Springer fan acting like somebody with sense?"

Ah, he made her smile. The kind of grin you give when you're feeling especially cute. "Close. I work for a magazine. News is pretty much my life."

"Sounds boring." He seized the latest issue of *Sports Illustrated* and turned to the center spread.

"I like my job." Unintentionally defensive, she wondered if this man without a past remembered what it was like to love what you do. "From what I hear, you liked yours, too."

"That's what they tell me. Don't remember it, but I miss it."

Weird, Navena thought. *How's that possible?*

"City College is looking for a basketball coach." There. She sounded in-the-know and empathetic. "We ran an article a few weeks ago about the change-up over there. You'd like living in Detroit."

"Where did you say you worked?" He slid the dog-eared copy of *SI* back into its previous slot.

"*Our Scene* magazine." She scanned the rows of covers for her familiar masthead. "Right . . . here."

She plucked the last copy from the rack and splayed its contents for Mack. He flipped quickly to the front of the book until he found the staff listing.

"Editor in chief. I'm impressed." He nodded. "Nice picture of you, too."

"Thanks. And look, here's a brief about you in our flashback section." Navena pointed at his head shot in the table of contents.

They admired their respective photos. Then he finally looked *at* her. Face-to-face, without hiding himself behind a magazine.

She absorbed the view. Indeed, seeing him from just one side had gypped her of half his incredibleness. Beyond beautiful, he felt . . . familiar.

As they looked into each other's eyes as if to compare faces to their déjà vu, energy surged between them, flushing Navena's cheeks with more than humility.

They frowned at each other.

"I'm new in town and bad with names." He launched into an apology. "Please don't tell me we've met recently. I'll be so embarrassed."

"No. Haven't been around your way."

It was his eyes—as deep as desert dunes. Navena sensed that if she peered into them any longer she'd be swept away in their sand storm.

"You have relatives who work at the hospital?" he asked, reading her mind.

Memories stirred. "Nope. We don't do traditional medicine."

"You have relatives here?" she asked.

"Don't know if there are McKnights in Detroit related to me." He wagged his finger and shook his head. "I can't remember anything, but I swear I know you."

"Guess a man never forgets a good pickup line, huh?"

They laughed. She tingled.

"Some things stick with you. Even across a million miles," he murmured. His cheeks went from warm beige to a gentle red.

"Are you okay, Mack?"

"I finally feel found."

Navena stood silent, knowing exactly what he

meant. "You were calling me. From out there." She pointed to the front windows.

"Maybe somebody's looking out for me."

"I'd say so. You are beyond lucky."

"What's meant to be will be, regardless of how we try to mess it up." Mack flashed a wistful grin. "If I'd taken a different flight . . . left Vee at home . . . who knows . . ."

"Do you remember—"

"Her?" He shook his head. "Not directly—like how she looked or sounded. But she left me feeling . . . cared for. It's hard to explain."

The faraway hollows behind his eyes narrowed and closed, changing their color from amber to brown. This moment seemed to be filling in whatever he'd lost in his ordeal.

"Why aren't you married?" Mack lifted her ringless hand for emphasis.

"I told you. Work." Dates in her semicelebrity status were plentiful. Yet none had ever come through the bookstore. Or felt so right.

She struggled for composure by lowering her gaze and redirecting the conversation. "Does this mean we get an exclusive on all your pre- and post-game coverage? If you take that job, I mean."

"Only if you'll have dinner with me tonight." He smiled.

"Exclusives come in all kinds of stories, you know. Headlines, fairy tales, yours and mine."

"So, these stories start with food?" She asked smartly.

"What better reason to bump into each other than to feed the heart and soul?"

"Wow. You're good."

"And to think. We're just getting started."

A MOMENT ON THE LIPS

PHYLLIS BOURNE WILLIAMS

Grant Price wants old classmate Melody Mason to work for his family's Boston investment company. Melody has retired from big business and is hiding. It is Grant's assignment to lure her back to the fast life. But when he arrives at her door, she doesn't look like the woman he remembers....

Melody has hidden herself away in rural Tennessee for a reason: she desperately needed a life change. So she has no intention of returning to a fast-paced lifestyle. Instead, she makes Grant an offer: stay, relax and find out what life is like without a hectic pace. Unfortunately, real life calls and Grant must return to Boston. Can Grant and Melody agree on what a good life truly means?

STRONGER THAN YESTERDAY

NICOLE KNIGHT

Faith's marriage is the kind written in fairy tales. Her husband, Gerard, is passionate, attentive and all hers. Then everything changes when Gerard's ex-wife tells him he is the father of her eight-year-old son—a child he never knew about. Now, the baby conceived on Faith's honeymoon seems unimportant—and Faith feels the same way.

Gerard is stunned at the news of his son's existence—and he's thrilled. After being abandoned by his own mother, he vows to be a real father to his child. What he can't understand is Faith's jealousy and insecurity. It will take all his patience to convince his beautiful wife that he has enough love for everyone in their new family—and especially her.